The Dream

by

Maria Savva

Printed and bound by Lulu.com 2011

Published by: Rose & Freedom Books
P.O. Box 55285
London N22 9EU
England, U.K.

A catalogue record of this book is available from the British Library

ISBN: 978-0-9564101-5-3

Acknowledgements:

Thank you to Darcia Helle, for being the first person to read the final draft, and for spotting lots of typos! Thanks for being such a great supporter of my writing, and a wonderful friend.

Thanks to Jason McIntyre for giving me your honest opinion about the book on reading the final draft. It means a lot that I have such supportive friends who would risk being hunted down like Nestor Maronski rather than see me publish a less than perfect book!

Thanks so much to Stacy Juba for your editing suggestions. Your tips were very useful and helped me to fine tune the final version. Thanks for your enthusiasm about the book!

Thank you to Joel Blaine Kirkpatrick for being so thorough and spotting all the extra spaces and missing punctuation! You have eagle eyes. And, yes, in the UK we say 'for ever' rather than 'forever' :) Oh, and a CV is a curriculum vitae. You call them resumes in the US. Most of all, thanks for finding Lynne's car... You were right it was at Sandy's flat!

Thanks to my wonderful friends, Calum McDonald and Julie Elizabeth Aldridge, for the final proof-reading and your helpful suggestions.

Thanks to all at BestsellerBound.com for the continual support and motivation.

Thanks to all the book reviewers/readers who have rated my books highly on Amazon, Goodreads, and other such sites. I am indebted to you.

Last but not least, thank you to anyone who has read and enjoyed any of my books. I'd like to dedicate this book to you.

Prologue

Lynne ran into the garden, carrying in her right hand her favourite toy—a small, brightly coloured car; red, orange and blue. It had large eyes and made a sound like a car racing along a track whenever she pulled it along the ground using the string attached to it. She found her favourite part of the garden, feeling happy that her sister was at a friend's birthday party so she could be alone and play with her toys. Her sister's favourite doll, Nancy, was in her left hand.

Lynne sat on the bench at the far end of the garden under the shade of the apple tree. She smiled and began to sing: 'Ring, a ring o'roses, A pocket full of posies...' Just then, she heard a sound in the next garden and hoped that her neighbour, Zac, wouldn't insist on climbing through the hole in the fence to play. At 4 years old, he was almost a year older than her, but he acted like a baby as far as she was concerned.

'Lynne, where are you?' shouted her mum from the patio doors at the back of the house.

'Here, Mummy!' she replied.

'Stay where I can see you,' said her mother, then disappearing back into the house.

It was a lovely warm day. Lynne began to run around in circles, feeling the breeze in her hair. Just then, she saw a white cat jump off the fence and realised that the sound she had heard coming from the next-door garden must have been the cat. She had never seen it before. It was completely white, with bright blue eyes. It had a collar with something hanging from it shaped like a fish.

'Hello,' said Lynne, excited. She ran towards her new playmate. It sat calmly watching her, seemingly unconcerned at the toddler who was now racing towards it.

Lynne stroked the cat. 'Do you want to play with my car?' she asked. 'What's your name?'

The animal began to purr, then laid down on the grass, allowing Lynne to continue stroking it.

Suddenly and without warning, it jumped up as if afraid. Its eyes turned very dark, almost black, and it backed away.

'Wait, little kitty, don't be scared, silly,' said Lynne. Then, she turned to her right, and saw her mother standing next to her.

'You scared the cat, Mummy!' Looking back at her new friend, she said, 'It's only Mummy, she won't hurt you.'

'Who are you talking to, Lynne?' asked her mother, seeing an empty grass lawn where Lynne was pointing.

'The cat, Mummy, look. Isn't he pretty? Can I keep it?'

'You and your imagination,' said her mother, sighing, unable to see the creature so clear and real in Lynne's eyes.

'Can I, Mummy? Please? He's so sweet.'

'It's time for dinner, Lynne, come on.' Her mother picked her up.

'Can I bring the cat inside?' She looked over her mother's shoulder as she was whisked into the house, and watched the cat in the distance, now further and further away from her. It continued to look at her with those hollow black eyes. Lynne began to feel a little frightened and held on tightly to her mother.

The cat never returned to the garden and Lynne was left wondering if she had imagined it after all. Like all events in a three year-old's life, it was soon forgotten. Two weeks later, her parents bought her a cat of her own; a black and white one. The mysterious white cat from the garden became a distant memory, never to be recalled.

Chapter One

I don't love him anymore, thought Lynne to herself, as she looked at Adam lying on the bed beside her. *We're supposed to be getting married in a couple of weeks time... eighteen days time.*

She jumped out of bed, ran into the en suite and closed the door. Reaching for the tap, she splashed her face with cold water. *Maybe I'm still asleep.* It was wishful thinking. Opening the bathroom door, water dripping from her chin, she took a deep breath and wiped her face with her pyjama sleeve. She walked into the bedroom and looked at the man lying on the bed. He was sleeping, his mouth slightly open. As she listened to the familiar sound of his breathing and the faint snore, a fear took hold of her; a realisation that she no longer felt anything for him. The sensation had crept up on her without warning. She tried to reach back into her past—even to last night—to conjure up some loving feelings. *I was still in love with him last night... at least I think I was.* They'd been laughing, as they watched a documentary on TV about a fourteen year-old girl who wanted a boob job, even though, at first, Adam had said he didn't want to watch it and they'd had a bit of a disagreement about that.

Lynne had been with Adam for over three years, and it was something she just took for granted that she still loved him, never questioning it. Okay, she knew it was no longer like in the first few months, when her heart would beat faster every time they met, but it was an unwritten rule, something that was just there. They were still together, so it had never entered her mind that she had stopped loving him. Not until today. Now, she knew for certain, that she had no feelings for him. *How can this have happened?*

Just last night, they had been talking about the plans for their upcoming wedding, and the honeymoon location, over a glass of red wine. Granted, she'd done most of the talking, but he was agreeing with her, and he seemed to be looking forward to it. Men weren't supposed to be particularly enthusiastic about planning weddings, so she didn't expect anything more from him. She'd felt happy.

Crawling back into bed next to him, she could see from the alarm clock that it was 7:21 am. The alarm was set for 7:30—the time Adam got up for work.

She thought back to his proposal, as she fingered the diamond engagement ring on her left hand. Her eyes drifted over to the wardrobe, within which her wedding dress was hanging. She'd noticed the dress a couple of months before Adam proposed to her, stopping in front of the shop window on her way to work to admire it. It was beautiful. As she'd stood in front of the shop window, she'd wished that Adam would pop the question so she could buy it. Her wish had been granted a few weeks later when Adam got down on one knee, at the top of the London Eye, in front of a group of smiling tourists, and asked her to marry him. He had tears in his eyes when she said 'Yes'. She'd felt so blessed, and sure that they were fated to be together. She tried to reach back in time and pull out those feelings, but they were gone.

As she turned to look at Adam, a strange emotion ambushed her; a feeling of deep regret. It was like the way she'd felt when she'd drunk too much at that party back in her university days, and had gone to bed with Stuart Redman, the most unattractive bloke on the campus; the one everyone said was most likely to join the Foreign Legion. It had been a feeling of instant regret, a feeling of uncleanness, when she'd woken up to find him dribbling all over his pillow next to her. She'd jumped into the shower straight away, and scrubbed herself until she had washed that night away.

The feeling was almost exactly the same now as she lay next to Adam; the gut wrenching sensation of having made the most horrendous mistake. But she couldn't jump into the shower now and wash away over three years of time. Somehow, though, that's what she wanted to do, as ridiculous as it seemed. *What's wrong with me?* she wondered.

Adam began to stir in the bed. Soon he would be awake. It was 7:29 am. She turned away from him and closed her eyes, pretending to be asleep. *How could I have just fallen out of love with him overnight?* Then she remembered the dream she had the night before last. In the dream she had been sitting alone in a bar and a man approached her. He looked familiar, but she had never seen him before. A white light shone around him, like an aura. He had said, *'You must not marry Adam, it will be a mistake'.* Then he disappeared, and she woke up. She was a bit shaken after the dream, especially as the man had seemed so real, and his voice remained in her head when she opened her eyes. But after a few minutes, when she had fully woken up, the dream had slipped away to the back of her mind, no longer significant. Then, Steve, her ex, had phoned her, out of the blue. She hadn't spoken to him for over four years. Could the dream, and the subsequent phone-call from Steve have caused her emotions towards Adam to freeze up now? Was that why she could no longer feel anything for him? She began to worry that perhaps she had never really fallen out of love with Steve, and his call may have awoken long dormant emotions, making her feel that her marriage to Adam would be a mistake. That would make more sense if Steve had called first and then she'd had the dream, but it had happened the other way round.

She could hear Adam in the shower. Usually, she got out of bed when the alarm went off, to prepare his breakfast; wanting to make the most of the time they had together, because Adam was often working abroad. Today, however, when Adam had said, 'Good morning,' she had rolled over and said, 'I'm tired. I think I'll lie in a bit today.' That had been the end of the conversation.

She lay in bed now listening to Adam singing in the shower. His voice sounded out of tune, but it didn't usually bother her. *I love Adam, I love Adam, I love Adam,* she tried to convince herself. Perhaps if she kept repeating that in her head, she would eventually believe it. She pretended to be asleep again as she heard him re-enter the bedroom to change into his work clothes.

Lynne had fallen in love with Adam at first sight. She had just come out of an awful relationship with that rat, Steve, and then she'd met Adam; sweet, kind Adam. He was handsome and gentle, and had been so good to her. Soon, she became besotted—almost obsessed. When he finally asked her out, after what seemed like an age, she'd been the happiest girl in the world.

People were jealous of Adam and Lynne's relationship. From the outside, they were the perfect couple. And even though their relationship was not as great as it had once been, Lynne still never doubted they would be celebrating their golden anniversary together one day. So, she could not understand how she could just wake up one morning and feel unable to even look at him.

Had she fallen for Adam on the rebound from Steve, transferring the feelings of love she'd had for Steve to Adam? Perhaps now that she had spoken to Steve again after so long, and realised she didn't love him anymore, she also no longer loved Adam; after all, he'd only ever been a substitute. Could it be that simple? But she felt sure that she loved Adam because he was Adam; not just because Steve had left her and she needed a replacement. Over the years, she had formed a strong bond with Adam; one she thought could never be broken.

The strange thing was, something at the back of her mind told her that she had probably known all along that she didn't love Adam, but had just not faced up to it until this morning. *I mean how could I have ever been in love with him?* Her mind now seemed clearer than ever before; more focused. It was as if a messenger had been travelling for over three years, desperately trying to get to her over a treacherous journey, wishing it had reached her sooner; it had still been catching its breath, after telling her, in no uncertain terms: 'You don't love Adam anymore.'

Thinking back, she realised that after the first few months of dating him, their relationship had become more like a companionship than anything else. With Adam away on business so often, she ended up spending the most important days of the year on her own: birthdays, Christmas, Valentine's day—an endless list of lonely occasions. But somehow this hadn't mattered to Lynne; she'd been busy, too, working as a secretary in an accountancy firm. She hadn't had time to ponder the strengths and weaknesses of her relationship. It was only really in the last few months, since she had been made redundant, that she had faced up more to the lonely days. This created some tension between her and Adam whenever he returned home. But she kept herself busy with the wedding arrangements, thinking that the wedding would wash over any of the inadequacies in their relationship. Since the engagement, she'd had a more positive outlook, brushing aside any arguments, believing that getting married would solve their problems. Now, she wondered whether they were too far down the line of incompatibility for that to work.

She took a deep breath as she heard Adam close the front door on his way to work. *What should I do? It would be better to tell him now, instead of standing him up at the altar.* But what about her family and friends? What could she tell them?

Chapter Two

When Adam had left for work, Lynne took her wedding dress out of the wardrobe and put it on, trying to remember how she'd felt when she first saw the dress in the shop window.

She picked up the phone and dialled her best friend's number.

'Hi,' said Sandra.

'Sand, are you busy?'

'Well, not really. It's been pretty quiet here for the past few months, but I still have to pretend I'm doing something, or I'll get sacked. It's so stressful, this recession.'

'At least you've got a job.'

'Oh, sorry, Lynne. But look, things are bound to pick up soon, and you'll get back into work. Anyway, I'm not feeling sorry for you. You're the lucky one; you're getting married!'

'Hmm.'

'You could sound a bit more enthusiastic!'

'I need to talk to you about the wedding,' said Lynne, smoothing the silk skirt of her wedding dress as she spoke.

'Yeah, okay. Do you want me to come over tonight?'

'Er... no, can we meet for lunch?'

'Sure.'

Lynne went into the kitchen to prepare her breakfast, in a daze. *Will Sand understand? She'll think I'm mad.* Then, she realised she was still wearing her wedding dress. There was a brief panic *Oh no!* But it was short-lived. Soon, a cloud of gloom enveloped her. *Who cares if I ruin the dress? I'm not marrying him, anyway.*

Common sense prevailed, however, and she went back to the bedroom to change her clothes. The dress had cost her five hundred pounds; money she could ill afford to lose. She had been made redundant over three months ago, and the job market was bleak.

Lynne sat eating her corn flakes, staring out at the blue sky. They lived in a tower block, and the view from the kitchen table was just sky, as far as the eye could see. There were hardly any clouds today. She would have preferred thunderstorms to fit in more with her mood. The sun was shining. In theory, that should have made her feel happier, but she was consumed with confusion. Her feelings for Adam had changed so quickly, so suddenly, so completely; like the wind changing direction.

It can't be... Her heart skipped a beat as she thought back again to the phone call she'd received yesterday. From Steve.

'I hear you're getting married,' said Steve.

Why is he phoning? Is he jealous? *Lynne couldn't tell. She wished she could see his face.*

'Yes, I'm getting married,' she replied, abruptly. 'Who told you?'

'Kevin,' said Steve.

Kevin was Sandra's brother. Every now and then, some news about Steve would filter through from Kevin to Sandra and then to Lynne. Usually, Lynne tried to ignore it. She didn't really want to hear about what he was doing. She didn't care. He had hurt her and it had taken time to get over him. She didn't want to listen to tales about him and other girls. Sandra knew this, so she usually only relayed stories that would please Lynne; like the time Steve sung karaoke at the local pub and someone had thrown a tomato at him; or, when a girl had thrown a glass of wine over him when he tried to pinch her bum. The last time Lynne had heard any news about him was over a year ago, when Sandra said Kevin had gone out with him on a stag night. Well, Sandra hadn't really told Lynne about this; she'd overheard a telephone conversation between Sandra and her brother, when Sandra had said: 'Oh you're going to the stag night then? Make sure you and Steve don't do anything stupid.'

'Why are you phoning me, Steve?' Lynne's brow furrowed.

'I wanted to wish you luck for your wedding.'

'Huh! Are you being sarcastic? I don't even know why I'm talking to you,' she snapped.

'Well put down the phone then,' he said.

'I will.'

'No, wait, Lynne. Can't we just leave the past in the past? We were close once, remember? I just thought that now you've moved on, it would be a good opportunity for us to call a truce.'

'Why would I want to be friends with you after what you did? How could I ever trust you again?'

'I'm sorry you're still so bitter about it, Lynne.'

'Oh... you are so self-righteous!'

'I know what I did was wrong, but it was years ago—'

'Is there a point to this conversation?'

'Why are you still so angry? I thought I'd be able to have a mature

conversation with you after so many years have passed. We had good times as well as bad.'

'What you did was unforgivable and I have a right to be angry with you, so get off your high horse!'

'Hmm... Maybe I shouldn't have called you. I am disappointed that you've not been able to forgive me. It might be too late for us to be friends, but I just wanted to let you know I wish you well.'

Could it really be possible that Steve had changed? Confusion swept through Lynne's mind. He spoke so calmly, and what he'd said really did make sense. In fact, she had thought she'd forgiven him and moved on, until he phoned and all the old emotions were stirred up when she heard his voice. That voice; it always did make her knees turn to jelly.

Hearing his voice now, she couldn't help feeling flattered and almost tempted; it sounded as though he wanted to rekindle their love. But she was supposed to be getting married to Adam in less than three weeks time; she could not afford to let herself feel this way. Taking a deep breath, she said: 'Steve, I don't think we should be talking.'

'Well, put down the phone then,' he said, for the second time.

'I will.' And this time, she did.

Surely, the phone-call from Steve couldn't be the reason she now found herself having second thoughts about Adam? *No, it can't be.* Steve had broken her heart over four years ago, when she caught him in their bed with another woman. Being so in love with him, she had almost forgiven his infidelity, but had been talked out of it by family and friends. He had been her first love. She had always thought she would marry him. It had taken a lot for her to walk away from everything they had together, but she had convinced herself that she made the right decision.

She'd received the call just after breakfast on Monday morning. She'd been getting ready to leave the house and go to the florists to make the final arrangements for the wedding flowers, when the phone had rung. She'd felt annoyed with herself after the call, and had phoned Sandra for moral support.

'Guess who just phoned me?'

'Who?'

'Steve.'

'Who?'

'My ex.'

'What? "Stupid Steve" phoned you? Why?'

'Can you believe, he wanted to wish me luck for the wedding!'

'How did he find out?'
'Your brother.'
'Oh, sorry.'
'It's not your fault. I haven't spoken to him since... you know. I wish I'd changed my mobile number!'
'He's a bastard, forget him. He's probably jealous.'
'Yeah.'
'He had his chance and he blew it. You're better off without him. Forget him.'
'Forget who?'
'Ha, ha.'

After the talk with Sandra on Monday, she relaxed a bit, but she couldn't help feeling curious about why Steve had phoned. For some reason, it made her feel good thinking he might be jealous. This worried her. Why should she care if he was jealous or not? Was she still carrying a torch for him? She went about her chores; organising the hen party, booking the hairdresser, beautician, and caterers, for the wedding... an endless list of "things to do". Every now and then, the memory of her conversation with Steve would pop up in her consciousness, forcing her to think about him. It was almost as if part of the flame had not been fully extinguished, and now a small spark threatened to grow. Had it already done damage by burning out some of her feelings for her fiancé? She had to face the fact that the phone-call and the sudden numbing of her emotions towards Adam might be linked.

⌛

Lynne met Sandra for lunch. They chatted. Lynne mentioned the dream, the phone call, and the feeling she'd had in the morning about not being in love with Adam anymore.

'Lynne, you and Adam have been together for over three years. You've lived together for ages, and I can remember a time you used to drive me crazy talking about how much you love him. Then, remember how happy you were when he proposed? You were over the moon; and that was only a few months ago. I really think you need to put things in perspective. Has anything happened to make you hate him? Something you haven't told me about?'

Lynne shook her head. She really could not recall any real problems between her and Adam. They'd argued more frequently in the past year, but she had always put this down to stress; what with

16

Adam being away so often. She'd never taken the arguments seriously. The only major disagreement they'd had was a couple of months ago, about where they should hold the wedding reception. She wanted a hotel with a sit-down meal, but he wanted a buffet so they could invite more people. One thing led to another and they started arguing about the cost of things. Adam made a reference to the fact that she was out of work and wouldn't have to be paying for anything. This hurt her because she had offered to use her redundancy payment towards the wedding if they needed extra money. They both had savings which were going to be used to pay for the wedding, and Lynne felt that Adam was being insensitive about her current predicament. He'd also slammed her for buying such an expensive wedding dress when she 'didn't know if she'd ever work again'. They'd slept in separate beds that night, and she remembered wishing she'd never met him. But when the initial anger had subsided, Adam had been very apologetic and said he'd been stressed out because there were rumours that there might be some redundancies at his office. She'd forgiven him, and completely forgotten about the disagreement, until now, when she was racking her brain to find some loose link in their relationship. 'Adam's a bit of a grump sometimes. Also a typical man, as he doesn't communicate very well; but that's just Adam, and I know him, so I put up with all that. He's always been really good to me,' she said.

'So, you're going to throw away a good man because of a dream you had, and a phone call from an ex, who—in case you've forgotten—was a complete prick, and totally broke your heart. I was the one who stayed up with you until the middle of the night, listening to you crying. Remember?'

'I know, I know.'

'Adam is worth ten of Steve. Even if you could get back together with Steve, you're not seriously telling me you would, are you?'

'No!'

'So, what's this all about then?'

'I just felt really sure this morning that I don't love Adam anymore. I can't explain it, but I was so sure. I'm not so sure now, though. It seems to have changed again. It's like a light flickering on and off. But, it's scary. I don't know if marrying him is the right thing to do. What if it's true that I don't love him anymore? When I think back, I can't really remember having any real conversations with Adam. He's always so busy. It's only recently that we have been sitting down to dinner together to discuss the wedding arrangements. Mostly, he's away or working, and I'm eating dinner for one in front of the TV.'

Sandra nodded and smiled a sad smile. 'I have to say, this was the last thing I expected you to say to me today. I always thought you and Adam were so close, and so right for each other. If you want my advice, I think you should give it another chance. I think maybe you were just really surprised to hear from Steve again, and all your emotions got mixed up. You used to love him, and maybe you never really closed the door on that. But as your friend, I have to tell you that I've always thought Adam is the best thing that's happened to you, and I've always been envious of your relationship.'

'I know you're right. I just don't seem to be thinking straight at the moment. It must be all the stress of arranging the wedding, and losing my job. Oh, I don't know. There's something else—' She stopped, feeling unable to continue; not sure if she could tell Sandra. They shared all their secrets, but this just seemed... almost crazy.

'I'm waiting,' said Sandra, smiling. Her forehead creased, however, showing that she was not sure she really wanted to hear any more.

'Okay. Well, since this morning, I've been trying to think of a reason why I would suddenly stop being in love with Adam. The only thing I can think of is that there's someone else I'm in love with, and my dream might be trying to tell me that. I mean, dreams come from our subconscious, so maybe I've met someone else who I've fallen for subconsciously.'

'We're not still taking about Steve, are we? Because—'

'No, definitely not!'

'Thank God for that!'

Lynne played with the stem of her wine glass.

'You're not hiding anything from me, are you?' asked Sandra. 'Have you met someone else?'

'No. I've been out of work for months, and spend most of my time indoors. I hardly go anywhere. Besides, I would have told you if I'd met someone; I always tell you everything.'

'I know, it's just that this has reminded me that you spend a lot of time on those social networking Internet sites, don't you? I remember you making a joke about a man you met on one of them sites, and saying that you could hook up with him if you ever split up with Adam.'

'That was a joke, Sand. I hardly use those sites anymore. It was just a novelty when I lost my job and had time on my hands. Recently, I've been so busy preparing for the wedding. The only other men I'm likely to meet are in my dreams!'

Lynne sipped her wine, and then realised what she'd just said: "In my dreams". A chill rushed through her as she recalled the man who had appeared to her and told her not to marry Adam.

Sandra smiled at Lynne. 'Just spend time with Adam this evening. Really concentrate on the positive stuff. Try to forget about the way

18

you felt this morning. Lots of brides get scared before getting married. Lots of them think about how they could be marrying someone else—someone like Brad Pitt, instead of Joe Bloggs—it's normal to have doubts. I just don't want to see you throw away something good. Promise me you'll give him a chance before you let him get away.'

Lynne nodded.

By the end of lunch, Lynne started to feel more relaxed. She realised it was most likely that the negative feelings she'd been having this morning were probably just because of the shock of speaking to Steve after all this time. It had been good to talk to Sandra about it; she had known Steve, and had been such a rock after the break-up. She knew everything that Sandra had said was true: Adam was worth ten Steves.

That evening, Lynne cooked a lavish meal for Adam, and they had a romantic evening together in the candle-lit living room. She tried to focus on the positive, like Sandra had advised. Almost like a first date, she was getting to know him all over again. They talked about the wedding, and how much they were looking forward to the honeymoon and finally being able to spend time together. As usual, he wasn't very communicative; but at least he'd agreed to leave work early and join her for dinner. Lynne's insecurities began to fade, and she realised that she would be a fool to let such a good man go. So what if the fireworks weren't there anymore? That didn't matter. He was familiar, and he was safe. She found that she really liked Adam. He had so many good qualities, it would be easy to fall back in love with him; it would just take a little time.

As she began to fall asleep in his arms, she relaxed, and was at peace with the world again; thankful that she had not reacted impulsively on the irrational thoughts she'd been having that morning.

Chapter Three

Lynne woke up and took a deep breath. 'It was only a dream,' she said to herself, in a whisper, feeling a sense of relief flood over her. Then, as she looked at Adam, she suddenly felt a strong sense of foreboding. The wedding loomed only a couple of weeks away. The image from her dream returned to her in a flash and then disappeared. She sat up quickly, and got out of bed.

Once in the kitchen, Lynne sat on the bar stool nearest the door, staring into the distance, not even bothering to turn on the light. She sat in the half-darkness—the only light coming from the moon—and watched the numbers on the oven clock changing. It was the middle of the night, but she did not want to go back to sleep. The dream she had just had was so clear in her mind; frightening her. The man in the dream had appeared to her again, exactly as he had done the night before Steve phoned her. *'Don't marry Adam'*, rang in her head.

She heard a movement in the corridor. 'Lynne?' Adam's voice, sounded groggy; sleepy. 'Lynne? Where are you?'

Jumping off the bar stool, she switched on the kitchen light and looked up to see him.

'Wh... What were you doing here in the dark?' he asked.

'I came to get a glass of water. I didn't want to wake you, so I left the lights off. I did wake you though, didn't I? Sorry.'

Adam frowned. Reaching out towards her, he touched her face. 'Let's go back to bed.' He took her hand.

She lay awake for the rest of the night, refusing to close her eyes, in case the dream returned.

Chapter Four

'It's just last minute nerves, Lynne,' said Sandra. 'Forget about it.'

'But...'

'No buts,' said Sandra, shaking her long mane of scruffy red hair as she spoke. 'You are not going to let me down. I've waited thirty years to be a bridesmaid. I've never been a bridesmaid before. I've always wanted to be. Funny, they say: "Three times a bridesmaid, never a bride", but I've never heard: "Never a bridesmaid, never a bride"; that would be more accurate in my experience.'

'What?' Lynne was still thinking about her dream, and hadn't really been concentrating.

'I'm jealous. You're getting married. I want to get married, but it looks as though it'll never happen. Then here you are, complaining and moaning every day about having cold feet. I'd gladly have the cold feet if I could walk down the aisle in a beautiful gown.'

'Oh, you'll get married one day.'

'Yeah.' Sandra shook her head doubtfully.

'You're still young, Sand.'

'Just about.' Sandra tutted.

'Anyway, we're talking about *me,* not you. *I'm* the one who needs advice.'

'I gave you my advice the other day, and it remains the same. Marry Adam. Look at it from my perspective: I've got the chance to wear a fancy, lacy dress, and walk down an aisle as a bridesmaid. You're not going to ruin my fun.' Sandra giggled. 'You are getting married, even if I have to drag you down the aisle myself. I want to be a bridesmaid! It's the nearest I'm likely to ever get to being part of a wedding party.'

'Sand, stop joking around for a minute, and listen!'

Sandra sat down. 'Sorry. I... I didn't realise you were being serious. I mean, we talked about this at lunch the other day, and I thought it was sorted. Look, as I say, it's probably just cold feet. I've read a lot about weddings—being a wannabe bride—and I know that some people get cold feet just before the wedding. That's all it is. You just have to ride it out.'

'No. It's more than that.' Lynne stood up. 'I've had the same dream three times this week.'

'Okay, so it's a pretty bad case of cold feet syndrome; but I'm

21

telling you, that's what it is.'

Lynne appeared lost in thought for a moment, before continuing: 'It's really... I don't know. The dream is so vivid. This man looks like an angel, with a halo and everything.'

'Yes, I know; he tells you not to marry Adam.'

'Yes.'

'The really freaky thing was, last night the man said more. He said, "You shouldn't marry him; you're making a mistake. Someone else needs you." I started to wonder who the other person was; the "someone else". I thought of Steve. I mean, he's the only other man I've ever dated properly. Steve phoned me the day after I had the first dream.'

'Damn that Steve. I'm so angry that he phoned you, messing up your head. He's a jerk. Can't you see he is making you feel like this; confusing you. It's probably some sort of game he's playing.'

Sandra picked up the pink bridesmaid dress. She walked over to the mirror and held the dress up in front of her. 'You don't think the colour clashes with my hair, do you?'

'Sandra, shut up!'

'What?'

'Sorry. I'm just not in the mood for this.'

'For what?'

'Talking about the wedding.'

'Lynne, I hate to break this to you, but you are getting married in a couple of weeks time. If you don't want to talk about it now—'

'Am I getting married?' She stared at her friend.

Sandra's face dropped.

'I might not be.'

'Lynne.'

'Sand, this dream is so real. It's getting to the stage where I'm too scared to go to sleep at night.'

'Lynne, sit down.'

She sat on Sandra's bed. Sandra placed the bridesmaid dress back on the bed where it had been, and sat next to her friend. 'Do you still feel that you don't love Adam?'

'Adam is so kind. He's lovely.'

'You haven't answered my question.'

'I think I still love him. It's just not as strong as when we first started going out together.'

'You can't expect that. Do you still get on together?'

'Yes. Well, most of the time.'

'Well then.'

'What?'

'If you still love him, you should marry him,' said Sandra.

Lynne sighed.

'Do you still love "Stupid Steve"? Is that it? Because—'

'No!' Lynne looked at Sandra, angrily.

'So what's the problem then?'

'I haven't told you everything.' Lynne touched her knees, appearing almost too frightened to continue speaking.

'Come on then,' coaxed Sandra.

'Last night, in the dream, the man said that if I marry Adam, my soul mate will die.'

'Oh, Lynne!' Sandra stood up. 'I can't believe we're having this conversation. I mean, I know you're stressed out about the wedding, but... but this is ridiculous.'

'Is it?' Lynne seemed to be questioning herself, eyes down, looking at her hands.

'Oh, I don't know what you want.' Sandra sighed. 'I think you're lucky to have someone like Adam. I wish I could find someone like him.'

'Adam is lovely.'

'Well, are you going to let a few last minute nerves ruin everything? I don't think he'll be very happy if you announce you can't marry him because a man in your dream told you not to.'

'I know, but if *you* had the dreams, you would understand why I'm feeling like this.'

'Okay, okay. Why don't you go and see Steve? Get it out of your system. See him one last time. That will prove that you're making the right decision.'

'I don't know.'

'Come on... I'll come with you.'

'I don't know where he lives.'

'Kev does. He still sees him sometimes. I'll get the address. All of this is Kev's fault. If he didn't tell Steve you're getting married, you wouldn't be having these freaky dreams. He's messed with your head, calling you like that—the two-timing rat. He obviously hasn't changed. You used to love him, and he's opened up old wounds by phoning you just before you're about to commit your life to another man. Anyone would be having bad dreams after that. Even the thought of Steve Reynolds is enough to give me nightmares.'

'Sand, I had the first dream before I spoke to Steve.'

'Yes, but you had the others *because* you spoke to him. Trust me, as soon as you see him again, you'll remember how much you hate him.'

Lynne remembered how her old feelings for Steve had bubbled up to the surface when she heard his voice on the phone. Hesitantly, she followed Sandra out of the house.

Chapter Five

'Do you want me to come in with you?' asked Sandra.

Lynne sat in the passenger seat of Sandra's car and stared out towards Steve's house. It was a big house. Semi-detached. *I bet it's got a big garden,* she thought. Steve had obviously done well for himself in the past few years. It was a far cry from the one-bed flat they had shared when they were living together. But he had been studying to be a lawyer, and she'd heard that he'd secured a lucrative job in the city, so she wasn't too shocked or surprised at seeing his house.

She sighed and looked at Sandra, who was using her rear-view mirror to adjust her make-up. 'I'm a bit nervous, Sand. Do you think that's stupid?'

'No. Look, you don't have to go and talk to him. But... I think it would help.' Sandra paused. Then, shrugging her shoulders, she said: 'I'd be quite happy to drive away if you'd prefer. He gives me the creeps. Ooh... just thinking that we're outside his house makes me feel so... ugh.'

Lynne took a deep breath, opened the car door, and stepped out. 'I won't be long.'

'Okay.' Sandra looked at her with a concerned frown.

'I am doing the right thing, aren't I?' she asked, turning back to look into the car.

'Yes.' Sandra nodded, but she appeared unsure.

Lynne smiled nervously and shut the door behind her. Standing next to the car, she stared at Steve's house, trying to make up her mind whether to go ahead, or turn back. After a few moments, she braced herself and began walking towards the door.

It was 9 pm. The lights were on. With each step she took, she could feel her heart beat faster.

Her hands trembled as she rang the door bell. *What am I doing here?*

A woman opened the door; her face looked familiar. Lynne racked her brains trying to remember where she'd seen her before.

'Hello,' said the woman, not appearing to have recognised Lynne at all. She seemed eager to get back to whatever she had been doing when the doorbell had rung; a look of impatience on her face.

'Um... Is Steve in?' asked Lynne.

'Yes. Who are you?' asked the woman, narrowing her eyes.

Lynne's eyes widened as she suddenly remembered who the woman was. Alicia. The last time Lynne had seen her was over four years ago, when she'd caught her in bed with Steve. 'Just say I'm an old friend,' Lynne answered, bluntly, as if preparing herself for a showdown at the door when Steve appeared. Why did this woman still make her feel this way after so many years? *I've moved on; I'm marrying Adam in a couple of weeks,* she reminded herself. She forced a smile at Alicia. Almost a grin. Too much of a smile.

Alicia didn't return her smile. Her face was hard, her eyes distant, as if she were trying to remember where she had seen Lynne before. 'I'll go and get Steve,' she said, walking away. Then, turning back towards Lynne, she asked, 'Um... what's your name?'

'Lynne,' she said, almost dramatically, as if she were an actress playing an award-winning role; as if she were hoping that as soon as she said her name, Alicia would fall to her knees and apologise for ruining her relationship. But it didn't happen. Alicia seemed oblivious to her; just as she had been when Lynne had opened her bedroom door on that wet May afternoon, all those years ago, and caught her in the act with Steve.

For months after she had caught them together, Lynne often had flashbacks. Alicia's face would appear to her; the face of a woman in the throes of wild abandon. This image had become imprinted on Lynne's mind. The flashbacks became more distorted as the months went by, and the look in Alicia's eyes—full of joy and smiling, when she had sat up in bed looking towards Lynne at the door—became Alicia laughing at her. Lynne had always felt somehow inferior to her ever since that day, because Steve had chosen her.

Lynne stood waiting at the front door, her stomach churning. Somehow, the fact that he was still with Alicia made it all worse; proving to Lynne that she *was* inferior to Alicia. The woman had managed to steal Steve and keep him. Lynne turned around towards Sandra's car. *Why am I still here?* She questioned herself. Initially, she had thought Steve phoned her because he was alone, and jealous about her impending marriage; but she'd been proved wrong. There seemed no point in her staying here, prolonging her humiliation. She walked away towards the car; towards a place of refuge.

'Hello, Lynne?' Steve's voice called out to her just as she reached the gate.

Her plan to escape had failed. She turned around slowly to face him, and walked back towards the door, her head bowed. As she got closer she dared to look up at him, and saw Alicia standing behind him.

'Lynne!' He seemed surprised to see her. 'What are you doing here?'

'Oh, I was just passing.' She looked over towards Alicia; a subconscious reflex.

Steve followed her eyes and he appeared embarrassed for a moment. He coughed.

'Aren't you going to introduce us?' asked Alicia.

'This is Lynne. Um, Lynne, this is Alicia.' Steve shifted uncomfortably as the two women smiled falsely at each other.

'How do you know Steve?' asked Alicia, her cold, expressionless gaze fixed on Lynne.

'We're old friends,' said Steve quickly.

'Oh.' Alicia stared at her with glazed eyes, as if lost in thought momentarily. 'You do look familiar. Have we met before?'

'No,' said Lynne.

'Were you at the wedding? Is that where I've seen you before?' Then turning to Steve: 'Was she at our wedding, honey?'

Lynne froze. Her eyes were drawn towards Steve's hand and sure enough she saw a gold band. Alicia and Steve were married.

'I really must go,' said Lynne, staring into the middle distance. 'I really must go.' She turned around and walked quickly towards Sandra's car, wanting to run. Opening the door of the car, she cried out: 'Drive!'

Sandra's eyes widened in shock at the abruptness. 'What? What happened? Did you see him?'

'Just drive, will you!'

Chapter Six

'Are you going to tell me what happened?' asked Sandra, parking the car outside the tower block that housed Lynne's flat. 'Lynne?'

Lynne looked at her friend, and then back at the window.

'You haven't said a word since we left Steve's place.'

'Don't say his name,' snapped Lynne.

'Well, at least that got a reaction,' said Sandra, sighing. 'You've still got feelings for him, haven't you?'

'No,' said Lynne to the car window.

'Yes, you have. Look, it's your life. I know I gave you a hard time about it earlier, but if you've decided you can't marry Adam, it's really up to you.'

'He's married,' said Lynne.

'Who? Adam?' Sandra looked at her, wide-eyed.

'No, stupid, Steve.'

'Oh, "Stupid Steve"; yes, I know.'

'You knew? Why didn't you warn me?' Lynne's brow furrowed and her mouth fell open. 'You allowed me to go there, to his home, and make a fool of myself! What sort of friend are you? You had so many opportunities to tell me he's married! What were you thinking?'

'Calm down... I...' Sandra shrugged her shoulders.

'Why didn't you tell me he's married?'

'The main reason I brought you to his house is so that you'd see he is all settled with a wife, and he'd moved on. I'm sure I told you he's married.'

'Well, you didn't! And it's *her* of all people!'

'Who?'

'Alicia! The girl he was having an affair with!'

'Oh my God. Sorry, Lynne. I didn't know he'd married *her*. If I had, I swear I would never have brought you here. Are you okay?'

'I'll live.'

'Sorry. But, look it this way: you didn't want to marry him, so she's welcome to him.'

Lynne remained silent.

Sandra's eyes widened. 'You're not telling me you were considering getting back together with him, after what he did?'

'No!' exclaimed Lynne. 'That's not it!'

'Good. You had me worried there for a minute. Anyway, I think

28

this has done the trick; I doubt you'll be having that weird dream anymore. You can marry Adam now, and live happily ever after. No more doubts.'

Lynne smiled sadly. 'I suppose you're right. I know you're going to think I'm mad for saying this, but I think I was having doubts because I was still wondering "what if" me and Steve had got married. I used to really love him, you know?' Lynne opened the car door to leave, a lump in her throat.

'It's okay, Lynne. I knew that. I was sure that you going to Steve's, and seeing he'd moved on, would set you free.'

Lynne looked back at her friend. 'It's not that I don't love Adam. I do, but...'

'I know,' said Sandra, noticing the tears forming in Lynne's eyes. 'You just needed to know whether you still had any feelings for Steve.'

'Something like that,' said Lynne, as she stepped out of the car.

Lynne cried openly as soon as she got inside her flat. She felt grateful that Adam was away for a work conference this weekend; it would give her time alone to deal with her emotions. She recalled the thoughts she'd had after the first dream, when she felt sure that she didn't love Adam anymore. The edges were blurred now. There were no cut and dried feelings; nothing was black and white.

As her tears subsided, a sense of freedom took their place. It was as if the tears had lined a pathway taking her further away from her pain. She had finally let go. She could close the door on her feelings for Steve. There was no more to be said between them. Theirs had been a close relationship once, but it had come to an end; even if it was an end that she had not wanted, having once believed that they were destined to be together for ever. She wiped the final few stray tears from her eyes, as she sat at the kitchen table, sipping a cup of tea and staring out at the starless night sky. The realisation struck her that she should be happy she was being given another chance at love: Adam wanted to marry her. They were moving ever closer to that day. A joyful feeling soothed her, almost like the sun coming out from behind grey clouds after a storm. At last, she could finally let go of the past and look towards the future, without wondering what might have been. And she realised that she did love Adam. It *was* that stupid dream, and then Steve's phone-call, that had put any seeds of doubt in her mind. It *had* been "cold feet", pure and simple; just as Sandra had said.

As she thought of Adam, his warm smile and his loving arms, she knew she was lucky to have him, and she wished he could be here with her now.

Chapter Seven

'If I have one more drink, I'll fall over,' said Lynne.

'It's your hen night, you're supposed to get bladdered,' said Lucy, her friend and former work colleague.

'I don't want a massive hangover on my wedding day. It's supposed to be the best day of my life. I want to remember it.'

'Oh, you'll have the photos to remember it by!' said Lucy, laughing and taking a quick snap of Lynne, as she sat bleary-eyed at the bar.

'That's another thing, I have to look half-decent in the wedding photos.'

'Don't worry, it's amazing what make-up can do these days. Here you go, drink up,' said Kelly, Lynne's sister, handing her another drink.

'I'm going to have to head back home soon,' said Sandra, looking at her watch.

'Poor Sandy, designated driver. Missing out on all the fun. You must be dying of boredom watching us drinking!' said Lucy, almost falling off her stool.

'No, I'm okay. I don't really drink that much, anyway,' said Sandra.

'Okay. We'll have one more dance, then we'll leave. What's the time?' asked Kelly.

'Three o'clock,' said Sandra.

⧗

After dropping Kelly off at her house, Sandra parked the car outside Lucy's flat. 'Bye, Luce. See you again soon,' shouted Lynne from the car as Lucy stumbled up to her front door.

'Am I glad to see the back of her,' said Sandra.

'Oh, she's okay once you get to know her.' Lynne giggled.

'Yeah, if you like alcoholics,' sneered Sandra. 'She didn't stop drinking from the moment we set foot in the club.'

'She's just happy for me,' said Lynne, looking at her hands.

'Yeah, sorry, Lynne. I must sound like a moody cow.'

'It's okay, I'd be a bit peed off if I'd been the only one who couldn't have any alcohol all night. You did enjoy it, though, didn't you?'

'Yeah, it was great. I think I'm just getting a bit too old for clubbing. The music was so loud!'

'Oh, don't be silly, you're never too old for clubbing.'

'Well, everyone else in there looked about sixteen.'

'So do you,' said Lynne, smiling.

'Thanks.' Sandra smiled back.

'I knew I could get a smile out of you somehow.' Lynne laughed.

'So, tomorrow's the big day,' said Sandra, driving away from Lucy's flat.

'Yeah. I'll be an old married woman.'

'Are you excited?'

'Yeah, I suppose so.' Lynne looked out of the car window. There were no more doubts in her mind about her love for Adam. She hadn't had any more of those dreams. Yet, there was something, a feeling, like a distant drum. It refused to go away.

They arrived at Sandra's flat after 4 am.

'Hardly seems worth going to sleep,' said Lynne, looking at the clock. 'We'll have to get up soon.'

'Yeah.' Sandra nodded, yawned, and fell onto the sofa. 'Oh, I'm really going to miss this.'

'What do you mean?' asked Lynne, feeling confused.

'Well... you staying at my flat after a night out. You won't be able to do that when you're married.'

Lynne smiled. 'Don't be silly, nothing's going to change just because I'm getting married.' As she said it, she averted her eyes from Sandra's gaze. Then, turning away from her, she said: 'I'm tired. I think I should go to bed.'

'Okay. Er... Lynne, are you all right?'

'Yes, I'm just tired.'

'You're not having second thoughts again?'

'No, that's in the past.' She turned back towards Sandra and smiled, feeling like a fraud. Something wasn't right.

'So the dreams have stopped?'

Lynne shivered then, as if someone had opened all the windows letting in a chilling breeze. Although that sensation only lasted for a couple of seconds, she was left shaken, and an eerie presence seemed to pervade the room. 'Y... Yeah,' she managed to say. 'I haven't had any more of those.' The strange feeling had passed as suddenly as it arrived. She sighed deeply, and continued: 'You were right, Sand, it was just a touch of cold feet.' Then, as if trying hard to convince herself: 'I'm fine, really. I've just had one too many drinks.'

31

Chapter Eight

'You look beautiful, Lynne.' Her mother smiled at her reflection in the mirror as she stood behind her. Tears were in her eyes.

Lynne smiled back at her mother's reflection. 'Thanks, Mum.' *It's true*, she thought, *I do actually look 'beautiful'; nothing like my real self. Exactly what I wanted. The beautician is a miracle worker.* A tear threatened to fall as she surveyed her appearance, but she stopped herself, for fear of ruining her mascara. Feeling the silk skirt of the ivory dress between her fingers, she tried to keep her mind on the present time, not wanting to think of anything that could ruin the day. *I have to get through this,* she said to herself.

Sandra ran into the room, holding the skirt of the pink bridesmaid dress in her hands to stop herself tripping over it. 'Hurry up!' she said quickly. 'We'll be late!'

'The bride is allowed to be late,' said Lynne's mother.

Sandra stood beside her and looked at Lynne, her mouth wide open. She appeared almost frozen in time for a few seconds. 'You're so lucky,' she said, eventually.

'It'll be you next,' said Lynne.

'Yeah,' Sandra replied, dejectedly. 'It might happen, one day, I suppose.'

'Oh, Mum, you haven't met Sandra yet, have you? She's my closest friend.'

'Yes, you have spoken about her before. Nice to meet you, dear.' She smiled at Sandra. 'So, you're unmarried? Are you seeing anyone?'

'Er... not at the moment.'

Lynne could see Sandra squirm, and was about to interject and save her friend from the interrogation, when her mother started talking again.

'These things don't just happen, Sandra, dear. You have to help them along. You don't have time to waste. You'll be left on the shelf if you're not careful. You can't just wait for Mr. Right to knock on your door; you have to look for him. You have to kiss a lot of frogs before you find your prince charming.' Then, looking at Lynne proudly, she added: 'Look at my lovely daughter. Don't you wish you were getting married today?'

Sandra appeared to be stunned into silence.

'She doesn't mean any harm,' Lynne whispered in Sandra's ear as they walked out of the door. 'She's just proud that her daughter's getting married.'

Sandra sighed. 'The sad thing is, she's got a point. I am thirty now. I'm running out of time.'

'No you're not,' said Lynne, as they walked together towards the white Rolls-Royce waiting outside the door. 'You've got plenty of time. And, you're pretty; you could have your pick of men.'

'I don't know. I haven't had much luck in the past.'

'Don't let my mum get to you. She's obsessed with marriage. It's not the be all, end all.'

'I know, but I wish I could find someone special.'

'You will.'

They sat in the back of the car, next to Lynne's dad.

'I've been waiting here for fifteen minutes. We're going to be late,' he grumbled.

'It's okay, Dad; the bride's allowed to be late.'

Chapter Nine

Lynne had tried so hard that morning to put the dream to the back of her mind; but now, as she walked down the aisle towards Adam, she could almost hear the voice in her head: "Don't do it."

After she and Sandra had returned home from the hen night, Lynne had fallen into a deep sleep on Sandra's sofa-bed. She'd woken up in a sweat, only an hour later, with heart palpitations. The dream had returned; only this time the "angel" appeared so real, as if he were in the room with her.

'Lynne, you are making a mistake. Adam is not right for you. He doesn't love you. If you marry him, you will regret it, and your true love will die...'

She had sat up in bed, shaken; unable to comprehend why she was having these dreams. Somehow, she did fall asleep again, and thankfully her other dreams were pleasant enough. In the morning, she put it down to yet more cold feet, and tried to concentrate on other things. Surely, once she married Adam, all of these thoughts of doubt would go away? Nervously, anxiously, she willed the clock to move forward, so that she could get to the church and get the wedding over with.

Standing at the altar, Adam was beaming. Lynne couldn't help stumbling over her words, and had to fake a smile throughout the ceremony, to the point that it felt like her face would become permanently fixed in this false, plastic, half-smile. She kept noticing Adam's best man, Paul, frowning at her. Did he sense that her heart wasn't in it? She tried very hard to disguise her thoughts. Sandra, who stood beside her, whispered, 'Are you all right?', on more than one occasion, and seemed very concerned. Somehow, Lynne got through the wedding, but was trembling as she walked with Adam, arm in arm, out of the church.

Breathing deeply to take in the fresh air, Lynne felt grateful that it was all over. The atmosphere in the church had been stifling.

Sandra happily threw confetti over the newlyweds. 'You have to throw your bouquet now... Remember, aim at me!' She winked.

Lynne nodded towards her and practically handed her the bouquet. Sandra seemed so happy to actually have it in her hands, that she didn't even appear to notice that Lynne hadn't thrown it. Sandra held the bouquet aloft, like a trophy, for all to see.

Feeling overwhelmed, Lynne just wanted to be anywhere else, away from the hundreds of eyes that were looking at her and expecting her to be happy and smiling. Her gut feeling was, 'Oh my God, what have I just done?'; but there was no rhyme or reason for her feeling like that... just the bitter aftertaste of a recurring dream. Nothing tangible; just thoughts and feelings.

Chapter Ten

At the wedding reception, Lynne drank too much champagne. At first, she liked the way the alcohol relaxed her, and helped her to dispel the disturbing thoughts she'd been having. The horrible sense of regret that had been tugging at her, faded with each sip of the fizzy liquid.

Soon, she was stumbling and finding it hard to keep her balance on the 4-inch heels of her new shoes, so she sat down and ate some food in the hope that it would neutralise the effect of the alcohol. After eating just one canapé, she felt as though she might throw up, so she made an excuse to Adam that she had to go to the toilet. *Where's Sand?* she wondered, determined to find her friend; needing to speak to someone who could help put things into perspective.

As she stood up, the whole room seemed to change and move around her, like it was spinning. It took a moment before she found her bearings. As she walked unsteadily away from the bridal table, she spotted Sandra talking to Paul, Adam's best man, in the far corner of the hall. It looked like Sandra was flirting with him. Lynne smiled, almost forgetting her worries. Perhaps Paul and Sandra would get together. She had never seen Paul with a girlfriend in all the years she'd been dating Adam. *Paul is such a nice, gentle man. Sandra could do a lot worse than him.*

Then she saw Sandra walk away towards the toilets. Paul looked in Lynne's direction. Again, he wore a frown on his face. He began walking towards her.

'Hi, Paul,' she said, trying hard not to slur her words.

'You've been drinking all evening,' he said curtly. 'You're making a spectacle of yourself. Have some respect for Adam.' He walked away in a huff.

Lynne was left open-mouthed. Her face began to get hotter and hotter, until she thought she might combust. Looking around her, she saw the smiles on the faces of guests on the dance floor turning to concerned frowns. She became aware of her slouched posture, caused by trying to stay upright on her heels. Doing her best to straighten up, she smiled her well-worn plastic smile, as she walked embarrassed towards the toilets.

Lynne found Sandra washing her hands.

'Er... you look very, um... merry!' said Sandra, giggling, but at the same time managing to look like her mother usually looked when Lynne was a teenager returning home from a night out clubbing.

Lynne caught sight of her reflection in one of the mirrors, and had to blink to make sure she wasn't seeing things. Her hair had long since fallen out of its style. It had been neatly pinned above her head with a few ringlets hanging down on either side; but now it was lopsided, with bits of stray hair falling this way and that, so it looked more like a bird's nest. Her mascara had somehow become smudged over one of her cheeks, and her lipstick had also been smudged.

'I look like a clown,' she said.

'Yes, you do,' agreed Sandra, laughing. 'Let me sort you out, Mrs. Green. I've got my make-up bag here. You'll be looking beautiful again in two ticks. So, how does it feel to be a married woman?'

Lynne's face dropped.

'Lynne?'

'I *have* done the right thing, haven't I?' She appeared to be asking herself, as she looked in the mirror.

'Has something happened between you and Adam since last night?' asked Sandra, confused. 'I thought you were excited about getting married. What has he done?'

'*Him?* No. It's me. I'm the one having doubts again. What's wrong with me?' She sat on the bin, which was one of those large bins with a lid; just the right height for a seat (if you are drunk).

'Ugh... Lynne, get off there. There are so many germs on bins. You'll ruin your dress.'

'I had the dream again last night,' she said, standing up and wobbling, so that Sandra had to put out her arm to stop her falling over.

'It was so real. It freaked me out. He said I shouldn't marry Adam.'

'Okay,' Sandra said, softly. 'Look, you're married now, and everything's fine. The world hasn't come to an end. No one's died. So, just put it down to cold feet.'

'You keep saying that: "cold feet, cold feet"; but it doesn't make sense. I've been with Adam for the last three years; why have I only been having these dreams in the last few weeks?'

'It's about the wedding,' said Sandra. 'As it was coming nearer, you were getting nervous, and maybe you were even scared. Some people have a deep fear of commitment. Marriage is more of a big deal than living together. You were scared to get married, and your dreams reflected that. You were trying to convince yourself not to marry Adam. But as I say, you're married now, and you haven't suddenly grown an extra head; so, I'm sure you won't be having those dreams anymore. Trust me, I've watched enough daytime TV to know what

I'm talking about! You have faced your fear now, so it's over.'

'I hope you're right.' Lynne smiled a crooked smile. It couldn't be commitment phobia, she reasoned, because she'd always wanted to get married. The dream had left her shaken, and had turned what was supposed to be the happiest day of her life into some sort of waking nightmare.

'Just have sympathy for *me*,' said Sandra, as she fixed Lynne's hair. 'I'm officially unlucky in love. Even though I caught your bouquet, I'm having serious doubts I'll ever find my knight in shining armour. The bridesmaid is supposed to get off with the best man, right?'

'Oh yeah, I saw you chatting with Paul,' said Lynne, as she reapplied her lipstick.

'Hmm... Yeah, I was thinking: here's a nice man; he's single, about my age. Why didn't you tell me he's gay?'

'Gay?' Lynne turned to look at Sandra, and accidentally drew a red line of lipstick on her cheek in the process. She grabbed a tissue and began wiping it off. 'Paul's not gay!'

'Oh come on, it's written all over him. He didn't fall for any of my flirting techniques.'

'Er... just because he didn't flirt back, doesn't mean he's gay.'

'Believe me, he is gay. I read once in a magazine, foolproof ways to tell if a man is gay. I tested him, and he is definitely gay.'

Lynne laughed. 'He's just a nice man, Sand. He's a bit shy; hasn't had much experience with women. You probably scared him.'

'Well, at least I made you laugh,' said Sandra. 'I'm glad my failed love life is of benefit to someone.'

'Do you want me to tell Adam you like Paul? Then maybe we could go out on a double-date?'

'Er... no, thanks. I think he'd prefer Adam to me; he's more his type.'

'Sand!' Lynne laughed again. 'No wonder you're still single!'

Chapter Eleven

Two weeks into their honeymoon, Lynne and Adam were on the beach.

'Time flies,' said Adam, rubbing some sun cream onto his shoulders. 'I wish we didn't have to go back to England.'

'Yeah,' said Lynne, looking up from her novel (the murdered girl's best friend, Suzanna, was just about to enter the hotel room, where her poor friend had been killed. It was nail-biting stuff). Lynne had been so engrossed in the story that she hadn't heard what Adam had said. *It probably wasn't important, anyway*, she thought. She looked at him and smiled blankly. It occurred to her that they hadn't really spoken at all for the past two weeks. Had they been together too long to have anything new to say, or were they just so relaxed in each other's company that they didn't need to talk? She was glad she'd bought the two novels with her that she saw on special offer at the airport, otherwise she would have been so bored.

This was the first time in a long time that they had really been alone together, without their daily routines of work and home-life. Adam's work involved a lot of foreign travel, so he had no interest in taking annual holidays. Lynne usually went on holiday with her friends or her sister. For about six months of the year, Adam and Lynne hardly saw each other. Adam would fly abroad, here and there, on business, returning home for a few weeks; but even then he worked for over ten hours a day. At the beginning of their relationship, Lynne thought this was the best of both worlds: she had her man, but she always had time for her friends. She'd looked forward to, and cherished, the time she spent with Adam. She used to think his frequent absences helped keep their love alive; but now, years on, she realised that they didn't really seem to have much in common. The time they had spent apart had caused them to drift further and further in different directions.

She knew she still fancied Adam. He could still make the butterflies in her stomach go wild when the mood was right. But there was definitely something lacking in their relationship. Even on this short honeymoon, he had kept his mobile phone close at hand, waiting for important calls from work. Very unromantic. She wondered if it was naïve to still expect romance after a three year relationship. She felt unsure, but decided that she must stop analysing things so deeply.

You'd find problems with any relationship if you looked hard enough, she reasoned. *All that really matters is, we're sitting here together, thousands of miles from home, on honeymoon. Surely, that's proof that he loves me? Maybe I'm asking too much; I mean, no one has a perfect relationship, do they?*

Leaning back in the sun lounger, she allowed herself to relax as her eyes took in the white sands and crystal clear ocean. Sighing deeply, she tried to hold on to this feeling; a much longed for moment of peace. The recurring dream had stopped, but the memory of it was still there and made shutting her eyes for sleep a tough task every night. The fear remained, but thankfully it became more distant with each passing day.

Lynne thought back to their wedding night, and disappointment reared its head again. They were supposed to be spending a romantic night together at a posh London hotel before flying out to their honeymoon destination the next day. She had bought a sexy, black night-dress, made of real silk. She loved the way the dress accentuated her curves, and couldn't wait to see Adam's face when he saw her wearing it. Lynne went up to the hotel room to change, whilst Adam went to the hotel bar to get some champagne for their room. When Lynne heard a knock on the hotel room door, she assumed it must be Adam, as he'd been gone over half-an-hour already. The door to their room was unlocked; she'd left it unlocked for him. Standing at the door to the en suite, posing in her new night-gown, she called out: 'Come in, it's open'. She waited in great anticipation as the door opened. Into the room walked a middle-aged woman, whose eyes widened as she caught sight of Lynne. The woman appeared to stifle a laugh as she said, 'Oh, sorry, I must have the wrong room. I was looking for my friend's room. Sorry.' She walked out the door, covering her mouth with her hand.

Adam didn't turn up until 3 am. By that time, Lynne had fallen asleep. He apologised the next day, saying he'd met his best man, Paul, down in the bar, and as they hadn't seen each other for so long, they'd had a lot of catching up to do.

Lynne sighed, and looked at Adam fiddling with his mobile phone as he sat next to her on his sun lounger. What did it matter if they hardly had sex anymore? They had been together for over three years; it was normal, wasn't it?

Adam turned towards her. 'I've had a text from work. I'll probably have to fly to New York the day after we get back home. Urgent business.'

'Okay,' said Lynne. And there the conversation ended. She was soon hooked on her novel again. *How will Suzanna react when she finds Chloé's body? I bet Brian killed her...*

Chapter Twelve

'Did you have a good honeymoon?' asked Sandra, taking a sip of her coffee.

'Yes, the weather was great. Nice beach. Oh, and I read two great books, I'll have to lend them to you. One's a murder mystery, the other's a romance,' replied Lynne.

'Hmm... reading books, great tan... not really the sign of a good honeymoon, if you know what I mean.' Sandra raised her eyebrows.

'Ha, ha. Unfortunately, we're not in the *honeymoon* stage of our relationship. But that's not to say we didn't get up to anything.' Lynne winked.

'And where's the groom? Back to work, straight off the plane?'

'Oh, he had to fly to New York on business.'

'He's away an awful lot. Don't you miss him?'

'Well, I'm used to it now, I suppose. Um... you said you had some news for me when you phoned.'

'Yes, I have,' Sandra smiled. 'I've met a man.'

'Ooh, how? When? Tell me everything!' Lynne's overexcited reaction to Sandra's news was to cover up her true feelings: she found herself feeling strangely jealous. Thinking back to her honeymoon, she realised that the romance had long since fizzled out of her own relationship. Even when they did spend the night together, the sex was more mechanical and routine, than sensuous and exciting. She thought back to when she'd first started dating Adam and how every moment spent with him would make her feel special and feminine. All of that had changed. Looking in Sandra's eyes, she recognised the sparkle of new love, and wished she could feel that once again with Adam.

Lynne had been looking forward to the wedding as something that could maybe re-ignite the spark in their love life, but sadly it had only served to mark the passing of time and to remind her that they had been really happy once.

Sandra fiddled with her red hair as she gushed, 'His name is Matthew... Matt. I met him last week at the gym. We've been out to the theatre, and dinner. He's really nice.'

'The gym? I didn't know you went to a gym.'

'I've had membership for about six months and paid loads of money, but never used it. So, I thought I'd give it a go. I'm glad I did!'

'So, what does he do for a living?'

'He's a personal trainer.'

'Oh.'

'He's gorgeous. I want you to meet him and let me know what you think. He's having a party next week for his thirtieth birthday, and he said I could bring a friend. Will you come?'

'Okay, Adam's out of town, so I'm free.'

⌛

Lynne sat on the sofa in the stuffy living room. Matthew's flat was very small. The tiny living room was the largest part of it; but even with the minimalist furnishing—a three piece suite, a small coffee table, and a unit housing a wide screen TV—there was hardly any room to walk around. Lynne wondered how he expected to host a party in here. The guests could hardly make use of the other rooms. His bedroom was only just big enough to fit his double bed; the even smaller bathroom, consisted of a shower, a toilet, and the tiniest wash basin Lynne had ever seen. The kitchen was almost non-existent, being a 2 foot square, tiled floor, surrounded by fitted cupboards.

People began to arrive for the party and the flat became very noisy and crowded, with the guests tripping over each other every time they moved.

Lynne fidgeted as she sat on the sofa. She had been joined by a young couple, Ned and Sue. They only looked about 20 years old. They were constantly hugging, kissing, and giggling. Lynne suddenly felt very old.

The room started to get smoky as more of the guests lit up cigarettes.

Sandra and Lynne had been the first to arrive. Sandra had offered to help Matthew prepare for the party and she wanted to introduce Lynne to him before all the other guests arrived.

'Hello, Matthew, nice to meet you,' Lynne said.

He'd shaken her hand and replied, 'Call me Matt,' flicking his long blonde fringe from his eyes. He was very handsome, like a model; with crystal clear blue eyes, tanned skin, and rippling muscles. Sandra had grinned from ear to ear as she introduced them. Matt handed Lynne a glass of champagne and then he and Sandra had disappeared into the kitchen, leaving her alone.

There didn't appear to be any food at the party, apart from a couple of bowls of nuts and crisps, some beer cans, and champagne. Lynne wished she had eaten before she came. She could hear her stomach rumbling as she began to feel more and more hungry.

After about 20 or so guests had arrived, the living room began to look more like a commuter train at rush hour. Matt appeared from the kitchen and pushed through the crowd. He leaned over Lynne. 'Sorry, Susan,' he said to her. She didn't know whether she should correct him; but then realising that if he and Sandra were an item now, they would be seeing a lot of each other, she said, 'I'm Lynne.'

'Oh, sorry! I've never been very good with names.' He laughed. He reached behind her and pressed a button on the stereo system that she now noticed she was sitting in front of. Dance music started playing. 'Sorry there's not much room in here,' Matt announced to the guests. 'Just getting you in the mood. We'll head off to the club in about an hour.' He then proceeded to turn up the volume on the stereo.

Loud music blasted from the speakers behind Lynne. Her eardrums were pulsating with every beat. She wanted to get up off the sofa, but the room was so tiny, and full of people, it seemed that it would be an impossible task. She leaned forward and put her hands over her ears.

After a few minutes, she began to feel as if her head would explode, and decided she would have to leave. Sandra was too busy with Matt to notice, anyway. Standing up, Lynne pushed through the crowd, apologising for nudging people and for making them spill their drinks. As she reached the living room door, she bumped into a tall man. Looking up, she saw that he was a not only tall, but dark and handsome. He looked a bit like Johnny Depp. She'd once had a serious crush on Johnny Depp, so she couldn't help but be mesmerised by this young man.

He smiled at her. 'Hi,' he said, his dazzling white teeth causing her to stare even more.

As she lost herself in his deep brown eyes, she couldn't help smiling back. *The champagne must have gone to my head,* she thought. *Lynne you're a married woman, so start behaving like one.*

But her eagerness to leave the party became a distant memory, and all she could do was look in awe at this fine specimen of a man. *A bit of flirting never hurt anyone,* she thought to herself.

'I'm Jason,' he said.

She was standing a bit too close to him for comfort, but given the fact that there were so many people crammed into the place, with little room to move, there was nothing she could do about it. The smell of his after shave, fresh and musky, filled her senses. *Why doesn't Adam smell like this?* Lynne had never liked Adam's after shave, it was too strong; but as much as she would complain about it and ask him to try other ones that she bought him for Christmas or birthdays, he always reverted to the bitter, pungent smelling fragrance that he liked.

'I'm Lynne,' she said to Jason, noticing that she was fluttering her eyelashes. She blushed in embarrassment.

'Would you like a drink?' he asked.

'Um... yes, okay.' Unable to avert her eyes from his gaze, she tried to remember the last time she'd met someone and felt so instantly attracted to them. With a touch of guilt, she realised it must have been when she first met Adam.

Jason soon returned, pushing his way through the crowd. He handed her a plastic cup. 'They only had champagne left, hope that's okay?'

'Yes, that's fine.'

They were having to shout at each other to hear themselves over the loud music.

'Listen, Lynne, do you want to go somewhere else? It's a bit too noisy in here and I don't fancy going to a club. I'd much rather get to know you a bit better. Fancy going to get a bite to eat?'

'I'm a married woman,' she said, giggling from the effects of the alcohol on an empty stomach.

'That's okay. I won't tell if you don't,' said Jason, smiling.

He took her by the arm and led her out of the front door. She followed, in high spirits, exhilarated by this adventure. *What harm can it do to have a bit of fun?* she thought, *Okay, I'm married, but I'm not dead! I'm young; I deserve a bit of romance. I'm not intending to sleep with him, so I'm not doing anything wrong.*

Walking along the street with Jason, Lynne couldn't help noticing the envious looks she was getting from women passing them by. *No one ever looks at me like that when I'm with Adam.* But Adam didn't look like he could be a Hollywood film star. He was just Adam. Plain, ordinary Adam. She bit her lip as she realised that she was starting to feel just a smidgeon of regret about marrying him. Her mind went back to the doubts she'd been having before the wedding; but she didn't want to think about any of that, having been sure she'd resolved it all in her mind. *I wouldn't have gone through with the wedding if I'd had serious doubts... surely...* But then another thought entered her mind: *Maybe I just married him because it was easier to do that than to rock the boat.*

'So, you're married?' said Jason, with a twinkle in his eye.

'Yes, I got married a few weeks ago.'

'Oh. So, why are you out on your own, picking up single men at a party?'

'My husband is away on business.' Lynne giggled again.

'So, while the cat's away...' said Jason.

'It's not like that. I just thought that your offer of going out for a meal sounded better than being holed up in that flat. I could hardly breathe in there. There was no food. I didn't eat anything before I came. I expected there'd be food at the party.'

'Hmm... my brother's never been very good at putting on parties.'

'Your brother?' Lynne winced. *Matt is Jason's brother?* They didn't look anything alike. She suddenly felt terrible about complaining about the party... It would get back to Matt now. And Sandra.

'Yes, Matt's my brother. We've got different dads, which is why we don't look alike.'

'Sorry... I didn't mean to say I wasn't enjoying the party.'

'It's okay. I'm his brother, and I wasn't enjoying it. I won't tell him you said anything.' Jason laughed. 'Right, let's get something to eat.'

They went to a Mexican restaurant and enjoyed a tasty meal, and a bottle of wine. Lynne felt as though she might have drunk too much, as she was feeling happier than she could ever remember—almost buzzing. Jason was a breath of fresh air. She found herself wishing she'd met him years ago.

'I guess us meeting up like this is bad timing, huh?' he said, as he walked her home.

'What do you mean?'

'Well, if you weren't married we could have had some fun together. I think you're cool.'

Lynne smiled at him, and couldn't help feeling that stab of regret again. *If only I hadn't married Adam. Maybe that's what the dream was about,* she thought, *Some sort of premonition that I'd regret marrying Adam because I was about to meet the man of my dreams.* She sighed and realised that there wasn't anything she could do about it now. Her choice had been made. She'd married Adam.

'What are you thinking about?' asked Jason.

'I suppose I was thinking I'd really like to be able to turn back time.' She surprised herself that she'd said it aloud. *It must be the alcohol.* She really needed to get back home and have a black coffee.

'Ha, ha.' Jason laughed.

He walked her to the entrance door to the tower block.

'Thanks for walking me home, Jason.'

'No problem. It was my pleasure.' His gaze lingered for a bit longer than was comfortable, and the next thing she knew they were locked

46

in an embrace. His lips met hers in a soft, passionate kiss. She wanted to pull herself away, but at the same time she couldn't help enjoying the sensation of this gorgeous man holding her, and wanting her. *It's only a kiss.*

After what seemed like a few minutes, but was probably only a few seconds, they parted, and she stared into his deep brown eyes, the colour of chestnuts.

'Thank you for a wonderful evening, Lynne.'

'Thank *you*,' she said.

Watching him walk away, was like watching the life she could have had, disappearing into oblivion.

Chapter Thirteen

After her night out with Jason, Lynne was embarrassed to admit even to herself that she felt like a teenager again. He had made her feel so special. Just like Adam used to. But even more so, because she would never have imagined that someone like him would even look at her, let alone kiss her. His words were still resounding in her head; he had said that if she wasn't married they could have been together. At the memory of this, she felt unsure whether to laugh or cry.

With sadness in her heart, she realised that she could not see Jason again. It would have been good to be his friend, but she couldn't risk it; the attraction was too strong, and she didn't want to tempt fate by meeting up with him again. It had only been a kiss, but she hadn't wanted it to end.

He had keyed his mobile phone number into her contacts in her mobile, while they chatted at dinner. She smiled to herself as an image of that moment came to mind, but she quickly brushed off any amorous thoughts and decided that the best thing to do would be to delete it. *I can't see him again, no matter how much I want to, it wouldn't be fair on Adam.* There was something positive she could take out of the experience, though, that made her feel glad she had gone out with Jason: her ego had been well and truly massaged; her confidence level boosted.

She searched for her mobile in her bag, thinking that as well as deleting Jason's number, she would have to send a text to Sandra, to let her know why she left the party so early. *Not that she would have even noticed I wasn't there.* Lynne's thoughts reverted to how lonely she'd been in that crowded flat, when Sandra had disappeared off with Matt.

Looking at her mobile, Lynne was surprised to discover that she had three missed calls on her phone and three voicemail messages—all from Sandra.

Message 1: 9:45 pm: *Lynne, where are you? Give me a call as soon as you get this.*

Message 2: 9:55 pm: *Lynne. Where are you? I'm outside the club. Come outside to meet me. I'm going home.*

Message 3: 10.53 pm: (sounding as though she'd been crying) *Lynne, I'm at home. Matt's a bastard. Where did you go? Oh well, I hope you had a better time at the party than I did. Call me when you get this.*

The timing of the calls meant Lynne had been in the restaurant with Jason when Sandra had phoned her. She didn't hear the phone ring at all. It must have been the music in the restaurant, or the fact that she was hanging on Jason's every word and didn't have space in her senses for anything else. She felt sorry for Sandra. Another failed romance... And she had really fallen for Matt. *What could have gone wrong?*

She dialled Sandra's number.

'Hi,' said Sandra. 'About time. Where have you been?'

'Sorry, Sand. I just got your messages. You sound as though you've been crying. Are you okay?'

'I couldn't find you at the club, Lynne, I looked everywhere.' Sandra began to cry.

'Sorry, Sand. I just felt a bit out of place at the party in Matt's flat, and I wasn't in the mood for clubbing, so I left early.'

'Why didn't you tell me you were leaving?' Sandra sniffed.

'You were with Matt.'

'Don't say his name, the bastard!'

'Er... What happened, Sand?'

'I really need to talk to you, can I come over?'

Lynne looked at the clock, it was midnight. 'What? Right now?'

'Yes.'

'Okay.'

Half an hour later, Sandra turned up at Lynne's door and began crying openly before she'd even stepped into the flat. 'I... thought... he was... different,' she said, incoherently, between sniffles and sobs. 'He's the... same as all... the others.'

'Calm down, Sand. Come on, tell me all about it.' Lynne put an arm around her and led her to the sofa in the living room.

When Sandra had used up the box of tissues in the living room, Lynne brought out a new box and placed it on the table in front of her. 'Okay, now, are you going to tell me what happened?'

Sandra sighed and nodded glumly.

'His ex-fiancée was at the party. She was flirting with him at the club, flaunting her plastic boobs. He ended up snogging her. Then he made an announcement to everyone that they were getting back together... And this is the best bit: he said that he wished they'd never broken up in the first place, and he'd never stopped thinking about her!'

'Oh my God... I'm so sorry, Sand.'

'And at the end, he winked at me and mouthed the word "Sorry", as if that's meant to make me feel better!'

'What a nightmare! I should have been there.'

'I really thought I'd fallen on my feet when I met him. I should have known it was too good to be true.'

'Well, I know this won't sound like much consolation, but at least it happened now when you've only recently met him, rather than a few months or years down the line.'

Sandra nodded. 'I know you're right, but it still feels like a kick in the teeth.'

'You'll find someone else and then you'll forget him.'

'They looked so good together, you know. The perfect couple. I was kidding myself thinking I'd be able to keep someone like that.'

'Hey, it's not all about looks, Sand. What he did to you was cruel. You need to find someone with a good heart.'

'Like your Adam?'

'Yes.' Lynne smiled, and then realised what it sounded like. 'Hang on a minute, Adam's not that bad looking.'

Sandra giggled. 'I didn't mean it like that.'

'See? You're laughing already,' said Lynne. 'You'll be over Matt in no time.'

'Don't say his name!'

'Okay, maybe it'll take a bit longer for you to get over him, but believe me, soon he'll be a distant memory. You'll laugh about it.'

'Yeah, right.' Sandra frowned. 'But, I know what you mean, Lynne. I need to look deeper than just looks. I always go for the good-looking ones and they're always the bastards.'

Lynne thought of Jason. 'I wonder if that's always the case?' she thought, out loud.

'It is,' said Sandra. 'Believe me, I know.'

Lynne wished she could tell Sandra all about her night out with Jason. Usually, she would have been telling her. But how could she? Matt and Jason were brothers. It would have to remain a secret.

Chapter Fourteen

Lynne woke up to the sound of her phone ringing. She felt groggy. She'd stayed up with Sandra until 3 am talking about her failed love life. They'd finished off a bottle of red wine between them, which on top of the other alcohol she'd consumed yesterday evening, made for a terrible headache. Reaching for the phone, she noticed the time on her alarm clock. 11:30 am *Oh my God!*

She picked up the phone. 'Hello,' she croaked.

'Lynne, dear, are you all right? You sound like you have a cold.' It was her mother.

'Oh, I'm fine.' Lynne coughed. 'I had a late night, so I've only just woken up.'

'Really? I've been up since eight. I've done some gardening and been shopping. You've missed half the day already. You really should get into some sort of routine. Just because you're out of work, doesn't mean you can give up on life. You've got to keep motivated.'

Lynne had put the cordless phone on loudspeaker and sat it on the bedside cabinet. She was used to her mother's lectures—she liked the sound of her own voice.

'Lynne? Are you still there?'

'Yes, Mum.'

'Right, well the reason I phoned is I have some bad news.'

Lynne sat up and picked up the phone, switching off the loudspeaker. 'What's happened?'

'I didn't want to spoil your honeymoon, so I waited until you got back before phoning you. Alex is dead.'

'Alex?' Lynne could not recall anyone called "Alex".

'Yes. Aunty Rachel's son. He died on your wedding day. That's why they weren't there. Remember me saying that it was strange they hadn't turned up?'

Lynne actually remembered her mother saying: *'I'll kill that Rachel, sending me an R.S.V.P. saying she was coming with her husband and son, and then not turning up! That's three extra meals we've paid for!'* But she thought it best not to remind her mother about that.

'It's such sad news,' continued her mother.

'How did he die?' Lynne remembered Alex—they used to go to the same school.

'He accidentally drank a glass of bleach. He was on his own when it

51

happened. So, by the time they found him it was too late to do anything. Such a waste of a young life. When they found him they thought it was suicide, but then Rachel remembered that she'd put the bleach in an empty water bottle. So he must have mistaken it for water.'

'But Mum, bleach smells like bleach. Maybe it *was* suicide?'

'No, he had a lot to live for. He was a very successful businessman.'

'If he was so successful, why did he still live at home with his parents?'

'There's nothing wrong with living with your parents.'

'I'm not saying there is, but if he was successful he'd have been able to afford to move out.'

'What does it matter now? He's dead. We went to the funeral last week. Such a sad day. He had so many friends. You two used to be close once, perhaps you could send a wreath to Rachel, or something?'

'I hadn't seen him for fifteen years.'

'Rachel and I used to say you two would get married one day. You used to play together as children.'

'I'll send a card to Aunty Rachel.'

When Lynne put down the phone, she lay on her bed for a while just staring at the ceiling. It was a shock to hear of someone her own age, who she used to know, dying. She remembered how Alex had once asked her out on a date when they were about 12 years old. She'd lied and told him she already had a boyfriend. At the time, she'd thought they were related, so she thought Alex a freak for asking her out; after all, she'd always called his mum "Aunty Rachel".

Alex wore NHS spectacles at the time—the ones with the ugly plastic frames—and he had acne. He had been bullied at school, but she'd always stood up for him, thinking they were related. Later, she found out that they weren't related; her mother had made her call his mother "Aunty", when she was a toddler, and the name had stuck.

They lost touch after secondary school, and "Aunty" Rachel didn't visit very often. Lynne thought back to the last time she'd seen her. Rachel had visited her mother, when Lynne still lived at home, about eight years ago. She'd shown them a photograph of Alex, which she kept in her purse. Lynne remembered that he'd looked quite handsome in the photo; nothing like the gangly teen she had known. After that, she found herself hoping he would visit one day with Rachel. But he never did. Soon after that, she'd moved in with Steve and forgot all about Alex.

Memories of playing with Alex as a child sprang up to the forefront of her mind, causing a tear to fall from her eye. She made a mental note to buy a card and send it to Rachel as soon as possible.

Sitting up in bed, Lynne placed a hand on her head, which was throbbing from her hangover. Reaching over to the bedside cabinet, she picked up the glass of water and drank it down in one go. Soon, she became aware of noise coming from the living room. At first she felt scared, thinking someone had broken in, but then remembered that Sandra had stayed over last night and was sleeping on the couch.

Just then, her bedroom door burst open and in walked an angry looking Sandra.

'When were you going to tell me?' she screamed, throwing something onto Lynne's bed.

'Tell you what?' Lynne looked down to see her mobile phone on the bed.

'That you are dating Jason!' Her cheeks were flushed.

Jason. Suddenly she remembered his face and couldn't stop herself smiling. But then she saw Sandra's reaction to that.

'What's wrong with you, Lynne? You're a married woman!'

Lynne tried her hardest to put on a straight face. 'You've got it all wrong. I'm not dating him!' Her smile returned.

'Why are you smiling? This is serious!'

'Sorry, it's just such a ridiculous accusation, it makes me laugh.'

'He just phoned you! Your phone was ringing, and I was going to bring it in to you, then I saw his name come up, and recognised the number. He's that bastard's brother!'

'I know. Look, calm down. I met him at the party yesterday. We went out for a meal, that's all. Nothing happened. I was going to tell you, but then you split up with Matt.'

'Don't say his name!'

'Sorry. Look, calm down, Sand. Sit down.'

Sandra took a deep breath and sat on the edge of Lynne's bed.

'So, if nothing's going on, why is he calling you? How has he got your number?'

'I didn't give him my number. He took my phone and saved his contact details in there. He must have phoned his phone with mine to get my number. I meant to delete his number from my phone last night, but then I saw your messages and I forgot.'

'Oh come on, do you expect me to believe that you were going to delete his number?'

'I'll delete it now! Look!' Lynne took the phone and deleted the number. 'See? It means nothing to me. Satisfied?' Strangely, she felt a bit reluctant to delete it, and regretted it afterwards, but she knew it had been the right thing to do.

'Why did you go out with him in the first place?' said Sandra.

'Look, he's good-looking, and he was flirting with me. I was flattered, and I'd had a bit too much to drink. We went out to dinner. I didn't do anything wrong.' She thought back to the long, lingering kiss, and blushed.

'Well, why did he call you this morning if there's nothing going on?'

'He's persistent, I'll give him that. But I told him I'm married. There's nothing going on.'

'Lynne, telling a man you are married is like a red rag to a bull. Did you know that loads of men fantasise about having sex with a married woman?'

Lynne laughed. 'I'm not having an affair. I've only just got married, for God's sake.'

'Yes, but Jason's last girlfriend was a married woman. I've heard he's a player.'

'Sand. Come on, this is me you're talking to. Do you really think I'd cheat on Adam?'

Sandra hesitated, as if she were trying to think of the right thing to say, then she replied: 'I didn't think you would, up until a few weeks ago when you started having doubts about your relationship.'

'Yes, but that was only because of Steve phoning me, and that stupid dream, warning me—' Lynne froze.

'Lynne, you look as if you've seen a ghost! Are you okay?'

Lynne shook her head slowly.

'Lynne? What's wrong?'

'Alex,' was all she could say.

'Who's Alex? Lynne! What's wrong?'

The colour had drained from Lynne's face. 'He died on the day of my wedding. My mum just phoned me and told me.'

'Who's Alex?'

She decided to tell Sandra all about it, in the hope that she would somehow feel better getting it off her chest.

'Lynne, I really think you're getting this all out of perspective. There's no way anyone could have stopped Alex dying; whether you'd married Adam or not, he still would have died. It's not as if Alex was anything special to you, anyway. You said yourself that when he'd asked you out at school, you'd rejected him.'

'Yes, but that's when we were kids and I thought we were related. I just can't help thinking about how I got a sort of crush on him when I saw his photo ten years later, before my relationship with Steve. What if Alex was the one I should have married? What if that's what the dream was trying to tell me?'

'Okay, even if it was, can you turn back time? No. And it really won't do any good for you to beat yourself up about it.'

'I am being a fool, aren't I?'

'No, you're just a bit shocked by the news of his death, and obviously still a bit shaken up by those dreams; but look, the two are not connected in any way. I mean, you hadn't seen Alex for years. You've got to try to forget about it.'

'You're right.'

When Sandra had left her flat, Lynne decided to visit the cemetery and take a wreath. Somehow, she felt she had to do something to try to shake off this irrational guilt she was feeling.

Her mother had told her where she would find Alex's grave. It was quite close to her grandfather's grave. Lynne took some flowers and placed them on her grandfather's tombstone. The memory of his funeral, six years before, flashed into her mind. She had visited his grave quite a few times, as she had been quite close to him. At the age of 90, he had still been strong, and looking after himself. He'd died in his sleep, and was found by a friend who used to visit him and help out with shopping. Lynne often thought that her grandfather was the only member of her family who understood her. He was always very kind and non-judgemental. She'd never had an argument with him. When she'd been living with her parents, she often spent the weekends with her grandfather, just to get away from the tension at home.

As she sat on the bench next to his grave, reminiscing, she almost forgot that she had actually visited the cemetery to see Alex's grave. When she remembered, she stood up slowly, feeling a bit nervous. She felt reluctant to actually go and place the wreath onto the grave. The more she thought about it, the more she felt hypocritical somehow. The last time she'd seen Alex was over 15 years ago, so why was she here pretending she cared? It didn't make sense. Sighing, she dragged her feet in the direction her mother had told her to go. After a short while, she came to an open area of the cemetery which had newly dug graves. She knew she would find Alex's here. Hesitating for a moment, she took a deep breath and walked on, carrying the wreath in front of her.

Soon she saw the wooden cross which had been placed as a temporary marker until the gravestone could be laid: Alexander Robert Ward 12.04.1979 - 06.06.2009 R.I.P. So here it was in black and white. *He is dead*. As she reread the wooden cross, she realised she never knew he had a middle name. She didn't know much about him at all. A tear came to her eye as she placed the wreath next to the rest of the flowers on the muddy ground. As she stood up again, the new grave next to his caught her eye. The reason she noticed it was because the man who had been buried next to Alex happened to be the same age as him... as her. Michael Anthony Taylor 01.01.1979 - 07.06.2009. They were only 30 years old. Their lives had been so short. She found herself wondering why this Michael Anthony Taylor had died. Was it an accident, or had he been ill? Maybe he had killed himself. She began to feel very morbid, so decided to leave the cemetery.

On her way back home, she bought a "With Sympathy" card for Alex's mum. She relaxed a bit when she had written it and put it in the post. The fresh air had brought her back to her senses, and she told herself that it was time to stop dwelling on Alex's death. Adam was due back from New York tomorrow. She decided she would cook him a special meal in the evening and really try to rekindle some of her old feelings for him. Meeting Jason at the party had reminded her how great it felt to be in love. It wasn't impossible for her to feel that way again with Adam, and she would try her best to make it happen.

Just as she was thinking about all of that, her mobile rang. It was Jason. She'd found a text message on her phone from him after Sandra left. **Hi sexy, I've been thinking about you. Call me, Jason X.** She'd smiled, flattered by the attention; but then she felt ashamed of herself, knowing that if she hadn't been drinking last night, she wouldn't have been so flirtatious. Had she inadvertently led him to believe that she wanted to see him again? Of course, she knew that if she had been single she would have jumped at the chance of being with him; but she had to be sensible, so she ignored the message. Now, though, the phone was ringing, and it was him. He obviously wasn't just going to go away.

'Hello,' she said, nervously.

'Hello, gorgeous,' he said. 'How are you?'

'I'm okay, thanks.'

'I had a great time last night and I was thinking about you. Wanna do something later?'

'Um... Jason, sorry, I really like you and I had a great time last night, too; but I'm married, and my husband is coming back tonight, so I can't. Sorry.'

'Oh, I thought you said he was coming back tomorrow.'

'Er... yes, he was. There's been a change of plan.'

'Okay, well, let me explain. I'm not really concerned that you are married. That really doesn't bother me. In fact, I find it quite a turn on. I only date married women. Less hassle. All the fun, but no ties, see? So, you really don't have to worry about anything. I'm always discreet. It's just, I think you and me could have a lot of fun together.'

56

Lynne felt surprised that she was actually tempted by his offer. It really would be dangerous to meet this man again. He seemed to have some sort of hold on her; a charm that left her without control of her senses. 'Really, Jason, I think you're a great guy, but my marriage vows are important to me.'

'I admire your loyalty. Especially as I got the impression that you're not very happy in your marriage.'

'What gave you that idea?' Her mind was reeling: how could he have seen through her so easily? Was it that obvious to everyone?

'Come on, Lynne, you don't have to be Einstein to work that out.'

She thought again of the kiss they'd shared, and blushed.

'Look, you're a beautiful woman, and you deserve to be happy. If you change your mind, you've got my number. I'll be waiting for your call.'

Lynne couldn't decide whether Jason was the most obnoxious person she'd ever met, or the most exciting man to ever have entered her life. She decided to save his number on her telephone, though, not really sure why she was doing it. She couldn't see herself cheating on Adam. It just wasn't something she would do, no matter how stale things were between them.

Chapter Fifteen

Adam returned from his business trip the following day, and went straight to work after dumping his luggage at the door. 'See you later,' he called out to Lynne, who was in the kitchen making a cup of tea. She ran to the door to see if she could catch him in time to say hello, but he had already gone. For the first time in a long time, she'd actually missed him, and had been looking forward to his return so that they could spend some time together. Something inside her was screaming out for some normality in her life; that's what she needed right now, more than anything else. Adam wasn't exciting or new like Jason, but he was like an old pair of slippers—comfortable. After the recent events, she was feeling fragile; she needed something to hold on to, to help her through the mire of of her unpleasant thoughts.

When she returned to the kitchen, she decided to phone Adam on his mobile.

'Hi, Adam.'

'Hi, Lynne. Sorry I couldn't stop. I'm late for a meeting. I'll see you tonight.'

'How was New York?'

'I was working, it wasn't a holiday.'

'You must be tired; jet-lagged?'

'No, I'm used to travelling.'

'I'm cooking your favourite meal tonight; spaghetti bolognese,' she said, to try to add some sparkle to the dying conversation.

'That's not my favourite meal,' he snapped.

Disappointment enveloped her. 'But... but you like it, though? I went out and bought all the ingredients.'

'I'll eat it.'

'What's your favourite meal?'

'I don't have a favourite,' he blasted.

She put his short-temper down to the lack of sleep. He was always travelling, and she was used to his moods.

'It used to be spaghetti bolognese,' she said absentmindedly.

'I don't remember that,' came his taut response.

'Adam, I'm making an effort here. We don't spend enough time together, so we don't really know each other any more...'

'Er... we just spent two weeks away together on our honeymoon.'

'Yes, and we hardly spoke.'

'That's an exaggeration,' he boomed.

'Adam, I've missed you. I'm looking forward to seeing you tonight.' She tried hard to stop her voice breaking, and could feel the tears in her eyes.

'You don't usually miss me.'

'Of course I do,' she replied, knowing it wasn't true.

'Look, Lynne, I have to go or I'll be late for my meeting.'

'See you tonight,' she said to the dialling tone (he'd already hung up).

Lynne's mood became sullen after the call. The romantic evening she had planned for tonight had been in an effort to try to start afresh. She wanted to put all her doubts and regrets behind her; but in the pit of her stomach she knew it was in vain. Adam was being as unresponsive as ever. The realisation that she wasn't the only one who regretted getting married, loomed over her like a cloud.

Adam arrived home from work at 7:30 pm. He walked into the kitchen, where Lynne was busy preparing the food.

'Hi, Lynne.'

'Hello.' She put down the wooden spoon and wiped her hands on her apron. 'The food will be ready soon.'

'You look beautiful,' he said.

Lynne was taken aback by this: firstly because she couldn't remember the last time he'd called her beautiful, and secondly, because she was sweating from the heat in the kitchen and some of her hair had stuck to her face. She'd already noticed that her mascara was running when she'd caught a glimpse of her reflection on the oven door a few minutes earlier. With a confused half-smile, she met his gaze.

He walked towards her and reached out his arms, hugging her. Then he kissed her forehead. 'I started thinking—after you called me this morning—that I've been neglecting you recently. I've been so busy at work.' Adam kissed her gently on the lips, then walked over to the door, where he'd left his briefcase. Opening it, he pulled out a box of chocolates. 'These are for you, darling.'

Darling? Her mind was agog. She couldn't recall him ever using the word "darling" before. As she took the box of chocolates from him, she started to worry. This morning he'd been so abrupt with her on the phone, and now he was buying her gifts. For some reason, she remembered something Sandra had once said she'd read in a women's magazine: *When a man starts buying you gifts unexpectedly, they're probably having an affair.* Lynne tried to put that out of her mind. Perhaps he was just trying to make up for the way he'd spoken to her on the phone earlier, and maybe he felt guilty for being away so often. It was nothing more than that.

He stood behind her as she put the spaghetti on to boil.

'That smells delicious, honey,' he said. 'I didn't know you could cook so well. Just to think, I've been missing all this home-cooked food while I'm away.'

She really was starting to feel disconcerted now. He'd never called her "honey" before, either. Not that she objected to such names, but it just wasn't Adam's style.

'Um, the spaghetti will only be about five minutes, so you can sit at the table if you like. I bought some wine.' As she walked over to the fridge, she noticed he was following her. She took out the wine and handed it to him.

Usually, Adam would make some remark about how she should have left it to him to buy the wine because he knows more about it. Or, he would look at the bottle and sneer slightly, before saying: 'That will do, I suppose,' just to show his superiority. She'd got used to it over the years and it didn't bother her; it was just another one of those rituals couples have to put up with to be able to live together. But today was different. The new improved Adam said: 'Great, I couldn't have chosen better myself! This will really complement the red meat. Good choice, darling.'

She couldn't smell any alcohol on his breath. He would have driven home from work, so he couldn't be drunk. But something was definitely up. He had changed. Lynne looked out at the night sky half-wondering whether there was a full moon tonight.

He kissed her again on the cheek and then sat down at the table with the wine. 'Where's the corkscrew, darling?'

'In the cutlery drawer, I'll get it,' she said.

'No, no!' he said, jumping up. 'I'll get it, sweetheart, I insist.'

Oh my God! Who is this impostor? Adam—the *real* Adam—would never have "insisted" on doing anything if she could do it herself.

She tried to think of other occasions, in the past, when he'd been so kind and courteous towards her, but her mind was a blank. The nearest would probably have to be their first few dates, when he used to open doors for her and ask her if she was "okay" every so often. Even then he'd never called her darling, honey, or sweetheart! She wasn't used to all this special treatment. It didn't feel right.

One of the things she'd fallen for at the start of their relationship was how casually he behaved with her. He never tried too hard, or put on airs and graces. She'd been so head-over-heels in love with him that it hadn't mattered to her if she had to do everything for him.

They sat down at the kitchen table to eat. He took one mouthful and began making noises to show he was enjoying it 'Mmm'. When he'd swallowed it, he said, 'That is the best spaghetti bolognese I've ever tasted. It's amazing. You know, honey, I think you have now convinced me that spag bol is my favourite meal. As long as *you* cook it, that is!'

Lynne took a sip of her wine and eyed him suspiciously. 'Adam is something wrong?'

He almost spat out his wine. 'Sorry? Why? What do you mean?'

'Not that I'm complaining, or anything, but you're acting differently. You've never called me honey, or sweetheart, or darling. Why now?'

He looked down at the table, and she felt guilty for saying anything. Had she spoilt the evening? She'd been the one moaning at him earlier about the fact that they didn't spend enough time together. He had made an effort and she'd thrown it back in his face.

'I just thought,' he started, 'that I've been away so often and working such long hours, that you must feel neglected. I was trying to make up for being so distant.'

'Sorry, Adam. I'm just not used to all the attention, I suppose.'

'I probably went a bit overboard. I just want you to know that I love you, Lynne.' His eyes were sad.

'Please, don't apologise. I'm sure I could get used to it.' She smiled, trying to recapture some of the earlier mood.

He smiled back, but she noticed a distance in his eyes. She was kicking herself for killing the moment.

They finished their food in relative silence, only having a brief conversation about the weather.

'I'll wash the dishes,' he said. 'I really do want to start helping you out as much as I can when I'm home.'

'Okay, I'm not going to argue about who's doing the washing up, that's for sure.' She giggled. 'I'll dry.'

Lynne began to feel more comfortable with him again, standing beside him as he washed the dishes. The conversation became more natural as he told her about his work travel plans for the month ahead. He said he also wanted to catch up with some of his friends, as he hardly ever saw them.

'Have you seen much of Paul?' she asked. She'd been thinking about telling him that Sandra had fancied Paul at the wedding. Now, that she'd been dumped so horribly by Matt, Lynne felt it was a good time to set up something where Sandra could meet Paul again. *He's a nice man,* she reasoned, *Sand needs someone like him.*

'Who?' asked Adam.

'Paul, your best man.'

Adam accidentally dropped a glass in the sink and it shattered. 'Oh shit!' he said. 'I'll have to get that cleaned up. Glass goes everywhere. Get out of the kitchen, Lynne. I'll make sure there are no shards lying around anywhere.'

'It's only a glass, Adam. Leave it for a minute, I just need to ask you something about Paul.'

Adam took off the washing up gloves and sighed. 'What?' The old Adam had returned, it seemed.

'Well, it's just, you know my friend, Sandra?'

'Yes, unfortunately.'

'Don't be cruel.'

Adam looked at his watch. 'Is there a point to this conversation? I have to get up early tomorrow.'

'Adam! Why are you being like this? I thought you were going to try to be nicer to me.'

'Sorry,' he said.

'Anyway, Sandra's single again, after a traumatic break-up. She's always falling for the wrong type of man. I know she fancied Paul at the wedding. I just thought they'd be good for each other.'

'I'm not sure,' said Adam. 'I think Paul's already seeing someone.'

'Oh, that's a shame. Do you think you could find out whether it's serious? It's just that I'd really like to help Sand.'

'I don't know. I don't see much of him, but if I do bump into him, I'll ask.'

'Oh, come on Adam, you could phone him. He was your best man at the wedding. You must be close if you chose him as your best man.'

'I'm just not sure Sandra would be his type.'

Lynne thought back to what Sandra had said at the wedding. Was that what Adam's defensive behaviour was about? He didn't want to reveal that his best mate is gay?

'What do you mean, not his type? She's a woman, he's a man. They're both the same age. Both quite good-looking.'

'Look, I've said I'll ask him if I see him, okay?'

'Is he gay?'

Adam looked at his feet. He took a deep breath. There was silence for a moment, and then he started laughing. Very loudly. So loudly, in fact, that Lynne worried the neighbours would complain. There wasn't much soundproofing in their block.

'Adam, what's so funny?'

'You,' he said, pointing at her. His face was completely red. 'You are funny! Imagine thinking Paul's gay! You're really strange, Lynne, I think you should get your head tested.'

And that was that. The laughter stopped, and Adam yawned. 'I'm tired. Jet lag I think. I'm going to bed.'

'I thought you didn't get jet lag?' she said, sarcastically.

'Goodnight, Lynne.'

She shook her head as he walked out of the kitchen. So here they were again. Back to the minimalist conversation level they'd started with. *Why did he say Sandra's not Paul's type? He doesn't like Sandra very much. He's only met her a few times.* It seemed he'd concluded that her friend was not good enough for his friend. That said something about their relationship. Looking resignedly at the shattered glass in the sink, she put on the washing-up gloves and began to clear up. She was seething inside.

Chapter Sixteen

The following day, Adam met Paul for lunch.

'Hi, I'm sorry I've been putting off this meeting,' said Adam, only briefly making eye contact with Paul as he entered the house.

Paul nodded his head. 'Don't worry about it. Come in. I've made us some spaghetti bolognese. I remembered you saying you like pasta, when we were talking at the hotel.'

Adam's mind went back to the evening before, and the drama that had occurred after the spaghetti bolognese Lynne had prepared. He could smell the beefy sauce and was reminded of the anxious thoughts that had been running through his head. 'Pasta is fine, thanks.'

He followed Paul through the narrow hallway. He'd visited Paul's house before, but this time was different. It felt almost as if the walls were closing in on him.

'Take a seat,' said Paul, indicating the chair at the head of the dining room table. 'I'll just go and get the food.'

Adam smiled, and sat down, watching Paul as he walked out of the room. He was surprised that on seeing Paul again he had not really felt much emotion. It was hard to know how to behave, now that they had taken such a big leap forward in their relationship. The last time they had seen each other was at the hotel in London where Adam was supposed to be spending his wedding night with Lynne, but instead, spent most of the night between silk sheets with Paul. On seeing him again today, he had only felt awkward, and was sure he could sense some reservation on Paul's part. Their friendship was important to him; he didn't want to lose it because of this. Adam remembered an old friend of his, back in college, who had warned him against starting a sexual relationship with a close friend. *'When the flames die, in most cases the friendship does too'*, she had said. As he waited for Paul to return to the room, he almost wanted to run and get away before disappointment had a chance of stealing what little joy there was left in his memories of their last meeting. He inwardly chided himself for being so negative about everything; after all, they were only at the start of their relationship, why was he predicting doom before giving them a chance?

Paul returned to the dining room with a tray containing two bowls of spaghetti bolognese and a bottle of red wine, with two crystal wine glasses. Adam thought back to how he had tried to compliment Lynne on her choice of wine for their evening meal, trying to make up for being a bad husband. That's in essence what he felt like. He knew that he'd been deceiving her from the start. He'd been a bad boyfriend, a bad lover, and now a bad husband to Lynne. Sitting here with Paul, it was clearer than ever to him that he had never really loved her. Shame burned through his being. He hated himself for all the lies and duplicity. Here he sat, sharing an intimate meal with his co-conspirator in the plan to end his marriage, but he wasn't even sure that ending the marriage was what he wanted.

Paul placed a bowl of food in front of Adam and handed him the bottle of wine, in an almost repeat performance of last night, except that the players were different this time. 'I hope you approve of the choice of wine.'

Unlike with Lynne, Adam could always rely on Paul to choose a good wine. 'Excellent choice, as always,' he said, still not quite able to meet Paul's eyes; strange, after such a passionate encounter only a month before. Perhaps it was the time that had passed between them that now made the night of ecstasy seem like something imagined and shrouded in uncertainty; uncertainty about how Paul felt. Paul had tried to contact him since, but Adam had been shellshocked after their night together. He had never slept with a man before. It was something momentous. He wanted to continue seeing Paul, but had felt such guilt all through his honeymoon with Lynne. She was so blissfully unaware. He even considered telling her everything, and on a couple of nights he came close, but he always stopped himself. After all, what did Paul think of his performance? Had he lived up to his expectations? Paul must be infinitely more experienced in such things. And, as much as he realised he was living a lie, he also knew that the lie was still there for a reason: protection. He lived in a world he considered to be against him; a world that just wouldn't understand. He had never been part of the gay scene, so he didn't have any other gay friends. He felt alone. Alone, except for Paul that is. But even Paul sent out mixed messages, because although he had told his friends and family that he is gay, he did not make a habit of flaunting his sexuality; he did not tell strangers, and hadn't told his employers and colleagues. Paul had lived two separate lives for many years—gay in his inner circle, but heterosexual in the eyes of the world at large. Much like Adam now. Except, Paul was the only one who knew the truth about Adam. He had a powerful hold on him now. A power that frightened Adam and had caused him to avoid his texts and calls.

Paul sat down opposite him, as Adam poured the wine. His hand was noticeably shaking, but Paul pretended not to notice.

'I'm so happy you're here,' said Paul. 'I was beginning to think you were avoiding me.' He laughed.

Adam joined in with the laughter, but there was a sense of sadness behind the façade. 'You know what it's like. I was just so busy at work, and then there was the honeymoon.' He wound the spaghetti on his fork, over and over, as he spoke; his eyes fixed intently on the food, unable to meet Paul's gaze.

'It's okay, Adam, we can talk about the night at the hotel. Look, if it makes you feel better, I was a little shaken up by the whole thing, too.'

Adam looked up, his eyebrows raised. Their eyes met for a few moments. Paul smiled at him, and he could feel the warmth emanating from his smile, putting him at ease.

'You're married remember?' said Paul. 'I don't make a habit of sleeping with men on their wedding nights. When you didn't respond to my calls, I felt terrible, as if I'd forced you into something that you didn't want. I've always had feelings for you, but I thought you were straight. I thought you were off limits, and I'd come to an acceptance of that. What happened between us was really unexpected. I didn't plan it.'

'It wasn't your fault. It wasn't anyone's fault, it just happened,' said Adam.

The two men ate their food in silence for a few minutes. Paul, reached for his wine glass and Adam looked up, catching his eye.

'Do you regret what happened?' asked Paul.

'No, of course not. It was just so... unexpected, as you say.'

'Adam, you've known I'm gay, for years.'

'Yes, but—and I know this is going to sound pathetic—I thought you'd get married eventually, to a woman, like I did.'

'It doesn't sound that pathetic. I have thought about doing just that. It would be easier; but I couldn't live a lie like that and risk hurting another person.'

Adam thought of Lynne and blushed.

'Sorry, Adam, I'm not having a dig, but that's just the way I see it. Personally, I couldn't do that to someone.'

'You think I'm a bad person,' said Adam, the weight of his guilt falling upon him again.

'No, I think you haven't faced up to who you are. You're not comfortable with it. That's okay. I'm not really there yet myself, and I've been trying to deal with it for longer than you. It's just you can get carried away listening to what the world view of *normal* is, and when you realise that you fall outside that description you can feel isolated. I've been there. You'll do almost anything to fit in. I used to date women, you know. Even though I wasn't attracted to them. I can fully understand you marrying Lynne. Your situation is different to mine. My family and my close friends know I'm gay. I don't have anything to prove.'

'Why aren't you openly gay? What's stopping you if your friends and family know? I mean, you've never dated other men publicly; well, not as far as I know.'

'I go to gay clubs,' answered Paul, 'but I tend to go to places out of town, where I'm less likely to meet anyone I know. You have to understand that where *I* grew up, being gay was unheard of. It was treated like having a disease. I had an uncle who was gay, but he married a woman. I never saw him smile. He hardly said a word. It was like he was living in a prison of his own making. He went senile at a young age; he was only in his sixties. All that bottling up inside did him no good.'

'How do you know he was gay if he never told anyone?'

'Well, there were the rumours, of course. But I also know that he had an affair with a local man, George. I caught them at it once, in my uncle's garden shed. I was young, so I didn't really understand what they were doing until later. Anyway, when my uncle went senile he was put in a home, and George used to visit him all the time. When I went to visit, I'd find him sitting by my uncle's bed, holding his hand with a really sad look in his eyes. Quite romantic really, in a tragic kind of way.'

'That's a sad story,' said Adam.

'More wine?' asked Paul, noticing that Adam had emptied his glass.

'No, thanks, I've got to get back to work soon.'

'Anyway, that story answers your question as to why I'm not comfortable being openly gay. I'm not sure that I ever will be. The way Uncle John was so ashamed of his sexuality, rubbed off on me, I suppose. Also, the way my parents used to talk about him. They'd say it was because he was gay that he went "mad", and that it was a terrible sin, and that was his punishment for unnatural behaviour.'

'But you said your parents know you're gay.'

'Yes, they do; but just because they know, it doesn't mean they're happy about it. They're not about to go shouting it from the rooftops. In fact, I'm under strict orders not to tell any of my other relatives. They say they'll be a "laughing stock". I actually overheard my mother crying, and saying it was a curse on the family, because her brother (Uncle John) had been gay. So, you can see that the reaction from my own family about my being gay is not exactly positive. In many ways, I'm like you.'

'I remember when you first told me you were gay,' said Adam. 'You told me not to tell anyone. And you know, I haven't told anyone, not even Lynne, and *we* must have had countless chats in the past about you, and about how she's never seen you with a girlfriend.'

'Thanks. Yes, whenever I tell anyone, I always say I don't want anyone else to know. I've always been like that. I'm ashamed of myself for being such a hypocrite. I wish I could just come out with it and let everyone know, but I've never really lived in a "gay friendly" environment. Even in my job, I'm sure if I said I'm gay, I'd be sacked. Maybe I wouldn't, but it's the way it feels; do you know what I mean?'

'There are laws against that sort of thing, these days,' said Adam.

'I know, but there are also many employers who would not take on someone they know is gay. Why do you think the laws were made in the first place? It's like a vicious circle, because even if I was sacked and took my employer to a tribunal, I'd probably end up having to go back there and work. Or, the alternative is to try to apply for another job after that; and if you have the reputation of taking employers to a tribunal, many of them wouldn't want to employ you, anyway.'

'You're right there.'

'There's still a lot of prejudice and ignorance out there,' said Paul. He stood up and cleared away the plates into the tray. 'I'll just get the dessert.'

Adam watched him walk out of the room and his eyes caught sight of the clock on the wall. He realised that he had been there over half an hour, but still hadn't told Paul what he'd come here to tell him; that he had decided to leave Lynne.

Paul walked back into the room carrying a tray with a cafetière of fresh coffee and two servings of profiteroles.

'Mmm, that looks lovely,' said Adam, as Paul placed the dessert in front of him.

'Only the best for you, Adam.' He sat opposite him again, and poured his coffee. 'So, I've been wondering: when we parted at the hotel, you said you were going to make a decision. Have you decided yet?'

Adam took a sip of coffee. 'Last night, I was feeling guilty about betraying Lynne. I mean, we are married now. I tried to do the "good husband" routine, but it was so fake; she saw right through me. And then, when she asked if you're gay, something snapped.'

'She's guessed I'm gay?' Paul's eyes widened.

'Well, I'm not sure she has. She asked if I would set you up on a date with her friend, Sandra, but I said she wasn't your type.'

'Who's Sandra?' asked Paul.

'She was the chief bridesmaid at the wedding.'

'Oh, the redhead. She was flirting with me.' He giggled.

'Well, she has good taste,' said Adam.

Paul smiled.

'I don't love Lynne,' said Adam. 'I've known that all along, but what I realised last night was—' He paused, unsure if he could continue.

Paul had a mouth full of profiteroles, but was so on edge, intrigued by what Adam was about to say, that he spoke: 'What?' Some of the cream splattered out of his mouth and onto the table. He laughed and wiped it with a serviette. The tension had been broken.

'Paul, I love you.'

Paul smiled. 'You love me? Really?'

Adam nodded, a strong wave of emotion taking hold him. He wanted to reach out and take Paul in his arms. 'I think so. You have to understand, I was caught off guard by my own feelings when we had sex that night. My wedding night, of all nights.' Adam shook his head. 'You know, I've suppressed my real sexuality for so long, because my family and friends just wouldn't understand.'

'Why didn't you ever tell *me*? I mean, you had the ideal opportunity years ago, when I told you I'm gay.'

'I know, but at that time, I was still in denial. I had feelings for you then, but I didn't want to face them. I'm ashamed of myself. I should be able to face up to it, but I find it so hard. I was brought up in a culture that abhors homosexuality. It's considered a mortal sin. I've been fighting it for so long. I've only ever dated women, and I've convinced myself I love them, even though all my sexual fantasies have been about men. It's absurd.

'Anyway, the way I feel at the moment, the way I feel about you; I want to tell the whole world. But I have a dilemma because I've basically done an unforgivable thing. I've married Lynne, knowing full well that it would be a sham; a cover-up, to make me appear *normal*, whatever that is. In a funny way, it's the best thing I've ever done, because it's made me finally face the truth. I've gone too far living a lie, and getting married showed me that. On the other hand, I know I'm going to break Lynne's heart when I tell her, and I don't want to do that. I've had a relationship with her for over three years, and a relationship is so much more than just sex. We have a history and a past together. It's going to tear her apart to learn the truth.'

'So, don't tell her the truth,' said Paul.

'But I can't go on living like this.'

'I know, Adam, but you don't have to tell Lynne the real reason you're leaving her. You have to try to make it easier for her. If you tell her you're gay, and she realises that she's lived a lie for years, it could break her.'

'What if I say that I've only just discovered I'm gay?'

'Hmm... not very convincing.'

'I can't lie to her.'

'You've been lying to her for years.'

Adam pursed his lips and sighed. 'I feel so bad about that. I like Lynne. Don't you think that maybe if I sit down with her and tell her the truth, give her a real reason, it would be better than just making up another lie?'

'Just say you've met someone else. It happens all the time. She'll get over it. From what you've told me, your relationship is a bit rocky at the moment.'

'It hasn't been good for a while. In fact, I did wonder whether she'd even turn up to the church for the wedding, she'd been acting so cold towards me for weeks.'

'Well then, there's nothing to fear. She might even be relieved that you're calling it a day.'

Adam shrugged his shoulders. 'I just don't want to hurt her. She's a good woman.'

'I'm sure you know Lynne inside out after so many years. You are the only one who can decide what to tell her. If you think she can handle the truth, then tell her.'

'Paul.' He reached out and touched his friend's hand across the table. 'What happened that night... between us; did it really mean anything to you?'

'I've already told you, I have deep feelings for you. If I'm honest, this has all really shocked me, because, as I said, I thought you were straight. I'm kind of thinking this is too good to be true.' He pulled his hand away from Adam's. 'But at the same time, I'm not sure you're comfortable enough with your sexuality, so I'm a bit worried you might just be caught up in the novelty of this, and are just experimenting. You might turn around one day and decide you're not gay. I don't want to be your guinea pig. Also, this would be my first real relationship. I've slept with men before, but only as one night stands and very rarely. As you know, I haven't fully found my comfort zone. It's all very much "hush hush" for me, too.

'There are only a few trusted people, close to me, who know I'm gay. If we start a relationship, everything will be out in the open and I'm not even sure that I'm ready for that. Do you know what I mean?'

Adam looked at him. 'I have to admit that I'm a bit surprised. I'd sort of taken it for granted that you'd be ready to start a relationship when I was. I suppose because I've known for years that you're gay, I was under the impression that you were comfortable with it. But it looks as though we're more alike than I thought. I really didn't imagine you'd have the same doubts as me. I thought you'd hate me for being a hypocrite.'

'You're not a hypocrite. You're just a victim of this intolerant society we live in, just like I am.'

'What if we were to leave town? Start a new life, somewhere else, where no one knows us. Away from the people and places we grew up in. Somewhere we'd feel more accepted. If we moved anywhere else as a couple, we'd probably feel more accepted, because no one would know our pasts.'

Paul smiled. 'I like that idea.' He took Adam's hand. Then, his smile turned into a concerned frown. 'Do you think you'll be able to leave Lynne?'

'I love you, Paul. I want to share my life with you. I feel like I've found what I've been looking for all my life. I wish I didn't have to hurt Lynne; but if I'm ever going to be happy, I have to leave her.'

'When are you going to tell her?'

'I'm not sure. Soon.'

Chapter Seventeen

A few days after Lynne had sent the card to Alex's mum, she received a phone call.

'Hello, can I speak to Lynne, please?' said the woman.

Lynne didn't recognise her voice immediately. 'Speaking.'

'It's Rachel here. Alex's mum.'

'Oh, hello Aunty. It's been a long time since we spoke. How ar—', but she stopped herself, realising that "how are you?" might not be the most appropriate question, so soon after the death of her son. 'I was so sorry to hear about Alex.'

'I want to know what kind of game you're playing, sending me a card, when you are responsible for my son's death.'

Lynne gasped. 'Wh... What are you talking about? I hardly knew your son.'

'He died because of you. You led him on and then married another man. What sort of person are you?'

'I still don't understand. In what way do you think I led him on? I... I... I hadn't seen him for fifteen years!'

'Oh, don't lie to me. Just stay away from me and my family. If you ever contact me again, I'm calling the police.' With that, Rachel put down the phone.

Lynne was left open-mouthed, wondering if this was some kind of joke.

Picking up the phone, she dialled her parents' number in a daze. Her brow furrowed at the injustice of being accused of doing something wrong, and yet not quite sure what she was being accused of. 'Hi Mum, have you heard from Aunty Rachel since the funeral?'

'Yes, dear. I had a call from her this morning. She asked for your telephone number. She said she'd received a card from you.'

'Mum, did Rachel say anything to you about how Alex died?'

'I told you, Lynne, it was an accident.'

'So, he didn't kill himself?'

'No, of course not.'

'She just phoned me now, and sounded really strange.' Lynne paused, unsure whether she could face telling her mum that Rachel had accused her of killing Alex. It sounded so surreal.

'Well, she's going through a hard time at the moment. What do you expect? She's not going to be her usual self,' said her mother.

Lynne took a deep breath. 'She... It sounded as if she was saying he killed himself, or maybe someone killed him.'

'No, you've got the wrong end of the stick, dear. I was at the funeral, and both Rachel and her husband, Peter, told me that he'd accidentally drunk some bleach.'

'Maybe they've found out more? Maybe there were tests done on the body?'

'No, no. If there was to be an inquest, he wouldn't have been buried so soon, would he?'

'Mum, I think you should phone Rachel. I'm worried about her. Then, can you phone me back and tell me what she says? But it's very important you don't tell her that I asked you to phone. She might think I'm interfering. Just pretend it's a social call. But can you try to find out more, please?'

'If you think she needs help, I'll call her. Come to think of it, she sounded a bit odd when she phoned me this morning. I just put it down to the grief. I'll phone her now, and I'll call you back.'

Lynne put down the phone, feeling nervous; her pulse rate was faster than normal. She took a deep breath and sat at the kitchen table, looking out at the cloudy sky, trying to calm herself down.

Rachel's accusation resounded in her head. It didn't make any sense. Lynne began to panic, uncomfortably aware that it was not unheard of for people to end up in prison for something they hadn't done.

She prayed her mother would find out more. Waiting by the phone, anxiously, she felt as though she would not be able to breathe properly again until this was resolved.

Fifteen minutes passed. If her mother and Rachel were still talking, it was a lengthy conversation. Were they discussing *her*? Would Rachel explain what she had meant by Lynne being responsible for Alex's death?

Lynne decided to make a cup of tea, to give herself something to do instead of sitting, waiting for the phone to ring. As she stirred the milk into the tea, a few minutes later, she looked at the clock. *If Mum doesn't phone back in ten minutes, I'll call her.*

She sat down with the cup of tea that she wasn't even intending to drink. Just then the phone rang, startling her. Everything had been so silent in the kitchen for the past twenty minutes or so; the ring tone broke through that like a crack of lightning.

She stood up and picked up the phone.

'Lynne, dear, I've just been speaking to Rachel. She's very angry with you.'

Lynne's stomach clenched, as if she would vomit. 'Why?' She held her breath.

'She says that she was going through Alex's things yesterday and she came across some photos of you. She also found his diaries for the past few years. The last entry in his diary was the day before he died. He wrote, "*I can't live without Lynne. Why did she choose to marry someone else? I feel like ending it all.*" Do you know anything about this?'

'Mum, the last time I saw Alex, we were teenagers.' She swallowed, her mouth dry.

'It seems he was in love with you and couldn't bear the thought of you marrying someone else.'

'But that's not normal. He hadn't seen me for fifteen years. This entry in his diary... maybe there's another girl called Lynne that he was in love with?'

'No, it was you. There are several entries in his diaries about you, some include your surname. And he had recent photos of you. One of the photos was in his wallet.'

'Recent photos? How?'

'You tell me. Are you sure you didn't go out with him for a while?'

'No, I didn't!'

'Rachel says that when they received the wedding invitation, he told them he didn't want to go because you'd broken his heart. She thought he was being silly at the time, so she included his name in the R.S.V.P. Lynne... She thinks you led him on and then hurt him by marrying Adam.'

'That's ridiculous! So, is she saying he killed himself now?'

'Yes. Apparently, Alex did kill himself. At the hospital they found that he had taken a vast amount of prescription drugs, as well as drinking the bleach. Rachel told everyone at the funeral that it was an accident, because she wanted to bury him with dignity. She's a proud woman, and she didn't want people talking about him. She didn't want the shame of it. She knew people would judge him and call him weak and selfish if they knew the truth.'

'Oh my God! That's terrible. I feel really bad about him killing himself, but I swear it had nothing to do with me. I feel sick that Rachel is so angry with me when I haven't done anything.'

'There are several entries in his diaries, spanning the last three years, saying, "Seeing Lynne". That means you would have been cheating on Adam.'

'Mum, whose side are you on? Do you think so little of me that you're willing to believe this? I'd never cheat on Adam.'

She thought back to her recent close encounter with Jason. Then she focused her mind on the accusation being thrown at her. 'I'm totally innocent in all this. It sounds like Alex was a loony. He asked me out when we were twelve years old. I turned him down. Maybe he never got over it? Who knows? It sounds creepy. I think I'm going to have to go to see Rachel.'

'What good would that do?' asked her mother. 'She's grieving the loss of her son, and she thinks you caused it. You'll only upset her.'

'But I haven't done anything, I have to explain that to her.'

'Why? Who will benefit from that? Think about it. You are the only one who would benefit, because you'll clear your name and Rachel won't hate you anymore. But she's already lost a son, and she has good memories of him. Do you want to take that away from her, too? If she finds out that her son was pining over someone who didn't love him, and that he was obsessive and delusional, what sort of memory of her son would she be able to cling on to?'

'A tragic one,' said Lynne, angrily. 'So you'd rather let her think of your own daughter as a cheating slut who led him on and broke his heart?'

'Maybe it's part of her grieving process, Lynne. She needs someone to blame for this unexpected and terrible tragedy. I know you are upset, but please don't do anything rash. I will explain everything to her in good time. Give her time to mourn his death.'

Lynne took a deep breath. 'You do believe me, though, don't you, Mum?'

'Of course I do, sweetie. I'm sure when you've had time to think about it, you'll see that what I'm saying makes sense. I will tell Rachel the truth, I promise. But not right now. Just leave things as they are for now. I'll tell her when I think she's ready to hear it.'

'I don't know. It's all so weird. How did he get recent photos of me? Was he stalking me? I feel really freaked out by this.'

'Lynne, there's probably some rational explanation.'

'Yes, the explanation is: he was a madman.'

'Haven't you ever been in love with someone from afar? Someone you couldn't have? That's probably all it was,' said her mother. 'Maybe he had a dream that you'd get together one day.'

'I still think I should go to Rachel's house. I want to see the diaries and the photos for myself.'

'Curiosity killed the cat.'

'It's not curiosity. How am I ever going to have any peace of mind, knowing Rachel can blame me for something so terrible? I need to explain everything to her.'

'Leave it to me, darling. Next time I see her, I'll try to tell her; and I'll ask her to call you.'

'Okay, thanks, Mum.'

Lynne felt unsettled when she put down the phone. By the sound of it, Alex had been obsessed with her, keeping a diary of make believe meetings. Again, her mind went back to the dreams she'd been having before the wedding. Could it really be possible that she was meant to marry Alex? She shuddered at the thought.

He had obviously been emotionally unstable to be so infatuated with someone he hardly knew, and to kill himself. That was not the sort of man she would want to settle down with. She felt sorry for him, in a way, but at the same time she felt a revulsion. *How did he get recent photos of me?* That still puzzled her. Wouldn't she have been aware of him following her around taking pictures? But then it occurred to her that, these days, there are all sorts of long range lenses on the market; he could have taken shots from some distance without her knowing.

She still felt a need to visit Rachel and explain things; but would Rachel believe her? She'd formed an opinion of her as the bad woman who had killed her son. *'If you ever contact me again, I'm calling the police.'* Lynne shivered as she recalled those words. Rachel had sounded so bitter.

Lynne knew she would have to play a waiting game. Her mum was right; it would be better coming from *her*—she'd always been good friends with Rachel. Her mum would explain everything to her in due course, and then one day Rachel would realise her mistake... She could only hope.

Chapter Eighteen

In the days following the disastrous spaghetti bolognese evening, Lynne tried to do her best to avoid further arguments with Adam. It was difficult because this basically meant not talking to him. He had, as far as she could see, turned into a person she despised. She couldn't even say, *'He's not the man I married'*, because nothing had really changed since they'd got married. They couldn't communicate with each other then, and they couldn't communicate now. He would get home from work after 9 pm, bringing a takeaway meal (for one). He would sit in front of the TV, watching whatever she was watching, but invariably commenting every so often that he couldn't believe she'd choose to watch such rubbish. Then, when they finally went to bed, he would fall asleep as soon as his head hit the pillow. She began to question, more and more, why she had married him.

The warning signs were there, long before they got married. She realised that she had just been too blind to see them; or maybe she just chose not to see them, refusing to allow the idea to enter her mind that she would have another failed relationship after Steve. Somewhere deep inside her, she wanted to believe that the Adam she met was still there, underneath all the layers, and one day she would find him again.

The downward spiral in their relationship seemed to come as soon as they were engaged. It was as if, before then, she had still been unattainable in some way, and Adam had to make an effort to keep her. Soon after the engagement, things began to get stale, as if he had stopped caring about her. Their conversations became shorter and he became more distant.

Looking back, she was not surprised that she'd been having cold feet before the wedding. Even the dreams made sense. It was like some part of her unconscious mind had been crying out for her to wake up and realise that the best of their relationship had long gone; but back then, she'd been starry-eyed, believing that marriage had a magical quality that would somehow bring them closer together. She told herself that once they were married, any past problems would disappear and they could start afresh. But here she was, a month later, staring at the brutal truth: their relationship was never going to be good again.

Was this the best she could hope for? Sitting on the sofa, watching

TV, and occasionally being able to laugh together about something?

In the past, whenever she had a moment of clarity and realised that she should perhaps leave him, she'd always panicked. She didn't want to be alone. Since the end of her relationship with Steve, she'd had a deep-rooted irrational belief that something must be wrong with her, because he left her for another woman. As a consequence of this, she wanted to prove that she could make her relationship with Adam work. So, whenever they faced a hurdle, she would do everything she could to get over it with their union still intact.

As she looked at Adam, eating his Chinese meal on the sofa, she realised that it had always been her who had given in after an argument, backing down and letting him think he was right. All this time, he'd never had to make an effort. No wonder he'd stopped trying; he never *had* to try.

Lynne didn't want to contemplate living the next thirty or forty years of her life like this.

Just then the telephone rang.

'Can you get that?' she asked.

'I'm eating,' he said.

'Please, Adam. We've been getting these prank calls all day. Whenever I pick up the phone, the person at the other end hangs up.'

'So, don't answer it. They'll soon get bored,' he said, turning up the volume on the TV.

'I thought you didn't like this programme?'

'I don't, but if I have to watch it, I might as well hear what they're saying.'

The telephone stopped ringing.

'See? They've gone away,' said Adam.

Lynne sighed and grabbed the remote control to turn down the volume on the TV.

'It might have been an important call,' she said, annoyed.

'Well, why didn't you answer it then? The phone's next to you. Besides, if it's important they'll call back.'

'If they call back, you have to answer it. If it's this prank caller, it's best if they hear a man's voice. Sometimes, if they think a woman lives alone, they try to intimidate her by calling and hanging up.'

The phone began to ring again. Lynne picked up the cordless phone and held it towards Adam. 'Answer it,' she said, agitated.

He sighed, put down his fork, and took the phone from her. 'Hello,' he said. His eyes widened. 'What? Who is this?'

Lynne looked at him, intrigued.

He hung up the phone and handed it back to her. 'It was the wrong number,' he said.

'What did they say?'

'Nothing.'

'But you looked shocked. Was it a man or a woman?'

'I don't know.'

'You're lying to me.'

He stood up. 'I'm going to bed.'

Adam left his takeaway meal on the table and walked towards the kitchen to get a glass of water, feeling stunned. In a way, this was ideal. Great timing. He couldn't have planned it better if he tried. So, why did he feel so despondent? He'd been intending to ask Lynne for a divorce, so he could be with Paul. Now, the opportunity for his dreams to come true had presented itself in a very unexpected way. He should have been grabbing it with both hands. *Why am I hesitating?* The caller on the phone, a woman, had said: *"Lynne's been having an affair behind your back for years."*

Instead of confronting Lynne, he'd let the opportunity slip away. Was it because he didn't want to face up to finding out that Lynne had never loved him? If he was honest with himself, he would have to admit that he'd never loved her; so, no, that couldn't be what was bothering him. Lynne had always been someone who was convenient. He had got together with her to show the world he was a real man; a man who could be accepted in the tough business world he had chosen for his career. He needed a woman behind him for appearance sake.

It had been easy enough to convince himself that he loved her in the early days of their relationship, when he was still trying to fight against his true nature. He had forced himself to be the best boyfriend a woman could have, building a disguise that could not be infiltrated; no one could ever find out the truth.

It was when Paul had revealed that he is gay; that's what had started this roller coaster. That had come out of the blue. He'd known Paul for almost ten years at the time, since his college days. Back in college, Paul had been one of the lads, making jokes about gay men, along with the rest of the boys. Adam had not matured enough at that stage to even have questioned his own sexuality, so he assumed he was straight and that he would marry and have children. Anything else just wasn't something he ever considered.

By the time Paul revealed his true sexuality, Adam had already developed his first crush on a man, but he had countered this by diving into a relationship with a woman. He'd even proposed to her, just to prove he wasn't gay. Their relationship didn't last, but after it, everyone saw him as heterosexual. That was what suited him best.

So, after Paul's revelation, Adam almost fell out with him. He didn't want to be associated with a gay man; afraid his own mask would slip. He avoided being seen with Paul and avoided his phone calls for some time.

Soon, he found out that Paul hadn't told the world about his homosexuality. He'd only told his parents and his closest friends. He'd even asked Adam not to tell anyone else. Adam began to miss Paul. They had been good friends. He realised that he was developing deeper feelings for him. He fought against it and decided that the best thing he could do would be to find another girlfriend, then he could stop thinking about Paul. That was when Lynne had appeared on the scene.

Adam made his way to the bedroom. *Surely, the thing to do would be to confront Lynne, about her infidelity, have an argument with her, and then leave?* But there was something stopping him. He loved Paul, but he still wasn't sure if he was ready to "come out", as they say, and have a full blown public relationship with a man. It could affect his career. His family might disown him. Everything would be turned on its head. It would be a big step. He'd mentioned to Paul about leaving town and starting again somewhere else; but how easy would that be in reality? They were in the midst of a recession, so finding work would be hard. And he loved his job.

I could maybe just see Paul, on the side, without Lynne having to know. After all, as far as I'm aware, she's already having an affair.

His mind was made up. It wasn't exactly the bravest decision in the world, but it was the one that suited him for now. *Maybe it is possible to have the best of both worlds?*

⧗

Lynne was left fuming as she heard Adam shut the bedroom door. She looked at the remains of his Chinese takeaway meal on the coffee table. *Why am I always left to clean up after him?* Her annoyance at this distracted her for a moment from the main thread of her thoughts—the fear she'd had a few days ago had returned; *Is he having an affair?* He had been very distant, more so than usual. Apart from the romantic meal she'd planned for them, which had gone terribly wrong, there were the silent phone calls. She was sure the caller had said something to Adam. But if he was having an affair, surely his lover would be calling his mobile phone? *Unless she wants me to find out about their affair.* Lynne gritted her teeth. Sometimes she felt like giving in and leaving Adam. He was such hard work. But in her current predicament, she would not be able to support herself financially if she left him. Momentarily, she thought about going to stay with her parents, but this thought flittered in and out of her consciousness; it was not an option. She knew how overbearing and judgemental her mother could be at the best of times; she would never forgive her if she left Adam, especially so soon after the wedding. Lynne knew that if it came down to a choice between her parents' house and Adam, she would rather suffer in silence with Adam.

Maybe I should go and stay with Sandra for a while? A sense of calm replaced the tension. Sandra would understand. She picked up the phone, went into the kitchen and closed the door. She dialled Sandra's number. There was no reply on the home phone. *Is she in bed already?* Lynne looked at the clock, it was 10:30 pm. She decided to try her mobile. 'Hi, Sand, sorry it's late.'

'That's okay. It'll have to be a quick call, though; I'm busy.'

'Oh...' Lynne hadn't expected that. She really needed to talk. 'I'll try to be brief,' she continued, in a whisper. 'I'm thinking of leaving Adam.'

There was silence on the line.

'Sand? Are you there?'

'Sorry, Lynne, I'm just having a hard time getting my head around it.'

'I know it sounds crazy. We've only been married a month, but I don't think I can live with him anymore. He's driving me mad. And I think he's having an affair.'

'*Adam?* Having an affair? What gives you that idea? And, why are you whispering?'

'I don't want Adam to hear me; he's at home.'

'Oh.'

'A few things have happened lately. He's been acting weird. Although maybe he's always been weird and I've just never noticed. Anyway, I was calling to ask you a favour.'

'Okay.'

'Can I come and stay with you until I decide what to do?'

'Er... I don't think that's going to be possible, Lynne. Sorry. Usually I'd say yes, but things have changed. I'm seeing someone.'

'I won't get in your way. I just need somewhere to stay.'

'Dave and I are going to be moving in together. I'm looking to rent out my flat; so, I'm sorry, but I can't let you stay there.'

'Woah, slow down. You've known this new man for two seconds and you're moving in with him? You've only just broken up with Matt.'

'I've known Dave for a while. We work together. He's been asking me out for months, but even though I really get on well with him, I've always thought he's not my type. I have to keep my voice down because he's upstairs. When I broke up with Matt, Dave and I got chatting, and he asked me out again. He's no Brad Pitt, but he's a really kind man and I can trust him. What we were talking about after Matt's party got me thinking. Remember when I said that I always fall for good-looking men but they always let me down? Well, guess what? I think my Mr. Right has been under my nose for ages and I just couldn't see him, because I wasn't really looking.'

'But don't you think it's a bit soon to be moving in with him?'

'No, it makes perfect sense. He only lives a few streets away from me. His house is so much nicer than my flat. I can rent out my flat for a bit of extra cash, and we can travel together to work, saving money on petrol. It will be great. I'm always at his house these days, anyway, so we thought it would be a good idea.'

'Well, you kept *him* a secret,' said Lynne.

'Yeah, as I say, I never really considered him boyfriend material until after Matt. We'll have to get together, so I can tell you all about him,' she gushed.

'But it sounds like you're on the rebound, Sand. You might regret it.'

'No, Dave is so sweet. Wait until you meet him, you'll know what I mean. I'm kicking myself for not getting together with him sooner.'

Lynne wanted to sound more enthusiastic. She did feel happy for Sandra; it seemed as though she'd found someone she could rely on, after a string of undesirables. But her happiness for Sandra was dampened by the state of her own relationship, which was slowly dying; her feelings being washed away like water spiralling down a drain.

'I can't wait for you to meet Dave. I'll phone you when I'm free. Sorry, I've got to go, I can hear him calling me.'

When Lynne put down the phone, she realised that she hadn't managed to explain to Sandra why she wanted to leave Adam. She'd wanted to hear what Sandra thought of the latest developments. She needed some moral support. But Sandra was too busy with her own life now, to have the time to listen to her problems. Perhaps she should phone her sister, Kelly? But she hated bothering her. Kelly had enough on her plate, with two small children to look after. And Lynne had never really got on with Kelly's husband, so she couldn't ask if she could stay with them.

By this time, Lynne had gone off the idea of moving out. The thought of packing her stuff and living out of boxes or suitcases, was not appealing. *This flat is as much my home as Adam's.* She had also just remembered that he would soon be jetting off to Germany or France for a few weeks on a business trip, so she wouldn't have to put up with him for much longer.

As she pondered this, a disturbing thought came to mind. The more she thought about it, the more plausible it seemed. She'd never questioned Adam when he set off on his business trips; she'd never even gone to the airport with him to see him off or to collect him. For all she knew, he could be living a double life. What if he had a mistress and spent half his time with her? But then she recalled she'd seen his passport a few times and it had many stamps on it; and she'd seen his bags with the airline stickers and labels on them when he'd returned from his trips. He definitely did travel. But did he travel as much as he said he did?

It would be easy for him to pretend he was going away sometimes, when he wasn't. The other possibility was that he travelled with someone else; a PA or secretary. He could be having an affair with her.

Lynne hated herself for thinking this. She didn't have any proof. Surely, even Adam deserved to be innocent until proven guilty? She had an urge to find his mobile phone, to check his recent calls. He'd gone to bed, so it would be easy enough for her to get it. He usually kept it in his jacket pocket, which he always hung on the back of the bedroom door.

Lynne exited the kitchen and walked along the corridor. She slowly turned the handle of the bedroom door and listened to hear Adam's light snoring. *He's asleep.* Stepping inside the room, she reached into his jacket pocket, taking out the mobile. She closed the door behind her and went to the living room.

Once on the sofa, she slid open the phone and clicked the menu until she found his recent calls. He'd had three calls from Paul in the last two days. Nothing unusual there. She looked at the list of calls he'd made. There were numerous calls to "Sharon". Her heart begin to beat faster, as if she were about to discover a deep dark secret. Writing down Sharon's number, she noted it was a landline rather than a mobile. She decided to ring it. It seemed like a familiar number for some reason. By the time she had dialled the first five digits, she remembered why it was familiar: it was his work number. Sharon must be his secretary, and he probably had to call her when he was out of the office. But it still didn't rule out the possibility that she could be his "bit on the side".

Lynne checked his text messages. Sure enough, the texts he'd received from Sharon were all work related, and didn't look suspicious at all. Perhaps she *was* just imagining his infidelity?

The most recent text he'd received was from Paul. It just said: *See you at mine tomorrow, lunch x*

Scrolling through the texts Adam had sent, she saw one addressed to Paul, saying: *I'm looking forward to it x*. She blinked to make sure she wasn't imagining things; but sure enough it was there—a kiss at the end of the message. *That's odd*. Scrolling down a bit further, she noticed another text to Paul: *Lunch was great thx we must meet again soon x*. Again, he had ended it with a kiss. There was also a kiss at the end of the next message Paul had sent him. *Maybe that's just the way they sign off when they text each other? They have been friends for years*. It wasn't very *macho*. She had a giggle to herself.

She took the phone back to the bedroom and decided she would turn in for the night. As she lay next to Adam, listening to him breathing, she began to get a bit annoyed that he'd agreed to meet up for lunch with Paul, and yet whenever she suggested they meet up for lunch he always said he was too busy. He'd rather spend his lunch hour with his friend than his own wife.

Thinking about it, she realised that whenever they'd had a meal together recently, they'd ended up arguing, or sitting in silence; no wonder he preferred having a meal with his friend instead of her. Maybe he told Paul his marriage problems, in the same way that she told Sandra everything? A tear fell from her eye, as she found herself longing for their relationship to go back to how it was in the early days. Over the years, they'd had good times and bad times, but for the past few months, it all seemed to be bad times. Silently, she cried herself to sleep.

Chapter Nineteen

When the alarm clock sounded at 7:30 am, Lynne got out of bed straight away. She undressed and went into the en suite. Adam usually pressed the snooze button a couple of times before he got up, so she knew she had time to prepare. She'd been lying awake for a couple of hours thinking about how everything had gone wrong in the marriage, and concluded that she would have to make an effort if she wanted to save the relationship. She filled the bath with scented oils and stepped in.

A few minutes later, Adam knocked on the bathroom door. 'For God's sake, Lynne! You know I have to get ready for work, what are you doing in there?'

'Come in,' she said, as sweetly as she could, trying not to let his sour mood get to her.

He pushed open the bathroom door, and saw her lying in the bath, covered in bubbles.

'I thought you could do with a bit of relaxation before you go to work,' she said. Then she stood up slowly, to reveal her naked body.

'What are you doing?' he said.

'Just trying to add a bit of sparkle to our love life. Come in, the water's nice and warm. I'll scrub your back.' She smiled, and blew him a kiss.

'I'll use the main bathroom, thanks. I haven't got time for this!' He slammed the door behind him as he left, leaving her feeling exposed and a little bit foolish.

Left alone in the bathroom, tears welled in her eyes, but she fought to stop them falling. Usually, she would go and make breakfast for him, but after what had just happened, she felt more like poisoning him. *He didn't have to be so rude about it.*

She dried herself off, pulled on her dressing gown and stepped into her slippers. Dragging her feet, she walked out of the bedroom, along the corridor, and into the kitchen. His voice could be heard as he sang in the shower. *What gives him the right to be happy, when he's just ruined my day?* Feeling scorned, she burnt his toast and made him a coffee with cold water. *That'll show him!*

When he walked into the kitchen, he saw her sitting at the table, staring out of the window, as if in a trance.

'Sorry about earlier,' he said. 'You know I'm grumpy in the

mornings.'

She looked at him and smiled. 'I've made you some coffee and toast.'

'Thanks,' he said, eyeing the charcoal coloured toast, 'but I've got an early meeting. I'll grab something on the way. See you later.' With that, he disappeared, slamming the front door behind him.

The tears that had been threatening to fall earlier, were now streaming down Lynne's face. Standing in front of the sink, staring at the world beyond the window, she felt trapped. *He must be having an affair; we haven't had sex since the honeymoon, and he didn't bat an eyelid when he saw me naked this morning. There's no other explanation.*

The sound of the letterbox flapping open and closed, roused her from her deep thoughts. She heard the post fall onto the front doormat, and walked out of the kitchen. There were two envelopes addressed to Adam, and two for her. Leaving his on the sideboard in the living room, she went over to the sofa to read hers. The first was a rejection letter for a job she'd applied for at the local council. Disappointment furrowed her brow; she had thought she'd at least get an interview for that, but no luck. Sighing, she scrunched the letter into a ball and threw it. She had been aiming for the wastepaper bin in the corner, but missed. Irritated, she stood up, picked it up grudgingly, and put it in the bin. When she returned to the sofa, she put her feet up and opened the other envelope, knowing what it was before she opened it: her credit card bill. *More good news,* she thought, as she looked at the balance. Sighing again, she stood up and placed the bill on the pile of other bills to pay, which she kept on the sideboard and paid at the end of each month. As she put the bill down, her eyes were drawn to the envelopes addressed to Adam. One was obviously junk mail, but the other was a white envelope with his name and address printed on it. It looked more personal than official. Curiosity overwhelmed her. She didn't usually open his mail, but these were desperate times: she wanted to find out what he was up to.

Even though the envelope was quite thin, when she held it up to the light she couldn't make anything out. *I'll have to steam it open,* she thought, frustrated.

As she waited for the kettle to boil, she drummed her fingers on the kitchen counter. When the kettle boiled and she saw the plume of steam rise into the air, she held the envelope there for a few moments. It took longer than she'd expected for the envelope to open. Finally, she was able to pull out the contents. Inside, she found a folded piece of white paper. She unfolded it and stared in disbelief at the words:

YOUR wife *Lynne* is HAVING an **affair** *she* is making **a fool of you I have the proof**

It was a poison pen letter. The words were cut out of newspapers and magazines and stuck onto the paper.

Lynne had to sit down as she was starting to feel faint. *Who could have done such a thing?* Who hated her that much? The only person she could think of was Rachel. But would she stoop so low as to do such a crazy thing? Perhaps she had lost her mind now that Alex had killed himself. Lynne didn't like the idea that Rachel was planning a vendetta against her.

She thought back to the prank calls, and now this. Someone was out to break up her marriage.

I'll have to tell Adam about it. Warn him. But if she showed him the letter, he would know that she'd opened his mail.

She picked up the envelope, and noticed the postmark was from a sorting office in Hertfordshire. Rachel lived in London. Could it have been sent by someone else? But who? *Jason. It could be him.* She remembered how he had phoned her the day after Matt's party and had said he wanted to go out with her again. Had he lied about preferring married women? Maybe he was trying to break up her marriage so she would go out with him again. She shook her head, realising how ridiculous that sounded. *Jason is young and good-looking. He could have any girl he wanted. Why would he become fixated with me?* Then she recalled how Alex had supposedly become obsessed with her. *Is there something about me that makes these weirdos become infatuated?*

Perhaps Jason was just not used to girls turning him down, so he may have taken offence. But Jason also lived in London, so maybe he didn't send it. Then again, it would be easy enough for someone living in London to take a trip to Hertfordshire to post the letter, to cover their tracks.

As she placed the letter back into the envelope, she realised her hands were shaking. She considered throwing it away, but there was a part of her that wanted to see Adam's reaction to this letter. Would he believe it? His reaction would reveal if he really cared about her. If it was true that *he* was having an affair, then surely this sort of news about her wouldn't bother him. She went into the spare bedroom, which they used as an office, and found some glue to stick the envelope shut. Feeling satisfied that Adam wouldn't be able tell it had been opened, she returned to the living room and put it on the sideboard on top of his other mail.

She sat on the sofa, staring over at the envelope. It was scary to think that someone had something against her and wanted to hurt her. She felt glad she'd opened the envelope; at least she now knew what was going on. Adam may have been embarrassed by the content and may not have told her.

An unwelcome thought invaded her mind: *What if Adam is doing this? What if he is having an affair and wants to leave me? This poison pen letter turning up is so convenient for him. He'd be able to blame me and walk out. No, that's too far-fetched; and besides, the prank calls happened when he was in the room.*

Her mind turned everything around: *What if Adam has received one of these letters before? Or more than one? What if that's why he's behaving so strangely towards me?*

Soon, she realised that all she was doing with this speculation was giving herself a headache. The only solution would be to wait until tonight and watch for his reaction as he read the letter.

She tried phoning Sandra to see what she made of it all, but both her mobile and her work phone went onto voicemail.

Lynne decided to go online and concentrate on trying to find a job, to take her mind off everything. It was like having a clock ticking in her head, as she waited impatiently for the time to pass, and for Adam to come home.

⧗

Adam walked in at 7:30 pm, and hung his jacket on a coat hook by the side of the front door. Lynne was sitting on the sofa, watching TV.

'Hi.' She spun around to greet him, with a smile on her face.

'Hi,' he replied, walking over to the sofa and sitting down. He frowned, finding it so hard to deal with his emotions. Keeping up the façade that he loved her was important, so that they could remain married. If she left him, he would be forced into a decision he was not yet ready to make; there would no longer be any excuse he could give to Paul.

'Lynne, I am really sorry about this morning.' He kissed her hand.

'Oh, I've forgotten about it,' she said, even though that was far from the truth. She looked at Adam, feeling determined not to spoil this again, like she had the last time he had tried to be nice to her. It was imperative that he was on her side, because soon he would be opening that poison pen letter. As she anticipated what his reaction would be, she trembled. Reaching out, she hugged him. 'Adam, I know things have been a bit rocky between us recently, but I really want to put all that behind us and get back to how we used to be.'

He smiled stiffly, and pulled away from her. 'I know I've been a bit distant, but I've had a lot on my mind, and it's just the pressure of work and because I'm away so often. Things are fine between us apart from that, aren't they?'

'Yes!' said Lynne, worrying that she may have said it a bit too quickly and enthusiastically.

'As you can see,' he said. 'I haven't brought a takeaway meal tonight. I thought it would be nice to take you out to dinner. That's if you haven't already eaten? I should have called, but work—'

'No, I haven't eaten.' Lynne had been feeling sick after reading the poison pen letter, and had hardly eaten a thing all day. 'It would be nice to go out somewhere.' She smiled. There was a glimmer of hope somewhere now, that things could get back to normal. Maybe Adam did still love her. All her doubts might be unwarranted.

'Great!' he said. 'I just need to check a few e-mails, and I'll be back. You get changed. Dress up, if you want.'

She watched him walking towards the office, and held her breath as she saw him pick up his mail from the sideboard on the way. Just when she had a bit of hope that they could get closer, that letter would be overshadowing the evening. *He might call off the dinner date now*, she thought, glumly. Or, he might not mention the letter, and then she would be thinking about it all evening unable to enjoy herself.

She stood up and walked towards their bedroom, passing the office room on the way. He had closed the door. The sound of the keyboard could be heard as he typed something on the computer.

She walked into their bedroom, feeling as though she were carrying a weight on her shoulders. Opening her wardrobe door to look for something to wear, she noticed all the dresses and tops that she'd bought over the years, that she'd hardly ever worn. They rarely went out as a couple, these days.

She picked out a black dress with silver trimming on the neckline, that she'd last worn when she'd been out with Sandra a few months ago. Her lips tightened, as she realised those had been happier days. When she put on the dress, it felt very tight around the waist; she'd gained a bit of weight since being made redundant, as she wasn't so active. *I've got to start doing some exercise.*

She took off the dress and put it back into the wardrobe, opting instead for some loose fitting trousers and a dressy top, which covered the unsightly bulges, and actually made her look slimmer.

The bedroom door opened and Adam walked in holding the familiar piece of paper. 'Look what I've received in the post.' He handed it to her.

Trying hard to act as if she hadn't seen it before, Lynne held onto the poison pen letter for a short while, giving the impression that she was reading it. 'Oh my God!' she said. *Was that convincing enough?* she wondered.

'Well, I don't believe it for a moment,' he said. 'Our marriage is built on trust and I know you would never cheat on me, no matter what other failings there may be. I just thought you should see it.'

'Okay,' she said, feeling confused by his reaction. There didn't seem to be any emotion there.

'Is there someone who hates you, who might want to break us up?' he asked.

'Er... no. I can't think of anyone. I'm just shocked at seeing this. Who could do such a thing?'

'Someone who's angry about something. Maybe we should keep it, in case anything else happens; the police might need to see it.' He took the letter from her. 'You said there had been some prank calls yesterday?'

'Yes.'

'Right, okay.' He looked at her. 'Nice outfit. Are you ready?'

'Yes.' She smiled.

As she followed him out of the room, she was left feeling numb. Somehow, she had expected either a heated argument, or for him to keep the letter secret from her. This was a very unusual way for him to behave after receiving information that his wife may be cheating on him. It left her feeling as though he didn't really care.

As Lynne sat in the passenger seat of the car on the way to the restaurant, she started to think that maybe Adam had just been really shocked by the letter, and maybe he feared that she *was* having an affair. He might be afraid to act angrily in case she left him for this other man. She hoped that was the real reason he had shown no emotion, and not because he just wasn't bothered either way.

By the end of the evening, on their way back in the car, Adam and Lynne were chatting away happily about the meal they had just shared and the waiter who had served them. An observer would have thought they were a very content couple who had never had a disagreement in their lives.

They arrived home and went into the bedroom. Adam held her in his arms and kissed her. It was a soft kiss; a brief kiss. She was left wanting more, but he put a hand in front of his mouth to stifle a yawn, and said: 'I'm getting up early tomorrow, my flight leaves at nine, so I'll have to be at the airport by seven. Don't bother waking up to make my breakfast, it'll be too early.' He proceeded to set his alarm clock and began getting changed into his pyjamas.

Lynne walked over to her side of the bed, disappointed at how the evening had ended. Everything had seemed to be going so well. Why didn't he want them to be close? The last time they'd had sex was during the honeymoon, and even then, it was only once and had been over in a few minutes; not satisfying for her at all. Was he just not attracted to her anymore?

'Goodnight,' he said, when she got into bed beside him.

'Adam?' she said.

'Lynne, I really need to get to sleep.'

'Adam, we haven't had sex for weeks. That's not normal, is it?'

'Do you want to have sex?' he said.

'Well, once in a blue moon would be nice.'

'Okay, get undressed.'

'What? That's not very romantic, is it?'

'It will have to be quick. I have to get up early.'

Lynne had now gone off the idea. 'Don't bother,' she said, turning away from him.

Chapter Twenty

Lynne couldn't sleep. She kept thinking about how unconcerned Adam had been about the poison pen letter, and then how he just didn't seem to be interested in her anymore. He was so cold.

Everything pointed to him having an affair. It kept popping into her mind; a nagging voice that wouldn't go away. She needed some proof. He was due to go to the airport this morning. If she followed him, she could find out for sure where he was going. But she couldn't follow him in her car; he might see it. Ideally, she needed to borrow someone else's car. The only person she could think of calling was Sandra; but ever since starting her new relationship, Sandra had been hard to get hold of. Lynne had been unable to get in touch with her when she'd tried earlier that day, and Sandra hadn't returned her voicemail message.

I'll call a cab, she thought, *and I'll get the cab driver to follow him.*

Carefully, she wriggled out of bed and went into the living room on tiptoes, aware that any sound might wake Adam. As she fished for her mobile phone in her bag, her eyes scanned the room for the yellow pages so she could look up a telephone number for a local cab firm. It was 3 am. Adam would be leaving at about 6 am, so she would have to order the cab for 5:30 am to be on the safe side.

She knew that if she spoke normally on the phone, there was a risk Adam would hear her; the walls in the flat were paper-thin. *I'll have to go outside.* Grabbing her handbag, she opened the front door very slowly. She pulled it shut behind her, cursing as it creaked slightly.

It was chilly outside, and Lynne wore only pyjamas bottoms and a vest top. She shivered as she dialled the number.

'Hi, can I order a cab for 5:30, please?'

She gave the man her address.

'Where will you be travelling to?'

'Um... I'll tell the driver when he gets here.'

'Sorry, Madam, we need to know the destination.'

'Okay, Heathrow Airport.' She hoped Adam was going there.

Lynne arranged to meet the driver downstairs, outside the main entrance to the tower block. Adam would be getting his car out of the parking area at the back, so hopefully their paths would not cross.

As she reached inside her bag, her mind went back to the evening before and a picture flashed in her mind of her keys lying on the sideboard inside the front door. *Oh my God!* She panicked and poured the contents of her bag out onto the ground. *My keys are always in here!* But they were not in there. She shook her head, remembering that she'd opened the door last night when they got back from the restaurant, because Adam couldn't find his keys. She had obviously forgotten to put hers back in her bag.

Looking around her, she began to feel frightened. This was no place to be stranded at 3 am. The tower block was notorious for drug dealers and violent gangs. Her heart skipped a beat as she heard footsteps coming from the stairwell, not too far away. Her imagination began to run wild.

She quickly gathered up the items from her handbag that were now scattered on the ground, and pressed the doorbell, urgently. After a couple of seconds, she pressed it again. The footsteps were now going in the opposite direction. She sighed with relief.

Adam appeared at the front door. He looked at her as if she had gone mad. 'What... Lynne, why?' He rubbed his eyes.

'I must have been sleepwalking,' she lied. 'I used to sleepwalk as a child. It must be all the recent stress that's brought it back.' Unable to meet his eyes, she pushed past him into the flat.

'You never told me you used to sleepwalk.'

That's because I've never sleepwalked. 'Yes, yes. I used to do it all the time,' she said, as she walked back into the bedroom.

Adam followed her. 'You do realise that I have to get out of bed in less than two hours?'

'I didn't do it on purpose,' said Lynne, sheepishly.

'Yes, I know, sorry,' he said. 'I just need to get some sleep. Goodnight.'

''Night.'

Lynne knew she would not be able to sleep. She would have to be ready to meet the cab driver in a couple of hours time, and try to somehow get him to follow Adam's car. This was going to be tricky.

Chapter Twenty-One

Lynne met the cab driver as planned, outside the tower block at 5:30 am. She had to sneak out of the flat without Adam seeing her. She'd waited until he was in the kitchen, and then grabbed her bag and keys and ran out of the door. He wouldn't look for her. He never went back to the bedroom once he'd left there in the mornings. He'd think she was fast asleep.

'Hello,' she said to the driver. He was a large man. His stomach almost touched the steering wheel. He had a round, friendly looking face, and a dark complexion.

'Hello, Miss,' he said, in a foreign accent she couldn't place. 'Heathrow Airport, yes?'

She got into the back of the cab and closed the door. 'Er... no. Can we just sit here a while, please? I'll pay you extra.'

'Oh, you want extra services? I don't usually do that sort of thing, but you are pretty lady, so I say yes.' His eyes were almost popping out of his head with excitement.

'No, no!' she exclaimed, feeling disgusted at the thought. 'You've misunderstood me. I want you to follow a car. He'll be leaving these flats in a few minutes. I'll show you the car, then I want you to follow him, please. As I say, I'll pay you extra.'

'Okay. I do it. This is your boyfriend you are following, yes?'

'No. I'm following him for a friend. It's her husband. She thinks he's cheating on her and I need to find out where he is going.'

'Ah! This sound like fun. I always wanted to be a detective.'

They sat in silence for a few minutes. Then the man said, 'You know, if your husband is cheating on you, he would be a mad man. You are lovely lady. If we find out he is cheating, then I take you out. I make you feel better.'

'It's not my husband.'

'So, you are single?' He turned around in the driver's seat to face her.

'No, I am married.'

'Oh, that is a pity, I am looking for a wife.'

Just then, Lynne spotted Adam's car pulling out of the car park. 'It's over there!' she said. 'The silver BMW.'

'Hmm... Nice car,' said the cab driver. He began to follow Adam's car, and Lynne could feel herself perspiring, unable to believe she was doing this. She remembered only yesterday how Adam had reacted to the poison pen letter: *'Our marriage is built on trust,'* he'd said. What if she'd got this all wrong? By following the car she was proving that she didn't trust him at all.

'Where is he going, Miss?'

'He said he was going to Heathrow Airport.'

'He is going the wrong way for Heathrow. He should have taken the road on the left to take the motorway.'

'Okay, just keep following him, please.' So, it looked as though he was lying. As she began to think again about all the silent phone calls she'd been receiving, her nerves jangled. Fear crept into her heart as she anticipated what she might be just about to find out. Did she really want proof that he was cheating? A memory she thought had long since gone, came cascading into her mind... She remembered how she'd felt that day, all those years ago, walking into the old flat she used to share with Steve and seeing him on the bed with Alicia. That gut wrenching feeling of inadequacy in the face of his betrayal. Did she really want to subject herself to something like that again?

She knew now that she had been hoping Adam would just go to Heathrow and get on the plane he was supposed to get on. Then there would have been something to build on, some hope to keep their relationship alive. *Perhaps he's going to a different airport.*

After only driving for ten minutes, Adam parked his car in a residential street, outside a semi-detached house. He got out of the car and walked to the door of the house. Shortly, the door opened and Paul stood there. The cab driver had parked on the opposite side of the street, but she could see them clearly, and felt almost too conspicuous. She leaned down in the seat so that if Paul or Adam looked over at the car, she could quickly hide. Luckily, they seemed engrossed in a conversation, looking only at each other, oblivious to anything around them. Then something very unusual happened. Adam embraced Paul, and they kissed each other... on the lips. It wasn't a brief kiss; not like the kiss he had given her last night. This was the sort of kiss she had been hoping he would give her; the kind of kiss he used to give her at the start of their relationship. All she could do was stare.

'So, it look as though your friend's husband is cheating on her then,' said the cab driver.

Lynne could feel the tears running down her cheeks. 'Can we go now, please?' she managed to say.

Once back at the tower block, she paid the cab driver. 'Thank you,' she said. She had dried her tears, and hoped he couldn't tell that she'd been crying in the back of the cab.

'I meant it when I say you are a beautiful lady,' he said. 'My offer is still open, if you want a real man.'

Lynne didn't know whether to laugh, or to cry again. She waved good-bye to him and watched as the cab disappeared off into the distance. Then she just stood there for a while, outside the tall grey building that housed the flat she shared with Adam. It no longer felt like home. That part of her life had been shattered. *What do I do now?*

Chapter Twenty-Two

Lynne stepped into the lift, and stood there. She just couldn't seem to concentrate for more than a few moments at a time without her mind recalling what she had seen. The passion in that embrace between Adam and Paul was obvious, even from her position behind a car window, across the street.

She couldn't help feeling regret that she had not waited to see what happened after. Would Adam have gone back to his car on his own? Would Paul have brought out a set of luggage and travelled with him? Would Adam have taken his luggage into Paul's house to spend two weeks there, rather than going away on a business trip? She would never know. What did it matter? All the evidence she needed was there in that kiss. That was why he had been behaving so coldly towards her. *He doesn't love me. He loves Paul. He probably never loved me. How long has he been seeing Paul? They've been friends since college; have they been seeing each other secretly since then? Why did he ask me to marry him? I thought he loved me.*

Eventually, the lift door closed and jolted Lynne back to the present. She pushed the button for the fifth floor. What would it feel like, walking into a place where she had shared memories with someone who had been lying all along? How could he be gay and still have married her? *What was he thinking?*

Years ago, she had heard about a friend of a friend, who'd been engaged to a man and found out he was gay. When Lynne heard the story, she'd said, *'Oh my God! That's so terrible. How could you ever get over something like that? I don't think I could.'*

The words resonated in her mind now. She found herself wondering what had become of this friend of a friend, as she realised that she hadn't really cared at the time. It was someone else's life. That sort of thing only happened in other people's lives.

The lift stopped at the third floor, and one of her neighbours got in. Mrs. Phillips. Lynne didn't know her first name. They didn't know each other at all, apart from what they could hear going on through the walls dividing their flats. Lynne was sure that Mrs. Phillips must have heard all the arguments she'd had with Adam; especially recently.

Mrs. Phillips was elderly, and lived alone with her cat; so, apart from being able to hear her talking to the occasional guest, Lynne didn't have a clue about what went on in her flat. Adam and Lynne lived at number 93, and Mrs. Phillips lived at 95. Lynne knew the name of her cat was "Bubbles", as she often heard the old woman calling him at random hours of the day and night.

The only reason Lynne knew her surname was "Phillips", was because an envelope addressed to number 95 had accidentally been posted through Lynne and Adam's letterbox about six months ago. Lynne realised that it was possible her name wasn't Mrs. Phillips, after all. The envelope could have been addressed to the wrong person, or to a previous occupier of the flat.

Lynne hardly ever saw "Mrs. Phillips" out and about. She remembered a brief conversation she'd had with her about a year ago.

'Oh, hello, dear.' The old woman looked at Lynne and smiled.

They'd both stepped out of their front doors at the same time.

'You must be on your way to work,' continued Mrs. Phillips. 'I'm off to the shops.'

'It's very early for a shopping trip,' said Lynne, yawning and wishing she could go back to bed. She was thinking: I'd never get up this early just to go shopping.

'I have to leave early, so I can get back early; before all the youngsters get back from school. It's quite intimidating. Have you heard about the gangs around here?'

'Yes, it's worrying.' Lynne nodded, wanting to be polite, but knowing she would be late for work if she didn't leave in the next couple of minutes.

'We have to be careful,' continued her neighbour. 'Last week, an elderly gentleman was beaten up on the second floor, for a packet of cigarettes.'

'Oh, dear,' said Lynne, looking at her watch.

'It's so scary what you hear on the news,' said the old woman. 'Sometimes, I wish I didn't have to leave my flat at all. It's not like it was in the old days.'

'No, that's a shame. Sorry, I have to dash.'

Lynne lowered her head in shame as Mrs. Phillips hobbled into the lift, realising that that had been the longest conversation she'd ever had with her, and all she'd wanted to do was get away. Thinking back, she was quite sure that the old woman had introduced herself then, as it had been just after Adam and Lynne had moved into the flat. She'd probably even told her her name, but Lynne realised, to her chagrin, that she'd not been paying attention.

Looking at Mrs. Phillips now, who appeared frail and at least 80 years old, she felt bad that she'd not even tried to talk to her, or listen to her, or visit her, over the past few months. Being out of work, she'd had ample opportunity. Mrs. Phillips didn't have many guests and would probably have been glad of the company.

'Hello, Lynne,' she said.

She had remembered her name, so this was confirmation that they must have introduced themselves to each other at some stage; or, maybe she'd heard Adam shouting her name during one of their rows. Lynne blushed. 'Hello,' she said with a big smile; overcompensating for being a bad neighbour.

'You're up early, dear,' commented Mrs. Phillips.

'Yes,' said Lynne. She looked at her watch and saw that it was just after 6:15 am. 'My husband went to the airport this morning.'

'Oh, that's nice. I've just been visiting a friend, who's not very well. She lives on the third floor. I thought I should keep an eye on her. She's 92. Her children and grandchildren hardly ever visit, even though they only live a few streets away.'

'Oh, that's terrible,' said Lynne.

'It's heartbreaking. It makes me almost glad I never had any children of my own.' Mrs. Phillips shook her head. 'Do you know what Edna said to me today? She said that she can go for days without saying a word, all alone in that flat. Sometimes she feels like she's going to forget how to speak.'

'That's so sad. But surely she can phone her children?'

'Young people don't have time to talk these days; they're so busy. Never grow old, dear. People don't want to know you when you're old.' The old woman laughed, but Lynne could sense a sadness behind it.

The lift stopped at the fifth floor and Mrs. Phillips got out. 'Aren't you coming, dear?'

As the number 5 flashed above them in the lift, Lynne's mind had gone back to thinking about Adam; she'd been there again, watching the kiss, unable to comprehend what was happening.

'Oh... yes. I am,' she said, disorientated. She hurried out of the lift and said a quick good-bye to Mrs. Phillips, eager to get away, to be alone. Lynne ran along the corridor, trying in vain to escape the images in her mind's eye. As soon as she stepped inside the flat, her tears began to fall.

Chapter Twenty-Three

Two days had passed since Lynne had witnessed Adam and Paul kissing. She had not left the flat for two whole days.

When she'd returned from her momentous trip in the cab, her mind raced at one hundred miles per hour; she was trying to recall every previous meeting she'd had with Paul; trying to work out whether this affair was a recent thing, or if it had been going on for ever. Eventually, she'd gone to bed and fallen asleep through sheer exhaustion caused by the sleepless night before.

She didn't wake up until the late afternoon. The first thing that popped up in her mind was the image of Adam kissing Paul. Again, she wondered whether it was even possible to get over something like this. She thought of phoning her old friend; the one who'd had a friend who'd been through a similar experience. Maybe she could get in touch with that girl and find out how she'd coped.

As nausea swept over her, she began to wonder whether she'd only dreamt it. Had it really happened? Had she really followed Adam in a cab? It all seemed like something someone else had done; so displaced in her mind. She wanted to black it all out, erase it so that it never existed.

In a way, she was glad she'd seen it. At least she knew the truth. Adam might never have told her. He could have kept on seeing Paul secretly, like some men have mistresses. She may never have discovered that she'd married a gay man.

But why didn't I realise he's gay? she asked herself. *Surely, anyone else would have known.* She wondered who else knew. Was everyone laughing at her behind her back? Suddenly, all her friends and acquaintances were potential conspirators. Had Sandra been trying to tell her on her wedding day, when she said that she thought Paul is gay? Paranoia took over Lynne's mind. Perhaps this was what it felt like to go mad; to lose touch with reality completely and let your mind run away where no one would ever find it.

She didn't eat anything that first day; she just lay on the bed. She cried and slept, then she ran it all through her mind again. After that, she cried again. Then, she slept again and awoke with the feeling she was going crazy. More crying ensued. It was like a never ending cycle of despair.

The next day, she felt sick from not eating, and very thirsty. She ventured out of the bedroom to fetch a glass of water. Once in the kitchen, she decided she should at least try to eat something. She stood staring at the cereal boxes in the cupboard for a while; not really looking at them, but more wondering how her life had ended up like this. Shaking herself out of her musing, she opted for corn flakes; but when she looked in the fridge, she saw there was no milk. She had meant to go and buy some milk yesterday, in that other lifetime, when ignorance was bliss. How she longed to return there, like an old, familiar holiday destination. But she knew she was looking back and remembering her past life as perfect, ignoring the great big black holes that were already making their mark there. Even if she hadn't discovered Adam's affair, she doubted their marriage would have survived much longer. It had been like a flower left outside on a sunny day without being watered; it had been slowly wilting and would have soon died, there could be no doubt about that. But still, the end of anything has to be mourned; so here she stood, enshrouded in doom and gloom, wishing the end of the world would hurry up and take away the pain.

The chocolate cheesecake that she'd bought a few days ago when planning another reconciliatory meal with Adam, stared out at her, tempting her taste buds. There would be no reconciliatory meal now. Sighing, she took the cheesecake out of the fridge and grabbed a spoon. *Why bother with a plate?* she thought, *I'm going to eat it all.* After removing the packaging, impatiently, she used the spoon to cut up the cake. After a few mouthfuls of the rich chocolate cake, with the smooth, cream cheese filling, she began to feel a bit better. But soon, the richness of the dark chocolate and the heaviness of the cheese made her a little queasy. Her mouth began to feel sticky. Becoming dizzy as she stood up, she steadied herself by holding onto the table, and then walked over to the sink to get some water.

The familiar image, which seemed to be imprinted on her mind, reappeared, more vivid than ever: Adam and Paul in an embrace. Kissing. Unable to stop herself from throwing up, the half-digested cheesecake appeared in front of her in the sink.

She stumbled back to the table, grabbing some kitchen towel on the way, to wipe her mouth. The tears began to fall. She desperately needed to talk to someone; but who? Who would be able to understand this? And, was it even real? Had she gone mad and imagined it? It all seemed so unlikely. *Adam and Paul? No, it could never have happened. Adam is not gay. He married me. We've been living together for years. I would have known.*

Her tears continued to fall.

She sat in front of the TV for the rest of the day, watching, but not really concentrating on the flashing pictures and the empty words. Nothing really meant much anymore.

She forced herself to eat some baked beans on toast in the evening, and managed to keep that down. Eventually, she fell into a deep but troubled sleep, whilst sitting on the sofa in her pyjamas, which she had been wearing all day.

Her dreams were of Adam, but he was far away and she could not get to him, no matter how hard she tried to reach out her arms or call his name. He kept drifting further away. She felt frightened, and kept seeing Paul's face; he was talking to her and trying to apologise. She wasn't listening. All she wanted to do was to get through to Adam, but he wasn't listening. Then she saw herself sitting on the sofa, next to Paul. The phone began to ring. He was saying: *'Aren't you going to answer that?'*, but she kept saying: *'What are you doing in my house? Go away!'*

Then, she woke up and realised that the phone was actually ringing. She almost didn't answer it; not yet feeling ready to face the world. But she knew that she had to try to stop herself falling deeper into this mire of self-destruction. She had to talk to someone, anyone, just to distract her mind from the dead end street of painful memories.

As she reached for the phone, she wondered if she was still dreaming. 'Hello,' she said, her voice hoarse.

'Lynne? Is that you? You sound like you've just woken up.'

'Yes, I have just woken up.'

'Oh... do you know what time it is?'

It was Sandra on the phone, but with this line of questioning, it could have easily been her mother.

'It's nearly midday,' said Sandra.

'Oh, I've sort of lost track of time.'

'I know, it can get like that when you're out of work.'

Lynne began to feel more hopeful, hearing Sandra's voice. She knew she could tell Sandra everything. It would be a relief to get it all off her chest.

'Are you busy today, Sand?'

'Well, actually, I was calling to see if you wanted to meet for lunch. Maybe one o'clock?'

'Okay. Could you come here? I'm not really up to going out anywhere,' said Lynne, looking down at her pyjamas stained with dried vomit and a few dry baked beans.

'Um... okay. But listen, don't go to any fuss, don't cook; we'll bring a takeaway. Is fish and chips okay?'

'Yes, that's fine.'

'Great, see you soon. I can't wait.'

Lynne felt a bit brighter, and more optimistic, when she put the phone down. Sandra sounded happy. She would definitely help to lift her spirits. She'd know what to say.

Lynne went into the bedroom to get changed. She took out a pair of jeans and a t-shirt from the wardrobe. As she closed the wardrobe door, she caught sight of her reflection in the mirror and almost didn't recognise herself. Her hair was sticking up all over the place, and her eyes were red and puffy.

She jumped into the shower in the en suite hoping to wash away the past two days, imagining it all spiralling down the plug hole as she rinsed the lather from her body. Feeling refreshed when she stepped out of the shower, she wrapped a large soft towel around her and took a deep breath, resolving to put it all behind her. She blow dried her hair, washed her face and applied some make-up.

When she went into the kitchen to get some plates ready for the fish and chips, she saw there was still some vomit stuck on the side of the sink. The smell made her want to throw up again. She noticed the remains of the half-eaten cheesecake on the table. It had melted. The room was a mess. There were some trodden baked beans on the floor, and bread crumbs all over the kitchen work surface.

Before she could tidy up, she heard the doorbell ring. She quickly found two plates, knives and forks, and placed them on the living room table. As she shut the kitchen door, she wished she had a lock for it, and prayed that Sandra wouldn't go in there.

Sandra stood grinning at the front door, but she wasn't alone. *I should have guessed,* thought Lynne. Standing beside Sandra with an arm around her, was a tall, smiling man, holding a large bag of fish and chips. As much as she wanted to believe he was just a fish and chips delivery man, Lynne knew that wasn't the case.

'Hi, Lynne,' said a beaming Sandra. 'This is Dave. I've been dying for you two to meet!'

Chapter Twenty-Four

Sandra and Dave were both holding a chip when Lynne said it, and they were now both still holding their respective chips, with their mouths open. Lynne knew the reason their mouths were open was not because they were going to put their chips in their mouths; it was because of what she'd just said.

Sandra and Dave were now both putting their chips back onto their plates, and both staring at Lynne as if she had said, 'Don't eat those chips, I've put rat poison on them.' But of course, that's not what she'd said. What she had actually said—the thing that had obviously put them off their food—was: 'I've just found out that my husband is having an affair with a man.'

Sandra was the first to speak. 'Lynne. Did I just hear you say that Adam—'

'Is gay. Yes. Well, technically he's bisexual, but hey, what does that matter now? My marriage is over!' Lynne stood up.

Dave shifted in his seat. He coughed and stood up. 'Er... I should be going. I have a meeting at 2 o'clock. I'll leave you two alone.' He picked up his briefcase and walked towards the door. 'It was nice meeting you, Lynne.' His face had turned bright red.

Lynne sighed with relief when he walked out of the door. 'Thank God!' she screamed. 'Why did you bring him here? I asked you to come here because I wanted to tell you about Adam! You should have come here alone!' She was storming around the room.

Sandra stood up and tried to follow her. 'Calm down, Lynne. I told you when we last spoke that I wanted you two to meet, so I thought it would be an ideal opportunity. I had no idea—'

'No idea that my husband is gay? Well, funnily enough, neither did I until a couple of days ago!' Lynne sat down on the armchair next to the sofa, and noticed the half-eaten meal. Dave had hardly had a chance to start eating. Her fault, she realised with a pang of guilt. One minute they'd been talking about how Sandra and Dave had met, the next minute she'd dropped the bombshell. But she just couldn't sit there and listen to their lovey-dovey memories. Her mind was thinking, *Yeah, yeah, wait until two or three years down the line, when you'll hardly ever have sex, and things that make you laugh about each other now, will make you want to strangle each other, or cry. And the odds are that one of you will be sleeping with someone else.*

Having an affair. Maybe, Dave, it'll even be with a man!

She looked at Sandra and realised she had managed to wipe the smile off her friend's face. Lynne lowered her eyes in remorse. Sandra had been happy when she'd walked into the flat, but now, for once in her life, she looked like she didn't have anything to say.

'Sand, sit down and finish your lunch,' she said. 'I'm sorry I shouted. I haven't been sleeping, or eating, since I found out. I just don't know what I'm going to do.'

Sandra sat on the sofa. 'I shouldn't have brought Dave here,' she said. 'Sorry.'

'He probably thinks I'm a lunatic,' said Lynne.

'Oh, don't worry, he already knows you're a lunatic; I warned him before we came,' said Sandra, daring to laugh, not sure what Lynne's reaction would be.

Lynne laughed, and the tension in the air began to lift. 'Thanks for coming over. I really needed to talk to someone.'

'I'll call in and take the afternoon off work,' said Sandra, taking her mobile out of her bag. 'They owe me some time off.'

Lynne listened to Sandra's telephone conversation, grateful her friend would be staying. She didn't think she would have been able to spend another day alone in this flat.

Sandra put her mobile back into her bag and reached for her plate. 'Well, we might as well finish our lunch,' she said.

They ate in silence, looking up at each other every so often. Soon Lynne began to feel better. Then, when she had eaten as much as she could, she said, 'Poor Dave didn't get to eat his lunch.'

'Oh, he'll be okay. There's a cafeteria at work.' Sandra smiled.

'He seems nice,' said Lynne. But then her emotions got the better of her. The tears were falling, and there was nothing she could do to stop them. 'Sand, Adam fooled me.'

'He fooled everyone, Lynne.' Sandra reached out a hand and touched Lynne's shoulder. 'Everything's going to be okay, you'll see.'

Lynne looked up at her. 'I don't know if I can get through this, Sand. I really don't.' Her emotions were so overpowering, she wondered if she might be on the brink of a nervous breakdown. She no longer felt in control of her tears, her sobs, or her speech.

Sandra gave her a tissue and kept repeating that everything would be okay and it wasn't her fault. Soon, Lynne began to feel like herself again.

'What's wrong with me, Sand?' She stared, wide-eyed. 'Why does everyone leave? Why does everyone I love, leave me?'

'Lynne, I'm still here. And I'm not going anywhere.'

They sat in silence for a few moments.

'Sand, I feel really bad about saying all this in front of Dave. Please apologise to him for me. If I'd been myself I wouldn't have said anything until we were alone. But I just had to get it out. I don't know what I'm thinking these days.'

'Don't worry, Dave will understand. It's not an easy thing to find out your husband is gay. I still can't get my head around it. I had no idea.'

'You guessed Paul is gay, though. I didn't believe you.'

'Paul?'

'The best man at the wedding.'

'What's he got to do with this?'

'He's the one Adam's having an affair with.'

'No!' Sandra's eyes were like saucers. 'Unbelievable.'

'Yes. In this case, instead of the bridesmaid getting off with the best man, it's the groom!'

'Adam and Paul?' Sandra shook her head. 'I would never have guessed.'

'It's all such a mess, Sand. D'you know, those dreams I was having before the wedding must have been my subconscious telling me not to marry Adam. I should have listened to my intuition. At some deeper level, I must have known he's gay. I don't think I ever really loved Adam, you know. I only thought I did. I think I was still in love with Steve.'

'Lynne—'

'I know, Steve's a rat; but you can't help who you fall in love with.'

'True, look what happened with me and Matt.' Sandra frowned.

'When Steve phoned me before the wedding, I started to think about him again,' continued Lynne. 'I was devastated when I found out he was married, but it kind of put closure on it for me. I thought I could make a go of it with Adam then. The truth is, I got together with Adam on the rebound from Steve, didn't I? I didn't give myself enough time to get over Steve.

'Things haven't been right between me and Adam for a while, but I kept trying to make things better. I didn't want another failed romance.'

'How did you find out about the affair... That's if you don't mind taking about it.'

'No, it's okay. I *need* to talk about it.' Lynne paused. 'I was suspicious that he was having an affair, so I followed him when he said he was going away on business. He drove to Paul's house and they kissed on the doorstep.'

'So, what did you do?'

'I came back here, and I've been in here for two days; hardly

106

sleeping, hardly eating. Generally deteriorating.' She laughed, dryly.

'You should have called me. If you were feeling so low, you should have told me. I would have come over.'

'I just wanted to be alone, I suppose.'

'So, all you saw was a kiss? What if he was just saying good-bye to Paul? Some men kiss each other when they say good-bye,' said Sandra.

'On the lips? Passionately? Whilst embracing each other?'

'Oh, I see.' Sandra nodded.

'Come to think of it, I found some texts on Adam's mobile the other day, between him and Paul; they ended their texts with kisses. I laughed when I saw that... didn't think anything of it. I wouldn't have ever guessed if I hadn't seen them with my own eyes.' She shook her head, the memory of those texts flashing in her mind.

There was silence, as if both women were trying to make sense of a particularly complicated conundrum. Then Lynne spoke again: 'It's such a shock, Sand. I don't know how long it's been going on. I mean, what if Paul has AIDS or something? Oh my God! I could have AIDS!'

'Lynne, you're overreacting. Just because he's gay, doesn't mean he's got AIDS.'

'I know that! But I don't know where Paul's been! He might be promiscuous. And AIDS is more common in the gay community, isn't it?'

'I don't know. Maybe you should have a test.'

'I'm going to. And I have to test for other STDs. Adam could have been sleeping around with other people, too. Ugh... I feel so sick. Why did he marry me? He stood there in a church and said vows that didn't mean anything. And Paul was standing right beside him. His best man. They've made such a fool of me.'

'Maybe the affair started after the wedding,' said Sandra.

Lynne stood up. 'Do you know, I don't even care anymore. I just have to get a divorce and move on. I have to put it behind me.'

Sandra stood up. 'Okay, let's go out this evening. We'll get dressed up and go out for a meal. We can go to the theatre maybe, or cinema. Something to take your mind off it.'

'I don't know, Sand. I'm out of work, I shouldn't be spending any money.'

'Okay, we'll get a takeaway and a DVD. My treat. We'll go to my flat and you can stay over. I'll call Dave and let him know I won't be home tonight.'

'I thought you'd rented out your flat?'

'I'm still looking for tenants.'

'Oh, okay. I could do with getting out of this place.'

Chapter Twenty-Five

The next day, Lynne was feeling much better. She woke up in Sandra's flat and found a note from her in the kitchen.

Gone to work. Please feel free to stay as long as you like. I've left the spare key on the table in case you need to pop out for something. There's some food in the fridge. Help yourself. I'll call you later, Sand x

Being in Sandra's flat, away from the things that reminded her of Adam, was like a form of therapy in itself.

The night before, she and Sandra had watched *Thelma & Louise* on DVD, whilst eating pizza and drinking wine. It had been just like old times; before Steve, and before Adam. Somehow, she wasn't sure if it was the wine or the whole mood of the evening taking her back to happier times, but soon she was feeling less needy and more centered. She began to realise that there was nothing she could do about the past, but she still had a future; her choice was either to be miserable and blame Adam for ever, or to close the door, and find out what new windows of opportunity would open to her.

Sandra had been organised enough to buy some essentials for the fridge and food cupboards. Lynne sat at the kitchen table and ate breakfast, flicking through the local paper, and hardly thinking about Adam at all. The pain was still there, but now she was able to ignore it and let the wounds heal, rather than picking at them and causing them to bleed over and over again.

Her mobile rang. She could see from the caller display that it was her mother. She made a mental note to act as if everything was fine, and not let on that there were any problems.

'Hi, Mum,' she said, trying to sound as cheerful as possible.

'Hello, dear. Why didn't you pick up your phone?'

'Er... I have picked up my phone.' Lynne's brow furrowed.

'No, I mean the house phone.'

'I'm not at home.'

'Oh. Have you found a job?'

'No, not yet. I'm at Sandra's flat.'

'I see. Well, the reason I'm phoning is, I've spoken to Rachel.'

The spectre of the memory of her last conversation with Rachel cast a shadow over Lynne's mind. 'Oh, really? Did you explain everything to her?'

'I tried, but she seems to think you are hiding something.'

'What?' Lynne stood up and began to pace the kitchen.

'She says that she remembers Alex talking about you quite a lot over the years, and she still thinks you were dating him.'

'But didn't you explain to her that I've been living with Adam for years, and then Steve before that?'

'Yes, but she says that you must have been having an affair with Alex, and that he thought you were single. She's still very angry about it all.'

'She's barking mad if you ask me.'

'Lynne, have some respect, her son has just died.'

'Oh, so it's okay for her to call me an adulterer, but if I say anything against her—'

'Look at it from her perspective,' interrupted her mother. 'You have to admit this does all seem a bit odd. Why would Alex have kept a diary and lots of photos of you, if nothing was going on?'

'So you believe her, over your own daughter? I've already told you, anything that was going on was in Alex's imagination. Oh, I'm not in the mood for this.'

'But Rachel says that there are other people who saw you together. She says one of them told her she was going to tell Adam that you've been having an affair. She said she tried to stop her, but she thinks this girl is going to write to Adam.'

'What girl? Mum, no one saw us together, because we were never together!' Lynne remembered the poison pen letter. *So, Rachel sent the letter!* 'Oh, that makes sense!' she said, thinking aloud.

'What makes sense?' asked her mother.

'You can tell Rachel that Adam received her letter, and he doesn't believe her lies.'

'Oh, well I'm glad to hear that it didn't cause any problems. Rachel wanted me to warn you. She was worried that Adam might leave you if he got that letter.'

'Mum, Rachel sent the letter. She *wants* Adam to leave me.'

'Nonsense. I know Rachel is upset with you, but she wouldn't do something like that.'

'Wouldn't she?'

'Of course not. Her son has just killed himself because he couldn't bear the thought of you with someone else. Why would she risk hurting Adam by lying about you having an affair? It doesn't make sense.'

109

'Nothing Rachel does makes sense.'

'Don't be disrespectful, Lynne. Rachel is in mourning. Have some compassion.'

'Compassion? For someone who is hell bent on destroying my marriage?'

'Darling, she was trying to warn you about the letter, to stop Adam reading it. She cares about you.'

'Well, her warning was conveniently too late.'

'Is everything okay between you and Adam, dear?'

'Y... Yes, fine.'

'He's such a good man,' continued her mother. 'When you find someone like that, you have to try your best to hold on to them. They are like gold dust, these days. There are many men like your ex, Steve, out there, but there are not many like Adam.'

'No,' agreed Lynne. 'There are not many men like Adam.'

'He's such a gentleman; so kind and considerate. Do you remember that time he offered to take me to the hospital when there was no one else available?'

Lynne began to feel nauseated. She didn't think she could listen to much more of this without spilling the beans about precious, wonderful, Adam.

'He's so—' Her mother was about to start up again about Adam's virtues.

'Yes, anyway,' interrupted Lynne. 'Thanks for calling, Mum. I'm busy.'

'Busy? What are you doing?'

'Lots of things. Anyway, I have to go.'

'Right, well, you and Adam must come over to dinner one evening. Maybe next week?'

'Er... Adam's away on business.'

'Oh, of course, I forget that he's away so often. Well, whenever it suits you both, call me, and I'll cook you a nice meal.'

Lynne hung up the phone and sighed. Rachel was turning out to be a real witch. She'd obviously called her mother hoping to hear that she and Adam had split up because of the poison pen letter. Well, she would be hearing about a split, all right, but for completely different reasons. Strangely, she almost wanted to stay with Adam now, not to give Rachel the satisfaction of seeing them split up.

Lynne could feel her blood pressure rising. She sat at the kitchen table to try to calm herself down. Her thoughts turned to how her mother had spoken of Adam, as if he were a saint or something. He'd managed to fool so many people. Even the thought of him repulsed her now. Living a lie and dragging her into his dirty, deceitful world.

For some reason, known only to himself—and maybe to Paul—he'd wanted to keep his sexuality a secret; even going as far as marrying her. Why, in this day and age, didn't he feel able to just come out with it and tell everyone he is gay? Why had he used her as a pawn in a ridiculous, childish game? Well, he had gone too far. She knew she was holding the ace card, because she could reveal to the world what he desperately wanted to keep hidden. The knowledge of that power made her feel stronger, suddenly. She was no longer the victim in all of this. He thought he could play her for a fool, but he was going to find out what it's like when your whole world falls to pieces. She would make sure of it.

Chapter Twenty-Six

Lynne caught the bus back to her flat later that afternoon. She had decided that she was going to get legal advice before doing anything rash. After all, Adam wasn't aware that she knew about his affair, so she could keep that to herself for as long as she needed to. It was as if a weight had been lifted from her shoulders overnight.

Talking everything through with Sandra had made her see that her relationship with Adam had been far from perfect. So, she had made up her mind to stop wasting time crying over its demise. She could look forward now; forward to a future that suddenly seemed a lot less daunting. Things could only get better.

As she sat on the bus, she flicked through her mobile, checking her recent messages. It had been ages since she had cleared the phone's memory and there was so much rubbish on there. She stopped when she came to the message she had received from Jason after their night out together. It had been so refreshing to be out with someone who wasn't afraid to express himself. So different from being with Adam.

A smile played on her lips as she realised that if she wanted to, she could go out with Jason again, and this time she didn't have to feel guilty. A free agent once more, she could do whatever she wanted and see whomever she chose to see. Her mind was so caught up in her dreams of the new adventure awaiting her, that she almost missed her stop.

Once inside her flat, she sat on the sofa and phoned Jason.

'Hi,' she said, when she heard his deep, luscious voice on the other end of the line.

'Look, babe, stop bothering me. I've told you I'm not interested.'

Lynne was taken aback. She almost hung up and resigned herself to her fate, alone and unloved.

'Alice, I think you should go back to your husband,' continued Jason.

'Er... this isn't Alice.' She sighed with relief as she said it.

There was an embarrassed silence, then he spoke. 'Okay, who is this? Sorry, but my phone doesn't recognise your number.'

'It's Lynne.' She waited. Would he remember her?

'Lynne?'

He didn't. Of course he didn't. She knew she was being a fool to expect him to. Someone like Jason probably dated 100 girls a week. Why would he remember her?'

'We met at Matt's party,' she said glumly.

'Oh, sexy Lynne,' he said.

She could picture his broad white-toothed grin. Smiling to herself, she replied: 'Yes, that's me.'

'Hey, babe, I knew you wouldn't be able to resist me. So you wanna hook up?'

Lynne paused. Unsure. He seemed so overconfident. 'Who's Alice?' she asked.

'Exactly!' he said, laughing.

'No... I want to know. You thought I was Alice, just now. Is she an ex-girlfriend?'

'She's no one important, hon. Just a girl who keeps harassing me. I took her out a couple of times thinking she was cool, but then she gets all needy and heavy. That's just not me. She phones me about three times a day. I thought she was happily married, but then she goes and leaves her husband for me. We only had sex once! That's just weird. Anyway, she wasn't really my type; a bit boring, you know? And she wasn't sexy like you.'

Lynne wondered what she was about to get herself into. He obviously wasn't someone who could offer her a secure future free of worries. She'd never be able to trust him. But right now, she wasn't looking for a new husband; she just wanted to go out with someone and feel special again. There were no illusions with Jason; she knew it wouldn't be for ever. She would just "hook up" with him and see what happened; take it a day at a time.

I've always been too sensible when it comes to relationships in the past, and look where that's got me, she reasoned. She'd always thought that she started a relationship with Adam too soon after breaking up with Steve. She'd never done the dating thing; meeting different people, going out and having fun, no ties. *Maybe it's time to try something different; take a leaf out of Jason's book and live a little.*

'So, when are you taking me out?' she asked, in the most seductive voice she could muster.

'Wow! Are you serious? I thought you were out of reach. I'd even deleted you from my phone contacts. Shows how much I know! How about tonight; you free? Hubby away on business again?'

'Yes, he is,' she said.

'Fantastic! Shall I pick you up at eight?'

'Okay.'

When she put down the phone, she wondered if she was wrong to mislead Jason this way. He had no idea that her marriage was over.

But she felt better when she thought that she wasn't about to become all "heavy" like that Alice girl. She was just after a good time, and that's exactly what he wanted. What he didn't know couldn't hurt him.

Chapter Twenty-Seven

When Lynne woke up, she was surprised to see Jason still lying in bed next to her. She had expected him to be the type to sneak out of the room as soon as his latest conquest had fallen asleep. But here he was, all 6 foot 2 of him—rippling muscles, golden tanned skin, stunning good looks—lying next to her. He'd spent the whole night with her. It was like something out of her wildest dreams.

She hadn't intended to sleep with him, but he'd obviously had a lot of practice getting women into bed. He'd probably used those lines on hundreds of women before her, but she didn't care. She needed to be with him so she could forget about Adam once and for all.

As she lay here, looking at the sleeping adonis next to her, she was glad she had spent the night with him. It had been so perfect. She finally knew what all the fuss was about. This was what she needed—someone who could give her an orgasm just by looking at her in a certain way.

As she thought about the magical night she had spent with this man, a sadness enveloped her. She realised that it wasn't real. It wouldn't last. Jason had already laid his cards on the table. He didn't love her. He just wanted a bit of fun. No ties.

I finally meet the man of my dreams and he's a commitment phobe.

She knew she was playing with fire here. She wasn't the type to sleep with someone if she didn't expect it would go anywhere. Deep down inside, she knew that she'd been hoping he would fall in love with her and finally realise that he didn't want to live a hollow life of one night stands, and affairs with married women; he'd be ensnared by her charms, and she'd get to keep him for ever. But, in the cold light of day, she knew it was very unlikely that someone like Jason would ever change.

With the memory of last night still fresh in her mind, she wanted to wake him up and do it all over again. When they had been making love, she had almost said, 'I love you.' She had managed to stop herself just in time, knowing he wouldn't want to hear that. Thinking about it now, she realised that she did have feelings for him.

In her mind, she recalled how he had spoken to her on the phone when he thought she was Alice—the "needy" girl. He'd been able to break up with that girl so easily and disregard her feelings. She had

115

meant nothing to him; she was just a pest, a hanger-on, someone to be discarded. Lynne felt a kinship with the faceless Alice now, aware of how easy it would be to become totally obsessed with Jason.

A panic took hold of her as she realised she was in too deep. She couldn't just sleep with someone and then get on with her life as if nothing had happened.

Jason began to stir in the bed.

Lynne trembled. Last night had been a big mistake. She had dived in, not thinking of the consequences, just because she wanted to get that image of Adam and Paul out of her head. Now, it was possible she had fallen for someone who would not only be able to break her heart, but could shatter it into a thousand tiny pieces so that nothing and no one would be able to put it back together again.

'Hello, sexy,' he said, interrupting her thoughts.

She looked at him and smiled.

'How was last night for you? I was better than your hubby, I bet.'

'Much better,' she said.

'Are you okay, hon? You seem a bit tense.'

'Sorry.' She tried to put on a more realistic smile, but could feel her face stiffen. The regret about last night had crept up on her slowly, but was suddenly all she could feel. 'I don't make a habit of sleeping around. I guess I just feel a bit...'

'Guilty?' asked Jason, laughing. 'Don't worry, it'll pass. You've got to loosen up, Lynne, baby. Enjoy your life while you're still young.'

'Yeah.' She nodded. 'But I wasn't feeling "guilty", just a bit out of my depth.' She looked into his eyes, and couldn't believe she was lying here with him. *Why can't it last for ever?*

'Do you want to do it again?' he asked. 'I don't have to be at work for another hour.'

'Er... yes... okay,' she said.

Soon, she forgot all about her concerns, and was once again in ecstasy. She drifted far away as he held her close and kissed her in all the right places, taking away her worries. He was like a magician who could make all the pain disappear and replace it with sensations of light and joy. She was so transported by his powers, that she didn't hear the front door open.

Lynne had decided to bring Jason to Sandra's flat, last night. She still had the spare key in her bag and knew that Sandra wouldn't mind. Also, she didn't want to sleep with Jason in the bed she had shared with Adam; it wouldn't feel right. On top of that, over the years, Adam had sometimes returned from his business trips unexpectedly early, and she didn't want to risk him coming home and finding them in bed together.

What Lynne didn't know was that the local estate agent also had a key to Sandra's flat so that it could be shown to potential tenants. So, as Lynne and Jason were enjoying themselves, oblivious to the world around them, the estate agent—a young man who appeared to be in his early twenties, with very short hair and large spectacles, which looked too big for his face—burst into the bedroom.

'This is the bedroom,' he boomed. He was followed into the room by two young females.

Lynne and Jason, hearing the noise, turned around slowly to face the three unexpected guests. Lynne grabbed the duvet, which had almost fallen on the floor, and quickly covered up.

'Who are your friends?' asked Jason, smiling at them. 'Aren't you going to introduce me, Lynne?'

The estate agent had turned a shade of red which Lynne didn't know was possible for someone to turn. His head looked like a tomato. He seemed to be rooted to the spot momentarily. Then he said, 'Sorry.' The two girls began to laugh, and they were soon ushered out of the room by the man. He could be heard repeating the word "sorry" as the party made their way out of the front door.

Jason began to laugh. 'Who were they? Was that your husband?'

'No!' she said.

'This is your flat, right?'

'It belongs to a friend. She's trying to rent it out. It was probably an estate agent. Oh my God! What if Sand finds out?'

'Who's Sand?'

'Sandra, my friend who owns the flat; she used to go out with your brother.'

'Doesn't she know you're here?'

'No, but that estate agent is bound to say something.'

'Oh, he won't, Lynne. Did you see his face? He was so embarrassed. More than you were!'

'So, weren't you?' she asked.

'No. Why should I be?' He shrugged. 'He's the one who burst into my bedroom. He's the one who should be embarrassed. You really need to chill out, babe. You're coming across as really uptight. You could put me off you. I thought you were cool.'

'We have to go,' said Lynne, getting out of bed and pulling on her dress. She couldn't find her underwear, and began to panic, imagining that it would be found by the next estate agent. Finally, she found it under the edge of the bed.

'What are you doing?' asked Jason, as she leaned down to retrieve her knickers.

'Getting rid of the evidence,' she said.

'So, is your friend as uptight as you?' he said, laughing.

Lynne rolled her eyes.

'Is she married?' asked Jason.

She looked at him then, confused. 'Why do you ask?'

'Well, she could join us next time. I'm always on the lookout for new thrills, if you know what I mean.'

'Um... no, she's not married.'

'Oh, that's a pity.'

Lynne began to realise that she didn't really like Jason.

'I'm not really married either, technically. I'm getting divorced.'

'What?' Jason turned his head around quickly to face her.

'I'm leaving Adam.'

'Woah! Hang on a minute. I know I'm good in bed, but you can't leave your husband for me. I'm not the marrying type. I thought I made myself clear.'

'But we can still see each other for sex, right?' she said, wishing she'd kept her mouth shut.

'No, I'm sorry, babe. I don't date single women. I can't take the risk. You'll fall in love with me and then it all becomes complicated.' He grabbed his jeans and headed out of the door.

'I'll call you,' she said, sarcastically.

He popped his head around the door, and said (obviously missing the sarcasm), 'No, Lynne. Don't call me. I'm sorry; it's over.'

With that, he was gone.

A sadness engulfed her as she watched him go. Why had she let him know she was leaving Adam? Okay, so Jason was obnoxious, but he was good-looking, great to be seen out with, and the best sex she had ever had. It was too late; she had frightened him away, and now she was alone again. For a little while, he had made her forget Adam, but now it was all there in her mind again. The stark truth had to be dealt with: Adam would be returning from his business trip in two days time. She would have to be prepared.

Chapter Twenty-Eight

Lynne received a phone call from Sandra at 5:30 pm that day. 'Lynne I'm on my way home from work. Is it okay if I pop round to see you?'

'Ye... Yes, okay.' She blushed. *Does she know about earlier?*

'We need to talk,' continued Sandra. 'Have you had dinner yet?'

'No, not yet.'

'I'll bring a takeaway. See you soon.'

Nothing else was said. When Lynne put down the phone, she couldn't help wondering whether the estate agent had said something to Sandra, and whether she had put two and two together. Sandra had sounded quite formal on the phone. Was she coming over to give her a lecture about not using her flat as a place to bring stray men she picked up?

She wondered whether Sandra would guess it was Jason who had been at the flat with her. Then she realised that she was being paranoid. Sandra was probably just coming over to make sure she was okay after everything that had happened with Adam.

Sandra arrived shortly after 6:30 pm. 'Hi, I've brought some Thai green curry, hope that's okay?'

'Yeah, great. Come in, I'll get some plates.'

They sat together by the kitchen table looking out at the grey skies of London.

'So, I guess you're coming to check up on me, to make sure I haven't slit my wrists or anything.'

'I know you wouldn't do anything like that,' said Sandra, but there was a look in her eyes that seemed to be saying, *'Oh, my God, I hadn't thought about that. I'm going to have to keep an eye on you.'*

'I'm okay, really,' said Lynne, trying to convince her.

It didn't work; Sandra still looked concerned.

'This isn't going to be easy for you. You won't be able to get over this overnight. I just want to let you know that I'm here for you. I don't want you to do anything stupid.'

'I won't,' said Lynne.

Sandra still didn't appear convinced. 'I know about this morning,' she said, sighing.

'Oh, I was wondering if—'

'Yes, the estate agent told me. Well, he thought it was *me*, actually. I'd never met that particular agent before. He phoned me and said, "Sorry for interrupting you this morning, I should have phoned before I came." So, I said I wasn't at the flat, and he said, "Oh, it's just that I accidentally walked in on a couple in your bed... um... you know." Well, I was shocked, I have to admit; it's so soon after you found out about Adam. It's a natural reaction, I suppose, to sleep with the first man you find when you go out, trying to forget about Adam; but these days you have to be careful.'

Lynne sat open-mouthed. 'Is that what you think of me? That I'd just go out and sleep with the first man I meet?'

'Oh... sorry, I didn't mean that. I just assumed...'

Lynne was fuming. She hadn't planned to tell Sandra that she'd slept with Jason, wanting to spare her, in case she was still hurt about splitting up with Matt—but now Sandra had offended her: 'It was Jason, Matt's brother, okay? So, I didn't just meet him.'

Sandra turned red, but soon regained her composure. Looking at Lynne, she took a deep breath and said, 'Well, at least it wasn't a complete stranger.' She carried on eating her meal.

'So, you're not bothered that I slept with Jason?'

'Why should I be?' Sandra smiled at her. 'I'm well over Matt. He's an arsehole. I'm happy with Dave now.' But then her demeanour changed slightly, and she narrowed her eyes. 'Are you two an item now?' Her eyes exuded alarm.

'No, it was a one off. He only dates married women, so when he found out I was splitting from Adam, he ran a mile. It's probably for the best.' Lynne shrugged.

Sandra appeared relieved, her shoulders relaxing. 'He wasn't good enough for you. I told you about his reputation before, didn't I?'

'Yes.' Lynne nodded and took a sip of wine. She leaned back in her chair. 'How the tables have turned.'

'What do you mean?' asked Sandra, finishing off her rice.

'Just over a month ago, you were jealous of me getting married. Now look at me! And you're all cosy with Dave.'

'That's just life. We never know what's around the corner.'

'True. Oh, what am I going to do?' Lynne leaned forward and put her wine glass back on the table. 'Adam's back in a couple of days and I haven't decided which way to play this. Do I tell him I've seen him with Paul, or do I let things continue?'

'Well.' Sandra sat forward in her chair. 'I've had a word with Kev. He's a lawyer, as you know.'

'Sand!'

'Don't worry, I was discreet. I didn't mention your name. I just said I was enquiring for a friend. I asked whether you could get a divorce so soon after getting married, and he said you have to wait a year.'

'Hmm... I knew that. I remember Steve saying something about it when he was studying. Kev knew I was getting married last month. How many other friends do you have that got married recently? He'll know it's me you were asking for, and then Steve will find out, and—'

'So what if he does? It's none of his business. And Kev has to be confidential about his clients; he would lose his job if he went around telling other people about his clients' private affairs. He won't say anything to Steve.'

'Why should I care if he finds out?' said Lynne. 'You know, sometimes I don't know what's wrong with me.'

'Come on, you've been through a lot in a short space of time; you're bound to feel confused about stuff.'

'What do you think I should do? Tell Adam? It's just that it's come at a really bad time for me. I'm out of work; otherwise I'd just go and rent somewhere.'

'I wish I could help out more, but I really have to rent out my flat. I would offer for you to come to stay with me and Dave, but it's his place...'

'Oh, no. I don't want to impose. Anyway, after our recent meeting, Dave probably thinks I'm half mad!'

Sandra laughed. 'No, he doesn't. I explained it to him. He said Adam is a low life.'

'Hmm... Dave sounds nice, Sand. I'm really happy for you. I'm sorry I can't be more enthusiastic about your new boyfriend, but it's only because I'm in the middle of all this.'

'Well, look, I'd say you should sit on this for a while. As you say, Adam doesn't know you've seen him with Paul; so you can think about what you're going to do and then plan your moves. Kev mentioned something about annulment being an alternative way to end a marriage without having to wait for a year. He's not a specialist in divorce, so he's not sure if your case would qualify, but he thinks it's worth you taking advice on it. It's a more long-winded way of getting divorced because you have to give evidence, but—'

'I don't like the sound of that. I just want to get it over with quickly.'

'It's still worth taking advice, though. You should go and see someone.'

'Maybe. I've been thinking I'll probably put off telling Adam. He wouldn't notice if I avoid him completely, anyway. We hardly talk, these days. And he's away on business so often...' She paused. 'Or, with Paul!' She shook her head.

'If you think you can handle living with him, after, you know...'

'Yes, I can. I mean, to be honest, I had a feeling me and Adam would split up soon. I was fooling myself, thinking the marriage would be a fresh start, but all the time the relationship kept getting worse. I think I've come to the point where I can accept it now. Okay, it was a shock finding out he's gay.'

'Yeah, a real shock!'

'Oh well, it's not worth crying over,' said Lynne.

'Good, so at least I don't have to worry about you all the time. You seem to have come to terms with everything.'

'Yes. Although, having said that, I don't know what I'll be like by Wednesday when he's due back. You might need to stand by your phone!'

'I'm free any time of the day or night. Just call, okay?'

'Thanks, Sand.'

Sandra looked at her watch. 'I'd better be going,' she said.

'Okay, well thanks for checking up on me. Oh, and I'd better give you back your spare key for the flat.' She ran into the living room and found her handbag. Returning to the kitchen she met Sandra at the door and handed her the key.

'Thanks, Lynne. Listen, I've just had an idea; why don't you apply for housing benefit and rent out my flat for a while. We could kill two birds with one stone. I'd have a reliable tenant, and you'd have somewhere to stay, away from Adam.'

'I'm not sure. I like this flat, and I don't see why I should be the one to leave. We rented it in both our names, and I bought some of the furniture. I need to find out what my rights are. I want to stay here. I'd prefer *him* to leave. I'm not the one who's done anything wrong.'

'I can understand you feeling that way, but let me know if anything changes.'

'Okay, Sand.'

'Kev could probably recommend a good divorce lawyer, so if you want me to ask him—'

'I'll let you know.'

Sandra disappeared into the lift at the end of the fifth floor. Lynne stood at the front door staring out at the sky, losing track of time as she watched the clouds drifting by. When it started to get dark, she made her way into the flat. Switching on the kettle to make a cup of tea, she caught sight of the moon outside the window. The clouds had become thick, obscuring the stars, and the moon was shrouded in a grey foggy covering, making it look almost scary, like in a horror movie. She hoped it was not a portent of things to come.

Chapter Twenty-Nine

Lynne went to bed early on Tuesday night. Adam was due back from his business trip the next day. *Or, from Paul's house*, she thought to herself as she lay staring at the ceiling. *It wasn't supposed to be like this. I was supposed to get married and live happily ever after, not marry someone I didn't really love and then find out he's having an affair, with a man!*

She felt angry and frustrated. Knowing he was coming back changed everything again. The thought of having to keep quiet and behave as if she wasn't aware he was cheating on her, was almost too much to bear. She desperately wanted to scream at him, and tell him what a mess he'd made of everything, and throw him out.

What would it be like having him lying in bed next to her, knowing what she now knew? *I can't keep up the pretence... I'm going to have to say something.*

But then, she thought it all through again. It would be another ten months or so before they could get divorced, and she didn't want to lose her rights in this flat. But, it would be hell living with him after telling him she knew about his affair. *Perhaps he'll go and live with Paul?* But he wanted to keep his sexuality a secret, so he probably wouldn't go and live with him. *Then, why was he kissing Paul so openly on the doorstep, where anyone could have seen them?*

Her mind kept going around in circles. *It's all such a mess.* A tear trickled down her cheek. *I wish I could go back in time; back to when I first met Adam. I'd walk straight past him and never look back.* She grabbed a tissue from the box on the bedside cabinet and wiped her eyes. Soon, she fell into a deep sleep.

When Lynne woke up the next morning, she was trembling. She had seen that man in her dream again; the man who had visited her in her dreams before the wedding. He had returned, and seemed so real and so lifelike, as if she could reach out and touch him. He said: *'I told you it would be a mistake. You shouldn't have married Adam. But you will be given another chance to do the right thing. When you wake up, it will January. The day Adam proposed to you. You will have the chance to turn him down.'*

'Who are you?' she screamed.

'My name is Mark Cribbs, I live at Churchley Rise, number 145.

It's in Hampstead, London.'

When she had woken up, the name and address were ringing in her head. She had an urge to write them down, so she wouldn't forget them. Sitting up in bed, she reached into the drawer of the bedside cabinet to retrieve her notebook, and wrote: 'Mark Cribbs, 145 Churchley Rise, Hampstead'. Just then, she heard Adam's voice. He was singing in the shower. He wasn't supposed to get back until the evening.

Looking over, she saw that his side of the bed had been slept in. As she looked at the bedding, she became confused and disorientated. In her mind, she could clearly remember changing the sheets the night before. She had put the clean red sheets on the bed, along with the rose patterned duvet cover. Now, she was staring at white sheets and the checkered duvet cover. *How could that have happened?* Adam wouldn't have been able to change the sheets without waking her. Turning around, she noticed that even her pillowcase was different. She looked down at herself and saw that she was wearing a different night-dress. She had gone to bed in the black nighty, but was now wearing the leopard print one.

As she looked around the room, she wondered if she was still dreaming. She noticed that everything looked different, somehow. Not in any real noticeable way, but, for example, the linen basket was full to overflowing and she'd only done the laundry a couple of days ago. When she'd gone to bed, the basket had been practically empty. *Perhaps Adam put all of his clothes from his trip in there?* She put the notebook back in the drawer, and got out of bed slowly. Feeling curious, she walked over to the linen basket. As she opened the lid, she could hardly believe her eyes: on top of the pile of clothes was her green jumper; the one that she'd bought from that designer store in New York a few years back. The green jumper had been ruined when Adam accidentally put it in a machine wash at 60 degrees a few months ago. It had shrunk to half the size; yet now it was back to its normal size and looking perfect. She picked it up and stared in disbelief. Her mind flashed back to the dream she'd had. *'When you wake up, it will be January.'*

It can't be true. Feeling cold suddenly, she went back to the bed, lifted the duvet, and climbed back in. Her eyes noticed the alarm clock: it was 7:40 am. For some reason she had a feeling that she should be getting ready for work. She shrugged and sighed at the thought. Every now and then, since she had been made redundant, she'd woken up in a panic, thinking she was going to be late for work, but then quickly realised that she didn't have a job to go to. Somehow, though, this feeling was different—more persistent. She covered her head with the duvet, to block out the light.

The en suite door opened, and Adam walked in. 'Lynne, aren't you up yet? You're going to be late for work.' He shook her. 'And, remember, we're meeting up in town later for dinner.'

As she slowly lifted her head above the duvet, she saw that Adam was getting changed. He reached over to the bedside cabinet and picked up his watch. The one with the brown leather strap that she'd bought him for his birthday last year. But how? That strap had broken a couple of months ago; she remembered him telling her that the watch had fallen off his wrist on his way to work.

'Adam, where did you find that watch?' she asked.

'What are you talking about?' He looked at her, frowning. 'You bought it for me.'

'I know, but you lost it.'

'Huh? I've worn it every day since you bought it. What are you on about? Are you still half asleep or something? I'll make you a cup of coffee.'

She watched him walk out of the room.

Something was definitely wrong. Had she lost her memory? Her mind went back to the dream again. Had she really gone back in time? *That couldn't happen, surely?*

Her mobile rang. She picked it up from the bedside cabinet. 'Hello,' she said.

'Hi, Lynne.' It was Lucy, her friend from work.

'Luce? It's nice to hear from you. It's been ages.'

'What are you on about? Oh, it's a joke, right? Ha, ha, very funny. Anyway, guess what? I've just found out the rumours are true. Sue just phoned me. She overheard Andrew talking to Evan last night, after work. She says they are definitely going to make people redundant. I'm worried it might be me.'

'Oh no. That's terrible. More redundancies? When I was made redundant, with Claire and Malcolm, I thought that would be it,' said Lynne.

'Oh my God, Lynne. I didn't know you'd already been told. Sorry. When did they tell you? Was it yesterday? Why haven't you phoned me? And on your birthday as well! The bastards!'

'Er... my birthday was—' She couldn't continue. The memory of her dream flashed before her vividly. Lucy had said her birthday was yesterday. The dream had told her she would wake up on the day Adam proposed... That had been the day after her birthday. The blood drained from her face. It must be true. She was either stuck in a lifelike, lucid dream; or, she really *had* gone back in time... As strange as it seemed.

126

Lucy continued talking as if she hadn't heard Lynne speak. 'Oh my God! I can't believe it. We were all sitting around the table celebrating your birthday at lunchtime yesterday. They are *so* two-faced.'

Lynne was anxious to cover her tracks now, just in case the dream had been real. 'Luce, what I meant to say was that I really thought I would be made redundant, with Malcolm and Claire, because we were... are the newest employees. They haven't said anything yet. It's just a guess.'

'Phew,' said Lucy, sounding relieved. 'Don't be silly, Lynne, you're the last person they would make redundant. Malcolm and Claire, maybe; they haven't been working there long. But, you're not one of the newest employees. You've been there longer than Denise. It's much more likely to be me, though, because remember that argument I had with Rolinda at the Christmas party? And we all know she's Andrew's favourite girl.'

'No, it definitely won't be you,' said Lynne, suddenly feeling like a fortune teller.

'Fingers crossed,' said Lucy.

'Um... Luce, I'm not sure I'll be in today. I'm not feeling very well.'

'You should make the effort, Lynne. If they're planning to get rid of people, they'll be looking for things like the number of sick days you've had, and how hard everyone is working.'

But Lynne already knew, and her motivation had left her. They were going to make her redundant, even though she'd only had one sick day that year, and she was one of the most loyal members of staff. She didn't owe them anything. 'Really, Luce, I'm not well. Tell Andrew. I'll probably not be in for the rest of the week.'

'Okay,' said Lucy, sounding concerned. 'Get well soon.'

Lynne put down the phone, and a fear gripped her. She could feel herself floating away from reality, and unable to comprehend what was happening. *I must still be dreaming, that's all. I'll wake up and everything will be explained.* Her thoughts soothed her momentarily, but then she noticed the date on her mobile phone: 19th of January. A day after her birthday.

She stood up quickly and opened the wardrobe. What she was expecting to find inside the wardrobe, wasn't there: the wedding dress. It wasn't there. Had she really gone back in time over six months? She caught sight of herself in the wardrobe mirror. Sure enough, her hair was shorter than when she'd gone to bed last night. Over three inches shorter. And it was still brown. She'd had it highlighted for the wedding, but there were no signs of highlights here.

She pulled on her dressing gown and walked out of the bedroom, down the hall and into the kitchen. She found Adam sitting at the kitchen table eating a slice of toast.

'Not dressed yet?' he asked.

'I'm not feeling well,' she replied.

'Oh no. You are still going to be able to meet me in town tonight, aren't you? I've planned something special for your birthday, seeing as I was working yesterday and we couldn't do anything.'

'Can't we just stay in tonight?' she said.

'Um...' His smile left his face, and she would have felt bad about it if she hadn't lived through the following six months. She remembered how (the first time around) she'd been happy he'd offered to take her out that night, after such a long period of time where their relationship seemed to have stagnated. Then, she remembered how wonderful she felt when he had asked her to marry him; it was like a new beginning, a chance to start afresh. *What a fool I was*, she thought, bitterly.

She studied his face; it was full of sincerity. There really wasn't any way she'd have been able to tell back then that he'd been cheating on her.

'Okay, Lynne. If you're not well, I'll cancel the restaurant and we'll get a take away instead, okay? I had also planned a trip to the London Eye, but the tickets will still be valid for another day.' He smiled. After taking a sip of coffee, he walked around the table towards her. 'Why don't you go back to bed for a while?' he suggested. He kissed her on the forehead.

She realised that he tended to kiss her on the forehead a lot, rather than on the lips. Perhaps that should have been a sign to look out for?

Soon he had gone to work.

Dragging her feet into the living room, she switched on the TV to watch the news. Sure enough, the news was over six months old. Somehow, as ridiculous as it seemed, she found herself back in time. She found herself wishing she had brought the lottery numbers with her.

Chapter Thirty

Lynne went into the bedroom to get changed. As she caught sight of the bedside cabinet, she remembered the notebook. She opened the drawer and fished it out, flicking through the pages until she saw the address she had noted down earlier: 145 Churchley Rise, Hampstead. It wasn't very far away. *It must be near the graveyard*, she thought. Churchley Rise, in Hampstead, was the name of the street where the graveyard was situated, where her grandfather was buried. She wondered whether this "Mark Cribbs" really lived on that street. Could it be possible for people to communicate telepathically with each other through a dream? It seemed unlikely, but she was ready to believe anything after the morning she'd had. She resolved to go and visit this address.

As she pulled a pair of jeans out of her wardrobe, she scanned the clothes, looking for the red t-shirt she'd bought in a sale a couple of weeks ago. *Where is it?*

When she had taken everything out of the wardrobe and put it back again, it dawned on her that if it really *is* January, she didn't own that red t-shirt yet. She'd only bought it in July. *This is ridiculous! People don't just go to sleep and then wake up in the past! What's happening to me?*

Deciding to wear a black t-shirt instead, Lynne began to question herself as to whether she had actually bought the red one or decided against it; or, whether she'd forgotten it in the shop. But she could distinctly remember seeing it in the wardrobe only yesterday. Then again, the wedding dress was in there yesterday, too.

Once in the kitchen, she made some toast and coffee. She drank her coffee, impatiently, pouring most of it into the sink; she felt anxious to get going, and to find this address. If Mark Cribbs did exist, and if she met him, things might start making more sense. Maybe she was having some sort of clairvoyant episode. She remembered that her father once told her his mother had been psychic and able to see the future. Lynne had never been interested in that sort of thing. Up until now, she had considered it gobbledegook. Suddenly though, paranormal experiences didn't seem so implausible. Part of her still held onto the hope that this was all some kind of practical joke; perhaps she had been set up by friends, and would be able to laugh at herself on a Saturday prime time TV show. Better still, she really wanted to be dreaming all of this, and wake up back in the present day. But what *was* the present day? The edges of time were suddenly quite blurry.

If Mark Cribbs did exist, would he recognise her? Had he been having similar dreams? It just sounded so absurd, like one of those stories on *Beyond Belief: Fact or Fiction.* As she laughed out loud at the thought, she began to worry—not for the first time that morning—that she may be losing her mind.

Her sat nav wasn't in the office where she usually kept it. *Where did I used to keep it in January?* she asked herself, irritated. Back then, she used to go and stay with Sandra a lot, as Adam had been away on his business trips quite often. She and Sandra often used the sat nav to navigate their way when they went out and about. It was most likely in her overnight bag. She went into the bedroom, and found the holdall on top of the wardrobe. Sure enough, the sat nav was in there. The battery was flat, so she would have to wait until she got into the car to put the address into the device.

She grabbed her handbag and noticed that she was still using the same handbag she'd been using in January. *Some things don't change,* she thought.

When she stepped outside the door, she felt shocked at how cold it was. *Yesterday was so warm.* Goose pimples erupted on her skin and she felt herself shiver. One of her neighbours walked past her wearing a scarf, woolly hat, and gloves. She noticed icy patches on the ground where snow had melted. Once again, she was reminded that it was (supposedly) January. She had dressed for July. The flat had been warm because of the heating, so she hadn't realised the change in temperature outside. Rubbing her arms to warm them up, she ran back into the house. She put on a jumper, her long black coat and Ugg boots. Her mind was in a daze, mystified as to how and why this had happened.

Once inside the car, she set up the sat nav, and punched in the address: 145 Churchley Rise. It was not recognised. A sense of relief washed over her: it wasn't a real address. She knew Churchley Rise existed, because the cemetery was located there. Switching off the sat nav, she headed in the general direction of the graveyard, where she'd been many times before to visit her grandfather's tomb.

It was a difficult drive to Hampstead. She almost turned back to go home, at least three times. Questions were running through her mind: What would she say to this "Mark Cribbs" if he did exist? What if he didn't exist? What would she do then? She turned up the radio, trying to block out her negative thoughts.

Finally, she reached Hampstead. She saw the familiar tall fence of the graveyard, which was a few hundred yards long, on the left side of the road. Lynne found a place to park, and looked around. There were no houses on either side of the road. The left side was the graveyard, and on the right hand side was a park. *Perhaps if I drive further along the street?*

Lynne continued driving, and soon reached the end of Churchley Rise. She saw another street sign, which read: Andover Road. She turned the car around and drove back, parking the car in front of the tall fence. Noticing an old woman walking along the street, Lynne got out of her car and approached her.

'Hello, er... sorry to bother you, um... I'm looking for a house on Churchley Rise, but there don't appear to be any houses along this road.'

The woman thought for a while, then shook her head. 'No dear, *Churchley Rise* is just the name of the cemetery.'

Lynne looked again at the imposing fence.

'There is a residential street along there,' continued the woman, 'called Churchley *Lane*.' She pointed a finger, indicating a street across the road, just beyond the park.

'Okay, thank you,' said Lynne.

The old woman walked away.

Not sure whether to just give up or continue on this wild goose chase, Lynne decided to walk over to Churchley Lane. Dreams weren't always accurate in regard to names. Maybe that was the answer. Soon, she arrived at the small entrance to the cul-de-sac, Churchley Lane. She walked towards the houses and looked at the door numbers. When she reached the end, she saw that the door numbers only went up to 110. There was no number 145. Turning around, feeling slightly relieved, she headed back to her car. Now that she knew the address in her dream didn't exist, she could move forward. But then she realised that she was back in the past, and there was no explanation for that. She'd hoped that today's trip would provide some kind of answer.

As she approached her car, she again caught sight of the street sign, Churchley Rise, and decided to visit her grandfather's grave. As she walked towards the cemetery gates, the memory of her last trip here—after Alex died—came to mind. She tried to think of something else, but the only other thought was just as unwelcome: her dreams. It suddenly occurred to her that there might be some link between her dreams and this graveyard. Could Mark Cribbs have been communicating with her from beyond the grave? She felt light-headed at the thought.

As a young girl, she remembered how she'd made up stories about

131

ghosts and had even pretended to communicate with one at school. Everyone believed her. That had all been child's play. Harmless. She also recalled how one night when she was about seven years old, she had awoken in the darkness and heard a loud booming voice say: *'I will haunt you'*. She recalled how in her dream that night, a man had told her his name and taken her to see where he was buried. She couldn't remember the name of the man from that childhood dream; but began to feel frightened now, as if it was all indeed coming back to haunt her.

She didn't want to find out that this man in her dreams, Mark Cribbs, was a real entity—dead or alive. She wanted to be able to go back to her car, drive away, and forget about it all. One thing was clear, though; she wouldn't have any peace of mind until she had an answer as to why she'd had the dream, and how she'd ended up back in time.

Walking through the graveyard entrance, she could feel her legs shaking with nerves. She had a feeling that someone—or something—was following her.

'Good morning.'

The voice startled Lynne. Turning to her left, she saw a middle-aged man sitting on a stool beside a flower stall. Breathing a sigh of relief, she smiled at him and walked over to buy a bunch of white roses for her grandfather's grave.

She carried the roses towards the pathway leading through the cemetery with hundreds of gravestones, making her way to her grandfather's tomb, with her dream still very much at the forefront of her mind. *Churchley Rise, number 145,* he had said. The thought occurred to her that the gravestones might be numbered. She looked at a couple of the headstones in front of her, but couldn't see any numbers.

A thought entered her mind: any one of these tombstones could be the final resting place of Mark Cribbs, and she might happen upon it at any moment. This thought caused her to shudder, and she could sense someone behind her, but when she twisted around there was no one there. An irrational fear gripped her and she didn't feel able to venture further into the graveyard.

As she turned back towards the entrance, she saw a small building that she hadn't noticed when she'd first walked in. As she got closer to the building, she noticed an arrow on the open door pointing the way to the 'Information Desk'.

Despite her fear, curiosity got the better of her. The dream was like a puzzle that had to be solved. Taking a deep breath, she walked into the building.

Behind the desk sat an old man. He looked up at her and smiled a restrained smile, as if he didn't want to look too happy. She realised that he was probably wary of causing her further anguish, knowing from experience that most people who came here were in mourning.

'Can I help you?' he asked.

'Er... yes, I hope so.' She couldn't believe she was about to ask for directions to a tomb for a man she'd dreamt about. 'I'm looking for a grave. Number 145.'

The man looked at her and frowned. 'That doesn't sound right. Our registered numbers begin with the surname of the deceased, and then an initial and a number. Each year, we start from zero again. So, for example, this year we are up to number fifteen.'

'Um... Okay, the surname is Cribbs, Mark Cribbs.' Saying his name out loud, felt like she was revealing a secret. 'I'm not sure of the date of death.' She lowered her eyes.

'Well, we have everything from 1995 on computer. I'll do a search for you. I can put in the information you've given me and leave the year blank.'

'Okay.' Lynne nodded.

'I won't be long,' said the old man. 'Take a seat.' He walked out of a door into the back of the building.

Lynne sat on the wooden chair next to the information desk and waited. It was eerily quiet. She kept looking around her, nervously. Cemeteries had never been her favourite places. The old man returned after a few minutes.

'There are a few Cribbs, but none with the initial M; and none of them have the number 145. I'm sorry,' he said. 'Perhaps if you can find out the year of death, and come back, I might be able to help you. Did he die before 1995? Our records on the computer only go back that far.'

'Um... possibly,' said Lynne, feeling embarrassed.

'I could do a manual search of our paper records,' he explained, 'but without a year to go by, it would take a long time; and I would have to charge you for it.'

'Oh...' Lynne thought for a moment. 'No, that's okay. I'll try to find out another way. Thanks for your help.' She walked out of the office.

She found herself feeling more confused than when she'd gone into the building. Looking down, she noticed she was still carrying the white roses intended for her grandfather's grave. Seeing that there were a couple of other people headed in the direction of his tomb, she felt a bit braver, and decided to go there before leaving the cemetery.

As she made her way towards her grandfather's grave, it felt almost as if she were wading through an invisible liquid. Everything seemed so fuzzy and unreal. *Perhaps it is all a dream?* she thought, wistfully. If so, it was a pretty realistic one.

She didn't stay long at her grandfather's tomb, just long enough to place the slightly wilting roses on the grave and wipe away some of the dust that had settled on the stone. The atmosphere in the cemetery was quite overwhelming; she didn't want to stay there any longer than she had to.

Her thoughts were revolving around and around, and always returning to the dream she'd had the night before. If she believed that this Mark Cribbs was somehow real, then he must be dead. After all, he had given her an address for a graveyard. And he must have died before 1995 because there were no computer records of his death. She felt cold for a moment. Who was he? And, why was he trying to help her? At least he appeared to be trying to help her, by sending her back to January. Now, she had a chance to leave Adam.

The more rational part of her mind thought that this Mark Cribbs was just a figment of her imagination. She'd known about the cemetery, and the address had obviously come into her dream from her subconscious. Maybe she'd been remembering her grandfather's death. He'd died the day after her birthday, six years ago; so, no wonder it was in her mind on this date. But that didn't really make sense, because when she'd gone to sleep last night it hadn't been January; it had been July. It was all so confusing.

Then she remembered her other dreams; the ones she had been having before she married Adam. Mark Cribbs had told her that if she married Adam, someone would die. Was that Alex? *If it really is January now, he'll still be alive.* She looked around her, warily. Was he following her? Rachel had said that he had recent photos of her. He must have followed her around. Her mind was suddenly fuelled with the desire to go to see him. Perhaps if she could meet up with him, face to face, she could nip his obsession in the bud.

As she got into her car, and switched on the engine, her eyes were drawn to the towering fence of the cemetery. Her heart began to beat a little faster as the fearful thought struck her mind again: somewhere in there, the body of Mark Cribbs could be lying. She prayed that this was just a nightmare, and that she would soon wake up.

Chapter Thirty-One

Lynne knocked on the door. It was a house she had visited as a child, with her parents: "Aunty" Rachel's house. Where Alex lived.

Rachel opened the door. Lynne hadn't seen her for about eight years, but she hadn't changed. There were photos going back to when Lynne was a child, and Rachel was there looking exactly the same as she did now. It wasn't that she looked young. She had never looked young. Somehow, she had always appeared middle-aged, even in her twenties.

'Hello, Lynne, what a surprise! I wondered when Alex would bring you over to see us!'

'Er... hello, Aunty Rachel.'

'Oh, please, call me Rachel, sweetie. We all know I'm not your aunty!' She was beaming.

Lynne followed Rachel indoors, and sat in the living room, waiting. Shortly, Alex walked into the room with Rachel. He appeared flushed; embarrassed. Perhaps he was worried that his little secret would now be revealed. Lynne couldn't help but notice how different he looked from that spotty teenager who had asked her out. He was very attractive. She began to wonder how someone this good-looking could have ended up obsessing over her. He could have his pick of girls. She was drawn to him, an almost maternal instinct, wanting to protect him. He was vulnerable; he'd killed himself over her. Yet, at the same time, that very fact repelled her. It was a strange mix of emotions.

'Hi, Lynne,' he said, scarcely able to meet her eyes.

'I'll leave you two lovebirds alone,' said Rachel, smiling. It was clear that she thought Lynne was Alex's girlfriend, and that he'd just never got around to bringing her to the house.

When she left the room, Alex sat next to Lynne on the sofa. 'It's great to see you again,' he said, looking at his hands.

He had a warm face, with almost boyish features. Again, she sensed that spark of attraction. She recalled how she'd felt about him when she'd seen his photo, shortly before she'd started dating Steve. For a short time, maybe two or three weeks, she'd wished she could go out with Alex. All of that had been forgotten when she began her relationship with Steve; but now it was there in the forefront of her mind. She wondered whether she had done the right thing in coming to visit him today. Things were never as cut and dried as they should be. She certainly hadn't expected to be feeling this way about him.

'I've been hoping you would come and visit,' he said, after a brief, awkward silence. 'I've missed you.'

'Really?' Her eyes widened.

'Yes, I think about you a lot.'

That statement should have freaked her out, considering she knew he'd been stalking her; but she didn't feel threatened by Alex at all. He seemed so placid.

Now that he was looking at her, she noticed how blue his eyes were. She had forgotten how clear and almost transparent they were. Her emotions were bewildering. She pulled her eyes away from his gaze, knowing this was wrong; she shouldn't have come. Her mission had been to try to make him see that she was not interested in him, but she was failing. Seeing him again took her back to a time long ago—her youth—before all the complications of failed relationships, and the responsibilities of life in general. He reminded her of her childhood; a time she'd like to revisit. Then she stopped herself, realising that it had been her desire to go back in time that had led her to this strange in-between world, where nothing made sense.

As she sat here, in the room she hadn't seen for many years, she began to wonder whether she was imagining it all. Would she wake up like Dorothy in *The Wizard of Oz* and realise that she had just been dreaming?

She couldn't get past the feeling she had in Alex's presence; a feeling of calm and familiarity, almost as though they'd known each other for ever. She just felt so at home with him. He was like an oasis in a desert, now that she had found herself in a strange place, caught between times. He was someone whom she recognised, and she wanted to hold on to that. He was an old friend, and she felt happy to see him again—despite everything.

Taking a deep breath, she tried to remind herself what a weirdo he was, stalking her and then killing himself.

'I remember how close we were when we were young,' he said. 'It's a shame we drifted apart.'

'Yes,' she said, finding her tongue, realising that she had hardly said a word since he'd sat next to her.

'Remember when I asked you out, when we were twelve?' He laughed.

She laughed along with him, to be polite, but couldn't read his face. It struck her as odd that he was joking about it; she'd always thought he must have been hurt by that rejection.

'I was such a geek in those days,' he continued. 'I'm not surprised you turned me down! When I look back at those photos...' He began to laugh and it was infectious.

She giggled along with him, at the same time trying to analyse him, knowing what she did about his future. *This man could be dead in a few months time.* She found it hard to believe, looking at him, that he could do such a thing. He came across as so normal and down-to-earth. He dressed well, she noticed; designer labels. And he was well-built, as if he really took care of his body, perhaps going to a gym.

'I'm so glad you've come,' he said. 'Can I get you something to drink?'

Immediately, she thought of the way he'd died, drinking bleach. It was the first thought that entered her mind. As she looked at this handsome, kind-looking man, her heart went out to him. She resolved to do everything in her power to stop him dying like that.

'Will you have a cup of tea?' he said.

'Um... okay.' She blushed when she realised she'd been so consumed with her thoughts that she hadn't responded to his first offer of a drink. All she'd done was stare at him, open-mouthed, as she contemplated how she could save him.

Watching Alex leave the room, Lynne reflected on the past few minutes. He seemed so completely ordinary, just like the Alex she'd known as a child. He didn't seem like an obsessive, suicidal stalker. Then, she remembered the diaries Rachel had said he'd written, and the secret photos he was supposed to have taken of her. Perhaps if she could find a way to get into his room, she could look for them and get a better idea of his frame of mind. But how?

He walked back into the living room with a tray containing two cups of tea, and fruit cake slices.

'I was just thinking, when I was in the kitchen, you never mentioned why you'd come today.' He stood with the tray in his hands, waiting for an answer.

'Um... I was in the neighbourhood, and my mum is always going on at me about how I should visit you and your mum more often.' She hoped that sounded believable.

'Well, I'm glad you're here. We shouldn't be strangers.' He handed her a cup of tea. 'No sugar, not too strong, and just a splash of milk. The way you like it.' He smiled at her.

Lynne was now feeling slightly spooked. *How does he know how I like my tea?* She hadn't told him.

'My mum says that you and I were so close as children,' he said, interrupting her thoughts. 'She used to joke that we'd get married one day.'

'Yes, er... I heard about that.' Then she realised that she'd only heard about it in the future, when she'd heard about his death.

'Help yourself to fruit cake,' he said. 'My mum makes the best home-made cakes.'

'Thanks.' Lynne remembered how, as a child, she had loved the cakes Rachel used to bring to her parents' house.

'I'm single at the moment,' said Alex, 'and if you are, too, I'd really like to get to know you better.' He smiled at her.

She looked at the cup of tea in her hand, not sure how to respond. Her instinct told her to say she is still with Adam, to make it clear to Alex that she is unavailable. But she remembered how he'd killed himself when he found out she was marrying Adam. She'd come here to save him, not to bring the date of his death forward.

'It would be nice to get to know you,' she said, avoiding any reference to her marital status. 'You seem nice.' *Nice? Nice? Why am I repeating words?* Then, a pang of guilt assailed her. *Surely, I'm leading him on now?* At least in her future life she had been blameless in his death, but now she was making him think she had some feelings for him; fanning the flames. 'As friends, of course,' she added, quickly, before he could speak.

'Oh, of course; friends. Yes, friends. We could see how it goes.' He appeared disappointed, as if he'd expected her to declare her undying love for him.

As she looked into his eyes, she knew it would actually be quite easy for her to fall for him. Maybe she was feeling vulnerable, having just got out of a bad relationship; or, it was a case of her needing comfort, and Alex being there offering kindness. Whatever it was, it left her feeling uncomfortable.

He smiled at her. 'How about I take you out tonight? You like Chinese food, don't you?'

He asked as if he already knew. *How would he know what food I like? First the tea, and now this.* Then she reminded herself that he was supposed to be stalking her. He must have seen her at *The Red Dragon Tree* restaurant with Sandra. They often went there.

'We'll go to this great place I know,' he continued. '*The Red Dragon Tree.*' He smiled.

Her tea almost went down the wrong way. She coughed. 'Sounds nice,' she said, realising he must have been in the restaurant in the past when she was there with Sandra. Watching her. Perhaps even taking photos of her.

She felt surprised by her emotions. As she sat here looking at him, she found herself feeling flattered he liked her so much that he would follow her around just to see her. It was almost romantic in a sick, stalker kind of way. She thought back to times in the past when she'd fancied someone, but had been too shy to say; when she would have done anything to see the object of her desire. Like the time when she had a crush on Ben at her college, and knew where he lived. She'd often taken a different route when out shopping, just to walk past his house, in the hope of seeing him. *What Alex is doing isn't that much different, really, is it?* she thought, almost as if she were trying to convince herself.

By the end of the afternoon, Lynne found that she was strangely looking forward to going to dinner with Alex. But she then remembered that she was supposed to be spending the evening at home, having a takeaway meal with Adam. And he was going to propose to her.

Chapter Thirty-Two

Lynne sat opposite Alex, eating king prawn fried rice, in *The Red Dragon Tree* restaurant. He had dressed smartly, and was clean shaven, wearing a gorgeous smelling after shave. After drinking two glasses of wine to drown her sorrows, she was finding him ever more attractive.

They talked about school, and the mutual friends they had known: *'I wonder what happened to so-and-so'*, and *'I heard that so-and-so is living in Hong Kong'*. Lynne found herself feeling nostalgic and wishing for the second time today that she could go back to her youth, when the only difficult decisions she had to make were things like, what clothes to dress *Barbie* in, or whether to watch *Top of the Pops* or do her homework. But again, she checked herself; she didn't want to do any more time travelling, unless it was going back to where she'd been before coming here. Okay, it might not have been a great existence, being unemployed and just finding out that your new husband is gay; but it was infinitely better than being stuck back in time, feeling afraid that you were losing your mind.

Somehow, despite her negative feelings about being caught in this time slip, Lynne felt comfortable here talking to Alex. It was easy to forget that he was actually, in reality, a suicidal stalker. There seemed to be a bond between them. They shared precious memories of growing up, and that made her feel close to him, as if he was someone she could trust. He came from the same background, therefore, he should—in theory, at least—have the same ideals.

She'd phoned Adam at work, saying that Sandra had asked for a lift to the hospital to visit a relative.

'I thought you were ill?' said Adam.

'Oh, er... I'm feeling much better now.'

'Well, if you're better, we can still go into town tonight,' he suggested.

'No, Sandra needs me...'

'What's wrong with Sandra's car?' he asked, grumpily.

'It broke down,' said Lynne.

'But, Lynne, tonight was meant to be special.'

He does a good impersonation of someone who gives a damn about our relationship, *she thought bitterly. She'd never thought of Adam as being a potential actor, but this was an Oscar winning performance.*

Granted, she couldn't see his face on the other side of the phone line, but still, he sounded convincing; as if he really would rather spend the evening with her instead of his lover.

'I know,' she said. 'Sorry. But we can have dinner together tomorrow, can't we?'

'No, I'm going to New York tomorrow.'

'Oh,' was all she could say, remembering back (or to be more accurate: forward) to when she had followed him, when he was supposed to be going on a business trip but had ended up at Paul's house. She had half a mind to follow him again, tomorrow, just to see how long the affair had been going on.

'I'll be away for two weeks. I really wanted to see you tonight.'

Lynne baulked as she realised that not too long ago, she would have believed him when he said that. 'Well, I'll be back by about eleven.'

'Hmm, well maybe we can have a drink together later for your birthday,' he said, still sounding grumpy.

'Okay.' She was dreading him asking her to marry him. She was going to say "No". She had to say "No". But then what? Everything would change. Her life would be taking a completely different turn. It was scary.

The waiter collected their plates. 'Would you like the dessert menu?' he asked.

'Yes, please,' said Alex, smiling at Lynne.

The waiter walked away.

'I could just do with an ice cream, now,' said Alex. 'That sauce was hot!'

'I'm on a diet,' said Lynne. She realised that she was always on a diet. But even so, it didn't stop her consuming vast amounts of chocolate, cakes, and ice cream, when she felt a bit down. Considering she'd been feeling down quite a lot lately, she had even more of a reason to be on a diet. But she wondered whether she would be able to resist the dessert menu.

'Oh, come on. Live a little,' said Alex. 'If you are on a diet, a bit of a treat won't hurt. And besides, I don't think you need to be on a diet. You've got a great figure.'

She couldn't help smiling at the compliment, as she wondered whether he was being honest or nice. Her dress size had gone up from a size 10 to a size 12 in the few months since she'd been made redundant. She knew she didn't look too fat, but the main problem was getting into her clothes. Then it occurred to her that she was back in January, and she had fitted into her size 10 black dress tonight without even trying. Looking down at her dress, she smiled, feeling a new lease of life. *I've literally lost a stone overnight! Now, where's that dessert menu?*

'I mean it, Lynne,' continued Alex. 'You look great.'

Lynne looked at him, tearing her eyes away from her reflection in the mirror to the right of the table; she couldn't help staring at her new svelte figure. 'Thanks,' she said. Noticing his eyes again, she realised that she really did love the colour of them. She knew she could fall for him. Blushing, she looked away.

The waiter brought them the menu and she chose the double chocolate cake with cream. Every spoonful tasted divine.

Alex had driven them to the restaurant. He drove them back to his house. It was almost 10:30 pm. As Lynne got out of the car, she said, 'Thanks, Alex, I really enjoyed this evening,' and, she meant it. As difficult as it was to put the negative thoughts to the back of her mind—knowing what she knew about him—somehow, she had thoroughly enjoyed his company tonight, and felt that she would like to see him again.

'I did, too,' he said, beaming. He locked the car. 'Come in for a cup of coffee,' he offered.

'No, no. I have to be going,' she said. In her mind she pictured Adam waiting for her back at the flat, ready to go down on one knee.

'Okay, Lynne, give me your telephone number, and I'll call you,' he said.

'Um...' She hesitated, not sure if it was a good idea. 'Okay,' she said, eventually, hoping she wouldn't regret it. They exchanged mobile numbers.

As she got into her car, the thought occurred to her that she might be over the limit. She'd had two glasses of wine, not too long ago, and usually avoided drinking at all if she knew she'd be driving. After battling with her conscience for a few moments, she shrugged; it was only a ten minute drive, and she didn't feel drunk. She had been eating and drinking at the same time, so the effects of the alcohol would be diminished. Nevertheless, she made a point of driving very slowly, and was glad that there were not too many cars on the road.

When she arrived home, she had a terrible guilt hangover. Her imagination had been running wild on the drive home, conjuring up thoughts of police cells and breathalyzer tests, courts, and even a jail sentence. She promised herself to stick to her "no drink" rule in the future if she was going to drive. The ten minute journey had taken almost twenty minutes at the slower speed. When she got home it was just before 11 pm.

Adam was seated on the sofa, waiting for her in the living room.

He'd placed a bottle of champagne in an ice bucket on the coffee table, and there were two champagne flutes sitting beside it. A large bouquet of red roses sat on the sideboard filling the air with a wonderful aroma.

He stood up to greet her. 'Hi, Lynne.' He grinned. 'I said I wanted to make this special, didn't I?' he said, pointing at the flowers and the champagne.

'It's lovely,' she said. *How am I going to do this?* She turned around to take off her coat and hang it on the door, wishing she'd stayed at Alex's house to have a coffee.

'Come over here,' beckoned Adam.

She left her bag on the sideboard, by the door, and walked over to the sofa, feeling awkward.

Adam reached out to her.

Smiling, as she sat on the sofa next to him, she tried to pretend that she hadn't noticed he wanted to hug her.

He sat down in front of her, on one knee, and reached into his jacket pocket, pulling out a box. A box she had seen before. The blue velvet one. She knew what was in there. The diamond ring. The one she had worn for over six months. She'd still been wearing it before her trip to the past, she realised; but looking at her finger now, she saw it wasn't there. It was still in the box.

'Lynne, we've been together for over three years. I think it's about time we took the next step.' He smiled.

She remembered back to how she'd felt when she'd heard those words before—the first time. The surroundings had been different; he'd taken her to the London Eye. But the words were the same. Even his suit was the same, and that too-strong after shave he always insisted on wearing. Back then, though, she'd been happy to hear the words that were just about to fall from his lips. She'd seen it as a positive step, a way forward; a way to glue together the cracks in their relationship.

'Will you marry me?' he asked. Then he opened the box to reveal *her* ring. She didn't look at it, not wanting to see it again. The first time she'd seen it, she gasped as it was so beautiful. She'd loved wearing that ring. But this time it would never be hers. She would never wear it. A sense of loss and sadness pervaded her mind.

Standing up, she said, 'I'm sorry, Adam, but you and I both know this relationship is over. Getting married won't change anything. We've had some good times. Let's remember those, and maybe we can still be friends.' She wasn't looking at him as she spoke. He remained on the floor, on one knee, holding the ring out towards her, as if stuck in a moment of time. She was staring ahead, into space. It looked like a scene from a theatre play where they were the only two actors on the stage.

'I'm going to bed,' she said, as she stared straight ahead of her. Walking away towards the bedroom, she could see him from the corner of her eye, still on one knee.

'Lynne!' He stood up, incredulous. 'Wait!'

She turned to face him, and as she did so, something snapped inside her. 'You're living a lie, Adam!' she shouted. There was a bit more anger in the way she said it than she'd intended, but she felt a release, as if she'd said everything she needed to say in those few words.

He stood open-mouthed, as if truly shocked. 'I... I... didn't know you felt like this,' was all he said. He said it to the sofa, unable to look her in the eye.

Lynne went into the bedroom, and heard the front door of the flat open and close. Adam had gone out. He didn't return to the flat that night.

Chapter Thirty-Three

Adam stood outside Paul's house. He hesitated before ringing the door bell.

Whilst driving to see Paul, he'd been sure of his motivation. The relationship with Lynne had been a façade. The only reason he'd asked her out was to try to put on a front for the world to show everyone he was normal; whatever that meant. He wasn't secure about his sexuality at the time, and he had done well in fooling others, and even fooling himself. Throughout his relationship with Lynne, he had never stopped thinking about Paul. He'd been lying to himself, thinking he could deny his true sexuality. He knew he'd always been gay, but the years of confusion had sent him in another direction, making him feel frightened. He had built a life for himself, based on another persona: the "Adam" that he had created to fit into the world around him. He used to be afraid of standing out, of being different; but now, he no longer felt the need to hide. It was time to put it all behind him.

When he'd started work at the bank all those years ago, he'd still been in denial about his sexuality. The colleagues he mixed with were all typical heterosexuals, getting married and having children. He had thought, rightly or wrongly, that he might lose his job if he told them the truth. There was no real reason for him to think that, but it had always been a fear. And then, two years ago, Joe Colver had started work in his department, and he was very openly gay. Adam envied Joe. Deep down, he wanted to stop hiding and "come out"; reveal his true self to the world. For years he'd been playing a role, acting as someone he was not. He wished he could be as brave as Joe, and because of this he became resentful. All his negative emotions at that time were aimed at Joe, even though Joe had done nothing to him. Adam would ignore him when they passed each other in the corridor, and he wouldn't socialise with him at work lunches, or after-work evenings. Whenever Joe asked him for help with something in the office, he'd say he was too busy.

Joe confronted him one day at the water cooler.

'Do you have a problem with me, Adam?'

Adam proceeded to fill his cup with water. 'I don't know what you mean,' he huffed. He was about to walk away, but Joe took him by the arm.

'Listen, just because I'm gay, doesn't mean I'm going to fall in love with you. You're not my type.'

There were some distant giggles, which could be heard from the secretarial pool.

'Let go of my arm.'

'Oh, and I haven't got AIDS either,' added Joe, dryly.

Adam turned to face him. 'I'm not homophobic.'

'No, you just don't like gays,' said Joe, bitterly. 'I know your type. You're not secure with your own sexuality. It's not a disease, you know. You can't become gay just from talking to me.'

Adam could only stare. If only you knew the truth, *he thought.*

After work, Adam went for a drink with two of his work colleagues, Jenson and Toby.

'That twat, Joe, cornered you at the water cooler, I hear,' said Toby, sitting opposite Adam and Jenson in the crowded pub.

'Um... yeah,' said Adam, feeling embarrassed.

'You know, the problem with gays—well, any minorities, for that matter—is that they have too many rights, these days,' said Jenson, sipping his beer.

'Er... well...' Adam was lost for words.

'Joe can get away with saying anything, but if we say something back to him, then we'll be considered homophobic and we could lose our jobs,' continued Jenson.

'True,' said Toby, looking at Adam. 'I hear he was accusing you of being a homophobe?'

'Yeah, I don't know where he got that idea from,' said Adam, playing with his coaster, feeling uncomfortable.

'Oh, come on, Adam,' said Jenson. 'You might as well admit it; there have been rumours going around about it for the last couple of weeks.'

'I'm not homophobic,' said Adam, for the second time in 24 hours. He felt sick to the stomach and as if he were trapped in a nightmare. What he wanted more than anything else was to finally break the chains and reveal his true identity, but he found himself being labelled as an enemy to what he held most dear.

Looking at the two men sitting at the table, he didn't feel this would be the ideal time to "come out". He'd heard Jenson joke about gay men before, and Toby had commented to him, when Joe first started work at the bank: 'I hope he doesn't bring his boyfriend to any work dos—I hate watching men kissing each other. It makes me feel ill!'

So, he was stuck, and had to listen to Jenson and Toby telling him Joe was "out of order" for speaking to him like that, and how he

146

should complain to the management, because 'those big wigs don't really like gays, and are probably looking for a good reason to sack him.' (According to Jenson). But then Toby said: 'What do you mean? Most of those big wigs are gay themselves! I wouldn't be surprised if Joe's having a fling with one of the managers.'

It was cringe worthy, but Adam had to sit through almost half an hour of their rantings before he found an opportunity to make an excuse and leave.

Adam thought back to those days. Joe Colver had left the bank quite soon after this all happened, to get a job in America. The truth was, Joe had never felt welcome in that environment, with people like Toby and Jenson, continually cracking jokes. They always added: 'We were only joking', or, 'we don't really mean it', at the end of their "jokes"; but the kind of things they said bordered on abusive. Adam had stood by and watched, wishing he wasn't such a coward.

In the aftermath of Joe's resignation, Adam went even further into his shell, feeling too fearful to come out with the truth. After all, he'd witnessed how Joe had been treated.

As he stood outside Paul's front door, he felt stronger; as if his reason for keeping up a pretence had gone. Lynne had dumped him. He was a free man; free to be with whoever he wanted to be with. He wanted to be with Paul.

Adam took a deep breath and rang the door bell. His nerves jangled as questions ran through his mind. Would Paul feel the same way about him? Would he understand why he'd had a relationship with a woman, denying his homosexuality?

He waited for a few minutes. There were lights on in the house, but Paul hadn't answered the door. Looking at his watch, he saw it was almost 12 am. It was late. But he was so psyched now, and just wanted to get it over with; tell Paul today, in case he clammed up again by tomorrow, and then he'd be forced to live even longer in this sham existence.

He rang the doorbell again, his hand shaking as he reached for it. This time, he heard some noise from inside. The door opened after a few moments, and Paul stood there in a short, silk dressing-gown. Adam's eyes were drawn to Paul's legs, and then to his bare chest. Adam turned crimson. He hoped Paul wouldn't notice his blushes.

'Hello, sorry to call so late,' he said, quickly.

'Um... Adam. I'm kind of busy at the moment.' He gestured with his head, indicating that there was someone upstairs.

Adam's mood changed. His shoulders slouched. The optimism had gone. It hadn't even crossed his mind that Paul would be in a relationship. Deflated and disappointed, he said, 'Sorry, I... I should have called first.'

'Wait,' said Paul, as Adam turned to leave. 'It must be something important, if you've come here at this time. Er... what time is it?' He held up his bare arm, to show he wasn't wearing a watch.

'It's midnight,' said Adam. 'No, listen, it's not important. I'll call you tomorrow, um, some other time.' With that, he turned and scuttled away, leaving Paul to wonder what was wrong with him.

Chapter Thirty-Four

Lynne woke up and switched on the radio, wanting to make sure it was still January. *Or did I just dream it all?* she wondered. She switched through the different radio stations until she found some news. Sure enough, the stories being related by the news team were things that had happened months ago.

She hadn't yet made up her mind as to whether she was happy with this strange turn of events. Her life, after the wedding, had been dismal. Part of her did feel glad to be somewhere else, even if it was in this undiscovered secret pocket of time. But she couldn't get used to it. It was like looking at the world through an invisible screen, not really living there, and not able to fully relax or be sure if she was awake or dreaming. She perceived herself as out of place, like a visitor from the future, and she kept expecting to wake up back in her former life. This unsettled her and kept her constantly on tenterhooks.

Her mobile phone rang. The first thing she noticed when she picked up the phone, was the date: 20th of January. This dispelled any lingering doubts that she was back in July. Sandra's name flashed on the phone. She always told Sandra everything; but *this*? Could she? She wasn't sure. It was still too early, and she was still in denial, feeling that it couldn't really be happening. Wouldn't Sandra think she'd gone crazy if she suddenly told her that she'd somehow travelled back in time?

'Hello,' she said, strangely nervous. *How can I be feeling nervous, speaking to Sand?*

'Hi, Lynne. Wanna meet up after work? I'm thinking of splashing lots of cash in the January sales, and then heading up West, for a show. Fancy it? Please say "yes". I can't face another night at home in front of the TV.'

Lynne remembered this exact same phone call from January. She'd been at work at the time, on her lunch break (instead of lying in bed at 12:15 pm). Lynne recalled their conversation:

'Yes, of course. I'd love to come! And, I've got some great news.'

'What news?' Sandra said. 'Don't keep me in suspense! Tell me now!'

'Okay.' Lynne beamed. She was so happy, and excited to be able to tell Sandra. 'Adam proposed last night! We're getting married!'

Lynne remembered how she'd gone shopping with Sandra that evening and bought lots of clothes in the sales, many of which she'd never worn. They'd found cheap, last minute tickets for *Hairspray*, the musical. They'd had a fabulous time, ending the evening being chatted up by two, rich businessmen in a wine bar. Lynne had bored everyone by talking non-stop about her wedding plans.

Thinking back, Lynne recalled that one of the men had been flirting with her. He'd been quite good-looking; young and fit, with gorgeous blue eyes. She'd thought to herself at the time: *If I wasn't engaged, I'd go out with him.*

She wondered if they'd meet him again if she met up with Sandra tonight. Suddenly, going back in time had its advantages.

'Pack an overnight bag,' said Sandra, interrupting Lynne's reminiscences. 'Stay at mine tonight. We'll drop your bag at mine before we head into town.'

Lynne realised she hadn't even spoken to Sandra yet. 'Okay, yeah... um... I've got some news.'

'What news? Don't keep me in suspense!' said Sandra. 'Tell me now!'

'Me and Adam have split up.'

'Oh my God!' Sandra's voice came out very high-pitched. 'Why? What happened?'

'It's a long story,' said Lynne. 'I don't really want to talk about it.'

'Right, okay... Well, maybe we can talk a bit about it tonight? You know I'm here if you need—'

'Sand, I'm okay. Really. Don't worry about me. The relationship had been dying for a while.'

'I'm sorry to hear that. I thought you two were good together. Listen, if you don't feel up to going out tonight, we can stay in and get a takeaway.'

'No, I don't want to ruin your evening. We'll go out.' Lynne remembered that great pair of black jeans she'd found in the sales for £10. She had to get them. They were her favourite pair of trousers. She also wanted to meet that man again... 'We'll have a great time, Sand.'

The early part of the evening unfolded much as Lynne had remembered it, except that she didn't buy as many clothes—leaving behind all those "bargains" that had never seen the light of day after being put into her wardrobe. Also, now that she had the knowledge she was going to be made redundant in less than two weeks, she didn't feel in the mood to spend money.

Lynne enjoyed *Hairspray* even more the second time, and couldn't help feeling chuffed that she'd seen it twice now, but had only paid for the tickets once. A great benefit of going back in time.

Finally, they arrived at the wine bar in Leicester Square. It was just as Lynne remembered it. She had a real déjà vu experience as she walked in and saw the blonde woman arguing with the barmaid about her change. It had happened the last time.

'Hey, are you blind or something?' the blonde woman said, loudly.

'Excuse me?' said the pretty barmaid, who looked much too young to even be in a bar, with her curly mop of brown hair and brightly coloured make-up, thickly applied. It made her look more like a child who'd been playing around with her mother's cosmetics. She looked as if she were about to cry.

The blonde woman was a good few inches taller than her, and probably weighed twice as much. 'I gave you twenty pounds and you've given me change for a tenner!'

'No,' said the bar maid. 'It was a ten pound note.'

'Get the manager!' screamed the blonde woman.

Meanwhile, all activity and most of the talking in the wine bar had ceased, as everyone looked over at the fracas.

The young barmaid went to find the manager.

Soon everyone started talking again. Lynne and Sandra bought their drinks, and went to find a seat amidst the crowd of people. The incident at the bar was soon forgotten. Lynne never did find out what happened the last time. As she and Sandra made their way to their seats at the back of the room in this replay situation, she realised that she wouldn't be finding out this time, either.

Sandra chose a comfy sofa at the back of the wine bar. The same place they had sat before. The bar was so busy, they had to squeeze in between two groups of designer-clad twenty-somethings. Lynne remembered them from the last time. All the faces were familiar. It was like going back to visit old friends, and she had to stop the urge to smile at them as if she knew them. *They've never seen me before*, she reminded herself. When she slipped up and smiled at one young man, he returned her friendly expression with a blank stare, then he looked away as if embarrassed.

Lynne's heart started to beat a bit faster as she realised that if all these people were the same, it wouldn't be long before the two businessmen they'd previously met, showed up. From memory, she recalled that they'd arrived about half-an-hour after Sandra and herself.

'I've had a great time tonight,' said Sandra, as she sipped her cocktail. 'Thanks for coming. *Hairspray* was good, wasn't it?'

151

'Yeah, fantastic!'

'Bargain tickets. We should do it more often.'

'Yeah.' Then she saw him. The hunk. He was laughing about something with his friend. Their eyes met across the room. She couldn't help smiling at him, and he started to walk in her direction, grinning from ear to ear; just as he had done the last time.

'Hello, ladies,' he said. His friend, a shorter man, stood behind him.

'Hi,' said Sandra, even though he was looking at Lynne.

He turned to face Sandra. 'Can I buy you lovely ladies a drink?'

'No, we don't accept drinks from strange men,' said Sandra, smiling. 'But thanks for offering.'

'Well, can we join you?' he asked, indicating his friend.

'Um...' Sandra looked at Lynne, and shrugged her shoulders.

'Why not?' said Lynne, still wearing the stupid smile that had appeared as soon as she'd set eyes on him.

'I'm Jack, and this is Aaron,' said the hunk.

They sat opposite Sandra and Lynne.

'So, are you two girls single?' asked Jack.

'Yes,' said Lynne. 'Are you?' She could feel Sandra's confusion. She knew she expected her to be pining over Adam, but that was history. Lynne just wanted to have a bit of a laugh, and forget all about it.

'No, we're married, but looking for mistresses,' said Jack, laughing loudly.

'Truthfully,' said Aaron, his up-until-now silent friend. 'We are city bankers. We don't get much time for dating. It's a hectic life.'

City bankers. That's why Lynne remembered that she'd thought they were rich. All those bonuses. She realised now, though, that these two were likely to either be made redundant soon, or they'd have their salaries cut—what with all the trouble the banks had been having lately in this recession.

'City bankers?' said Sandra. 'So, you must be rich.'

'Well, yes, I suppose you could say that,' said Jack. 'This suit is designer, you know.'

'It's nice,' said Sandra.

Lynne, having heard all this before, began to see it from a different perspective. Surely, someone who has money wouldn't have to talk about it so much? She'd been so happy to be engaged to Adam, the last time she'd met them, that she hadn't really been reading too much into the chat up lines. It had all been just friendly talk. She hadn't expected it to lead anywhere, so she hadn't been too concerned about the amount of truth involved.

'Banks are going through a bit of a rough time at the moment, aren't they?' asked Lynne. 'Aren't you concerned about your jobs?'

'No,' said Jack. 'Look, we're not really bankers, we're... we're successful businessmen. Are you sure you won't let me buy you a drink? Did I mention you've got beautiful eyes?' He looked at her.

'What's your real job, Jack?' she asked, smiling.

Jack appeared slightly embarrassed, but laughed and said: 'I'm a plumber and Aaron's an electrician. But it's not all about money, is it?'

'Well, exactly,' she said. 'So, I don't know why you were trying to impress us by saying you are rich.'

'Oh, it's just something we do for a laugh,' said Aaron.

Lynne giggled. She thought back to the last time she'd met them. Their conversation had been superficial, and had mainly revolved around the fact that she was getting married, and Jack had been flirting with her, saying: *'You can't marry him, you'll break my heart.'* Apart from initially introducing themselves as city bankers, they hadn't really talked much about themselves at all. Lynne hadn't questioned them then, and hadn't discovered the truth. She thought about how many times in her life she'd have loved the opportunity to dig a bit deeper and ask a few more questions to find out what really lies beneath the surface; the fragile lies that cover up and disguise most of what's true. Maybe if she'd asked more questions of Adam at some time, she would have found out about his homosexuality sooner, and not have had to go through with that charade of a marriage.

'Anyway, now that you know who we really are, do you still want to know us? That's the real question, isn't it?' asked Jack.

'I'm not sure I really want to know someone who blatantly lies about what they do for a living. I mean what was the point of that?' asked Sandra, looking suddenly serious.

'I'm sorry,' said Jack, standing up. 'I don't think I want to know someone who's obviously lost her sense of humour. Come on, Aaron, we're going.'

It just wasn't meant to be, was it? thought Lynne, as she watched him walk out of her life for a second time. 'Why did you have to frighten them away?' she said, looking glum.

'You're not telling me you were seriously interested in those idiots, are you?' Sandra looked at her, wide eyed. 'They were trying to play us for fools. Pretending to be rich! I mean, what sort of man does that?'

'Um... quite good-looking sorts of men, who are only having a laugh.'

'They were being dishonest,' said Sandra. 'How could you trust someone like that? You'd never know if he was telling the truth or

153

not.'

'Oh, Sand. I just thought Jack was really good-looking. It would have been fun to have a fling with him.'

'You're not thinking straight. You've just broken up with Adam. You were with him for more than three years. You can't just jump into another relationship, especially with someone like Jack, just because he's good-looking.'

'I know. I just thought a bit of fun would help me to stop dwelling on it all,' she said, thinking out loud.

'You'll be fine, Lynne,' said Sandra, putting an arm around her. 'Just take your time and find someone worthy.'

Everything Sandra said would have made perfect sense, if she'd been back in her old life and if Adam hadn't been gay. But somehow, this new "future-aware" life made her want to throw caution to the wind. It felt like she was invincible. After all, she knew that whatever she did, she'd still be alive in July... As far as she knew.

Chapter Thirty-Five

Lynne received the letter from her employer less than a week after her return to the past. She recognised the envelope and knew exactly what the content was.

Dear Lynne,
Unfortunately, due to the economic downturn, the firm has to make some employees redundant, and, with regret, you are one of the people being considered for redundancy.

A decision will be made in the next two weeks, and you will be notified of the outcome. In the meantime, if you wish to make any representations, please forward a letter to me by Friday 30th January...

As she read the letter, she remembered how shocked she had been the first time around. In her five years as an employee at the firm, she had always been punctual and hardworking, and had hardly ever taken a sick day. That loyalty didn't matter in the cold hard world of business. Shaking her head, she remembered the ember of hope that had flickered inside her as she'd written the letter in response, asking her bosses to reconsider. The tears fell heavily a week later when she got the final decision letter.

She thought of those who had been kept on by the firm: apart from her best friend at the office, Lucy, who was the only one who knew how to work the database and was therefore indispensable, the only other two survivors were Denise and Rolinda. Denise was a young girl, who had only started work at the firm the previous year. There were rumours that she'd snogged Evan, one of the partners, at the Christmas party; she kept her job, filing her nails and taking sick days whenever she pleased. Rolinda, who'd had a very open affair with Andrew, the senior partner (even though Andrew had been married at the time), survived the crushing blow of a redundancy in a recession. Even though her affair with Andrew was rumoured to be over, they still flirted outrageously at staff get-togethers, and no one could forget the embarrassment of hearing Rolinda and Andrew having sex in his office many times, and then having to pretend they didn't know what had gone on. It was a no-brainer that she would be safe from the axe.

Lynne remembered feeling hard done by when she'd received the final confirmation of her redundancy, but after her initial disappointment she thought it would be easy enough to find temporary work whilst looking for another job. However, after over five months of job-seeking she was still out of work. This put a different perspective on the letter she now held in her hands.

She felt frustrated and angry at how she'd just been dumped in a time of bleak prospects. Surely, the firm could have found a way to cut corners and keep their loyal staff on board during the recession? Tearing the letter into tiny shreds, as tears filled her eyes, she dropped the confetti-like pieces into the kitchen bin.

Blackness overshadowed her, a feeling of no hope. There was no point doing any job searches. She'd already wasted enough time over the past few months, filling in long-winded application forms and getting rejections, or just no response at all from recruiters. Even worse were the long interviews she'd had to endure, with written tests and presentations, and a hundred questions scrutinising her personality, only to find that after all the effort and nervous anticipation, the doors were closed in her face. She decided she would just ride it out and start looking for work properly in July, when she was back in real time; or at least *real time* as she knew it.

That made her wonder what her life would be like by July. There had already been big changes: she'd met Alex again, and she'd split from Adam.

Adam. As his name flittered across her mind, she remembered that he would be back from his business trip soon. She felt an urgency to sort something out before he returned. He'd come back to the flat the morning after she'd told him it was over, to collect his suitcase. Trying to avoid him, she'd stayed in the kitchen, but on his way out, he'd said: *'Lynne, we'll talk about all this when I get back from New York.'*

It was clear she wouldn't be able to avoid him when he got back. She didn't want to live with him anymore, and this made her feel like leaving. But she liked this flat; it felt like home. Why should she have to give up everything because of his lies?

The most sensible thing would be to stay here. Maybe Adam would agree to leave. But even if he didn't, he was away on business most of the time, so she wouldn't have to have much to do with him. A feeling of déjà vu flooded her senses as she remembered that she had been facing the same dilemma only recently (but in the future) when she'd found out about Adam and Paul, and had wanted to leave him, but had nowhere to go.

She heard her mobile phone sound to alert her she'd received a text message. It was from Alex: *Hi, r u free 2nite? x*

Since their night out together, she had been hoping (she realised, in vain), that Alex was one of those people who said things like: 'It would be great to see you again', or, 'We must keep in touch'; but was, in reality, too busy. She'd hoped they'd gradually lose touch and she wouldn't have to see him again, or she could just see him very occasionally. But it had only been a few days since their last meeting. It brought all her inner doubts to the forefront of her mind. She had wanted to believe that he wasn't going to get obsessed with her if he actually met her, but it appeared that he seemed to be heading in that direction.

She hoped she was just reading too much into it, because of what she knew from the future; imagining problems where there were none. After all, she'd thought he was really nice when they'd gone out to dinner.

She didn't want to ignore his text, because she still felt jittery about the fact that he'd killed himself (in the future), and she didn't want to be the cause of that again. So she replied: *I'm not sure.*

He texted back, immediately, and Lynne had visions of him sitting in his house, staring at the phone, waiting for her to text back. *There's a film I want 2 c at the cinema. Wanna go?*

What harm could it do, going to the cinema? she thought. *OK* she replied.

I'll pick u up at 7. C U. x

She dialled his number. 'Hi.'

'Hello, Lynne. I didn't know if you were at work, so I texted rather than phoned. How are you?'

'I'm fine.'

'I've really missed you,' he said.

Warning bells rang in her mind. They'd only seen each other a few days ago and she hadn't even thought of him in the meantime, but he'd *missed* her? It didn't make sense. He definitely sounded like a stalker. *Stop*, she scolded herself. *I'm overreacting again. He's just a nice man. It's just a nice thing to say.*

'Ahem, anyway,' she said, ignoring the comment. 'I thought I'd better phone you and give you my address, if you're picking me up tonight.' More warning bells rang in her head. *How can I give a known stalker my address? Wouldn't it be better to meet up somewhere else?* She shook the thoughts away.

'I've already got your address,' he said.

'How?' Her question came abruptly, her mind suddenly full of paranoid thoughts.

'Er... dunno, maybe my mum gave it to me? I definitely have it. I'll be there tonight at seven. Hope you like romantic comedies?'

'Yes, I do,' said Lynne, wondering how Rachel would have her address. Then she remembered she did have it when she sent the poison pen letter in the future, but that was after Lynne had sent her a condolence card and she'd written her address on the back of the envelope. She'd never kept in touch with Rachel, so why would she have her address?

'So, it's settled then,' said Alex. 'Our first proper date, tonight! I can't wait.' With that, the phone line went dead.

Proper date. Oh my God! Where did he get that idea?

Chapter Thirty-Six

Lynne was glad to get out into the night air after the movie. She'd felt claustrophobic in the cinema, sitting next to Alex, because every time she turned to get some popcorn from the box in between their seats, she would see him staring at her. It was freaky. He didn't seem to be at all interested in the film, he was just watching her every move. Each time she turned towards him, he'd give her a toothy smile, which looked eerie in the half-darkness of the movie theatre.

'So, what did you think of the film?' asked Alex, as they negotiated their way through the crowds of cinema and theatre goers on the West End street.

'It was okay,' she said, looking ahead of her, avoiding his gaze. She'd been unable to concentrate on the film, feeling his eyes burning into her.

It began to rain and she hadn't brought an umbrella. Looking around her, she thought about disappearing into the crowd and taking the tube home, leaving him behind; but it was after 11 pm, and even though he was a bit strange, she didn't think Alex posed a threat to her. She wouldn't feel as safe on her own at night on public transport. *I'll just take a taxi home*, she thought.

'Stay at my place tonight,' he said, interrupting her concentration. 'It makes sense. It's only a few stops on the tube. You can have my room, I'll sleep on the sofa.'

'But, I haven't brought anything with me.'

'That's okay. I'm sure my mum could lend you pyjamas, and we have a spare toothbrush. We buy them in bulk!' He laughed.

She didn't want to lead him on, but she didn't want to reject him, aware of his fragile state of mind. *How can I turn him down nicely?* Then the thought occurred to her that if she stayed at his house, in his room, she might be able to find the photos and diaries that Rachel had talked about. Curiosity got the better of her.

They went down the steps into the tube station.

'You look lovely tonight, Lynne,' he said.

This comment reminded her that he'd been staring at her all evening.

'Er... thanks,' she said, blushing due to excruciating embarrassment.

'Our first official date,' he announced, as they sat side by side on the train. 'How do you think it went?'

'I... I... Look, Alex, I... wouldn't call it a date as such...' She noticed the frown on his face, so she laughed to try to make light of it.

'Well, what would you call it?' he huffed. His face had reddened.

The train pulled into the station, so, thankfully, she could avoid his question, at least for the moment. He was getting very intense, very quickly, and it made her feel unsettled. She'd been warming to him after their first meal out together, but in the last few hours she'd seen a different side to him. He definitely showed signs of being obsessive, and maybe not quite right in the head.

Standing behind him as he unlocked the front door of his family home, she wondered if she'd made the right decision to accompany him here. They'd hardly said two words since they'd stepped off the tube train. It had been raining, so they'd run from the station. Her coat was matted from the rain.

'Step inside, beautiful lady,' he said, gesturing for her to enter before him. 'Let me take your coat,' he offered.

She removed her dripping wet woollen coat and he took it from her.

'I'll get a hairdryer,' he said, disappearing off down the hall.

Rachel appeared from inside the living room. 'Lynne! Darling!' she exclaimed. 'Oh, look at you, you're soaking wet! I'll lend you my hairdryer.'

'Um... Alex went to get it.'

'Ah... That's my Alex, such a thoughtful boy. Did you have a nice time tonight?'

'Yes, thanks.'

'Oh, I'm so glad you two got together. You are just the perfect couple! You used to play together as children. Your mother and I always said you'd get married one day! Oops, I'm jumping the gun, aren't I? Did he ask you?'

'Er... ask what?' Lynne was not really sure she liked the way this conversation was going.

'I thought he would pop the question tonight. Oh! There I go, shooting my mouth off again! Just ignore me... It must be my age!' She laughed, and disappeared into the living room. Poking her head around the door, she said: 'Lynne, dear, come in and sit down while you wait for Alex.'

'No, it's okay, I'll wait here. I'm tired, so I'll just dry my hair and then go to bed.'

Just then, Alex ran back towards her. 'Sorry for the delay, I couldn't find the hairdryer. Here you are.'

She took the hairdryer from him.

'Mum, can Lynne borrow some pyjamas? And she'll need a toothbrush.'

'Of course!' Rachel smiled.

'You can go up to my room, Lynne,' said Alex. 'It's the first door on the right. You can't miss it—it says "Alex's Room" on it!' He laughed.

'Thanks.' Lynne walked up the stairs, and when she got to the top she turned instinctively to look down and saw both Alex and his mum looking up at her. The claustrophobic feeling she'd had in the cinema returned. It was all very weird. She forced a smile at her audience, and said, 'Er... Goodnight,' quickly turning around to escape from their gaze; but somehow she knew their eyes were still upon her.

'I'll be up in a sec to bring you something to wear,' said Rachel, causing Lynne to shudder.

Lynne opened the door into Alex's bedroom tentatively. The sign on the door saying "Alex's Room", looked as if it had been there ever since he was a child; it was very old and had a picture of a robot on it.

She wasn't sure what she'd expected to find inside the room, but it looked like a normal bedroom. There was a double bed, a large wardrobe, a couple of tasteful art prints on the wall, bookshelves, and a computer desk in the corner. It was very tidy; everything in its place. The wooden floor was clean, and the walls were painted a violet shade. The curtains matched the duvet cover; a cream and beige striped design. As she took in the room, she heard the door open behind her.

'Here you are, Lynne, a fresh pair of pyjamas; they should fit, I think. I changed the sheets on the bed today because Alex said you'd be staying over. I've put a new toothbrush in the bathroom for you. It's just across the hall.'

'Thanks, Aunty,' said Lynne.

'What did we say about calling me "Aunty"?' Rachel giggled.

'Oh, sorry. I forgot. I'm so used to calling you that,' she said, smiling.

'That's okay, lovey.' Rachel placed the pyjamas onto the bed and took Lynne's hands in hers. 'I want us to be good friends now. You mean so much to my Alex, and I'm really grateful that he's found someone to love at last.'

Lynne squirmed when Rachel winked at her. Things were getting a bit too heavy. 'Um... Rachel... Me and Alex, we're just friends. There's nothing going on.'

'Oh no, I know you haven't slept together. He told me. You want to wait until you're married. That's admirable in this day and age. I suppose that's why you want such an early wedding? I thought June was a bit soon; but I suppose when you love someone, you just know, don't you? There's no point in hanging around.

'Of course, I shouldn't be telling you any of this, but I'm just so excited. My son's getting married! Please forgive me, Lynne. I've spoilt the surprise. When he asks you, just pretend you didn't know. Please will you do that for him?' She smiled and gave Lynne a big hug. 'Welcome to the family, darling. I've always wanted a daughter.' With that, she turned around and left the room as quickly as she had arrived.

Lynne was left speechless. *What sort of family is this?* Then she thought back to her future life; the way Rachel had spoken to her, and the poison pen letter. The unstable mind seemed to be a family trait.

It seemed she was destined to have Rachel as an enemy. If she turned down Alex's proposal, Rachel would hate her. Then, she had a chilling thought: *If I turn down his proposal, he will probably kill himself.* That's what she was trying to stop. How could she live with herself? She felt like a king at the end of a chess game. Checkmate. Trapped, with no more moves.

Chapter Thirty-Seven

Lynne lay in Alex's bed staring at the ceiling; the familiar woodchip ceiling paper that most ex-local authority houses were decorated with. She remembered how, as a child, in her own bedroom, she would often try to see patterns and make out shapes in the woodchip. Sometimes she would see faces, animals, people, and other such things. Many a childhood nightmare had evolved from this.

Now, however, she was an adult, facing a nightmare of a different kind. She felt sick to the stomach at the thought of marrying Alex, but there didn't appear to be a way around it. *Maybe I should just marry him and then lie about having to work abroad, like Adam did to me. Then I wouldn't have to see him...* The thought occurred to her that maybe she was just destined to marry a man she could not live with for one reason for another. In her "future" life it had been Adam, but in this life—because she had turned him down—it would be Alex.

She had been pondering her options for over an hour, and sleep refused to come; kept away by the workings of an agitated mind.

As she lay in the half-darkness, the bedside lamp still on, she heard the door handle turning. She pulled the duvet cover closer to her, and wondered who could be coming into the room at this hour. Alex's head appeared through the gap in the door.

'I saw the light was still on,' he said, grinning like a small child. 'D'you mind if I come in?'

'No,' she said, startled by the question, and unable to think clearly.

He rushed in and sat on the edge of the bed. He was wearing pyjamas. 'It's great, having you stay over. It's just like the old days, when we were kids, remember?'

'Um... to be truthful, I don't really remember much about those days,' she lied, trying to find a way of dampening his excitement.

'Oh, you must! You just have to think back. Most weekends we used to stay over at each other's houses. We used to sleep in the same bed!' He grinned again.

'Look... Alex, I'm tired' She faked a yawn. 'I'd like to get some sleep.'

'Okay, yes, but first I have something to ask you.'

Oh, no! Not the marriage proposal! She winced. 'Er... can't it wait until the morning?' The thoughts raced through her head. If he just went out of the room, she could pack her things and leave early, then he wouldn't have a chance to ask her.

'Not really,' he said. Then, he got down on one knee. He fished out a small box from his pyjama pocket and opened it. Inside, sat a beautiful, dazzling, diamond ring. Even nicer than the one Adam had given her, she thought.

'Lynne,' he said. 'I've loved you for a long time. I know that sounds weird, but it isn't really. I think you are my true love. I fell in love with you when we were children and have never been able to get you out of mind, no matter how hard I tried. You're like an obsession.' He stopped and stared.

She realised that in different circumstances, she would have been quite flattered and touched by this announcement. He was very good-looking. Blonde hair, blue eyes, a perfect smile. And, she had had a bit of crush on him at one time. But that was before she knew what she now knew about him. *How could I even think of getting involved with a suicidal, obsessive, stalker?* As much as she tried to deny it, there was undoubtedly an attraction. This going back in time was really playing havoc with her senses. *Oh, I have to speak to Sandra! She'd know what to do!*

'Will you marry me, Lynne?'

She heard his voice, and was again reminded of her predicament.

'I'm sorry, Alex...' she began. His face crumpled and his chin shook. He was going to cry!

'Please don't say no!' he said, standing up. 'It's all I've ever dreamed about! You are everything I've ever wanted! I don't know how I could live without you.' His voice became loud, and she was worried that soon his mother and her partner, would join them in the room.

'Calm down, Alex. Don't you realise it's all a bit too soon?' she said, in an almost-whisper, trying to get him to lower his voice, too.

'Too soon? Thirty years? How can that be too soon?'

'We're only thirty years old now. You haven't known me since I was born.'

'Haven't I?' he said. 'I feel as though I've known you for ever; since time began. Why can't you love me in the same way that I love you?' Then he did begin to cry.

Lynne knew she had to be careful. He was obviously very unstable, and could perhaps kill himself at any time.

'Please don't cry,' she said. 'I'm not saying I don't want you as a friend.'

'Okay,' he said, through tears. 'Can you accept this ring as a friendship ring?'

'Um...' She hesitated.

'What? You don't like it?'

'No, it's lovely. I just don't want to give you the wrong idea. I just want to be friends, that's all.'

'Yes, of course. For now. That's fine. Okay,' he said. 'But, maybe in a few weeks, you'll see things differently.' He seemed to be pleading.

'Keep the ring, for now,' she said. 'We'll see how things develop.' She reddened in shame. Wasn't she still leading him on by saying that; giving him something to hold onto that was not really real?

He appeared to calm down, and sat on the edge of the bed again. She reached out and took a tissue from the box on the bedside cabinet.

'Thanks,' he said, as she handed him the tissue.

She watched him dry his eyes.

'I'll leave the ring here,' he said, putting it on the bedside cabinet. 'You sleep, and let me know what you decide in the morning.' He stood up and leaned over the bed, giving her a kiss on the forehead. 'I love you, Lynne,' he said softly. 'I'll never love anyone else the way I love you.'

She watched in bewilderment as he walked out of the room. As soon as he closed the door, she got out of bed and reached for her handbag, knowing she would have to get out of the house as soon as possible, or end up a captive in a loony bin. Then she remembered the diaries and photos, the main reason she'd agreed to stay at his house.

Praying Alex wouldn't be coming back into the room, she began to open drawers in the computer desk. The drawers were full of the usual things you would expect to find: elastic bands, batteries, staples, paper, a calculator etc., etc. Then, in the bottom draw, she saw a box labelled, "My secret stuff".

She lifted the box out of the draw. *If it's so secret, why isn't there a lock on it?* she thought, mockingly. Then, she felt slightly guilty that she was in his bedroom, looking through private things. But, it was the only way she could find out if it was true, about the photos and the diaries.

When she opened the box, she almost fell over. On top of everything, lay a photograph of her. In the photo, she was drinking a glass of wine, in surroundings which looked very much like... yes, *The Red Dragon Tree* restaurant. *So, it's true, he has been stalking me.* Looking at the dress she was wearing, she realised that this had been taken when she was out with Sandra, when Adam had been away on business, probably around December or early January. Very recently... Well, *recently* in terms of the date she found herself at now.

Looking further into the box, there were over fifty pictures—all of *her*—all pretty much pictures of her face; close-ups! Her mouth fell open.

The diaries... the diaries... she thought, rummaging through the box. W*here are they?*

They were not in the box.

She looked through the wardrobe, making a bit of a mess, and trying to tidy up as she went, but to no avail. Everything had been folded neatly; now it was a messy pile.

Just as she almost gave up, her eyes were drawn to the only other possible place the diaries could be kept: the bedside cabinet. She took a deep breath and opened the drawer. Lo and behold, there were a pile of diaries, going back at least ten years.

An initial feeling of guilt was quickly erased from her mind as she picked up the diaries; she now knew that he had been invading her privacy over the past few years, so why should she feel in the least bit guilty about invading his?

She began with the most recent diary. He had marked their meeting last night with a scribbled heart, and had written: *Cinema with my true love! Time to propose to Lynne!*

There was a childish element to many of his entries that was almost endearing, looking at it from an outsiders point of view; but when Lynne slowly realised that all of this just proved his unhealthy infatuation with her, she could feel no warmth at all. He had been literally spying on her. Alex had marked in his diary many "dates" with Lynne, which had never occurred. The dates seemed to correlate with the dates when the photos of her were taken.

Initially, she had resolved to take the diaries and photos with her, but her instinct told her that he would probably guess that she had them. Given his fragile state of mind, he might do something stupid if he became aware that she knew about all of this.

She heard some movement on the landing, and worried that Alex would come back into the room. As quickly as she could, she put the diaries and "secret stuff" box back where she'd found them, keeping a few of the pictures as evidence. As she was putting them into her handbag, she heard the bedroom door handle moving. She jumped back into bed and reached over to turn off the bedside lamp when she saw Rachel's head appear through the gap in the door.

'Are you okay, dear?' she asked.

'Yes.'

'It's just that I couldn't help noticing your light is still on. Can we talk?'

'Er... I'm tired,' she replied.

'I won't keep you long, I just need to let you know a couple of things.' Rachel walked into the room, and sat on the edge of the bed.

Lynne sat up and noticed the time on the alarm clock; it was almost 2 am.

'I've been comforting Alex for the past half hour,' said Rachel. 'He's in a terrible state. He said that you are trying to put the wedding date back a bit, and he's so keen to marry in June. I mean, we've already booked the church and the reception hall. Won't you reconsider?'

Lynne could only gape, incredulous.

'Lynne, dear, I know getting married can be scary. I remember what I felt like the night before I married Alex's father. I was so nervous. But believe me, it was the best day of my life. And what it's taught me is that sometimes the things we're most afraid of are the things that happen for our own good. We just have to be brave.'

Lynne now believed that not only had she gone back in time, but she had ended up in a parallel universe where things happened randomly and made no sense at all. Maybe it was like *Alice in Wonderland* or something?

Sighing, she said, 'Aunty... sorry, I mean, Rachel; what you have to understand is, Alex planned the wedding without even asking me to marry him.'

'Oh, I know that, dear. But he said that as you two are so deeply in love, he was sure you'd agree to the June wedding. In fact, he says you led him to believe that's what you wanted. He's very upset.'

Led him to believe that's what I wanted? Lynne could only stare in disbelief.

'He told me that you'd been hinting about getting engaged, for ages,' continued Rachel. 'He said, just before Christmas, you'd made him stop outside a jewellers, and you'd shown him a diamond ring you liked. So, he went back the next day and bought it. And, he said you always told him that June is the best month to get married.'

A fear gripped Lynne's mind. Could it be possible that this new time she had found herself in, also included a new past? Could it be true that she had been going out with Alex and had agreed all of these things? How could she know? Nothing made sense anymore.

'But, I've only known him a couple of days,' said Lynne.

'That's a bit of an exaggeration! Okay, so you've only been to the house in the past few days, but Alex says you've been dating for years.'

'That's a lie.' It had to be a lie, didn't it? After all, she knew that he had lied before... in her "real" life... But what was *real*? She felt as though she were losing her grip.

'Are you calling my Alex a liar? Do you know how much he loves you? I've just spent over half an hour trying to stop him crying, because he's worried that you're not as serious about him as he is about you.'

'Rachel, Alex is not right in the head.' Lynne got out of bed and took her handbag from the bedside cabinet.

'What did you just say? How can you be so disrespectful? He'd die for you.'

Lynne shivered.

'I hope you're going to apologise, young lady.'

'I have to go home,' she said. 'I'll call Alex during the week.'

'No, you don't. Not so quickly! You'll stay here, and we'll all talk about this in the morning. You owe him an explanation at least.'

Alex's mum left the room.

Lynne stood in the middle of the bedroom, wondering what to do for the best. If she left now, he would be really upset and it could tip him off the edge. As much as she hated him at this moment, she didn't want to be the reason he killed himself. At least in her future life she hadn't played a role, but now she was very, *very* involved.

She really needed to talk to Sandra. Sandra would be a lifeline; a connection back to her sanity. She would be able to confirm that Lynne had absolutely no contact with Alex before the last few days; she could set her mind at ease.

Sand can come over and help explain everything to Rachel. Then, it occurred to her that perhaps Rachel's partner would be at breakfast in the morning, and maybe he wasn't as crazy as the rest of the family. Maybe he would believe her.

The more she thought about it, the more sense it made to stay and get everything out in the open at breakfast.

She texted Sandra: ***Sand, no questions, just get to 123 Firnwell Crescent, Enfield, as early as poss in the morning... I need you! Lynne x***

Chapter Thirty-Eight

Lynne woke up and looked at the alarm clock in the unfamiliar room. For a moment she didn't know where she was, but then "fully awake" mode kicked in, and the disastrous events of last night were now all she could think of.

She stepped out of the bed and realised that she would have to wear the same clothes and underwear she'd had on the evening before; and she didn't have any antiperspirant, face wash, moisturiser, or any of her make-up. Not wanting to borrow anything else from Rachel, she resigned herself to having to turn up to the breakfast meeting feeling less than confident. Sandra hadn't responded to her text, so Lynne feared that she'd have to face the crazy mother and son on her own.

The door handle turned without warning, as seemed to be the custom in this house. *Hasn't anyone in this family heard of knocking a door before entering?*

It was Peter, Rachel's husband. A tall man with grey hair and a beard.

'I thought I heard some movement in here,' he said, looking through the gap in the doorway. 'We're meeting for breakfast in ten minutes. I gather we are discussing the wedding plans. Rachel asked me to tell you.' He closed the door.

As she sat on the edge of the bed, Lynne's mind raged. Peter was Rachel's second husband. Alex's parents had divorced many years ago. Lynne had been holding out hope that as Peter wasn't related to Alex, he might not be as delusional as rest of the household, but now she felt totally on her own again. *They won't believe me; Peter seems as mad as the rest of them.*

Ten minutes later, she found herself walking down the stairs on the way to the kitchen, wishing she'd escaped the night before. She was carrying her handbag and the "secret stuff" box. Seeing her coat hanging on a hook by the front door, she again thought about escaping. Just then, the front door bell sounded, and through the frosty glass of the door she could make out the shape of a woman... *It's Sand! Thank God!*

Rachel walked past Lynne who was now at the bottom of the staircase. Turning to face her, Rachel said, in a curt tone: 'I'll just get the door, it's probably the postman. You go and take a seat; Alex and Peter are waiting.'

Lynne stood in the hallway, watching as Rachel opened the door.

'Hello, can I help you?'

'Hi, I'm here to see Lynne.' Sandra waved at her.

'Come in!' shouted Lynne, relief screaming out from her features. 'It's okay, Rachel, this is a friend of mine.'

'Sorry, but we have some very important matters to discuss,' said Rachel. 'You'll have to come back later.' She was about to close the front door.

'No, wait!' said Lynne. 'Sandra's here to help me. You see, I didn't think you'd believe me if she wasn't here.'

'Believe what?'

'Well, your son has been stalking me, he's obsessed. He is delusional. I haven't seen him for about fifteen years, but he's got all these photos of me.' She held up the "secret stuff" box. 'And he's been keeping diaries,' she continued, 'saying we're going out. It's all in his mind. Sandra can tell you—'

'I'm disgusted! How can you be so rude? You've been sleeping in my house. My son gave up his bed for you last night, and this is how you repay him? With these lies!'

'They're not lies. Sand, help me out. Have I been going out with a guy called Alex for years?'

'Er... Adam. You've been with Adam.'

'There! You see?'

'You're mistaken,' said Rachel, to Sandra. 'My son's name is Alex, not Adam.'

'I'm confused,' said Sandra, frowning.

'Okay, Sand, this is Rachel, one of my mum's old friends. She has a loony son called Alex—'

'I beg your pardon!' screamed Rachel. 'How dare you!'

'Anyway, as I was saying; Alex has taken all these pictures, look.' She handed Sandra the box of photographs.

'That's my son's private box!' said Rachel. 'Alex! Alex! Come out here!' she called.

Alex and Peter entered the hallway.

Sandra was looking through the photos. 'Oh my God! This is when we went for your birthday, last year. Look, there's my arm in the photo!' she said to Lynne. 'Where did you get these?'

'They were in his bedroom. He's been following me, taking photos.'

'You're joking?'

'I wish I was.'

'That's mine!' said Alex, grabbing the box, causing the photographs to spill onto the floor. He sat down and frantically tried to gather them all together.

'Why have you been taking photos of me without my knowledge or consent?' asked Lynne.

'Why are you doing this to me, Lynne?' He looked up at her with tears in his eyes.

Lynne looked at Sandra, as if for assistance.

'I don't really understand what's going on here,' said Sandra. 'All I can say is, I'm Lynne's closest friend and I've never seen Alex before. She was going out with a man called Adam for over three years, but they've recently split up.'

'So, you were seeing my son at the same time then?' said Rachel, glaring at Lynne. 'You are despicable. But now, your sleazy life has been revealed.'

Lynne sighed. 'Tell them, Alex! Tell them that this so-called relationship is all in your head! Go on!'

Alex stood up. 'I love you, Lynne. I'll always love you. I'll go to my grave being in love with you. Why must you humiliate me like this? What have I ever done to you, except be so in love that I could not keep away from you? I have all these pictures, see? Doesn't this prove that I love you?' His tears were falling now.

'Come here, Alex, you're too good for her. Two-timing, untrustworthy... It's best you found out before the wedding.' Rachel took him in her arms.

'He really needs help,' said Lynne, to Peter. 'He's imagined the relationship. You need to get him to a doctor. He's not right in the head. He might kill himself.'

'If he does kill himself, it would be your fault!' was all that Peter said. 'You should be ashamed of yourself, leading him on. He's such a sensitive, kind boy. You should leave now.'

'And don't come back!' said Rachel, grabbing Lynne's coat and throwing it at her as Lynne and Sandra walked out of the door.

'What was all that about?' asked a dazed Sandra as they walked away from the house, towards her car.

'I'm so glad you came, Sand! You're a life saver.'

'I still don't really know what was going on. Who were those people? Why were you there?'

'I went out with Alex last night.'

'Why was he so upset?'

'He thinks he's in love with me, but he's obviously got some sort of mental disorder. I felt sorry for him, because he killed himself—' She stopped, suddenly finding her bearings. 'What I mean is, he threatened to kill himself if I didn't go out with him.'

171

Sandra laughed. 'He did seem a bit intense. He was going on about being in love with you, but I've never seen him before. How long have you two been going out?'

'We've been out twice, only as friends, and he'd already booked our wedding and a reception hall. He freaked out last night when he asked me to marry him and I said no.'

'Oh my God, that's unbelievable.'

'You saw the photos, didn't you? I found them last night. All those pictures... They were taken without my knowledge. He's been stalking me and making diary entries, saying we've been meeting. It's all really weird.'

'You should go to the police,' said Sandra.

'No... no I couldn't.'

'Why? Who knows what he's capable of? He's been stalking you, so he probably knows where you live.'

'He does know where I live.'

'I don't want to scare you, but, he might—'

'He's more of a threat to himself than to me. I'm a bit worried, in case he kills himself.'

'Why would you care? He's a freak.'

'Well, Rachel is one of my mum's oldest friends, and Alex used to go to the same school as me. We used to play together as kids. I even had a crush on him at one point.'

'Oh, is that where he got the impression that you love him?'

'No... He didn't know about my crush.'

'So, what are you going to do?'

'I don't know. I was hoping you might have some ideas.'

Sandra shrugged her shoulders. 'I'm as confused as you are. But look, at least he knows where he stands now, right? You've made it clear that you're not interested in him.'

'Yes, but will he accept that?'

'Maybe you should go to the police. At least then they'd have a record of this.'

'I'm not sure.'

Chapter Thirty-Nine

The next day, Lynne woke up in her own bed, and after the initial daily check of the date on her mobile phone to make sure she knew what month she was in (a habit that had become compulsive), her first thought was of Alex. She couldn't help worrying about him, as if somehow she would now be to blame if he killed himself. *Should I phone him, just to make sure he's okay? But wouldn't that be leading him on?*

Just then there was a knock on the front door. She looked at the clock; it was 8:30 am. *It's probably the postman.* Reluctantly getting out of the warm bed, she pulled on her dressing gown and walked to the door. Looking through the spy-hole, she saw him: Alex. *Oh my God, what is he doing here?* Her first reaction was of fear. He was crazy and delusional; what if he killed *her* instead of killing himself?

He leaned down and called through the letter box: 'Lynne, I know you're in there, please open up, I just want to explain.'

He didn't sound angry. She knew she should be cautious though, so decided to leave the chain on the door when she opened it.

'Er... Alex. It's very early.'

'Sorry, I should have phoned before coming over. Can I come in? I just want to talk. I need to apologise, and I want to thank you for helping me.'

'Helping you?'

He looked at the ground, appearing embarrassed. 'I...' he said, still unable to meet her eyes. 'I have been a fool.' Then, he seemed to find some courage and looked straight at her: 'I was lonely, and I fell in love with you. I suppose my fantasy got a bit mixed up with reality for a while. I just want to say sorry.'

He was looking at her with those gorgeous blue eyes, and tears were threatening to fall from them. He seemed so sad, and so sincere. She wanted to hug him. It had taken some nerve for him to come here and apologise after everything that had happened.

She unhinged the chain and opened the door. 'I suppose you'd appreciate a cup of tea.' She smiled.

He sighed and nodded.

Lynne watched him sitting at the kitchen table, staring out across the misty, morning sky, as she made the tea. He was very handsome, he

173

would make a great model. If only he wasn't so mixed up in the head, she would have given serious thought to going out with him again.

Sitting down opposite him, she poured a cup of tea from the teapot. 'Do you take sugar?'

'Yes, two please, and milk. Thanks.' He was looking around the kitchen, then at his hands, seemingly unable to keep still. Then, he lifted up a carrier bag that he'd brought with him, and put it on the table. Opening it, he took out the "secret stuff" box, and the diaries. 'I want you to have these,' he said. 'I should never have taken these photos. It started off as a bit of fun at first, just because I thought you were really pretty and I wanted a picture of you. I hid behind a bin across the road from where you lived and took a photo. It came out really nice, look.'

The photograph showed her walking out of the communal doors at the flats she used to live in with Steve.

'That's one of my favourites,' he said.

Alarm bells began to ring for Lynne; this was not normal behaviour. She didn't know where to put her eyes as she noticed how Alex seemed to be admiring the photo. Again, her mind boggled as to how he had managed to take so many pictures of her without her knowledge.

'I like photography,' he continued. 'I don't only take pictures of you. I have loads of photos of places I've visited, and of random strangers. Most are on my computer now, as I have a digital camera. I'm thinking of doing a professional photography course.'

'Oh, that's nice,' she said, still slightly on edge and not sure how to react.

'Well, I just wanted to tell you that I'm sorry I took all the photos without your consent. I promise I won't take any more. I also want you to have the diaries. It's about time I face reality and realise that you and I are not going to get married!' He laughed, but his eyes were sad.

Lynne sighed, as if a great burden had been lifted from her shoulders. Smiling at him, sympathetically, she said: 'Thank you, Alex. I was feeling a bit bad after yesterday. I didn't want to hurt your feelings. I'm sure you're a very nice man, and you'll find someone to love.'

'Maybe,' he said. 'I think you've forced me to wake up. Hopefully, now I can try to focus on other things. It's funny, but I can appreciate now, how we can get obsessed with one thing and then that's all that matters, even though there are hundreds of other opportunities floating around every day. We miss them. We just don't see them when we're fixing our sights on an unreachable goal.'

'You sound like a philosopher,' she said, giggling.

Alex smiled at her, and again she sensed the attraction that she always felt when she was with him; but she fought it.

'Well,' he said, seeming to snap out of a trance. 'I must be going. I'll leave you in peace.'

They walked to the front door in silence.

He turned around as he walked out of the door. 'I really wish I hadn't messed it up by being so foolish,' he said. 'Can we still be friends?'

'Um... I...'

'Okay, maybe it's a bit too soon for that,' he said. 'But look, my door is always open. I really didn't mean any harm.'

'Take care of yourself,' she said, smiling, as he walked away. A tear came to her eye and she hoped he would be all right.

Chapter Forty

When Adam returned from his business trip, he woke her from her sleep at 6 am. 'Lynne, wake up, we have to talk.'

'Adam?' She looked at him, through hazy morning eyes. 'What's happened?'

'Nothing, I'm in a rush. I have to be at work in just over an hour, but I wanted to speak to you before I leave. We need to talk about what happened.'

Sitting up, disorientated, unsure whether she was in the past or future, she said: 'Wh... What happened?' hoping her question would provide the answer.

'Come on, Lynne! Don't make this harder than it already is. You turned me down when I asked you to marry me. I thought that was what you wanted.'

She sighed. 'Really, Adam, I've said all I need to say on the matter. You don't love me. This relationship is a farce. Oh! Look at the time! I'm going back to sleep!' She pulled the covers over her head, and lay down on her side.

'I don't know why you've suddenly come to the conclusion that I don't love you. Where has it come from?' He sounded offended.

She sat up in bed, agitated. 'Do you really need me to spell it out to you?' Her anger filtered out into the room. She'd never been a morning person, and she felt very tempted to just come out with it and tell him she knew about his affair.

'I know it's hard with me being away so often, but—'

'Why did you ask me to marry you?' she asked.

'Because we've been together for over three years. I... I thought it was time we... I thought you wanted to get married.' He shrugged.

She would have preferred him to have answered, "Because I love you". His reply just added fuel to her fire, making her all the more certain he was hiding something.

'So, there's no one else in the picture?' She narrowed her eyes.

'What? Are you accusing me of having an affair?'

'Yes!' she shouted. 'And I know all about it!'

'This is ridiculous!' he said. 'Who am I supposed to be having an affair with? I wouldn't have the time to have an affair even if I wanted to!'

'I know, for example,' she continued, angrily, 'that when you are

176

meant to be going away on business, you really go to your lover's house!'

'Wh... What! This is nonsense. Who's been telling you these lies?'

'Oh, don't patronise me, Adam. I followed you. I saw you kissing—' Then she stopped, realising that she'd only seen him kissing Paul in the future.

'Kissing who?' he demanded. 'I am really starting to worry about you. Would you tell me what the hell you are going on about?'

It irritated her that he could stay so calm whilst literally lying through his teeth. Something snapped inside her: 'You're gay, aren't you?' she said, looking at her hands, not wanting to face him. It still hurt her when she remembered seeing him with Paul, and all the pain that went along with him deceiving her for so long about his sexuality.

He didn't answer. 'I'm going to work,' he said, after a silence that contained palpable, unspoken, emotional confusion.

The front door slammed behind him a few moments later, and she began to cry.

⧗

Adam walked out of the flat, feeling paranoid. Somehow, Lynne had guessed; but he'd been trying so hard to forget about his feelings for Paul, and trying to lead a straight life. Was there something about him that pointed to the fact that he is gay? He'd always thought he passed for a heterosexual. None of his friends had ever had any suspicions. *Or have they?* Suddenly, he didn't feel as confident. What if everyone knew, but they were all just humouring him, wanting him to find his own way to come out of the closet about things, not wanting to rush him. Was it that obvious to everyone? All these years, while he had been trying to fool his friends and colleagues, had they secretly all had their doubts? Did they gossip about him? No, it couldn't be true. He'd always had girlfriends. He'd never had a boyfriend. *But how did Lynne guess?*

He reasoned that something must have happened recently to put the idea into her mind; after all, they'd been living together for ages, and she hadn't said anything to him before about any suspicions. As he racked his brains, nothing sprang to mind. *And, what did she mean about seeing me kissing someone?*

He resolved to talk to her about it this evening, after work, and get to the bottom of it. Whatever it was that had caused her to think this, he would put his foot down and act as if it were a preposterous suggestion. His stomach twisted with regret. He hated this life of lies

177

and deceit. Wouldn't it be for the best if he just revealed all to Lynne? She hadn't seemed angry about him being gay, but understandably angry that she'd been led astray. Despite everything, they were good friends, and he felt that he'd be able to explain everything to her. He wanted to be free of this burden. But his mind went back to the last time he'd seen Paul, just before he left for his business trip. Picturing him in his mind, in that silk dressing gown, he remembered how he had wanted to put his arms around him and never let go; but the reality was that Paul had been with someone else that night... A lover. Was it a one-night stand, or was it something more serious? Adam had felt so embarrassed after that meeting that he'd brushed it off when Paul texted him later.

Sorry I couldn't let you in last night, I was a bit er... busy. I felt bad after. Was it something urgent?
He found the text from Paul when he switched on his mobile after the flight to New York. He stared at it for a while, not sure how to respond. His relationship with Lynne was over, and he really wanted to tell Paul that he loved him; but he couldn't get it out of his mind that Paul had been with another man, and he didn't want to face a rejection.
Replying to the text, he wrote: **Don't worry. I'd just had a row with Lynne, and needed a bed for the night, I found a hotel. All is well now**.
When he clicked the send button, he sighed deeply. Lies... More lies to cover up lies... He hated his life.

One thing he was sure of, as he stepped into his car on his way to work, was that things had come to a head. He would have to talk to Lynne later and clear the air. Should he finally come out and leave the lies behind? Or, should he try to get her back—woo her again and marry her—blank out the truth and keep it hidden? His mind was in turmoil.

178

Chapter Forty-One

Lynne lay awake, tears filling her eyes. She didn't know why she was feeling so upset, but she couldn't shake the sense of desolation and loneliness. There was no doubt in her mind that her relationship with Adam was over. She had thought that she'd be relieved to finally send him packing, but somehow, she couldn't feel happy about it. It just brought back all the memories of the future life she had led; the hope she'd had on her wedding day, and the despair in finding out that he'd lied to her. Everything was lost.

Despondency encircling her, she forced herself out of bed and walked through the hall. As she passed the office room, she was reminded of the wasted time she had spent in there filling out job applications to no avail in her other life. Her mind just seemed to be drifting from one negative thought to another. Then, as she wondered whether she should try applying for some jobs she hadn't tried before, to take a positive step to get her life back on track, the words resounded in her mind: *back on track*. She remembered she had joined a social networking site called *getbackontrack.com*, in her previous life, trying to connect with people who could help her find a job. One man she'd met on there, Woody, had flirted with her. He'd come across as a nice man, but she'd been engaged to Adam. Well, here she was, newly single, and really needing a diversion, something to take her mind off everything. A sprig of hope spurring her on, she walked into the office and switched on the computer.

Lynne logged onto *getbackontrack.com,* in anticipation, but her details were not recognised. She hadn't set up the account yet in this time dimension. So, she registered with the site and looked up Woody's details. She added him as a friend, and smiled to herself. At least now she would have something to do, to distract from the mess her life had become. She made a mental note to come back later and check the website.

Making her way to the kitchen to get some breakfast, her mood began to lighten. Her mobile phone sounded from the bedroom, alerting her that she had missed a call. Turning around, she walked into the bedroom and saw the phone lying on the bedside cabinet. The caller display showed that Sandra had called.

In two minds as to whether she should phone back, she twirled the phone around in her hands. Every time she met Sandra recently, she'd been feeling increasingly odd. She really wanted to tell her everything about her current situation, but was worried that Sandra would have a hard time believing her. Would it jeopardise their friendship, if she told her everything? Theirs had always been a very open and candid relationship; they never kept secrets from each other, so this didn't feel right.

She sighed and dialled her number. 'Hi, Sand, I think I missed your call?'

'Yeah, I wanted to check up on you and make sure you're okay. I've been a bit busy since we last saw each other at that loony's house.'

'Yeah, I'm fine. I haven't heard anything more from him.' She bit her lip; lying seemed to have become a habit. Why hadn't she just told Sandra that Alex had come to see her and apologised?

'Great! Listen,' Sandra continued. 'I was thinking of going to the gym. Do you want to join me? It's just that we're in February, and my new year's resolutions about keeping fit are already down the pan.'

Lynne remembered Sandra's disastrous relationship with Matt, and thought she should really try to dissuade her from going to the gym. 'Um... gyms are expensive, aren't they?'

'Yeah, but they're worth it. I really need to shift some weight. And, on the plus side, we might get to meet some men. Er... how are things with you and Adam? Have you patched things up?'

'There's nothing to patch up. It's over.'

'Well, all the more reason for you to get out there.'

'I might have met someone,' said Lynne, thinking of Woody.

'Oh! You sly fox! Who?'

'Just someone I met online.'

'I didn't know you were dating on the Internet.'

'Well, it's not a dating site; it's a site for people who are looking for work.'

'But you've got a job.'

'Um... didn't I tell you? I've just been made redundant.'

'Oh, I'm sorry to hear that. It's happening everywhere. They're letting people go at my work, too. If you need any help with the job search, let me know.'

'I'm going to sign up at the job centre next week. It's really depressing.' Lynne recalled how much she hated that place. She was tempted not to bother claiming; but she would need the benefits now—especially as she was splitting from Adam, and couldn't rely on *his* wage anymore.

'So, tell me more about this online chappy,' said Sandra.

'It's nothing serious. We just get on really well.'

'You have to be careful about people you meet online. Make sure you find out as much as you can about him, and don't meet him on your own.'

'I think I'm old enough and ugly enough to look after myself, thanks.'

'Ha, ha. You know what I mean.'

'Yeah, thanks. Don't worry, I'll be careful.'

'So, do you think you'll join up to a gym with me?'

'No, sorry, Sand. I actually think you should maybe buy a DVD and do some exercises at home; it'd be a lot cheaper. You know how many people buy membership for gyms, but never use them,' she said, recalling the future conversation she'd had with Sandra.

'No, I'm on a mission to find a man, and gyms are supposed to be great places to meet them. Besides, I already bought annual membership in January as part of my new year's resolutions, and I was feeling guilty today because I've only been there once this year, and that was to sign up for the membership!'

Lynne thought of Matt again, and Jason. She knew she'd be kidding herself if she didn't admit that she wanted to see Jason again. But thinking about it, she realised that as she wasn't married this time, Jason wouldn't be interested in her.

'Well, I'd better go,' said Sandra, snapping her out of her reverie. 'Glad to hear that your stalker isn't bothering you anymore.'

'Yeah, okay, bye, Sand.' Lynne was left with the feeling that she would somehow have to tell Sandra about the future, if only to save her the heartache over Matt. But she wasn't sure she could do it. This future knowledge had given her so much extra responsibility. What if this new life she found herself in wasn't the same as the old one? What if Sandra and Matt would make a perfect couple in this life? Maybe his old flame wouldn't return. It might be like a parallel universe where things happened differently. She didn't want to have to make decisions for other people's lives. It would be safer to keep quiet and just be there for Sandra if she was needed.

Later that day, Lynne ventured into the office room, hoping to find a message from Woody. As expected, he had replied:

Hi, thanks for the friend request. I'm looking for work as a mechanic; be sure to let me know if you hear of any vacancies. What line of work are you in? I'll try to help out as much as I can.

She remembered finding that message from him before; everything was déjà vu in this life.

Hi Woody, nice to meet you. I'm looking for secretarial

work. Any help you could provide would be great.

She decided to leave it at that; that was the same message she had sent in her future/previous existence, so it should be enough. Her hopes of getting a relationship out of this were starting to wane; after all, she didn't really know anything about Woody. They'd been getting on well when they'd chatted online before; but was she setting herself up for disappointment? He'd flirted a bit with her on Valentine's Day, but that was about it. He could be married with kids, for all she knew.

Her eyes were drawn to the calendar above the desk: Valentine's Day was only a few days away. Just as that thought entered her mind, she heard the front door of the apartment close; Adam had returned from work. Some part of her wanted things to go back to how they were before the time switch. She almost wished that she'd agreed to marry Adam, and (as ridiculous as it seemed) she felt like going to greet him, and apologising for everything, in the hope that he'd take her back. It would be easier to bear than the upheaval she was anticipating. The fear caused by being lost in this alien world made her want to grab hold of anything familiar. This all seemed like some horrendously extended nightmare, where she was privy to certain information unknown to others, and unable to tell anyone for fear they would think her deranged or unstable. She felt trapped, and she felt like screaming; but she doubted that anyone would hear her screams.

⧗

Adam walked into the office room. He looked a bit cagey, not able to keep eye contact with her, as he said: 'Hi, I thought we should talk about this morning.'

She quickly logged off the website, feeling strangely guilty that she'd been hoping to get to know Woody with a view to a possible relationship. 'Er... yes, okay,' she said, standing up.

'I could cook some pasta for us, and we'll chat. I've brought some wine,' he said.

'*You* are going to cook?' Surprise was evident in her voice. He'd never before offered to cook for her.

'Yes, I've been thinking about our relationship, and I realise that I haven't been paying you enough attention. We haven't been spending enough time together. That's the real problem. We can get through this, Lynne. I...' He hesitated. 'I love you,' he said eventually, his eyes closed.

She had no way of knowing whether he'd really meant it. Why had he closed his eyes when he said it? Could it be because he was lying and couldn't look her in the eye, or was it because his feelings were so deep? Her mind kept going back to the kiss she had witnessed between Adam and Paul, but another part of her was saying: *That was in the other lifetime; things might be different now, maybe he's not gay this time.* She desperately wanted to believe him, wanted them to start over again. Maybe this going back in time was giving her another chance, and maybe she could make the rules this time.

She came out of her daydream to find that Adam had already left the room and was whistling a tune in the kitchen as he prepared dinner. Taking a deep breath, she walked out into the passageway and made her way slowly to the kitchen.

Adam was standing next to the cooker, wearing her apron; the one with the blue and white stripes, lacy edging, and an embroidered bunch of flowers on the pocket. She pushed away the thoughts that were entering her mind telling her that he looked effeminate wearing it. *It's just an apron*, she thought, *we don't own any other aprons; he has to wear an apron to cook.*

In the window behind him, the view of the setting sun was magnificent. She could only see the back of his head. He was still whistling a tune she didn't recognise, and seemed relaxed as he broke the spaghetti into the boiling water and turned towards the fridge.

As he turned, he noticed her standing at the door. 'Oh, Lynne, I didn't know you were there.' He made a face as if he had been startled.

'Sorry,' she said.

'I'm making spaghetti, with a garlic and prawn sauce,' he said, smiling at her.

'Great. Sounds lovely.'

Then, he said: 'You look gorgeous tonight, by the way.'

Her mind recalled the spaghetti bolognese evening, in her future life, when they'd had an argument after he kept paying her compliments. Would tonight end the same way?

'Thank you,' she said, in a half-whisper.

The next thing she knew, he had his arms around her and was kissing her at length.

Left flustered after being released from his hold, she absentmindedly wiped her mouth with the back of her hand as if rubbing away his kiss. Instantly, she regretted doing this, realising that he was still looking at her. His eyes lost their brightness for a moment. She smiled at him in an attempt to make up for unintentionally offending him. There was a look of relief in his eyes.

He continued cooking. With his back to her, as he stood at the cooker, he said, 'I think we need to talk about the misunderstandings and miscommunication lately. I was very hurt when you accused me of having an affair, and when you said that I—' He stopped, mid flow, and didn't say anything else for a couple of minutes. Then, he turned to face her. His eyes met hers: 'One thing I'm confused about is, you said you followed me and saw me kiss someone. I really need to know why you said that. We both know it's not true.'

Lynne looked at the floor, the vision of Adam kissing Paul as clear as day in her mind's eye. But she knew that had happened in a different lifetime; she couldn't accuse him of it now. Looking back at him, she saw that he appeared baffled. He must be telling the truth; he couldn't be acting.

She wasn't sure what to say. It didn't feel right just to say sorry; and she couldn't tell him anything about the future life, or seeing him with Paul. Her mind was full of muddled thoughts.

'Um...' she began. 'I just said that to try to get you to confess. I thought you were having an affair.' She stared at her hands as she spoke.

'Hmm...' He turned back towards the bench and continued chopping some garlic. 'Well, I'm not having an affair. All these misunderstandings are all my fault. I'm sorry. I intend to put things right.'

With his back to her, she couldn't see his expression. It was frustrating not being able to tell if he appeared sincere when he spoke. With all her heart, she dearly wanted to believe him.

'Adam?' she said, waiting; wanting him to turn to face her. But he remained totally engrossed in chopping an onion. Sighing, she continued, 'I have been feeling a bit unloved recently. I want to be able to trust you; but when you go away for weeks on end and then never want to go out with me, or even touch me, it can get a bit lonely.'

He turned to face her briefly. 'Sorry,' he said. 'As I say, things will change. I promise.' He continued with his cooking.

They spent a very pleasant evening with good food, nice wine, and polite conversation. In fact, Lynne couldn't remember the last time they'd spent such an enjoyable time together. That night, they made love, and Adam was very passionate, telling her repeatedly that he loved her and from now on things would be different. He seemed determined to make their relationship work.

Lynne lay in bed that night, listening to Adam's quiet snoring, and surprised herself by pondering their relationship and thinking: *If he were to wake up now and ask me to marry him again, I'd say 'yes', without a moments hesitation.*

Chapter Forty-Two

The next few days were a blur for Lynne. She kept questioning her conscience. Why was she back with Adam? She had witnessed him, first hand, kissing Paul; betraying her... But another part of her wanted to believe that now she had gone back in time, Adam wouldn't be gay anymore.

Adam was suddenly very attentive; he had changed. Nothing was too big or too small for him to do for her. She only had to ask him, and he'd do it. He'd taken a few days off work so they could spend time together. They enjoyed a romantic day in London, taking a trip on the London Eye at dusk. They watched the sun set over the city, and the view was beautiful. Lynne had been secretly hoping that he would propose to her. She found herself willing him to do it when they got to the top of the London Eye. But he didn't. He did give her a long, lingering kiss, though, and a group of tourists had stared at them afterwards. Lynne was sure she'd seen a look of envy in some of their eyes. She loved being part of a couple with Adam; tall, strong, handsome, Adam. Everything seemed perfect, except for the constant nagging at the back of her mind replaying the kiss between Adam and Paul and asking her whether she was crazy.

As much as she wanted to relax and enjoy this special time with Adam, the memory of that kiss remained a blot on the landscape. If only the going back in time could have erased it. Perhaps he was driven into Paul's arms before because their relationship wasn't going well? If she could just keep his interest, maybe he would stay with her, and everything would be okay. But her conscience kept telling her otherwise. She had a feeling of doom and gloom creeping up on her when she least expected it.

The day after their trip to the London Eye, they took the Eurostar to Paris. Walking hand in hand with Adam around the French capital, Lynne couldn't help the wide grin on her face. *Why can't it always be like this?* she thought. Then: *Maybe it can; maybe Adam has really changed...* But that doubt crept in again. *What about Paul?*

She made the decision to talk to him about her concerns, knowing that if she didn't she would never have any peace of mind.

As they sat in a lovely, little, traditional French restaurant that evening, Adam seemed engrossed by the view outside the window. She turned to see what he was looking at, and took in the lovely old-fashioned street lighting and the clear night sky; stars twinkling. There were fashionably dressed people rushing by towards the metro at the end of the working day. Turning back to Adam, she noticed that his eyes had a far away look in them, as if he was lost in thought. In this relaxed and peaceful setting, it felt like the right time to air her worries.

'Adam,' she said, softly.

He turned towards her as if she had roused him from a dream. His eyes were still distant.

'I need to ask you something,' she continued, 'and I want a straight answer. We have to be able to trust each other if we want this relationship to work.'

'Okay,' he said, smiling through a stiff face; appearing nervous.

'Are you seeing someone else?' she asked.

His face relaxed then, as if she had not asked what he'd feared she would.

'Of course not,' he said, brushing it aside.

'And you're telling me the truth? Because if I find out that you're lying...' She hesitated, not quite knowing what her threat should be; after all, she had already discovered him with Paul in their future relationship, and what had she done? She'd fallen back into his arms as if she couldn't live without him. She shrank back in her seat, almost ashamed of herself. Why couldn't she just walk away, leave him, and find someone she could trust? That way she could live her life without always looking over her shoulder.

'I'm telling you the truth,' he said, taking her hand from across the table and holding it. 'I love you, Lynne.'

He appeared sincere.

Reaching into his jacket pocket with his free hand, he brought out a small box. The box with her engagement ring in... She recognised it immediately.

She sighed deeply.

Smiling, he released her hand and opened the box, revealing the diamond ring. She felt brave enough to look at it this time. Perhaps things would turn out all right, after all? The shining jewel looked new and sparkling, not lacklustre as it had been when she'd worn it day in day out. It was just as she remembered when he'd first proposed: it was beautiful.

'I was going to wait until we went up the Eiffel Tower, to ask you, but somehow this restaurant seems ideal; it's so cosy and romantic. Will you marry me?' he asked.

As she gazed into his eyes for a moment, she couldn't help recalling the dream she'd had the night before returning to January. The man in her dream had said she was being given the chance to reject Adam's proposal. She remembered how she'd felt after seeing Adam kissing Paul; she'd wished for a chance to go back to when they'd first met and to walk right past him. So why was she now so uncertain?

She smiled at him, trying to silence her nagging doubts. *This time it will be different,* she thought. *This is my chance to make it work between us.*

The smile on his face slowly faded as he waited for her answer. He was still holding out the small box towards her.

'Er... Adam, can I think about it for a while?' She studied the checkered tablecloth, which she noticed was slightly frayed at the edges. She couldn't meet his gaze. All the events of the past few weeks were running through her mind.

He frowned and stared at the ring for a few moments, glumly. 'Of course,' he said eventually, closing the box and placing it back in his pocket.

The sound of the box closing resonated in her mind, like the closing of a door; a door that could have led the way to their future happiness. A sense of regret followed, with some anxiety in tow.

She watched him as he sipped his wine and finished his meal. There was no more conversation that evening in the restaurant, just silence. Had a moment to salvage her relationship just passed her by, or had she had a lucky escape? A sadness took hold of her and could not be shaken.

They next day, they returned to London in semi-silence; a reminder to her that their relationship was not perfect. As the Eurostar train took them home, she pondered her situation. Her thoughts were of frustration, loneliness, and uncertainty. She had still not answered his question, but she knew that she would not agree to marry him; she could not go back to living a life with someone whose heart was obviously elsewhere.

Chapter Forty-Three

The day after their return from Paris was Valentine's Day. Their romantic interlude had been spoilt by him proposing to her, and her procrastination. Ever since her non-reply to his proposal, there had been an icy distance between them. He seemed to be waiting for a "yes" from her before he would talk to her again, as if the news that she needed time to think confirmed that she did not love him. He didn't mention Valentine's Day at all, leaving the flat for work that morning without so much as a good-bye. Lynne sat up in bed at 8 am and sighed. She knew that he was offended by her putting off an answer to his proposal, but she could not be rushed into a decision. Although on the train ride home she'd been sure her answer would be "No", there was still that other part of her that wanted to believe their relationship could work. Her mind felt tangled and she wanted to find out more before committing herself; if indeed she would commit herself.

She stepped out of bed into her slippers and went into the en suite to take a shower. As she finished dressing, she heard the post arrive. Walking into the hallway, she wondered whether Adam had sent her a Valentine's card. She hadn't received one from him this year, in the other time dimension. He had forgotten all about Valentine's Day back then, but had apologised profusely and promised to take her out to dinner to make up for it. He never did. She was holding out hope that things might be different the second time around.

As she turned the corner from the hallway into the lounge, she saw the post lying on the doormat. There was just one item: a dark red envelope, which looked like a Valentine's card. A smile played on her lips, as she recalled how attentive Adam had been just a few days ago, before his proposal. She walked over and picked up the envelope. Turning it over, she noticed the handwriting. It wasn't Adam's writing. Her mind was foggy as she tried to guess who could have sent it. Opening the envelope hesitantly, she found a pretty card with a heart on the front, bearing the words 'I love you'. She opened the card and read it, her eyes widening as she did so:

'Darling Lynne, I think about you all the time, I have always loved you. You are beautiful. I will always love you. I can't

wait until I see you again. Please say you will be my Valentine.
I will come to your flat tonight at 8 pm and take you to dinner.
I've booked the restaurant. See you soon, my love.
Yours for ever, Alex XXX'

She was left feeling astounded. There was no logical reason for this. Turning the envelope over again, she noticed that it didn't have a stamp on it, so it must have been hand delivered. A feeling of dread invaded her mind as she began to imagine Alex loitering outside at this very moment. Panic and fear began to replace her previously relaxed mood. It was irrational that she should receive this card now. When they'd last spoken, not so long ago, he'd been so apologetic. Since then, she had allowed herself to believe that his infatuation had been nipped in the bud, but this card proved her wrong. He didn't seem to be someone in control of his mental faculties. He had killed himself in the other lifetime, so he was capable of doing that again. The more contact she had with him, the more nervous she became that he could perhaps turn violent towards her.

She found herself pacing the living room as she mulled things over. The card said that he would be coming to take her to dinner tonight! It was like hitting a dead end. What else could she say to Alex to make him see sense?

Deciding that she needed to eat something to help her think more clearly, she walked into the kitchen to make breakfast. Sitting at the table, eating her boiled egg and toast, she stared out at the grey skies of London and considered her options. Perhaps she should introduce Alex to someone else; fix him up on a date, so he could concentrate his thoughts on another person. But who did she hate enough to send on a date with Alex? He was obviously not the full ticket. She would hesitate in sending her worst enemy on a date with him.

She noticed the Valentine's card again, lying on the bench next to the cooker where she had left it when she walked in.

Her mind went back to happier times, when as children she and Alex played together. He had shown no signs of turning into an obsessive stalker back then. She had never seen him with a girlfriend when they were growing up, but he had looked pretty geeky, so she wasn't surprised. Her mother had said something about him having a girlfriend when Lynne was living with Steve, but she couldn't be sure if her memory served her correctly.

After breakfast, she washed up the dishes in a daydream, wondering how she was going to get around this problem. Suddenly an idea came to her from out of nowhere: *I'll tell Alex we'll just be friends. Maybe if I tell him we can be friends, and draw a line somewhere, I can help him? He admitted he had a problem separating reality and fantasy, when we last spoke. If we become friends, maybe I can convince him to seek professional help?* She wasn't sure it would work, but she didn't have any other options.

She found her mobile phone and called Alex's number.

'Hi, Lynne!' he said, excitedly, before she had a chance to say anything. 'I knew you'd call. Happy Valentine's Day! Do you like the card?'

'Alex, we need to talk,' she said.

'Of course we do, that's why I booked a lovely restaurant in the city. I know you like it because you've been there a few times. "*The Floating Garden*".'

'Alex, remember when we last met—'

'Of course I do; I never forget our meetings,' he said cheerily, before she had a chance to finish.

'I have decided we can be friends, but that's all,' she said.

'Didn't you like the card?' He sounded disappointed.

'We can be friends, Alex. If things were different, who knows? But I'm not free to be your girlfriend.'

'But I love you.'

'You have to understand, I'm already in a relationship.'

'Your friend said you'd split up from your boyfriend. Your friend, Sandra, when she was at my house... remember? She said you'd been seeing someone called Adam, but you split up.'

'Um... We're back together.'

'I love you more than he ever could, Lynne.'

She realised she was not getting through to him, and began to regret phoning. Agitated, she worried that she was now making things worse. 'I'll always be your friend.' She winced as she said it.

'Meet me tonight, Lynne. I'll pick you up at eight. We'll talk.'

'I can't meet you tonight; it's Valentine's Day and I'm going out with my boyfriend. Sorry.'

'Don't go out with him; go out with me. I asked you to marry me, Lynne. I'm the one who loves you, not him.'

'Alex—'

'Admit it, Lynne, it's me you love. That's why you called me now, isn't it? On Valentine's Day of all days. It's obvious you feel the same way about me as I do about you. You can't keep away from me. I feel the same about you. We can be together. For ever. I've already booked the church for the 6th of June.'

That date made her shudder; the date she'd married Adam in her previous life.

'I'll come to get you, Lynne, and we'll spend the day together. You don't have to deny your feelings anymore. I'm at home. I can be there in ten minutes. I'll get in the car now.'

'Alex, please. I can't marry you. I thought you understood that the last time we spoke.'

'I know you were just trying to be loyal to Adam. But Adam doesn't love you. I'm on my way to my car right now. I can't wait to see you again. Forget Adam. I'm the one who loves you. *He* hasn't asked you to marry him.'

'He has asked me—' Immediately, she regretted her words and wished she could retract them. For a brief moment, she'd panicked, imagining Alex coming to the flat. She'd felt backed into a corner, and the words had come out of her mouth before she had time to think it through. She put a hand over her mouth.

'He's asked you? To marry him?'

'Yes, but I—'

'You're a bitch,' he said, bluntly. 'You led me on, and now you're engaged to be married to someone else!'

'No, I'm—'

The line went dead.

'I'm not engaged to Adam,' she said, anxiously, to the dial tone. But, Alex had gone, it was too late for him to hear her.

Fear gripped her. She had to find him; he sounded so upset. *He might kill himself now!* Instead of avoiding it, she may have actually brought the time of his death forward. Trying to concentrate on her breathing, which was coming in short sharp gasps, she ran into the bedroom and grabbed her handbag. Her throat felt tight. Pulling her coat from the hook on the back of the front door on her way out, she almost tore the collar. She ran down the long flights of stairs to her car, not having the patience to wait for the lift. She almost knocked an old lady over in her haste. 'I'm so sorry,' she shouted behind her; she had no time to lose.

Out of breath when she got to her car, she had to sit in the driver's seat for a few minutes before setting off. The atmosphere had a density to it, as if the world was closing in on her. Winding down the window to get some air, she felt light-headed and feared she would faint; but she knew she had to be strong and continue on her mission. A picture entered her mind of Alex drinking a bottle of bleach. Pushing it from her mind, she tried to think positively: *I'll go to his house and talk to him; he'll listen, and he'll see sense.*

The traffic was horrendous. There were road works at the end of her street, and temporary traffic lights. The time changed on the clock in

191

her car: minute after minute. She waited, stuck in a queue, trying to keep hopeful that she would be meeting with Alex soon, and that he would be okay. As she sat in the unmoving traffic, she dialled his mobile number. It rang and rang, and went onto voicemail. 'Alex, hi, it's Lynne. I'm coming to see you. We'll talk. Call me back when you get this message.'

Almost twenty minutes later, she reached the high road leading to Alex's family home. She could hear the sirens as she turned into the crescent. *No! Please God, No!* her mind screamed. Everything moved in slow motion as she pulled up in her car a short distance away from the ambulance that was parked outside his house. She saw his mother, her hair unkempt, still in her dressing gown, looking frantic with worry. Rachel called out to the paramedics: 'Is he going to be all right?'

The stretcher contained a lifeless body, an oxygen mask on his face: Alex. She was too late. He had already done it; he had already killed himself.

All she could do was stare at the ambulance as it pulled away, and watch it as it turned the corner. Her attention then turned to Rachel, who stood like a statue, her back to Lynne, facing in the direction of the ambulance's path. Lynne suddenly realised that now the ambulance had gone, her car was very exposed. Rachel would only have to turn around and she would see her. It was too late to try to turn the car around, as that would cause a commotion and attract her attention. Lynne decided to hide in the car. Taking off her seat belt, she leaned down low so that she could not be seen through the windscreen. She stayed there in an uncomfortable crouched position for about five minutes, and then tried to peek over the steering wheel to check if Rachel had gone indoors.

When she sat up, she saw Peter leading Rachel out of the house; they were walking towards where her car was parked. Lynne gasped and crouched down again, praying they hadn't noticed her.

Shortly, she heard the sound of an engine starting up just behind her. When she was sure the car had driven past, she sat up and saw it disappearing in the direction the ambulance had taken. It was the same car that Alex had once driven her in.

Lynne sighed with relief that they had not spotted her, but then she felt an ambush of guilt as the image of Rachel walking to her car flashed into her mind: her coat was thrown haphazardly over her shoulders, revealing that she was still wearing her dressing gown underneath; her face looked harrowed. Peter had been practically keeping her upright as he led her with his arm around her. Rachel was now on her way to the hospital to find out her son had killed himself.

192

Lynne remembered the last words Alex had said to her. He thought she was engaged to Adam, and that had been enough to set him on his path to self destruction. *It's all my fault.*

Feeling torn, she wanted to go to the hospital to see Alex. Perhaps if he was still alive and she showed some interest in him, it would give him the will to continue living. But she knew that if she turned up at the hospital she would be met by Rachel and Peter, who would surely blame her for all of this.

She turned the car around and drove home. As she did so, she thought of everything that had happened since her strange return to the past. It made her feel small and insignificant. There was obviously a greater plan that could not be changed. Alex had been meant to die, and there was nothing that she or anyone else would have been able to do about it. In a funny way this made her feel better about it; she could not really have been to blame if it was fated or written in the stars. But even as she thought this, she could not shake the blackness that enveloped her when she wondered how different things would be if she'd just agreed to meet Alex. *It's all my fault*, she thought again, as the tears ran down her face.

Chapter Forty-Four

The phone call came the next morning at 10 am. Lynne's mum sounded very distressed.

'Darling, I have some bad news. Are you sitting down?'

Lynne braced herself, even though she already knew what her mother would say. She had spent half the sleepless night before, trying in vain to convince herself that he could still be alive; after all, he wasn't supposed to die until June. And, she kept telling herself that he hadn't killed himself until the wedding the last time, and he'd known she was engaged when his mother received the wedding invitation; so there was a chance that he had survived. She prayed for a little more time to try to help him. But her mind kept replaying the scene of his lifeless body on the stretcher.

'What is it, Mum?' she asked with a voice that betrayed her.

'Alex died yesterday.'

The tears came quickly; she could not hold the grief inside.

'Oh, darling. Don't cry,' said her mother, her own voice breaking with emotion. 'You two were so close. You must be devastated.'

Lynne took a tissue and tried to compose herself. 'It's really sad,' she said, her mind racing with negative thoughts telling her that she was the one to blame. She had known he was vulnerable, and yet she had hurt him badly with words that may as well have been daggers.

'The funeral is on Tuesday,' said her mum, softly.

'No, I can't go to the funeral,' she replied, speaking her thoughts as they came. How could she face Rachel and Peter?

'Oh, but you must, Lynne. I know it's hard for you, but I'll be there with you. And, Rachel is so distraught, she'll need all her friends and family around her.'

'Mum, I won't be attending. Sorry. I'll send a card and a wreath, but I can't go there. I already have plans.'

'Cancel your plans, and come to the funeral. You should be there. Rachel told me that you and Alex were planning to marry. I thought you were still with Adam. If I'm being honest, I never really liked that Adam; there was something not quite right about him.'

Lynne's brow furrowed. Her mother had always spoken highly of Adam, sometimes making her squirm with how many good things she said about him. 'I—'

'Why don't you keep me updated, Lynne?' continued her mother,

194

cutting her off. 'Do you know how embarrassing it was for me to pretend that I knew about you and Alex? You know, Rachel and I always said you'd marry when you were children.'

'This is getting ridiculous,' Lynne huffed. The need to cry had long since left her. 'I was never going to marry Alex.'

'But Rachel said—'

'You can't believe anything Rachel says.'

'But... you were dating him; Rachel said you were meant to be meeting up for Valentine's Day. She found your message on his mobile phone.'

'Mum, there was never anything between me and Alex! He was delusional.'

'Oh my, don't speak ill of the dead, Lynne, dear.'

'But you have to believe me, Mum, because now Rachel is going to think I'm to blame for Alex killing himself.'

'Killing himself? What? He didn't kill himself.'

'That's just what she wants you to believe. But he killed himself, because he thought I was engaged to Adam.'

'Engaged to Adam? Oh, I can't keep up with you,' said her mother, sounding suddenly cheerful. 'Well, I must say, it's about time he put a ring on your finger.'

'Um, a minute ago, you were saying you don't like Adam.'

'That when I thought he was just using you. You've been living together for so long, and there's never been any mention of marriage. I'm pleased to hear he has proposed; he's a good man. Better than that Steve you were seeing.'

'Mum, we're not engaged.'

'Well, why did you say—'

'What I said was: Alex *thought* I was engaged to Adam. That's why he killed himself.'

'Darling, Alex died in an accident. He didn't kill himself. He went onto the roof to adjust the TV aerial, and he fell off. He slipped. Rachel is beside herself because she was the one who was harassing him for weeks to get the aerial fixed.'

Lynne placed a hand over her mouth, stunned into silence. Could it be true that Alex didn't kill himself this time? Had it really been an accident?

'So, you see, dear, Rachel wants you at the funeral. She specifically asked if you would come. She blames herself for his death.'

Chapter Forty-Five

The day of the funeral was cold and windy. Lynne pulled her coat closer to her as she walked along the gravel path leading to the church steps. There were many people gathered outside, none of whom she recognised. Her parents were not outside; she wondered whether they were already in the church.

The row she'd had with Adam the night before was fresh in her mind; another worry to add to her list of worries...

'Oh, you're home early,' said Lynne, as Adam walked into the kitchen holding a bottle of wine.

'Yes,' he said, smiling.

She carried on stirring the sauce she had prepared for her oven baked pasta dish.

'I've brought some wine. I would like to talk tonight; we have to discuss the future. I'm leaving for Paris in a couple of days; I'll be away for two weeks. I don't want this hanging between us. I realise I've been cold towards you lately, but it's only because I feel a bit put out that you still haven't given me your answer.'

Lynne raised her eyebrows in surprise. He hadn't mentioned anything about the proposal since they'd got back from Paris, over a week ago. Since then, their relationship had been back in the distant and uncommunicative phase that was all too familiar. They'd hardly said two words to each other since returning from France, and she'd assumed that he knew what her reply would be.

She coughed, unsure how to respond to him.

'What are you cooking?' he asked. 'It smells delightful.'

'It's a pasta bake; I got the recipe from a pack of macaroni.'

'Great,' he said.

He sat at the kitchen table and began to whistle a tune.

'It'll be about half an hour,' she said, placing the baking dish in the oven, hoping he would leave the room and go and watch television. She was in no mood to make conversation with him today. All she could think about was Alex's funeral, which she would be attending tomorrow. The thought of having to see Rachel and Peter again, made her nervous. Adam didn't know anything about Alex, and it wasn't something she felt able to talk to him about.

'So,' he said. 'Shall we have a glass of wine before dinner?'

Lynne turned to look at him, and saw him stand up and approach the cutlery drawer. He took out the corkscrew and began to open the bottle of wine.

She walked over to the cupboard above the washing-machine and took out two wine glasses, hopeful that the wine might ease her worries and maybe make it easier to sit through a conversation with Adam.

He filled a glass and passed it to her.

'Thanks,' she said, taking a sip of the red wine.

'You look tired, Lynne.'

'I'm okay,' she said.

'How is work?'

She realised that she hadn't even told him she'd been made redundant. 'Um... it's okay,' she said, seeing no need to tell him anything; after all, their relationship was all but over.

'This recession is really biting,' he commented. 'We have very little new work coming in. But I suppose the plus side to that is, I was able to take a couple of days off to spend with you last week. It was nice.' He reached an arm towards her. 'It made me realise how much fun we have together,' he said, stroking her arm.

As she forced a smile at him, she could feel a headache coming on. Red wine sometimes had that effect on her. Drinking it on an empty stomach hadn't been a good idea.

'So, tell me, have you made a decision yet?' He looked her in the eyes. 'About us.'

Sighing, she replied: 'Sorry, Adam, I've had a lot on my mind since we got back from Paris. An old friend died last week, a boy I once knew.' As she said it, she could feel the tears form in her eyes.

'Oh, I'm sorry to hear that.' Adam appeared sincere.

'It's his funeral tomorrow. I haven't been able to think about anything else.'

Adam nodded. He stood there for a few moments, looking sympathetic, then he turned and left the kitchen. The television sounded from the living room a moment later, and the rest of the evening was spent in silence. Lynne ate her dinner in the kitchen while Adam sat with a lap tray on the sofa watching the news channel.

After dinner, she decided to go to bed early. Not having had much sleep since Alex's death, she knew she would need all her wits about her at the funeral. Her mother had said that Rachel blamed herself for Alex's death, but there was still a little voice in Lynne's head telling her that Rachel would find a way to implicate her. There was something she couldn't trust about that woman.

As Lynne walked out of the kitchen, Adam turned to face her. By now, he had finished off the rest of the bottle of wine, and he appeared

197

flushed. 'Lynne, darling, join me on the sofa,' he said, patting the space on the sofa next to him.

Her mind couldn't help but recall the spaghetti bolognese evening, when in their future life he had called her "darling" and it had all ended in misery.

'I think I'll go to bed,' she said.

'Oh, come on,' he said, not so patiently now. 'You are avoiding me, aren't you?'

'Me avoiding you? I'm not the one who doesn't even try to communicate. You've been sulking since we got back from Paris.'

'Yes,' he said, standing up unsteadily, quite obviously drunk. 'That's because you are supposed to be in love with me, but when I ask you to marry me you say you need to think about it. I've tried,' he said, walking towards her. 'I've tried everything I can think of, but it's not enough for you, is it?' He was standing in front of her now, his sour breath against her face. 'What do I have to do?'

'Sorry, Adam, I can't talk about this now. I have to go to a funeral tomorrow.'

'Whose funeral? Have I ever met him?'

'No. I used to know him when I was young. We went to school together. His mum and my mum are friends.'

'So, it's not as if you knew him recently. Don't tell me you're mourning his death, because I don't believe you. When was the last time you saw him?'

'About two weeks ago.'

'Oh, okay.' For a moment, he was lost for words, then he said: 'Look, you need to give me an answer, I won't wait for ever. If you love me then say "Yes" and we'll get married.'

'Why do we have to rush into this?'

'It's been over three years, Lynne. You either want to marry me, or you don't.'

'The question is, can I trust you?' she replied, not thinking.

'Oh no, what is this? Why do you keep accusing me of seeing someone else? You're neurotic, do you know that?'

She moved away from him, closer to the hallway.

'That's right, walk away. But this won't go away. If you don't give me an answer by tomorrow night then you can leave and find somewhere else to live.'

'Er... I pay the rent too.'

'The tenancy agreement is in my name,' he said, surprising her.

'It's in joint names,' she said.

'No, it isn't. I did all the negotiating, remember? And do you recall signing anything?'

'No, but—'

'Exactly. It's my flat, and if you won't marry me then you can stop wasting my time and get out.'

'I'm going to bed,' she said, feeling angry and duped. How could she have missed the fact that the tenancy for the flat was only in his name? If she said no to his proposal, she'd be out on the streets with no job.

As Lynne walked up the steps into the church, she was pondering her dilemma. She didn't want to marry Adam, knowing what she did about him, but she didn't want to lose the roof over her head.

'Lynne, darling!' a familiar voice sounded from the back of the church as she entered. 'So glad you could make it.'

She turned to see Rachel standing next to Peter, her parents not too far behind them. They were all watching her as she approached them. Feeling self-conscious, she looked at the floor.

Rachel gave her a hug when she stood next to her. 'This must be so hard for you, lovey. You look washed out.' Lynne was certain she saw a sarcastic glint in Rachel's eye, but it only lasted a millisecond, so she assumed she'd imagined it. Now, Rachel smiled; her blue eyes a sea of compassion.

'I was shocked to hear of Alex's death,' said Lynne, quietly, looking at her hands as she spoke.

'You'll get through this, sweetie; we all have to get through it.'

Looking up briefly, she saw the tears forming in Rachel's eyes, and felt a deep empathy. She hugged the woman for a second time and smiled at her. 'You'll be okay, Aunty.'

Soon, the funeral service began. After the priest had said his part, he invited Rachel to stand at the front of the church and talk about Alex.

'I have prepared a speech, actually,' said Rachel, taking a piece of paper out of her bag. 'Please excuse me, I need my glasses.'

The congregation waited in silence as she dried her eyes with a tissue and put on her spectacles.

'Welcome, everyone, to my dear son's funeral. I never thought I would ever say that. No parent ever dreams of outliving their child.' She read slowly and calmly from the sheet in front of her, her eyes down. 'Alex was my only child. He was my light in the dark, and he was my life. I really don't know how I am going to—' She paused, and it appeared she would not be able to continue. Already, there were tearful faces in the congregation.

Lynne stared at Rachel, feeling so sorry for her, wanting to go up and hug her again. Despite everything that had passed between them, here was a woman in distress; a woman who had lost her only child.

'So sorry,' continued Rachel, after a few moments. 'This isn't easy, but I have to get through it.' She sighed. 'My son was a kind, gentle, and loving man. He may not have lived very long, but in his time on this earth he was able to find something that most of us can only dream about. He found his true love, his soul mate; and he was going to get married to her. Lynne, was his true love.'

Lynne felt startled to hear her name, but then she took a deep breath and told herself that Rachel was bound to mention her as she remained under the misconception that Alex was going to marry her.

'She is here today,' continued Rachel, 'my son's soul mate. Please stand up, Lynne.' Rachel pointed her out with a flourish of her hand.

Nudged by her father, Lynne slowly stood up. With all eyes upon her, she turned scarlet.

'This woman, ladies and gentlemen, was going to marry my son. But now, she has been left alone. Her grief must be unbearable. You can sit down now, my lovey.'

Rachel's tone sounded sarcastic to Lynne, but again she told herself she must be imagining it.

Slowly, the interested faces in the crowd—curious as to what Alex's "soul mate" looked like—turned back towards Rachel, and Lynne felt less like a spectacle at a circus.

'My son did a lot of work for charity in his short life,' continued Rachel. 'He ran the marathon last year, and raised £3,000 for the local hospice where his grandmother died. He also took part in various projects and schemes to help the under privileged in society. He took a trip to Africa, a few years ago, to raise money for the AIDS charity, and he did voluntary work at the local RSPCA charity shop. He was a giver in life and he has now become a giver in his death. Alex had a donor card. He wanted his organs to be donated after his death. I have never been too sure about that sort of thing, but now I think it is nothing short of miraculous; a wonderful thing to do for another human being.' Rachel took off her glasses and wiped her eyes.

Lynne was surprised to hear about all of Alex's charitable work, and began to see him in a different light. There was obviously a lot about him she hadn't known.

'In this room today is a man called Michael. He is the cousin of a young man called Mark, the recipient of my son's heart. Mark had been waiting for a heart transplant for nearly two years, and when my son died, his heart was found to be a match. So, my son's heart will live on, dear friends, in the body of a wonderful person.' Rachel addressed a man somewhere on the other side of the church from where Lynne sat: 'Michael, I am so happy that my son was able to help your cousin.'

'Thank you,' came a deep voice, the owner of which Lynne could not see.

The crowd gathered in the cemetery and listened to the priest. Some cried and some looked lost in thought. Lynne felt sad, and could not help but remember that she had been here at this cemetery not too long ago looking for the gravestone of a man from her dreams. The memory made her shiver. She had been unable to stop herself from reading all the names on the tombstones today, as she wondered with a sense of dread whether she would spot the name, "Mark Cribbs".

As she tried to listen to the priest's words to distract from her thoughts, she noticed Rachel standing next to him. Lynne recalled her speech in the church, and found herself wishing that she had tried harder to get to know Alex. Behind the obsessive exterior, it seemed he was a good man.

When the service was over, Lynne stood for a while watching the others as they took turns in approaching Rachel, hugging her and speaking some well chosen words.

As Lynne stood, in a half-trance, she heard a voice that she had heard before. 'Hello,' he said.

She turned to see a tall, handsome man. He reminded her of a typical English gentleman like the type you would find in a Jane Austen film adaptation, with his windswept dark hair and sharp features. Blushing slightly, as he held out his hand to greet her, she said, 'Hello,' and shook his hand.

'I'm Michael, I wanted to introduce myself. I'm Mark's cousin—the heart transplant patient.'

'Oh.' She shuddered. This man appeared familiar, but she could not place him. Then, for some reason her mind went back to her dreams again; the recurrent dreams she had been having in another space and time, warning her not to marry Adam. *'If you marry him, your soul mate will die'.* She wished she could forget those memories. The unwelcome thought that Alex may have been her soul mate and that she had unwittingly caused him to die, reared its head again.

Michael reddened slightly. 'I'm sure you must be grieving deeply; you have lost someone who meant the world to you. I can relate to some extent, because my cousin has literally been on his death bed for the past couple of years, but now he has new hope thanks to your Alex. I wanted to let you know that he has done a wonderful thing by helping my cousin. Oh no, I'm talking too much again, aren't I? I'm just nervous, sorry... I didn't really know how to approach you. I'm sure that anything I say won't help in these circumstances, but—' He shrugged his shoulders and remained silent.

She realised that she had been standing looking ahead with a glazed expression on her face, and he must have thought she was not listening to him. But she had heard every word, and felt unworthy of his gratitude. Smiling through all the jumbled thoughts that were taunting her and making her feel like a fraud, she said, 'I hope your cousin gets well.' Then she wondered if that was the right thing to say.

'Mark's feeling great since the op, thanks. The doctors say his body is adjusting well. It's a waiting game, but we think he'll be okay. His own heart was about to give up any day now, so it was truly a Godsend when Alex—' He stopped. 'Sorry, I didn't mean to sound insensitive.'

'No, don't worry,' she said.

'Um, Lynne—you don't mind if I call you that, do you?'

'No, not at all.'

'I was going to ask whether you'd like to come to the hospital with me later when I go to visit Mark. I'm sure he'd want to thank you himself.'

'I'm not sure,' she said, feeling like a trespasser in all of this.

Michael nodded. 'I'll give you my business card, and you can call me if you change your mind.' He handed her a small card, which she read with curiosity: Michael A. Taylor, Solicitor. 'No pressure,' he said. 'Um... do you mind if I take your telephone number? Er... it's just that Mark is a bit unsettled at the moment and we want to make sure we keep him happy. He did mention that he wanted to thank the donor's family. I'd just like to be able to keep in touch if there's any news.'

She felt unsure about giving her number to a stranger, even such a handsome one, but then she remembered what he did for a living; perhaps a solicitor could be trusted with it. 'Um... okay, but I don't have a business card,' she said, feeling awkward.

'Oh, okay.' He took a pen out of his pocket, along with another business card. 'Here, write your number on this.' He smiled.

After she had written the number down, she handed him the card and he smiled as he took it. She couldn't help feeling drawn towards him, a strange, almost magnetic pull.

Just then, Rachel's voice distracted her: 'Lynne, we must talk.'

Lynne said good-bye to Michael and watched him walk away.

Rachel took Lynne's arm and led her away from the few remaining mourners at the graveside. When they were out of earshot, Rachel's face changed. She had an almost eerie, piercing look in her eyes. 'You have played the part of the grieving fiancée very well today; but we both know you never loved my son. He told me that you were engaged to another man. That's why he killed himself.'

Lynne gasped at the revelation.

202

'You murdered my son, you lying slut, and you have some nerve showing up here. Don't worry, I'll make you pay, one way or another.' The older woman walked away towards the grave.

Chapter Forty-Six

Adam shook her awake, and said: 'Lynne, I'm changing the locks tonight. You should pack your stuff and move out today.'

'Wh... Wh... What?' she stuttered, sitting up on her elbow, squinting to see him with foggy morning eyes.

'Oh, don't pretend you're surprised. I've tried as hard as I can, but it's clear you don't love me, so you're not welcome here.'

Feeling more awake now, she replied: 'You've tried? Oh, so spending two days with me in one year is trying, is it?' She coughed to clear her throat; her voice sounded dry and croaky and it was impeding her in getting her point across. It was absurd that he could just make a decision to throw her out when for years she had put up with his neglectful behaviour, and especially knowing what she did about him. Maybe she should just come out with it; tell him she knew about Paul? It appeared she had nothing to lose. Although she was tempted, she stopped herself: *What good would it do?*

Looking at Adam, she realised that the only reason she stayed with him was for a sense of security and stability. She had wanted to make the relationship work, but it just didn't seem plausible anymore. He was gay in the future life, and she was pretty sure that that sort of thing wasn't something that could be changed by a slip in time.

'I want you out,' he said, stubbornly. 'Pack your things. I don't want to see you here when I get back this evening.' With that, he left, and she heard the front door slam behind him.

It was just before 7 am. She slumped back down onto the bed and stared at the ceiling, incredulous. This felt like home to her. She had been sure they'd rented this flat as a couple, but he'd gone behind her back and put it in his name. This made her question the legitimacy of their relationship from the start. Had he been planning to ask her to leave even before they'd moved in together? Maybe he was already seeing Paul back then.

Her mind went back to the future, when she had been planning to leave Adam. At that time, it had been difficult to find anywhere else to go: Sandra and Dave had been moving in together, so she couldn't stay at her flat. Feeling more positive, she realised that Sandra hadn't started going out with Dave yet. It was only February, and Sandra hadn't got together with Dave until at least July. Maybe she could stay with Sandra. She fished in her handbag for her mobile phone and called

Sandra's number.

'Lynne?' She answered, whispering. 'Do you know what time it is?'

'Oh, sorry, Sand. Listen, I have a bit of a problem and I thought you might be able to help.'

'It's a bit difficult to talk at the moment.' She was still whispering. 'Can we meet for lunch?'

'Yes, sure.'

Lynne began to pack a suitcase, realising that she would have to just take some of her clothes and personal items for now, and come back to collect the rest. As she packed, she felt sad. Finding herself at the end of her relationship with Adam, she couldn't help thinking back over the times they'd spent together. She had really loved him, up until she'd seen him kissing Paul. She knew that. Since then, she'd felt numb.

As she sat eating her breakfast, staring at her suitcase, she wished she was going on holiday. Somewhere far away, where she could start a new life; like *Shirley Valentine*. The telephone woke her from her daydream.

'Hello,' she said.

'Hi, darling, it's Mummy.'

'Oh, hi.'

'Darling, I wanted to let you know that Rachel has just phoned me. She wanted your address so she could send you a thank you card for your attendance at the funeral. She sounded very upset, so I didn't talk to her for very long. I was going to suggest that you should visit her; maybe we could go together. I think she'd like to stay in touch with you because you were so close to Alex.'

'But, Mum, I already told you, there was never anything between me and Alex. Aunty Rachel is mistaken.'

'Yes, I know that, but she is a grieving woman. What harm could it do if you play along with her? Alex is dead. She'll never see her son again. Won't you visit her, at least once? Just to show that you care.'

'That's precisely it, I *don't* care. She's an evil woman. Do you know, she threatened me yesterday at the funeral?'

'She was so lovely to you yesterday, introducing you as Alex's true love...'

'That was all for show. Later, at the graveyard, she told me she blames me for his death and she'll make me pay.'

'I've never heard such nonsense.'

'Call her yourself, if you don't believe me.' With that, Lynne hung up, feeling too emotional to continue the conversation. She hated the feeling that Rachel blamed her for Alex's death. She'd felt like this before, she remembered—in her future life—but it was different this time. This time she was painfully aware that she really had somehow contributed to the factors that led to his suicide.

Lynne washed up the dishes, thinking about what her mother had said. Rachel wanted her address. She remembered the poison pen letter. For the first time that morning, Lynne felt pleased that she would be leaving the flat. She resolved not to give her mother Sandra's address, so that she couldn't pass on any information to Rachel.

The phone rang again, just as Lynne had finished the dishes and was on her way to the office room. She sighed and picked up the phone.

'Lynne, dear, it's Mummy.' She did not sound as happy as she had done earlier.

Lynne stayed silent.

'I've just come off the phone with Rachel,' she said, a disappointed edge to her voice.

'Really?' asked Lynne, disinterestedly.

'She phoned me again to tell me something about Alex. It's a bit distressing.'

A familiar feeling of desolation grabbed hold of Lynne. She recalled how she'd had a similar conversation with her mother in her life before the time slip.

'Lynne, dear, is it true that you stayed over at their house a few weeks ago?'

'I did, for one night. It was like the night of the living dead. They're crazy. It's like a madhouse in there.'

'Don't be so disrespectful.' Her mother paused, and then said: 'Rachel says you stayed over after a date with Alex.'

'How many times do I have to tell you? I wasn't dating Alex, no matter what Rachel says.'

'But Rachel told me that you both announced your engagement the morning you stayed at their house. Why would she say something like that if it isn't true?'

'Because she is crazy woman. It's all lies. You can ask Sandra.'

'Sandra?'

'My friend, Sand, you met her at the wedding. She was a bridesma—'

Lynne took a sharp intake of breath.

'Whose wedding, Lynne?'

'Oh, no, sorry I don't think you've met Sand, I was confusing things.'

'I haven't met your friend Sandra, but I do remember you talking about her before. How is she involved?'

'She was at Rachel's house on the morning that Rachel claims I announced my engagement to Alex. What actually happened was, I found out he had been stalking me.'

'Hmm... Well, I'm not quite sure what to believe,' said her mother. 'The main reason I'm calling is, Rachel told me something else. Are you sitting down?'

'Yes, what?'

'It wasn't an accident; Alex killed himself. Apparently, he took some prescription drugs belonging to Rachel and Peter, and he also drank some bleach.' She paused as if waiting for a reaction from Lynne.

'Oh dear,' said Lynne, trying to sound unaware.

'It's tragic. I'm sorry to say this, but Rachel says he was very upset that morning, because you had told him you were going to marry someone else. He had been storming around the house complaining to Rachel that you'd promised you'd marry him and now you were engaged to another.'

Lynne gulped. 'Alex was jealous of my relationship with Adam. I just don't think it's fair to lay the blame on me,' she said, trying to quieten the accusing voices in her head. 'Alex was a disturbed man. He obviously had mental issues. He needed help. It wasn't my fault.'

'Rachel says he was a sensitive soul. He was really hurt. I'm not throwing stones, Lynne, dear, but I think there is a lesson to be learnt here. You shouldn't play with someone's heart.'

'There was nothing anyone could have done,' said Lynne, unsure if she really believed that. A tear threatened to fall.

'Well, I wanted to put you in the picture and warn you that I don't think it would be wise for you to visit Rachel at the moment. She's grieving; and seeing you would only make things worse.'

⧗

Lynne met Sandra for lunch at a café near Sandra's office.

'You look terrible,' said Sandra, as they met at the door.

'I'm a bit tired. I've been through a lot in the past week or so, that's why I wanted to meet.'

'Oh, okay. Let's get a table.'

'So, tell me, what's been bothering you?' Sandra was frowning as they sat opposite each other in the softly lit café; the dim yellow lights making Lynne's features look even more drawn as the shadows fell over her cheeks.

'Well, the most urgent matter is that Adam has kicked me out of the flat, so I have nowhere to go. I wanted to ask if I can stay at your flat until I find somewhere.'

'You can stay as long as you like, you know that,' said Sandra.

A waiter approached them: 'Are you ready to order?'

'Um, yes, we'll have two chicken salads. Is that okay, Lynne?' said Sandra.

Lynne nodded at the waiter.

'Anything to drink?' he asked.

'I'll have some water,' said Sandra.

'Er... orange juice,' said Lynne.

The waiter walked away.

'Lynne, surely you have some rights. Adam can't just kick you out of the flat. I thought you were both paying the rent?'

'The tenancy is in his name only.'

'Oh... But, you've been paying rent and bills, haven't you?'

'Adam earns much more than I do, and we've had a joint account. Everything comes out of that.'

'I could ask Kev about it, he—'

'No,' said Lynne bluntly. 'I don't want your brother involved in this.'

'He won't talk to Steve about it, if that's what you're worried about. Client confidentiality, and all that.'

'No, Sand. I'd rather do this my way.'

'Okay, but I still say you should go and see a solicitor, get some advice.'

'Maybe. Oh, I don't know. Everything's gone wrong all at once.'

Sandra frowned. 'Don't get upset, Lynne. Everything always happens for a reason. We never know what's around the corner.'

'I've got an appointment at the job centre this afternoon. It's so depressing.'

'Hmm... Oh, well, I'm sure you'll find something soon.'

'Maybe.'

The waiter brought their food and they began to eat in silence. Lynne started to feel a bit better, knowing that at least she now had somewhere to stay.

'I've got some news,' said Sandra, with a curl in her lip, indicating that she couldn't stop herself smiling.

'Oh?'

'I've met someone.' Now, she really did smile. A grin, in fact; like the Cheshire Cat.

'A new man?'

'Yes. His name's Matt.' Her eyes sparkled at the mention of his name.

Lynne frowned, but then tried to look happy for her friend.

'He works at the gym I go to. He's a personal trainer. Very fit. Gorgeous!'

'Lucky you,' said Lynne.

'Er... that's where I was this morning, when you phoned.'

'What, at the gym?'

'No. With Matt. At his flat.'

Lynne remembered the pokey flat where he had hosted his birthday party.

'That's why I couldn't talk on the phone. He was still sleeping,' gushed Sandra.

'Just be careful, Sand. Don't get your hopes up. Don't fall in love with him before you find out what sort of man he is.'

'Oh, it's too late for that. I'm head over heels. Just wait until you meet him, he's too good to be true.' Her eyes were dreamy and distant.

Lynne sighed and realised that she could not do anything about this now; she would just have to be there to pick up the pieces.

Later that afternoon, she attended the local job centre and sat filling in forms for ages. Then, she sat going through the forms with a young man for about an hour. He gave her lots of pieces of paper in a small wallet and explained that she would have to come back every two weeks to sign on, and she would have to keep a record of her job search. She had not actually intended to do any job searching. In her future life, she'd still remained unemployed even after months of serious job searching. Now, though, she would have to keep a record of jobs that she applied for, so she would have to start the tedious process of putting together a CV.

She arrived back at the flat at 5 pm and used the computer to prepare a CV and search for jobs. She recognised the jobs she had previously applied for, and decided that she would make a note of those jobs as a record for the job centre, but she would not actually apply for them; after all, even if she did apply, and go to the interviews, she knew she wouldn't get the jobs. Her foresight proved very useful in this instance.

She logged on to the job networking site and found another message from Woody: **Hi, how's the job search going?**

She replied: **Hi Woody, it's a bit depressing. I've just got back from the job centre and am compiling a CV.**

Then she saw Woody was online and she got an instant message from him: **Hi Lynne. I hate the job centre, too, but keep your**

pecker up, you'll find something soon.

She replied: **Hi Woody, how's your search going?**

Woody said: **Oh, the job search isn't going too well, but the search for a kindred spirit is going well. Would you like to come out for a drink tonight? I see from your profile information that you live locally**.

When he had sent her that message the last time, she'd thought he sounded like a desperado. She'd also been under the illusion that she still had a good relationship with Adam, so she'd brushed him off. However, as she'd got to know Woody over the following weeks, she found that he seemed like a nice man. She decided to throw caution to the wind.

Okay, that would be fun, she replied.

Here's my mobile number, give me a call, he wrote.

As she wrote down Woody's number, she heard a key turn in the front door. *Shit!* She had planned to be out of the flat by the time Adam returned home.

Logging off from the website, she could hear Adam's footsteps. It sounded as if he had gone into the kitchen. The smell of fish and chips wafting through the flat made her hungry. It was unlikely he'd bought some for her, though, as he'd wanted her out of the flat by the time he got home.

After shutting down the computer, she tiptoed out of the office room, wondering whether it would be possible for her to slip out without Adam noticing.

Walking past the kitchen, she saw him, his back to her, as he placed his takeaway on a plate. She scrambled to the front door, slowly opened it, and stepped outside, breathing a sigh of relief. As she walked to her car, she decided that she would phone Woody and arrange to meet him. She smiled to herself, feeling positive about a friendship with Woody—and maybe more... But then, she stopped walking, suddenly realising that she had left the paper with Woody's number written on it next to the computer. She'd have to go back inside the flat. Most likely, she'd have to speak with Adam. Cursing, she turned back towards the flat.

Once outside the door, she took a deep breath and turned the key in the lock. She saw Adam on the sofa with a lap tray and his dinner. He turned to look at her as she entered the flat.

'Sorry,' she said. 'I forgot something, I won't be long.' She ran into the office room and retrieved the paper, placing it in her handbag.

Adam called out to her as she left the flat: 'Your keys!'

'But... I thought you were changing the locks?'

'I've changed my mind. Why pay money for a new locks when I already have perfectly good ones?'

'But, I'll need to come back to collect some more stuff,' she said.

'And when you do, I will open the door for you,' he said. 'Now, give me your keys.'

She fumbled with the key ring and eventually managed to get the keys off. 'Here,' she said, throwing them onto the floor.

'Thanks,' he said. 'I'm leaving for Paris tomorrow, so you can collect your other stuff when I get back, in two weeks.'

'But what if I need something during that time?'

'Sorry, but you should take anything you need now.'

'Enjoy the rest of your life, Adam,' she said, slamming the door behind her.

Adam leaned back on the sofa and sighed, feeling a bit bad about ending the relationship with Lynne in that way; but he knew he had to be cruel to be kind. He loved Paul, not Lynne; and the feelings were getting stronger. His every thought was consumed with his memories of Paul, and a desperate need to tell him how he felt about him. He resolved to invite him to the flat tomorrow. The worst that could happen would be that Paul didn't feel the same way. Again, he worried about whether Paul might already be in a relationship; the image of him standing at his door wearing his silk dressing gown, flashed into his mind. He felt envious knowing there had been another man in Paul's bed that night. Pushing that thought to the back of his mind, he told himself that he had always felt a special attraction towards Paul. Surely, Paul had felt it, too?

Trying to assuage his guilt about the way he'd treated Lynne, he thought: *At least she's free to meet someone else now; someone who can really love her.*

After he finished off his meal, he stood up to take the empty plate into the kitchen. Noticing Lynne's keys on the floor, he frowned as he recalled how easy he'd found it to lie to her about having to go to Paris on business. He picked up the keys and shrugged his shoulders.

Chapter Forty-Seven

When Lynne got to Sandra's flat, she hardly recognised the place. There were lots of people crammed into the small rooms, with loud music playing. The scene looked familiar, and she recognised some of the people although she knew instinctively that she'd never met them. The befuddlement made her feel cold and hot at the same time, as if she had a fever. She pushed through the people who were clogging up the hallway and tried to find Sandra, but she couldn't see her. Then, making her way into the living room she saw a couple who were canoodling on the sofa at the back of the room, and she knew instantly why she felt so strange. This wasn't déjà vu, but real repetition. Instead of being in Matt's flat for his birthday party, as she had been in her previous life, she found herself at the same party with the same people, but in Sandra's flat. That couple had sat beside her when she'd been to Matt's party. It was disconcerting.

In the hot and stifling atmosphere of the room, with loud music blaring, Lynne turned as if sensing someone at the doorway, and knew who she was about to see. There he stood, in all his glory: Jason. She caught her breath when she saw him again, remembering the times they had spent together and how he had made her feel. He looked in her direction and smiled a brilliant wide grin; his tanned face highlighting his white teeth. Should she go and speak to him? He was a familiar face; someone she could talk to amidst the crowd of nameless ghosts from the past. But when she remembered how it had all ended, the pull of desire she felt for him weakened. Trying to forget, she turned away.

Frantically, she scanned the roomed searching for Sandra or Matt, but couldn't see them. Suspecting they would be in the kitchen, she pushed her way towards the door. With the crowd of party-goers jammed so closely together, choosing a direction to move in seemed an impossible task. Once again, she ended up in front of Jason, just as she had done before. She smiled up at him, cautiously, then she noticed his eyes went to her hand. *He's looking for a ring*, she thought, knowingly. As soon as his eyes left her hand, he walked away in the other direction, without even saying hello. *That's not how it happened before*. She was amazed at how he didn't even acknowledge her this time, just because she didn't have a wedding ring on her finger. Paralysed by her disbelief, she stood in the same position, just watching him as he walked away.

When he'd disappeared from sight, Lynne shook herself out of her coma like state and began to search again for Sandra. Eventually she found her standing in the bedroom, chatting with a young couple. 'Hi, Sand,' she said, pushing her way past the people congregated in the small room.

'Oh, Lynne, hi!' she said, looking a bit flustered.

'I didn't know you were having a party,' said Lynne.

Sandra laughed, but didn't look very happy. She appeared harassed and tired. 'Well, actually, I didn't know until I got home! Matt invited his Facebook friends for a party. The plan is to take them to The King's Head when they all arrive.'

'You mean they haven't all arrived yet? How many people are coming? And what's the party for? It's not his birthday or anything is it?'

'No. Um...' Sandra sighed. 'Apparently, Matt loves parties and he has a lot of friends. He says: "You don't need a reason for a party".'

'Hmm...' Lynne frowned. 'So, are you going to the pub with them later?'

'Er...yes... I suppose I'll have to.' That laugh again. 'You'll come along, too, won't you?' Her eyes were pleading.

'Um... I don't know, I'm a bit tired. I was planning to have a quiet evening.'

'No, come; you need taking out of yourself. It'll be fun.' Sandra smiled and walked away as she saw Matt standing in the doorway.

Lynne suspected that tonight would be the night Matt dumped Sandra for his ex-girlfriend. Even though the last thing she felt like doing was going to a party, she knew she'd have to be there to comfort her friend. She decided to phone Woody and get him to meet her at The King's Head instead of the other pub he'd suggested. That way she could kill two birds with one stone.

Later that evening, Lynne stood at the bar of the now crowded pub, next to Sandra and Matt. Prior to their arrival there had only been about five people in The King's Head; now it was filled to the rafters, and very noisy.

Woody had texted her, saying he was running late. Lynne wondered whether she would be able to find him in this crowd when he arrived. She didn't know what he looked like.

A blonde barmaid approached them to ask for their order. Matt seemed over-familiar with the woman, and she was definitely flirting with him, leaving Sandra looking quite agitated. She took Lynne to one side.

'Let's find a table,' she said. 'I can't bear watching that trollop chatting Matt up right in front of my eyes; she knows I'm his girlfriend. I feel like punching her in the face. Plastic bimbo! I mean, that's obviously a boob job, don't you think?'

'Er... barmaids have to be friendly with the customers; that's their job. What's wrong, Sand, you're like a different person. You're not usually so... Well, so...'

'I know, I know,' said Sandra, looking distracted. 'I don't know what's come over me. Ever since I've been dating Matt, I've been so highly strung. I get jealous whenever he looks at another woman. I think it's because he's drop dead gorgeous, and I'm always worried he's going to leave me for someone else. I mean, have you seen the way the girls at this party have been fawning over him.'

'Well, if you keep thinking like that, he probably will leave you. Men don't like over-possessive women. And there are such things as self-fulfilling prophecies.'

Sandra sighed. 'I know you're right; it's just that I turn into this neurotic freak whenever other women start flirting with him. And the problem is, women are always flirting with him wherever we go.'

Matt approached them, pushing his way through the party-goers. 'Here you go, ladies,' he said, placing their drinks on the table in front of them. 'I'll just go and get my beer. Francesca's keeping it safe for me.' He winked and disappeared into the throng.

Sandra gulped down her vodka and orange, emptying the glass in record time. 'Am I just imagining it, Lynne? Was Matt flirting with that barmaid? I feel like I'm going mad. He's always flirting with women. Or is it just me thinking he's flirting?'

'Um...' Lynne worried about Sandra, unused to seeing her so het up. 'Perhaps you shouldn't be dating Matt if he's such a flirt. I mean, no woman would feel secure with a man who's always chatting up other women.'

'But I love him,' said Sandra, forlorn.

'Love is a strong word, Sand. You haven't known him that long.'

'Yes, but that's my problem. I meet a good-looking guy, and I fall in love with him. Then he breaks my heart, either because he turns out to be a cad, or because he dumps me. That's my life story, so far...'

'Sand, try to be realistic about this. You haven't known Matt long. Maybe he won't turn out to be what you expect.' Lynne's mind went back to the future again. Perhaps if she could just persuade Sandra to get out of the relationship early, she would save her the heartache. 'You have to kiss a lot of frogs before you find your prince, remember? He doesn't look like the settling-down type.'

'Oh, this is depressing,' said Sandra, looking into her empty glass. 'Let's change the subject. I need another drink. You?'

Lynne looked at her untouched drink on the table. 'Have mine. I'm not very thirsty.'

'Matt's a long time getting his beer.' Sandra frowned.

Just then, a bell sounded. 'It's only nine o'clock, surely it's not last orders already,' said Sandra.

'Maybe they have an announcement or something,' said Lynne, as the chatter in the pub died down.

Matt appeared, standing up on the bar. The blonde barmaid, looking uncharacteristically shy, was standing next to him.

'Everyone,' started Matt. 'I have an announcement to make. It's excellent news, I'm sure you'll all agree! Francesca and I are engaged again!'

Cheers sounded from the crowd.

'We should never have split up in the first place. I just wanted you all to know that I was wrong to leave this wonderful woman. I love her, and I don't think I ever stopped loving her.' He hugged the barmaid and gave her a long lingering kiss to the sound of wolf-whistles, cheers, and hand clapping from the crowd.

Then, Lynne saw Matt turn to find Sandra in the crowd and mouth the word 'Sorry' with an apologetic look on his face.

Sandra stood up and picked up Lynne's drink from the table. She pushed her way through to the bar. Lynne followed her, knowing she'd need her support. Lynne watched as Sandra threw the drink over the perfect blonde barmaid who was stepping down from the bar. There were a few sharp intakes of breath heard around the pub, and murmurs of disapproval.

'What the hell did you do that for!' screamed Francesca, looking like a contestant in a wet t-shirt competition.

Lynne could tell by the tears brimming in Sandra's eyes that throwing the drink hadn't had the desired effect of making her feel better. Everyone in the pub was looking at Sandra as if she were mad. A burly man walked over to her and escorted her out of the pub. 'You're barred,' he said, as he shoved her out of the door.

Lynne ran out of the pub after her. 'Sand!' she called out. She found Sandra crying openly.

'I told you it would happen, didn't I? He dumped me.' She looked at Lynne, through watery eyes.

Lynne put an arm around her and led her away from the pub. 'Let's go home. He wasn't the one, anyway. Mr. Right is out there somewhere. Don't worry.'

'I'm never going to fall for a good-looking bloke again, okay,'

215

snivelled Sandra. 'If I ever say I want to go out with a good-looking bloke ever again, you have to stop me.'

'Okay,' said Lynne.

Just then, a man walked up to them. He was quite tall, with a large beer belly making him look six months pregnant. He had a bald head, and a strange, unkempt, black beard, that grew all over his face as if to make up for the lack of hair on his head. 'Are you Lynne?' he asked, smiling at her, revealing gaps where his two front teeth should have been.

'Um... who are you?' she asked.

'I'm Woody,' he said. 'I recognised you from your online photo.'

You haven't got an online photo, she thought. *Now, I can see why.* Instantly, she felt terrible for judging him by his looks; but he was utterly unappealing to her, and she couldn't imagine ever going out on a date with him. He had been very flirty on the Internet, so he was obviously looking for a date. She pondered for a minute whether any of her emails could have given him the impression that she was interested in dating him. Frowning, she reddened as she tried to recall.

'I'm sorry I'm so late,' he said. 'I tried to get away earlier, but I had a last minute job. I'm doing some part time work for a friend until I find work.'

'Oh,' said Lynne. She could hear Sandra's sniffles beside her. Woody had looked at Sandra intermittently, but was either ignoring the fact she was crying, or trying not to be rude by mentioning it.

'Er... Woody, my friend here has had a bit of bad news. I'm going to have to take her home. We'll have to postpone our drink.' *Postpone! Why did I say that? Now he's going to expect to see me again!*

'I understand,' he said. 'Is there anything I can do to help?'

'No,' said Lynne, politely. 'I'll be in touch.' With that she walked away from him, looking back at him apologetically. *I'll be in touch? What? Why did I say that?* Then, she instantly felt terrible for snubbing him like that just because he wasn't attractive. She'd always thought she was the sort of person who wouldn't judge someone on appearance alone. Remembering their friendly chats on the Internet, she couldn't help feeling like a fraud.

'Is that the man you said you met on the Internet?' asked Sandra, bringing her mind back to the present.

'Um... yes,' said Lynne, embarrassed.

'I admire you, Lynne. That's the difference between me and you. I could never go out with someone like that. I always go for people who look good. That's my mistake, right? I'm going to try to be more like you.'

'Um... I'm not going out with Woody. He's just a friend.'

They continued walking back to Sandra's flat, both of them disconsolate; faces down.

'What am I gonna do, Lynne? My life is over!'

'You'll be okay, Sand,' she said, knowing that was true; *she'll get together with Dave*. Then, Lynne had an unpleasant thought: in the future life, Sandra got together with Dave quite soon after she split from Matt. If that happened now, she wouldn't be able to stay with Sandra for very long.

She began to feel insecure... Things in this time slip world were definitely happening at a faster pace than the future she had known.

Chapter Forty-Eight

The next day, Lynne decided to visit her parents, remembering that she had left spare keys to the flat with them when she and Adam had first moved in there. Her mother had suggested it. *'You know how absentminded you can be sometimes, Lynne. I'll keep spare keys here, just in case you lose yours.'* Lynne had felt a bit offended at the time, but thought it was a good idea to have spares somewhere.

Walking up the path to her parents' house, a guilty feeling washed over her; she had not been to visit them for ages, and the only reason she was going there today was to get the keys. Her mother often phoned her and invited her over, but somehow other things got in the way.

'Hello, love, what a nice surprise. Come in. Your father is in the back garden planting some herbs for me. It's such a lovely day, we were just relaxing outside.' Her mother led her through the house and out of the patio doors.

Lynne sat on a bench in the garden, chatting with her parents about the weather and gardening. Her intention had been to just go there, collect the keys and leave; but she thought it only right that she should spend time with her parents, realising she hardly ever saw them.

Her mother showed her photos of the barbecue they'd had when Lynne had been in Paris with Adam. 'It would have been so nice if you could have come, dear. You would have been able to see your sister and the children. The boys have grown so much, look,' she said, pointing at Lynne's sister's children in a photograph. Lynne realised, with a heavy heart, that she had never really spent any quality time with her nephews.

'Tommy looked bigger at the wedding; has he lost weight?' she asked, remembering her nephews, who'd both been page boys when she married Adam.

'What wedding, dear?'

Lynne turned her attention away from the photographs, and saw her mother's confused frown. 'Um... Oh, silly me; did I say *wedding*? I'm sure I have early-onset Alzheimer's, sometimes. I meant... the... Christmas party. You know, the last time we all got together... er... Tommy looked bigger at the Christmas party.' Lynne was babbling, she knew it; but for a moment she had forgotten she was back in time.

Her mother didn't look convinced. 'Are you sure you're okay,

Lynne?' she asked, removing her spectacles and placing the photo album on the bench beside her.

'I'm fine,' she replied, avoiding her mother's scrutinising gaze.

'Sometimes, when we have things on our mind, they just slip out. Were you thinking about Alex, dear?'

'Alex? Why would I be?' Lynne's cheeks reddened.

'Well... at the funeral, Rachel made a big thing about you two being engaged—'

'We were never engaged!' Lynne stood up.

'I know, dear. I didn't mean to upset you.'

Lynne walked away from her mother before she could say anything else. This new life she found herself in, did not seem real at times. She couldn't help but wonder whether she had been in a terrible accident and now existed in a coma, dreaming or imagining all of this. At other times, when she was feeling particularly morbid, she imagined that she had died, and reached the afterlife where you have to relive things that have happened to you in your mortal existence.

'You really should visit more,' said her father, shaking her out of her trancelike, contemplative state. She had been walking through the garden, in a daze, and now found herself standing next to him watching him water the plants.

'Yes, I should,' she said. 'I'm sorry.'

'You will stay for lunch, won't you?' asked her mother, who had somehow appeared by her side. 'I'll make some sandwiches.'

'Yes, okay,' said Lynne, reluctantly. She really just wanted to get the spare keys and go to the flat to pack some more of her stuff. It would take ages.

They sat at the kitchen table, Lynne and her parents, eating their sandwiches in silence. Every now and then a comment would be made, usually by Lynne's mum, and the others would nod or agree. Lynne fidgeted in her chair, feeling strangely uncomfortable sitting with her parents realising that she didn't have that much in common with them anymore.

'So, how's Adam? Working hard as usual, I suppose?' asked her father, surprising her, as he had hardly said a word for the past half hour.

'He's away on business,' said Lynne, leaving out the finer details. She knew she would have to tell her parents that she and Adam were separating, but today did not seem like the right time.

'I spoke to Rachel, this morning,' said her mother, unexpectedly. 'She phoned me,' her mother went on. 'I know this is a touchy subject for you, Lynne, but you must listen to me. Rachel is still very upset about Alex's death. She wants you to stop phoning her.'

Lynne stiffened. 'Wh... What?'

'Well, she says that when she hears your voice she remembers Alex. She remembers how upset he was because you left him. It's hard for her. I told her that you're probably just concerned about her, but she really doesn't want you to keep phoning her.'

'I haven't phoned her.' Lynne stood up. 'I can't believe she's saying I phoned her.'

'Sit down, dear.'

'Mum, I'm going to say this one more time, and I don't care whether you believe me or not. Rachel is a fruit loop; she's crazy.'

'Don't be so disrespectful,' said her father.

Lynne sighed. 'What do I have to say to get through to you? I'm telling you, she is certifiable. Her son was, too.'

'Don't speak ill of the dead,' said her mother.

'Oh...' Lynne could not hold her temper any longer and decided she should leave before she regretted her behaviour. 'Mum, can I have the spare keys to my flat, please? I've lost mine,' she said hurriedly, impatiently.

'You really should be more careful, Lynne. Where were you when you last had them?'

'I don't know!' she said, angrily. 'Where are the spares?'

Her mother looked at her with disappointment in her eyes. 'I'll go and get them,' she said, standing up.

Lynne walked to the front door and opened it, standing on the doorstep, taking deep breaths to calm herself. Her mind was reeling. She didn't like the thought of Rachel telling these lies behind her back, and the fact that her parents were so quick to believe her.

'Here are the keys, Lynne,' said her mother, walking up behind her.

Lynne turned around to face her. 'Thanks.' She took the keys and forced a smile. 'Mum, I have to go now.'

'All right. When will we see you next?'

'I'm not sure. Look, Mum, you have to believe me. I haven't phoned Rachel. I think she's just really upset about Alex dying and she wants to blame someone.'

'Maybe,' said her mother. 'I just think it's best if you keep away from her.'

'I have been keeping away from her! Haven't you just heard what I said?'

'Okay, well. It was nice to see you, love, you must come around more often.'

Lynne, shook her head in disbelief—sometimes it was impossible to get through to her mother. 'Bye, Mum.' She turned to walk away.

'Oh, and try not to lose those keys,' her mother called after her. 'Maybe you should make more copies.'

Walking away from the house, Lynne felt as though she had just been emotionally abused. Her parents obviously thought of her as a child and they were willing to believe a freak like Rachel rather than her. She tried to think of other things, but the thought of Rachel spreading all these lies about her, made her anxious and unable to concentrate on anything else.

Driving to the flat she had shared with Adam, her mind was distracted, and she almost drove straight into the back of a car in front of her at a set of traffic lights. Ruffled, she wondered whether she should deliberately cause an accident, then maybe she'd wake up from this living nightmare. Her head was overloaded with negative thoughts. Taking off from the traffic lights, she raced along the road at breakneck speed. *Perhaps if I drive fast enough, I'll break through to another time dimension*, she thought, almost laughing out loud. It was as though she were losing control of her mind.

As she approached another set of traffic lights, which were red, she suddenly came to her senses, and slowed down; as if the red light was a warning. Now, fully compos mentis, she sat at the traffic lights gripped by the fear of what might have happened. She had been seconds away from causing a major accident.

She watched as a mother helped her toddler across the road. Lynne's eyes widened in horror as images of what might have occurred flashed through her mind. She had been intending to drive straight through the lights. It seemed absurd to her, now, that she'd actually contemplated crashing the car in the hope of returning to her former life. Did she really want to go back there?

She remembered how intolerable her life had been before the time slip. Life was hard now, but she would still be in an unbearable existence even if she did return to her previous world. There was some reason she had been sent back here; that was the overwhelming feeling she'd brought with her. Although not comforted by the thought, it made her realise that she had to make the best of this situation. Somehow she had to get through this.

She parked outside the tower block and felt a yearning to be back inside the little flat, in the kitchen that overlooked the world from on high. She wanted to stay there for ever; live out the rest of her days as a hermit. But in reality, she did not have any right to live there anymore: Adam had made sure of that.

When she stepped out of the lift on the fifth floor, she saw Mrs.

Phillips. She remembered their recent meeting, in her former life. The old woman smiled at her as she approached. 'Hello, dear. Lovely day today, isn't it?'

'Er... yes.' Lynne's stiffened face cracked into a smile.

'I've been looking after a friend, who's not very well. I thought I should keep an eye on her. She's 92. Her children and grandchildren hardly ever visit, even though they only live a few streets away.'

'Oh, that's a shame,' said Lynne, eager to get to the flat, to be alone.

'It's heartbreaking. It makes me almost glad I never had any children of my own,' she said, shaking her head. 'Do you know what Edna said to me today? She said that she can go for days without saying a word, all alone in that flat. Sometimes she feels like she's going to forget how to speak. Young people don't have time to talk these days, they're so busy. Never grow old, dear. People don't want to know you when you're old.' She laughed her sad laugh.

Lynne remembered the old woman saying exactly the same thing when they last met. It was as if she had inadvertently stepped into a world where everything was scripted and characters would just turn up and say on cue what they had been told to say. Her mind thought of that movie: *The Truman Show*. She felt disturbed, just as the main character in that film had been feeling; trapped in a scripted world, without a script.

As Lynne walked towards the flat, she began to feel the injustice of not being able to live there anymore. Adam was hardly ever there, being away on business so much. She had put her heart and soul into the flat; choosing the furniture just as she liked it; cleaning the place; decorating; and arranging for the appliances to be fixed. It just seemed so unfair that he could turn around one day and tell her to leave. Sighing, as she placed the key in the lock, she wondered whether she should get some legal advice about her rights.

As she stepped into the flat, she heard music playing. It sounded like it was coming from the stereo in the bedroom. She thought she could hear Adam laughing, but then realised it wasn't Adam; it was another man. Had someone broken into the flat? Squatters?

Closing the door quietly, she ventured into the passageway that led to the bedroom. Sure enough, the music was coming from in there; a classical piece, which she didn't recognise. Should she go any further? Trembling with nerves, she hesitated. Perhaps it wasn't safe for her to confront whoever it was. Then, she heard his voice. Adam.

She knew in her heart what she was about to find, and she tried to prepare herself mentally. As she walked straight into the bedroom, she made direct eye contact with Adam and stood watching as his shocked face became redder and redder as he stared at her.

'L..L..Ly..Lyn..' He seemed unable to find his voice. He was naked on the bed, Paul lying beneath him, his head turned away from her.

Suddenly, Adam jumped out of the bed and grabbed hold of one of the sheets, wrapping it around him.

Lynne stood there, unable to speak. Although she had known he would be there with Paul, she hadn't appreciated how difficult it would be for her to see them together.

'What are you doing here?' said Adam, in a quiet voice.

'I... I came to get some of my things,' she said, shrugging off her feelings of abhorrence.

'How did you get in?'

'My mum had spare keys.'

'Oh...'

There was silence as the awkward trio stayed in their positions. Lynne became more aware of the smell of body odour in the room and began to feel sick. 'I need some air,' she said rushing towards the door.

She could hear them talking, as she sat in the living room, tears spilling down her cheeks. Walking in on Adam and Paul had brought back a painful distant memory... The time she had found Steve with Alicia. The pain was the same, and it tore through her heart. Betrayal, lies, deceit. *Why has this happened to me again?* Her mind was spinning.

After a few minutes, Adam joined her in the living room. Now fully dressed, he sat next to her on the sofa. 'Listen, Lynne, I am so sorry you had to find out this way. I... I thought you wouldn't be coming back here. If I'd known.'

'It's okay,' she sniffed, taking a tissue and wiping her eyes. 'I knew about you and Paul.'

'How?'

'It doesn't matter how.'

'I never meant to hurt you, Lynne.' He looked sad. His eyes were wet.

'You shouldn't have married me, knowing you're gay.'

'Married you?'

Confusion was written all over his face, and then she realised that she'd made a mistake. 'Sorry. I mean, you shouldn't have asked me to marry you.' She looked at her hands. 'I'm not thinking straight,' she said, standing up. 'It's not easy to come home and find your husband in bed with another man!'

Then she realised she'd said "husband" and turned away, unable to face him.

'We weren't married, Lynne. Okay, you're right; I shouldn't have asked you to marry me. I was in denial. I didn't want to face the fact that I'm gay. Okay... There I've said it. I felt ashamed. For years, I've known I'm gay, but I haven't wanted to admit it to myself.'

'How long have you been seeing Paul?' she asked, turning towards him.

He looked down at the floor. 'This is the first time we've ever... Well, you know.'

'Do you expect me to believe that?' Lynne thundered.

'It's the truth. I only told Paul how I feel this morning. He's felt the same way about me for ages, but he didn't know I'm gay.'

'Oh, it's so romantic,' she said, bitterly. 'So, you're going to settle down with him now, are you? And live happily ever after?'

Adam stood up. 'I... I love Paul, and he loves me.'

'I think I'm going to puke,' she said.

'Lynne, for what it's worth, I do care about you... If things were different—'

'So, you are throwing me out so you can set up home with your lover? That's just great!'

'About the flat, if you want I can transfer it to you. We can ask the landlord. I'm going to go and live with Paul, so I won't be needing it.'

Paul walked into the room, hesitantly, looking as if he was unsure how Lynne would react. He appeared almost frightened.

'I'd better go,' he said.

As Lynne looked at him, she could see again the image in her mind of him lying naked on the bed.

'I'll call you later, Adam,' he said, almost inaudibly.

'Okay.'

They watched Paul leave.

'So,' began Adam. 'Do you want to carry on living here?'

She shrugged her shoulders.

'Well, look, the tenancy doesn't have to be renewed for a couple of months yet; so, let me know. Take your time. And, please feel free to come here whenever you like. I've been feeling bad for throwing you out like that. I won't bring Paul here again.'

Adam walked out of the room. She heard him go into the bedroom.

Lynne decided to leave. She could come here anytime, after all. His guilt and shame had won her back the right of residence at the flat.

As she walked out of the door, it was almost as if she were walking into a new dimension. In her future life she had never confronted Adam about his affair or sexuality. Things were ominously different in this new world she had entered, and she was almost fearful of going any further.

Chapter Forty-Nine

Lynne returned to Sandra's flat. Sandra was still at work, but would be returning home soon.

Lynne decided to prepare dinner for them, feeling it was the least she could do after Sandra had offered her shelter; and she wanted to try to cheer her up after the disastrous break-up with Matt. As she cooked the pasta, she thought about Adam's offer for her to go back to live at the flat. She wondered whether she could go back there now, and sleep in that room, after seeing what she had seen. As much as she'd tried to put all emotions aside since finding out about Adam's true sexuality, she couldn't get past the fact that she still had strong feelings for him, and it had hurt her deeply seeing him with someone else. He had chosen someone else. She knew it would take time for her wounds to heal.

Sandra arrived home shortly after 6 pm. Lynne heard her open the front door, just as she was removing the pasta bake from the oven. She smiled to herself. *Perfect timing!* But then she heard another voice. Sandra was not alone.

Lynne walked out of the kitchen and along the hallway. Sandra and Dave were walking towards her.

'Hi, Lynne. This is a friend from work, he's just come to have a look at the toilet; you know I told you that it doesn't flush properly? He can fix those sorts of things, apparently.' She smiled and led Dave to the small toilet.

'I've made some dinner. Pasta bake,' said Lynne, when Sandra joined her in the living room.

'Oh, I'm going out for dinner,' she replied.

'Okay, not a problem, I can put yours in the fridge.' Lynne tried to sound upbeat, but was sure the disappointment showed in her face. She realised that Sandra's relationship with Dave was starting to develop, and that meant she would have to go back and live at the old flat again soon. She wouldn't have a choice.

'Listen, Lynne, do you want to come out to dinner with us?'

'Er... but won't you and Dave want to be alone?'

'No, it's not like that, we're just friends... Wait a minute, how did you know his name?'

'You must have mentioned it.'

'No, I didn't.'

'Oh, I heard you talking to him when you went into the toilet...
You said his name,' bluffed Lynne. It was hard keeping the present
and future/past distinct in her mind.

Sandra narrowed her eyes as if deep in thought. Then, still appearing
confused, she said: 'Right, okay.' Lowering her voice to almost a
whisper, and leaning towards Lynne, she continued: 'Er... just out of
interest, what do you think of him?'

'I don't know him, I've only just met him. Well, actually, I haven't
even really met him.'

'No, I mean looks-wise,' said Sandra, still whispering. 'He's not all
that, is he?'

'He's okay-looking, I suppose.'

'Um... It's just... He likes me. He's asked me out before, but I've
always said no. I've never taken him seriously. But now, I'm trying
to change my attitude; I'm going to try to find a good man, rather
than a good-looking one.'

'Well, that's a good attitude to have, but don't you think it's a bit
soon to start dating again after Matt?' whispered Lynne, in reply.

'Oh, Matt was just a fling. I've known Dave for ages, so I know I
can trust him.'

'That's good,' said Lynne, trying her best to be happy for Sandra.

'You look tired, Lynne. Are you okay?' Sandra's voice had now
resumed its normal volume.

'I've just got a lot on my mind. Well. Adam, mainly.'

'Oh.' Sandra opened her mouth to continue speaking, but then
hesitated, as though wondering if it was the right thing to say. Finally,
she said: 'Do you think there's a chance you two will get back
together?'

'No.' Lynne shook her head vehemently. 'It's definitely over
between us. I went back to the flat today to get my stuff and I found
him in bed with someone.'

'Oh my God!'

'He's gay.'

Sandra's brow furrowed.

'Yes, gay,' said Lynne. 'He was in bed with Paul. You were right—'
she stopped herself; she had been about to say "you were right when
you said he is gay". But of course, that had all happened in the
future/past life.

'Who's Paul?' asked Sandra, frowning.

'He's Adam's best friend. Well, they're more than that now,' she
said, bitterly.

'Oh my God. I don't know what to say, Lynne. You must be
devastated.'

226

'No. No. I'm actually okay with it. After all, my relationship with Adam was not really going anywhere,' she said, still feeling the sting of rejection.

'Yes, well, you seem to be taking it well,' commented Sandra, a frown still fixed on her face. 'I have to say, I had my suspicions about Adam. I read once in a magazine, foolproof ways to tell if a man is gay. I tested Adam one day and he showed all the signs of being gay. At the time, though, I didn't think it could be true because you and him were together.'

Just then Dave entered the room.

'I've fixed it, Sandy; you shouldn't get any problems with it now.'

'Fantastic! Thanks! You haven't met Lynne, have you?'

'Nice to meet you,' he said, approaching her and holding out a hand.

She shook his hand and smiled.

'So, Lynne, are you coming out with us?' asked Sandra.

'Er... no, I think I'll stay and eat my pasta bake,' she said. 'Shame for it to go to waste.'

'If you're sure,' said Sandra. Then looking at her, facing away from Dave, she mouthed. 'Are you sure you'll be okay?'

'Yes, fine.' Lynne nodded.

'Okay, well, I won't be out too late,' Sandra called out, as she left the flat with Dave.

Alone in the flat, Lynne began to think over everything that had happened. She couldn't decide whether her situation was better or worse now than before she went back in time. In the past, she'd often wished to be able to go back and do things differently, but now she was starting to believe that some things could not be changed. She didn't feel in control. It seemed that if something was going to happen, it was going to happen.

As she lay in bed that night, pondering her predicament, she realised that most of the future events she'd lived through before, had already happened again. She dearly hoped that meant there would be no more surprises.

227

The next morning, while in bed, still half asleep, Lynne heard Sandra leave for work. Through her groggy, sleepy state, she was also sure she'd heard a man's voice in the flat. Dave had obviously stayed overnight.

Sandra had given Lynne her bedroom and slept on the sofa bed. She'd explained that as Lynne was out of work she might want to sleep in in the mornings, and she wouldn't want to be sleeping in the living room because Sandra would have to walk through there from her bedroom to the kitchen to get ready for work.

As Lynne began to fully wake up, she was feeling a bit guilty for taking over Sandra's bedroom now that she had started a new relationship. She'd probably prefer some privacy.

Once again, Lynne considered moving back to the flat she had shared with Adam. She was reluctant to do so as it held so many memories, but now she felt that it was the only thing to do. Just as she contemplated getting out of bed to start packing her stuff, her mobile phone rang.

Still very tired, she slipped out of bed, a little shaky on her feet, and reached into her handbag to take out the phone. 'Hello,' she said, clearing her throat.

'Oh, hello. Is that Lynne?'

'Yes.' The voice sounded familiar but she could not place it.

'Hi Lynne, I'm Michael. Er... Michael Taylor. We met at Alex's funeral.'

In her mind, she could see his face and his warm features, and remembered the strange pull that had drawn her to him. She recalled, in a misty memory, how he looked like a fictional hero from a romantic novel: tall, dark and handsome. 'Hello,' she said again.

'Um... the reason I'm calling is because, Mark—my cousin—is getting much better, and he's going to be released from hospital today. I'm going to collect him. I know it's a bit short notice, but I wondered whether you would like to come with me? He has been talking a lot about how thankful he is to Alex's family. Alex's mum has been to visit him a few times, and she tells us that you have been talking about Mark a lot. I thought that perhaps you'd like to meet him.'

A familiar pang of frustration surged through Lynne's brain as

Rachel was mentioned. There she was, spreading more lies about her; this time to complete strangers. Lynne resolved that the best thing to do would be to go to the hospital and see him, so that she could find out if Rachel had said anything else about her. She intended to confront Rachel about all of this, but she needed to have the full story before she did that.

'Okay, er... What time are you going to the hospital?'

'I'll be leaving in about half an hour. Where do you live? I could pick you up on the way.'

Lynne gave him Sandra's address, and then hurriedly showered and dressed, nervously anticipating their meeting.

She sat nibbling a croissant, not really feeling able to eat anything as she was so anxious about the impending trip to the hospital. Hospitals had never been her favourite places; she always felt conscious of the over-sterilised smell to cover the scent of death and disease. She was just finishing a cup of coffee when the door bell rang. Jumping up, as if someone had set the floor on fire, she rushed towards the door.

Michael looked very handsome, in a grey pinstripe suit, white shirt, and blue tie. He seemed taller than she remembered. He smiled at her.

'Hi,' she said, blushing, and feeling awkward.

'Nice to see you again, Lynne.' He extended a hand to shake hers. 'Thanks for agreeing to come. It'll mean a lot to Mark.'

She followed him out to his car. A large black Mercedes; very plush. Michael held the door open for her to sit in the passenger seat.

They drove in silence for the first ten minutes and Lynne tried to concentrate on the view out of the window. She realised that they had nothing in common really, apart from Alex's funeral—and that was something she preferred to forget. Michael seemed to be just as unable to find anything to say. She knew that he thought she'd been engaged to Alex and had lost her "soul mate" when he died; so, he was probably expecting her to be grieving.

'So, how have you been?' he said eventually, as they sat at a particularly stubborn set of traffic lights.

'Fine, thanks,' she said, avoiding his eyes. 'How about you?'

'I'm fine. As I said on the phone, Mark is doing well and the doctors are optimistic. Of course, he has to look after himself. The next year will be crucial; he has to try to avoid any colds and flu because his immune system will be severely disadvantaged.'

'Yes, of course,' said Lynne.

The car took off, and once again silence resumed on the drive to the hospital.

Lynne was glad when they finally parked in the hospital car park.

The walk to the ward where Mark was being cared for, was

thankfully quite short. Lynne felt claustrophobic in the whitewashed, antiseptic-smelling atmosphere of the hospital. Soon, they arrived at the ward, which was more colourful: there were paintings on the walls, and blue striped curtains, giving it a more homely feel for the long-term patients.

A petite nurse greeted them as they walked through the door. 'Hello, Michael,' she said cheerfully. Her large green eyes sparkled as she looked up at him, as if he were a close friend. Then the nurse looked towards Lynne, and her eyes lost their sparkle. A look of disappointment momentarily pulled down her smiling features. This only lasted a few seconds and then she seemed to purposefully alter her appearance to a wide smile. Lynne wondered whether the nurse was a little upset to see Michael with a woman. Maybe she secretly fancied him. Lynne couldn't blame her; he was stunning.

'Mark's so excited about going home today. He'll be so happy to see you,' continued the nurse, slightly less cheerily than she had begun.

'Er... this is Lynne,' explained Michael as they walked through the ward. 'She was engaged to Alex; the heart donor who donated his heart to Mark.'

'Oh!' The nurse brightened. She stopped walking and stood in front of Lynne. 'Mark is so grateful. He'll be so happy to meet you at last. He talks about you all the time.' She put an arm around Lynne as they walked towards Mark's bed.

The next five minutes were a complete blur for Lynne—she knew it was five minutes because she had noticed the clock on the wall just before she turned to face Mark in the hospital bed. She neither heard anything or saw anything for a full five minutes after seeing Mark. When she came round, she was lying on a hospital bed in a different ward, with a cannula in the back of her right hand. She noticed the time on a clock on the wall opposite her bed.

'Lynne, are you okay?' asked Michael, who stood next to her bed, looking worried. A young nurse with bleached blonde hair and a tattoo of what looked like some sort of script, on her inner right forearm, took blood from Lynne's vein.

'What happened?' asked Lynne.

'You fainted,' said Michael and the nurse together.

'You'll be okay, darling, just relax,' comforted the nurse. 'We need to take some blood to find out what caused the blackout. Er... could you be pregnant?' she asked.

Lynne thought back to the last time she and Adam had slept together. 'Er... I don't think so,' she said.

'We'll need a urine sample, just in case,' said the nurse.

Slowly, over the next few minutes, Lynne's mind began to piece

230

together what had happened before she fainted. As soon as she'd seen Mark, she had fainted. It was him. It was Mark Cribbs. The man from her dreams.

Chapter Fifty-One

Lynne and Mark were released from hospital at the same time. There were no abnormalities revealed in Lynne's blood tests, and she wasn't pregnant. Lynne had already known the real reason she fainted; she didn't need the medics to tell her.

Seeing Mark Cribbs sitting there had just been too much. He was a real, living breathing person. Those dreams she'd had before her wedding to Adam, in her future existence, had been real in some way. Sitting in the back of the Mercedes, as Mark sat in the passenger seat with his cousin at the wheel, she couldn't believe she was in the same car as the man who had once haunted her dreams. It all seemed so fantastical. The line between reality and fantasy, which had been seriously blurred since the time slip, was now totally eclipsed. She didn't really know what to believe anymore, and found herself in a state of utter incomprehension. It was all she could do to go along with the tide and see where it took her.

Mark looked similar to Michael. He was handsome, and had the same black hair; but his eyes were deep brown, whereas Michael's were blue-green in colour.

Lynne began to wonder whether her dreams had been some sort of premonition. Could Mark be her "true love"? She had never been one of those people who believed in true love or soul mates. That was more Sandra's territory, and she'd often made fun of her because of it. Only since those dreams, had Lynne started to wonder about anything like that, because the dreams had been so real and so lucid.

Michael had arranged a surprise welcome home party for Mark, at Mark's parents' house. Unbeknownst to Lynne, he had invited Rachel.

They walked into Mark's parents' house and were greeted by a group of people all waiting anxiously to see him. Lynne felt overwhelmed as the chatter became louder with everyone asking him how he was feeling. In reality, she didn't want to be there, she wanted to leave. It was all too weird. She didn't feel as if she belonged there, and yet she knew that some bond existed, which she could not explain; it was as if this were somehow destined.

Lynne was in the kitchen, drinking a glass of water and eating a canapé, when Rachel walked in from the garden. A piece of tomato from her canapé fell onto the floor as the shock of seeing Rachel again caused her to lose control for an instant.

'Well, well, well...' said Rachel. They were alone, the other guests either in the garden or in the living room.

'Hello,' said Lynne, standing up after retrieving the tomato from the floor.

'You really are keeping up appearances, aren't you? Wouldn't it be terrible if everyone here found out what a fraud you really are?' She walked closer to Lynne, her eyes glaring. 'You broke that heart; my son's heart. His heart still lives on. Despite your best attempts to ruin him, my son is still alive as long as his heart beats on, and I will do everything in my power to protect him. I think you should go and make your excuses and leave the party, Lynne, dear; unless you want me to tell everyone the truth about you.'

'I was leaving, anyway,' said Lynne.

'Huh! A coward as well as a heartbreaker.' Rachel walked away from her, towards the living room. Then, she turned to face Lynne again, her eyes looking as if they were keeping a fabulous secret. 'I haven't finished with you yet, my dear. You can't just kill my son and get away with it, you know. I'm going to follow you until I die, and I'm going to make your life hell. You'll never be happy again, not as long as I have a breath in my body.' With that, she walked out of the room.

Lynne felt a chill inside her, and picked up her handbag, making her way out of the door, and along the hallway. Michael noticed her heading towards the front door.

'Leaving so soon, Lynne?' he said, rushing towards her and standing between her and the doorway.

'Er... yes, sorry. I have things to do,' she said, Rachel's threat still burning in her mind.

Michael looked glum. 'I suppose it was short notice. I should have told you about the party before. I really wanted you to spend some time with Mark.'

Lynne was aware of Rachel's presence as she turned briefly to look back into the living room. Rachel was watching her; her accusing eyes emanating hatred. 'I'm really sorry, but I have to go,' mumbled Lynne, walking around Michael to the door. 'Er... thanks for inviting me.' Looking briefly at Michael as she spoke, she noticed the disappointment in his eyes. 'Can you say good-bye to Mark for me.'

'Yes, of course. And this isn't good-bye,' he said. 'You must keep in touch. We owe you so much.' He smiled at her with a look of compassion.

Lynne bowed her head, ashamed of herself for not just coming out with the truth; but she didn't want to cause a scene with Rachel there.

'Okay, bye,' she said, awkwardly.

As she left the house, she realised that she didn't have her car with her. Mark's parents' house was miles away from Sandra's flat. She sighed. Staring at the ground as she walked, she made her way towards the tube station. She again thought of Sandra and Dave, and felt bad about taking up room in the flat now that they had started a relationship. Lynne resolved to go and collect her things from Sandra's and return to the flat she'd shared with Adam.

Later that day, she arrived at her old home.

Closing the door of the flat behind her, and sitting her suitcase down on the floor, she noticed some post on the doormat. As she picked it up, she spotted a familiar looking envelope. It was the one that contained the poison pen letter. Lynne shook her head and sighed deeply: Rachel seemed to be haunting her. The threats she had made at Mark's party were still fresh in her mind. What would it take to stop Rachel? She couldn't live her life for ever looking over her shoulder. Previously it had been Alex who was stalking her, but his mother appeared to have taken over from him in his wake.

Wheeling her suitcase into the bedroom, intending to unpack, Lynne noticed that the sheets were in disarray on the bed. They'd remained as they were the day she had caught Adam and Paul together. It upset her again, momentarily; but then she decided to disregard it. She would have to try to move on. It was not possible to change what had happened.

As she began taking the sheets off the bed, she heard the doorbell ring. She wasn't expecting anyone. Looking at her watch, she saw it was 4 pm; an odd time for anyone to be calling. *Perhaps it's one of those cold callers for the gas or electric companies*, she thought to herself, as she walked towards the door. When she opened it, she wished she hadn't. Standing outside was Rachel, a smug grin on her face.

'Can I come in?' she asked.

'I don't think we have anything to say to each other,' replied Lynne, stiffly.

'I warned you I would follow you; and I always keep my promises—unlike some people,' said Rachel, through clenched teeth.

'I don't want to be disrespectful,' started Lynne. 'But, I really think you should seek some help. It's hard for you—losing Alex like that—and I know you need someone to blame; but I didn't do anything wrong.'

'Oh, you are a prim little miss, aren't you? Butter wouldn't melt. Remember who you are talking to, Lynne. I know the *real* you. I know the truth.'

'I really think you should leave now,' said Lynne, agitated.

'Don't worry, I'm going. But I won't rest until I see you suffer. I'm going to make sure your fiancé knows the truth about you, pretty little girl. Then we'll see if he marries you, or if he breaks your heart like you broke my son's heart.' Rachel walked away.

Lynne was left feeling helpless. It seemed there was nothing she could do to stop Rachel trying to hurt her. Closing the front door, she walked back towards the bedroom in a daze.

As she began making the bed, she started to feel a bit better, thinking it all through. She knew Rachel wanted to split her and Adam up. If she could make sure that Rachel found out that they'd split up, maybe she would finally leave her alone. But would she give in that easily? It was worth a shot. She hadn't been planning to tell her parents about the split with Adam yet, but it seemed like the only solution.

Chapter Fifty-Two

When Lynne phoned her parents' house, there was no reply. They were probably out visiting her sister, she imagined; they often went there to spend time with the grandchildren. Feeling frustrated that she had not been able to speak to her mum and finally get Rachel off her back, she slumped down on the couch and switched on the television to distract her mind.

Her mobile phone began to ring. The first thought that came to her was that it might be Rachel phoning to threaten her again; she began to feel very harassed. Looking at the caller display, she didn't recognise the number. She decided to let it go onto her voicemail. A few moments later, the phone alerted her that she had a message. With trepidation, she dialled her voicemail inbox.

The message was from Michael. *'Hello, Lynne. Er... could you call me back when you get this message. I just want to ask you a few questions about Alex's mum. I'll speak to you later.'*

Her heart skipped a beat. Lynne wondered whether Rachel had said something to Michael today, after she left Mark's party. His voice had sounded concerned. Feeling anxious, she called him back.

'Thanks for getting back to me so quickly, Lynne,' he said.

'No problem... um... your message said you wanted to talk about Alex's mum?' She held her breath as she waited for a response.

'Yes,' he said, pausing. Then, he continued. 'I don't really know how to say this. Maybe it's best if we meet up in person? It's just, this time of mourning is hard on everyone, and people can behave out of character when they are grieving.'

'What has she said?' asked Lynne, quickly, unable to bear the suspense.

'Um... I really think this is best said face to face. Can you meet me this evening for dinner?' he asked.

Lynne felt flustered. 'Er... yes, I suppose so.'

'I'll pick you up at about eight then.'

'Okay,' she said.

After putting the phone down, Lynne felt nauseated. *What did Rachel say to him?* What would he be thinking now? Most likely, Rachel would have painted her as some kind of evil, insensitive bitch.

Lynne sat forward on the sofa, her head in her hands, dreading seeing Michael again for fear of what he would say. As she

236

contemplated how best to explain things to him, it suddenly occurred to her that he would be going to Sandra's flat to pick her up for dinner, not knowing that she was living *here* now. She was just about to call him back, but then she thought things through, and wondered whether it would be better for her to meet him at Sandra's, after all. Perhaps, taking Sandra with her tonight would be a good idea. Sandra had been a witness to Rachel's crazy behaviour.

She phoned her friend, at work.

'Oh, sorry, I can't come out tonight,' said Sandra. 'I'm meeting Dave. I think it's getting quite serious. I might be moving in with him.'

Lynne had heard this before, but tried to sound as if it was the first time: 'Really? Isn't it a bit soon?'

'No, I've known Dave for years, and it would make more sense. I could rent my flat out, and we could travel to work together, to save money. Um... it might mean you having to move out... Unless of course, you want to rent the place? Maybe you could get the rent paid by the DSS until you find work?'

'Um... no, that's okay, I've moved out. I'm back at my flat.'

'What! With Adam? But I thought he was—'

'Yes, yes; he's still gay, and we're not back together. He's gone to live with his lover.'

'Oh, nice,' said Sandra, the sarcasm evident in her voice. 'Listen, Lynne, I feel like a really bad friend because I haven't had time to sit and talk to you about... Well, about Adam, and you finding out he's gay.'

'That's okay, I'll live,' said Lynne, dejectedly.

'No, really, I'll arrange a free evening next week sometime, and we'll have a girlie night out, okay?'

Lynne tried phoning Michael when she'd put the phone down, but there was still no reply. Frustrated, she decided she would have to go and wait for him at Sandra's flat. She still had a key, so even if Sandra and Dave had gone out she'd be able to get in.

Later that evening, she sprayed on a little of her favourite perfume and looked at her reflection in the bedroom mirror. She was wearing her favourite black dress and had accessorised with pearls. As she studied her reflection, she began to worry about whether her hair looked okay. *It definitely needs a trim*, she thought. Then she wondered, momentarily, why she was making such an effort to look nice. Did she fancy Michael? In truth, she was still feeling a bit freaked out about seeing his cousin and recognising him from her dream. But for some reason, she hadn't been able to get Michael out of her mind since leaving the party. It wasn't Mark she was thinking about, but him. She'd always had an image of what her perfect man would look like, and she'd dated a string of men who all looked very similar: tall, dark, handsome. Michael, was all of those things, but there was something else about him. Something she could not define. A feeling. A sense that she was drawn to him in some way; the way she had felt when she first saw him at the funeral.

Sighing, she walked away from the mirror, reached for her coat and handbag, and walked towards the front door. When she opened it, something red caught her eye. Stepping outside and looking back, she saw that someone had written 'Whore' in red lipstick, on the front door. *Rachel. Oh my God, she's so... What a bitch!*

Lynne ran indoors and found some make up remover from her dressing table and rushed to clean the lipstick from the door. She was thankful that at least it hadn't been written in paint, or a spray can. *What if Michael had been coming here to collect me for dinner and he'd seen this!*

Composing herself, after cleaning the writing from the door, Lynne began to feel paranoid. What if Rachel was still around somewhere, following her?

Every step Lynne took, she looked over her shoulder, worried that Rachel was there. Once inside her car, she tried to calm down, telling herself that it wasn't possible for Rachel to be following her all day. She drove to Sandra's flat, looking in her rear view mirror a lot, trying to see if there were any cars trailing her. She felt like a nervous wreck by the time she got to Sandra's flat. Checking the time on the clock in the car, she saw it was 7:45 pm. Michael would be arriving soon.

Lynne stepped out of the car cautiously, looking around to make sure there were no other cars pulling up in the vicinity. Absurdly, she checked behind the bushes on the path towards Sandra's flat, shaking her head when she realised that she was becoming overly suspicious of everything.

She walked through the communal door and made her way to the flat. Once inside, she relaxed a bit. All was quiet inside, so Sandra and Dave must have already left. She poured herself a glass of water and sat on the sofa, waiting.

At 8 pm on the dot, she heard a car pull up outside. Walking over to the window, she saw the Mercedes, and a warm feeling took hold of her. She smiled broadly, as if he were her best friend and she couldn't wait to see him. Something was telling her that whatever Rachel had said to him, the truth would find a way out. She wouldn't let the lies come between them. Then she checked herself. Having just come out of a disastrous relationship, she didn't want to get involved with anyone just yet. Even if Michael did look like the man of her dreams, she would try to stay detached.

A few moments later, the doorbell rang. She walked with light footsteps towards the door, as if walking on air.

He looked as handsome as ever, if slightly unsettled. He was frowning, but also looking at her with sympathy. Now, she was worried; whatever he wanted to talk about concerning Rachel, was probably something she would rather not hear. His eyes seemed to have a look of almost pity in them.

She turned away and said: 'I'll just grab my coat.'

'Great,' he said.

A few awkward moments later they were sitting in his car, on the way to a restaurant.

Lynne was pleased that the restaurant Michael had chosen was very dimly lit, with candlelight being the main source of light. She sat opposite him at the table, feeling relieved that he would not be able to tell if she looked embarrassed at any point; their faces appeared a strange orangey-yellow colour, the real shades and tones masked by the candlelight.

They ordered their meal and talked about Mark and how he was feeling. They talked about the weather, and about the amount of traffic on the journey to the restaurant. They made small talk, neither of them wanting to be the first to bring up the subject of Rachel.

Things changed when the meal had been served. As soon as the waiter left the table, Michael began to talk.

'Lynne, the reason I asked you here tonight was to talk about Rachel.' He looked down at his food for a moment and then continued. 'Her behaviour was a bit strange at the party. I don't mean to sound disrespectful at all. I know that all of this; Alex's death; the heart donation... Well, it's been a strain for you, and for Alex's parents.'

'Michael,' Lynne interjected, 'I think I need to come clean about something. I feel as though I'm lying to you, and I don't want to do that.'

He raised his eyebrows.

'You don't have to worry about upsetting me when you mention Alex,' she continued. 'I wasn't engaged to him. In fact, I hardly knew him.' Lynne had been looking at her plate of food while talking, feeling very self-conscious. She slowly lifted her eyes towards Michael, to gauge his reaction.

He stared at her, wide-eyed. 'I don't understand. So why... Well, why were you at the funeral?'

'I knew Alex as a child; we went to the same school. We met up a few weeks before his death. His mother thought I was his girlfriend .'

'She said you were his fiancée... at the funeral.'

'Rachel is not the full ticket. Um... Sorry to sound so bitter, but she's caused me a lot of trouble over the past few weeks. She's got it into her head that I broke her son's heart because I wouldn't marry him, and that he killed himself because of that.'

The food on the table remained untouched. Lynne picked up her glass of wine, feeling as though she needed something to numb her senses. Her hands were shaking.

'I don't know what to say,' said Michael. 'This is all news to me. But it makes it a bit easier for me to tell you what I was going to tell you.' He took a bite of his steak, and seemed less awkward.

Lynne looked up at him, expectantly.

'Rachel said some things to Mark's parents today, which were a bit upsetting,' started Michael. 'She was saying that because Alex's heart is inside of Mark, he is still living through him. She called Mark "son" a few times, and she said that she wants to be involved in his life now because she feels as though she's his new mum.'

'Oh.' Lynne began to eat her food, remembering what Rachel had said to her at the party. She felt a bit better now that the conversation was not revolving around Rachel's lies about her.

'All of that might not sound too bad,' continued Michael. 'I mean, we all know she's grieving; but she just seems really hyper... A bit out of control. I feel a bit embarrassed saying this to you, but she warned us all about you when you left the party.'

Lynne, gasped and almost choked on the piece of meat she had placed in her mouth at that moment. She began to cough.

'Are you okay?' Michael looked as if he were about to stand up.

'Yes, yes...' she croaked. Then, unable to speak, she pointed to the water on the table and took the glass, drinking it down. After a few more troublesome coughs, she continued, 'Wh... What did she...' Lynne cleared her throat. 'What did Rachel say about me?'

'Er... it wasn't pleasant. She said you had deceived her son; that you'd been having an affair when you were engaged to him, and he'd been depressed. She didn't tell us he'd killed himself, but she said that you'd made him feel that his life wasn't worth living. She told us to avoid you.'

'So, why did you get in touch with me then?' asked Lynne.

'I don't know. I guess the way she was talking, and the way you are... it just didn't add up. You don't seem like that sort of person. And after the way she'd upset my aunt and uncle, I wasn't really warming to her.'

She looked into his eyes, and again she felt drawn towards him.

He turned away.

Just then, a waiter walked past their table, followed by a woman. It had happened a few times since they'd sat down for their meal that people had followed waiters past their table; but this was different. As the woman walked past her, Lynne smelt a familiar perfume, which she recognised as the same perfume worn by Rachel today. Looking at the back of the woman, she noticed that her hair was in the same style as Rachel's. Concerned that she was imagining things, Lynne took a sip of wine and tried to breathe steadily.

'You've hardly touched your meal,' commented Michael. 'Is it okay?'

'Oh, yes, it's lovely,' said Lynne, picking up her knife and fork and trying to forget what she had just seen. As she chewed her food, she looked past Michael's head and saw that the woman had been seated at the table behind him. The menu held up in front of the woman, obscured her face. The low lighting in the restaurant made it difficult for Lynne to make out anything that would confirm that she was Rachel.

'What are you looking at, Lynne?' Michael turned around to look behind him.

'Oh, nothing. I thought I recognised someone.' She felt too embarrassed to say that she thought Rachel was stalking her. After a few minutes, she noticed that Michael had finished his meal. 'Perhaps we should leave now,' she said. 'I'm not really feeling that hungry.'

'Oh.' He raised his eyebrows. 'If you're sure. I was going to order dessert.'

'Oh, okay, go ahead,' she said, feeling trapped.

At that moment, Rachel stood up and stared at her. Lynne's eyes widened, and this was not missed by Michael. He turned around to see Rachel walking towards their table.

'Good evening.' She smiled at Michael. 'What a coincidence. I wasn't expecting to find you here. How lovely to see you again. How's Mark?'

'Er... Hello, Rachel. He's fine, thanks.' Michael looked at Lynne, bemused.

'Why are you following me everywhere, Rachel? It's ridiculous.' Lynne stood up to face her.

'I just came over here to warn Michael about you. This girl, ruined my son's life, and now it seems she wants to do the same to you. Did you know that she's engaged to be married, yet she was dating my son behind her fiancé's back for three years. I thought it was only fair you should know what you are getting involved with. She's poison.'

'Well, thanks for the warning, but Lynne and I are only friends.'

Rachel turned towards Lynne, scowling. Then, she walked away.

'You see what I have to put up with? She must have followed us all the way here.'

'You should get an injunction against her. Harassment is a serious issue,' said Michael.

Lynne shook her head and sat down.

'I didn't know you were engaged,' he said. 'You're not wearing a ring.'

She looked up at him, and caught a twinkle in his eye. Why would he care if she was engaged or not? Did he like her, too? She shook herself out of her dreamlike state. 'Er... it's a long story. Let's just say I'm not engaged anymore.'

'So, you're single?' he asked.

'Yes.'

'I'm single, too,' he said, smiling at her.

Is he really interested in me?

'Er... I'm not really ready to get into another relationship,' she said feebly, regretting it as soon as she said it.

'Oh, no, I wasn't suggesting that, don't worry.'

She felt sad, a feeling that an opportunity may have just passed her by. 'Sorry,' she said. *Please still like me*, she thought.

'It's okay. Look, perhaps we'd better leave now.' Michael called the waiter for the bill.

They walked in silence to the car. She was sure that Michael wouldn't attempt to ask her out again. He drove her back to Sandra's flat in silence, as she stared out at the night through the passenger window contemplating what might have been. The more time she spent with him, the more she liked him. He might be just what she needed, to help her get over Adam. He might even be 'The One'. But now, it seemed, she would never get to find out.

Michael wanted to walk her to the door, so she had to explain that she didn't live there; that it was Sandra's flat and she'd only been staying over. Even though he didn't ask, she took out an old receipt she found in her handbag and wrote her actual address on it. As she handed it to him, she felt a bit foolish, and wondered whether she appeared too desperate. He walked her to her car and said he'd really enjoyed the evening. He didn't try to kiss her. She had wanted him to try to kiss her, because then she could make amends for telling him that she didn't want a new relationship. She did. With him.

When she returned to her flat, she noticed a small bit of red lipstick that she had missed on the door. The memory of the encounter with Rachel in the restaurant still lingered in her mind. She worried that

Rachel would be everywhere she went from now on, trying her best to ruin her life.

Chapter Fifty-Three

When Lynne woke up the next morning, she heard some noise coming from the kitchen. Her first thought was that Rachel might have broken in. She felt very vulnerable suddenly. Getting out of bed as quietly as possible, she began to get dressed. Then, she heard whistling. She took a deep breath and relaxed. It was only Adam.

She pulled on her cardigan and went into the kitchen.

'Oh, hello,' he said. He was seated at the kitchen table eating a slice of toast. 'I wanted to talk to you. I hope you don't mind me just coming in unannounced. I think I'll have to make arrangements to move my things out, so I don't have to visit here.'

He was babbling; something he always did when nervous. She found herself feeling sorry for him, even after all he had done. None of that mattered in this moment. Whether she was just pleased to see a friendly face after her run-ins with Rachel the day before, or whether she was just glad it was him in the flat instead of Rachel; somehow, the anger she'd originally felt towards him had dissipated.

'Er... yes, I suppose it would make sense if you moved your things out; but don't feel that you have to rush into anything.' She walked over to the percolator and poured herself a cup of coffee.

'Um... Lynne, how are you?'

'I'm fine,' she said, turning to face him.

'About the last time I was here.'

'Look,' she interjected, 'you're gay; I'm over it. Okay, it would have been better if we'd never had a relationship, but we've got to move forward. I don't want to keep looking back.'

'Great.' He seemed relieved. 'Thank you for being so understanding. I really didn't mean to hurt you. You'll always be special to me.'

'I know; if you weren't gay, I'd be the only girl for you. Right?' She laughed, trying to make a joke.

He laughed a weak laugh, too. 'Yes, something like that.' He smiled at her. 'So, does that mean we're friends again?'

'I suppose so,' she said wearily.

'Good, because I have some news, and I wanted to tell you first, so that you wouldn't hear it from anyone else.'

She sat opposite him at the table. 'What is it? Is Paul pregnant?' She laughed.

'Very funny.' He frowned, then said: 'Paul and I... We're engaged.'

'Oh.' Her mouth fell open in shock, and she was surprised at her own reaction. It was like she'd been thrown into reality. This wasn't going to be as easy to deal with as she had first imagined.

'Lynne?'

He appeared to be waiting for a reaction; perhaps for some words to show she approved and was happy for him. She could not give them. 'Congratulations,' she said, in a sarcastic tone. She stood up.

'Sorry,' he said.

'Look, I think you'd better leave,' she said.

'Okay. I'll go.' He stood up. 'I just wanted you to hear it from me. He walked towards her and touched her arm. 'I'd be honoured if you would come to the wedding.'

I'm sure you would, she thought, *then you wouldn't have to feel so guilty for tearing my life to pieces.*

'It's on the 6th of June. I'll send you an invite.'

Fantastic, she thought, bitterly. Then, the date *6th June* flashed into her mind; it brought back the painful memory of her last phone conversation with Alex; it also brought to mind her marriage to Adam in the real world—or was *this* the real world? She couldn't be sure anymore.

Watching as Adam walked away, she knew she had to stop grieving over the past. She could not change any of it.

Chapter Fifty-Four

Lynne stayed in the flat that day, as though she were hibernating. She had visions of Rachel approaching her in the shops or in the Post Office, so she avoided going out at all. The shopping could wait.

Every hour or so, she opened the front door, just to check whether there was any more graffiti scrawled on there. Each time, she felt a great sense of relief when she didn't find any.

She spent a short while on the Internet, checking emails. She was slightly disconcerted to find that Woody had left her three messages. *Is he stalking me, too?* she thought. *Am I some sort of magnet for loonies?* But then she reasoned that he had her phone number and hadn't been calling her; if he was a true stalker, he would have called.

She clicked onto *getbackontrack.com* to look at his messages. The first said: **Hi Lynne it was lovely to meet you, if somewhat briefly. I hope your friend is feeling better. By the way, she is very pretty. I wondered whether she is single. Sorry, to just come out with it like that, but I'm single and looking for a new relationship. She seems just my type.**

Lynne was surprised to feel a twinge of jealousy. Surely, she should be relieved that this very unattractive man wasn't interested in her? Somehow, the fact that he didn't find her attractive began to play on her mind. *What's wrong with me?* she wondered. Then she remembered how upset Sandra had been when they met Woody in the street. Her face had been streaked with mascara from her tears. She had not looked "pretty" at all. She reread his email: *'She seems just my type',* he had written. *Oh, so his type is a blubbering wreck?* She giggled to herself.

His next message had been sent a few hours later. **Hi Lynne, I just realised what I wrote in my last email. I didn't mean to offend you. You are pretty, too.**

Oh my God, she thought.

His final message, the next day, said: **Lynne, I hope my last two emails didn't offend you. Perhaps we could arrange to meet up again for a drink?**

She responded: **Hi Woody, thanks for your emails. My friend thinks you are attractive, too; but unfortunately she is already in a relationship. I'm also in a relationship**, she thought of Michael as she wrote it.

As she was stuck indoors, she spent a few hours tidying up the flat to give herself something to do, in between checking the status of the front door. By 4 pm, she began to feel like a prisoner. It was almost as if Rachel was keeping her hostage. Just as this thought entered her mind, the phone rang. It was her mother.

'Hello, dear. Rachel's just phoned me, she's in a right state. Apparently, she went to visit the boy who has Alex's heart, and his family called the police. She's at the police station now. She's been arrested. I wondered whether you have Steve's number. He's a criminal lawyer, isn't he? I know you two split up; but we need to find a solicitor to represent her. She hasn't got anyone.'

'No, I don't have Steve's number,' fumed Lynne, annoyed that her mother would even think of asking him for help after what he'd done to her. 'Why can't her husband find a solicitor for her?'

'He's left her, apparently. I couldn't really understand much of what she was saying; she was rambling on, and not making much sense. She was saying that the police were putting her in a section, or something, and that a solicitor had to get her out.'

'Section? I think maybe she's been sectioned. That's what they call it when they arrest loonies like Rachel.'

'Lynne! I won't have you talking about her like that.'

'Well, why do you think she's been arrested?'

'I have no idea. She said that the boy's mother wants to keep her away from her son. I think that's so ungrateful, considering he wouldn't be alive without Alex's heart.'

'You don't know the full story, Mum. She's making their life hell, saying that Alex is still alive in Mark, the donee.'

'Well, he is in a way... It's his heart.'

'Oh, Mum! The woman is crazy. Look, I'll phone Michael; he's Mark's cousin. I'll find out what's happened.'

On phoning Michael, Lynne discovered that Rachel had been to visit Mark at about 8 am that morning, and had been told she couldn't see him because he was sleeping. She then began accusing the family of trying to stop her seeing him. She had sat outside their door for most of the day, telling everyone who passed by that she had to try to get her son's heart back (a neighbour had relayed this to the family).

When Mark's mother tried to ask her politely to leave, Rachel had thrown a brick through the window and said she was not leaving without Alex's heart. They then called the police, and Rachel had been sectioned under the Mental Health Act. Michael had spoken to the police about it, and it seemed likely she would be sent to a hospital for treatment. As all the signs were that she had some form of mental illness. From the initial prognosis it was likely she would be in hospital for some time.

Chapter Fifty-Five

The next day, Lynne had an appointment at the job centre. She was intending to drive there, but when she got downstairs, she saw that all four of her car's tyres had been slashed. She knew at once who was responsible. This was Rachel's handiwork. And, if there had been any doubt in her mind about that, it was soon quashed when she found a piece of paper under her windscreen wipers. Another poison pen letter, reading:

I'M watching you.

Lynne took a deep breath and tore up the paper. She took comfort from the fact that Rachel was now safely inside a psychiatric ward. Part of her also felt sad about this. Obviously, Rachel suffered from a disorder. In all likelihood, it was probably something that ran in the family and had caused Alex to kill himself. It was such a waste of a young life. He could have been helped if only he'd been treated, the way Rachel would hopefully be treated now she was in hospital. A guilty conscience nagged at Lynne again, as she wondered if there was anything she could have done. Maybe she should have alerted a doctor to Alex's problem. Could she have saved him? She sighed, at the futility of her thoughts; she couldn't bring him back now. It was too late, and it wouldn't do to constantly torture herself with this sense of blame or failure that crept into her mind every time she thought of him.

After signing on at the Job Centre, Lynne called her insurers and a garage to get her car's tyres replaced. Fifteen minutes later there was a knock at her door. She opened it and saw Woody standing there. He seemed as surprised to see her as she was to see him. 'Lynne?'

'Hi... er... how did you know where I live?' She felt a sense of paranoia which was becoming all too familiar these days.

'I didn't.' He laughed. 'I'm here to change your car tyres. I've just got a job at the garage down the road. What a coincidence, hey?'

'Yes.' Lynne smiled, but all sorts of thoughts were whizzing through her mind. What if it was Woody who'd sent the original poison pen letter? What if he'd slashed her tyres as a ruse, so he could meet her again? She shrugged off the unwelcome thoughts.

Half an hour later, Woody had finished replacing her tyres. She knew it would be polite to offer him a cup of tea, but she didn't really want him in the flat. Her mind was all over the place. When he left, she chided herself for judging him like that. He had been so polite, and had not really seemed like a stalker.

She decided that she could do with a holiday. Perhaps getting away somewhere was what she needed, to clear her mind and help her to relax. Perhaps a weekend away.

She phoned Sandra.

'Hiya, Lynne.'

'Hi, how are you?'

'I'm fabulous! Dave and I are moving in together. Isn't that great?'

'Yes, that's fantastic,' said Lynne, trying to sound enthusiastic. 'Listen, Sand, the reason I'm calling is that I really need to get away for a few days.'

'Oh? Where are you going? Anywhere nice?'

'Um... I was going to ask whether you wanted to come with me. Maybe a city break. Paris?' But then she remembered that she'd recently been to Paris with Adam and didn't really want to go back; there would be too many memories. 'Er... no, maybe Rome, or Prague. We should be able to get a cheap last-minute deal.'

'Oh, sorry, Lynne, but I'm moving in with Dave this weekend. And next weekend we're going to a 50th birthday party. Then, the weekend after that—'

'Oh, okay; I get the picture,' said Lynne, dejectedly.

'Sorry. I'm sure you'll be able to find someone else to go with, won't you?'

'Yes, of course.' But Lynne couldn't think of anyone. Her sister was too busy with her children, and she'd lost touch with her work colleagues. She hadn't seen any of them since she'd gone back in time.

The next few weeks went by slowly for Lynne. She spent all her time alone. It was as if she had locked herself away from the world.

At the end of April, she received an invitation to Adam and Paul's civil ceremony. Unexpectedly, she began to cry when she read the invitation. Memories of her own wedding flooded her mind, taking her thoughts back to her life before the time slip. It reminded her of the dreams she had been having about Mark at the time, when he was telling her not to marry Adam. It all seemed so surreal.

As images of Mark flashed through her mind, she wondered whether she should get in touch with Michael and ask how Mark was doing. She hadn't heard from Michael since the day Rachel was sectioned. She had thought about him every day, though, and hoped he'd get in touch.

But she knew that the only reason he'd been in contact with her was because of Alex's heart donation. He now knew that she hadn't really been engaged to Alex, so he wouldn't really expect her to be concerned about Mark. It saddened her that their communication had come to an end so soon, before they'd had a chance to become friends. Over the last few weeks, as she had been thinking about Michael, wondering why she'd pushed him away when she would have liked to get to know him better; she'd also wondered about Mark, hoping he was okay. The dreams she'd had of him before she met him had created a connection between her and Mark, in her mind.

Underlying all of this, and her most persistent thoughts, revolved around the way Alex's life had ended. It was like an unresolved issue in her consciousness.

The link between her dreams and Alex, continued to haunt her. "Mark Cribbs", in her dream had said something about her soul mate dying if she married Adam. At one point she had thought Alex must have been her soul mate as he had died when she married Adam in her future life. Since his death, she had thought about him constantly. She couldn't get past the feeling that she had been involved to some degree in his decision to kill himself this time. Perhaps that was where all her recent feelings of vulnerability and paranoia were coming from? She knew she needed to make her peace with Alex somehow. The only way to do that would be to visit his grave again. She didn't really want to, but she had to try something. Perhaps if she went there it would bring some closure. Her rational mind knew that there was really nothing anyone could have done to save him, but it was a constant battle to make sense of it all.

Later that day, she visited the cemetery and bought two bunches of flowers from the seller at the entrance; one for her grandfather's grave and the other for Alex's. She walked along the gravel path leading to her grandfather's grave, wanting to put off the inevitable for as along as possible. She didn't know how she would react on seeing Alex's grave today.

Sitting on the bench opposite her grandfather's grave, after placing white roses on his tomb, she tried to settle the thoughts that were invading her mind. Eventually, she realised she could not put it off for ever.

Walking towards the place where Alex had been buried brought back memories of when she had last been there. That was when she had first met Michael and felt drawn to him as if she knew him from some other place and time. Then, she recalled the way Rachel had threatened her, and a blackness came over her like a shadow of pain.

She stared at the gravel path as she walked, listening to the wind through the trees, which sounded eerie somehow. There were a few other people milling around the gravestones, tending to flowers, picking out weeds, and cleaning dust from the tombstones.

Lynne looked up to make sure she was walking in the right direction, feeling a bit unsure. She saw a man walking towards her. Even though he was quite a distance away from her, she knew who it was as soon as she saw him. Mark Cribbs. *He must have come to pay his respects to Alex*, she thought. Soon they were face to face, and he smiled at her.

'Hello, Lynne,' he said.

His smile was weak. His face was pale. She began to worry that perhaps he might be unwell. Michael had said that he would be more prone to infection after the operation.

'Hello, Mark.' She wanted to reach out to him and hold him upright, to make sure he didn't fall. He looked so frail. 'How are you? Are you okay?'

'Oh, don't worry about me,' he said, still looking as though he might keel over. 'You've come to visit Alex's grave?'

Lynne nodded, staring at his eyes, which looked like deep sunken pits of blackness.

'Can we talk?' he said, pointing to a bench at the side of the path.

'Yes of course,' she said, wondering what he would want to talk to her about.

They sat together on the bench. Mark smiled at her with a weary look on his face. 'What was Alex like?' he asked. 'I'd like to know more about him. I have his heart, and it feels strange that I know next to nothing about him.'

'Oh... um... Well, he was...' Lynne couldn't think of anything. Then she remembered how she had once found him attractive. There was no reason for her to tell Mark everything about Alex; she could tell him the positive things. 'He was a very handsome man. Very sensitive. Yes. Sensitive.' She smiled, pleased that she had found something good to say about him.

'Michael told me that you weren't really engaged to Alex.'

'Oh.' Again, Lynne was unsure how to continue.

'It's okay, he told me that Alex's mum was a bit weird and she lied about you being engaged.'

'Yes, that's right. Alex was a friend. Nothing more. His mother is a bit overbearing, and she probably influenced him a lot.' *Enough, stop babbling*, she told herself.

'Mike likes you,' said Mark.

Lynne's eyes widened in surprise, and when she looked at Mark she saw a twinkle in his eye.

'He's just come out of a bad relationship,' continued Mark. 'Well, it was about three years ago. He really loved her, but she cheated on him and he never got over it. Since he's met you, he seems to have perked up a lot.'

Lynne blushed. She felt as if her face were burning, which made her even more embarrassed and unable to douse the fire erupting on her cheeks. The flowers she had bought for Alex's grave were still in her hands; she focused on those, trying to avoid looking at Mark.

'Sorry, I didn't mean to make you feel uncomfortable,' he said. 'I'm just saying, my cousin is a great bloke. Any woman would be lucky to have him as a partner. And, obviously, I want him to be happy. I've seen the way he's been since you... Sorry, I shouldn't be saying this.'

Lynne looked at Mark and thought that he would probably be blushing, too, if he had enough blood in him to colour his face. But he was ashen; white. *Deathly pale*, she heard the words in her mind.

He stood up. 'I'd better be off,' he said, nodding towards her. 'It was nice to see you again.'

She stood up and said good-bye to him, watching as he walked away. Then, she made her way to Alex's grave. When she reached the graveside, she looked back towards where Mark had been, expecting to see him further along the path; but he was gone. It was almost as if he had just disappeared. *That's odd*, she thought, *he couldn't have walked away that fast. He must have run!*

She turned her attention to Alex's grave and laid the flowers. Tears threatened to fall, but she was determined to try to face up to this, once and for all. She stared at the candles and wreaths lying on the grave. There was also a plastic covered photograph of Alex there. He looked so young and vibrant in the photo. *Much too young to die,* she thought. Then, she turned her eyes to the right and caught sight of a new wooden cross that had been placed in the ground over a newly covered grave. She gasped as she read the name: Mark Cribbs. Determined not to faint again, feeling light-headed, she tried to find somewhere to sit. She soon found her way back to the bench where she'd been sitting only a few moments before with Mark... Mark Cribbs... How could he have died and yet have been sitting here next to her? Memories of her dreams, and of the time she had visited this graveyard looking for his gravestone, swam through her mind. None of it made sense, and she was now really starting to believe that she was losing her mind. She tried to rationalise it: *If I really was mad, surely I wouldn't be thinking I'd gone mad, because I'd be too mad to question anything!*

She sat on the bench staring towards the graves: Alex and Mark, side by side.

What did it all mean? Why had she been dreaming of Mark for so long before she'd even met him? He seemed to be trying to pass a message to her, but his messages were difficult to understand. A white cat appeared at her feet. It was lying down and licking its coat. She hadn't noticed it before. There was something soothing about the creature's presence. She had always liked cats. Leaning forward, she stroked its back. 'Hello,' she said in the high pitched voice she reserved for use with animals and small children. Looking at the identity tag, she read its name: 'Misty.' The cat purred and then looked at her. At once, she was taken aback. Its eyes were not like a normal cat's eyes. They were deep, and black, almost like black holes; as if the cat didn't have any eyes at all. But they *were* eyes. They were just completely black. At once, she recognised those eyes as the eyes that had been staring at her a few moments before: Mark's eyes. She shook with fear.

She knew she had also seen this cat before, and racked her brains trying to remember where. Everything was so fuzzy from fear. Then she remembered: the cat had been outside the reception hall when she'd married Adam; it had been sitting on top of a commercial waste bin, highlighted by the light from the lamp-post above. She was so drunk then, that part of her memory had erased that image, and part of her had thought she'd imagined it. After all, there are no cats with black eyes; black like charcoal ball bearings.

How could this be? *I'm obviously imagining this,* she reasoned. But the eyes drew her to them, so she felt unable to look away. At last she pulled her gaze away from the cat's eyes, and picked up her handbag, standing up and walking away backwards. She was looking at the cat, as if wary of it; avoiding the eyes.

As she walked further along the gravel path, she soon felt as if she was at a safe enough distance from the cat to turn around. Sighing deeply, she began to wish she had never come to the cemetery. She tried to work out what the significance of the cat outside the reception hall and here at the cemetery could be. The reception hall was on the other side of town.

'Lynne!' She heard a woman's voice call out behind her. A shiver ran through her. The voice was unmistakable. She began to walk faster away, faster and faster, until she was running.

The woman called out: 'Lynne, stop! Wait, I need to talk to you!'

She continued running away from the woman, running as fast as her legs would carry her, wishing she had worn her trainers today instead of these heels.

Eventually, after what seemed like an age, she exited the cemetery. The flower seller at the gate frowned at her as she passed by. 'Are you all right, love?' he asked, concerned.

'I'm fine.' Lynne panted and puffed. Then, she had to stop running; she was out of breath.

'Did something scare you in there?' he asked. 'Wasn't a ghost, was it?' He let out a belly laugh.

'No, I... I'm fine, thanks,' she said, walking away from him.

She stopped dead in her tracks as she looked at her car and saw the same white cat sitting in front of it. Again she tried avoiding its eyes, but the pull was too great. Breathing a deep sigh of relief, she saw its eyes were normal. Blue, cat's eyes. *It must be a different cat,* she thought. She moved nearer and stroked the cat, and as she did so she saw the tag on its collar. It was the same as the tag on the other cat's collar, in the shape of a fish: "Misty". She gasped.

Unlocking her car door quickly, in a rush to leave, she felt a tap on her shoulder.

Turning around slowly, afraid of what she might see, she caught sight of Rachel. Her eyes widened.

'Sorry to startle you, Lynne. Please don't worry, I'm on medication now. I'm so sorry for the way I behaved before.' She looked down at the ground.

'I... I thought you were in hospital.' Lynne was not sure whether she should just get into her car and make an escape, or stay and listen... Was it possible that Rachel had changed? She opened the car door and held onto it, ready to make a quick exit if necessary.

'I was in hospital, but they released me yesterday,' explained Rachel, appearing to find it hard to keep eye contact with Lynne. 'I'm on medication, and I really feel like a different person; I'm much calmer. The anger has gone. I don't remember much of the past few months. Well, I do, but not in any detail. It's like foggy memories that come and go. The one thing I do know is that I needed help.' Rachel was speaking quickly, as if in a hurry to explain away her past behaviour.

Lynne was still unsure whether she could trust her. Was this another act, like the one she had put on at the funeral?

Rachel looked at the ground.

'Um, I'm happy to hear you're feeling better,' said Lynne, forcing a smile and opening the car door just a little more.

The movement prompted Rachel to start speaking again: 'Lynne, dear, I feel I have to explain something to you. I suffer from a delusional disorder.' She coughed, as if embarrassed. 'It was most probably made worse when Alex died. The doctors are still trying to diagnose the cause and whether there is any other underlying condition.' She sighed. 'Oh, I don't want to bore you with all this; you're probably not interested. Except, I wanted you to know that I asked the doctors whether it could be a hereditary illness. They think it might be. My Alex probably had the same thing. Which is why he... Well, it's why he did what he did.'

Rachel's face looked sad; her eyes were hollow and distant.

On the one hand, Lynne felt sorry for her; but she couldn't help the anxiety that was building up inside her as she recalled the earlier threats Rachel had made. She didn't feel comfortable in her presence.

'Er... I have to go,' said Lynne.

'Yes, of course. But I'm glad I bumped into you. I've been feeling so terrible about everything.'

Lynne nodded and got into her car.

She drove along the highway, hardly concentrating on the traffic, more concerned about trying to stay sane. There were so many questions in her mind.

As she stopped at a set of traffic lights, she felt something soft and feathery on her arm, and turned to her left to see the white cat climbing over onto the front passenger seat. She gazed at the creature in shock. The lights changed, but she was transfixed; mesmerised by this cat who seemed determined to follow her. It had obviously climbed into the car while she was listening to Rachel.

Car horns began to beep angrily behind her. She was shaken into action and sped off with her new passenger on board, feeling as if she were being watched. The cat washed its coat, apparently oblivious to all the noise of the traffic, or anything else for that matter.

⌛

Back at the flat that evening, Lynne wondered about the cat. After getting back from the graveyard, she had let it out of the car and it had wandered off quite happily. She hoped it would be all right, whilst also hoping she would never see it again.

As she stood in the kitchen, staring out at the blackened sky, stirring a cup of hot chocolate at 10 pm, her mobile phone rang.

Who's calling at this hour? she wondered. 'Hello?'

'Oh, hello, dear.' It was an elderly woman, by the sound of the voice. 'I've found your cat.'

'My cat?' Lynne frowned.

'Yes, "Misty". I got your phone number from the ID tag. He's been sitting on my doorstep all day. For the past hour, he's been meowing very loudly, as if he's lost. The neighbours have been complaining. Could you come and collect him?'

'Er... where are you?'

The woman lived downstairs in the tower block. Lynne got into the lift and went to the old woman's flat. She felt dazed. What was happening? Why was her telephone number on the ID tag? Had she lost her memory? Is that what all this time travel was about? Maybe she hadn't gone back in time at all, but had just forgotten who she was. Was this just amnesia on a grand scale? But no; that didn't explain everyone else's behaviour.

She saw Misty outside the flat when she stepped out of the lift. The cat walked towards her as if it knew her well. Looking at the tag on its collar, she saw her mobile phone number. How could that be? She toyed with the idea of taking the cat's collar off and throwing it away; that way she wouldn't get any more calls about the cat. Just then, the old women who had phoned her, stepped out of her door. 'Oh you found him, then,' she said, smiling at Lynne.

'Er... yes, thank you.' Lynne quickly picked up the cat and made her way back to the lift.

Puzzled, she knew she would have to take the cat home with her until she could work out what was going on.

As she walked through her front door, holding Misty in her arms, she knew that she wasn't looking forward to spending a night in the flat with the creature. A spooky feeling enveloped her. Even though she knew it bordered on animal cruelty, she decided to lock it in the kitchen overnight.

The next morning, when Lynne walked into the kitchen, she could smell the cat before she saw it. Misty was sleeping in the corner. She opened one of the windows to let in some fresh air, even though it was cold outside. Why had this cat followed her? All night, she had tossed and turned unable to sleep knowing that it was there in the flat, worried that at any moment it would appear in her bedroom. Those black eyes haunted her as she remembered seeing Mark in the graveyard. The cat began to stir as she looked at it. Then it stretched and walked towards her, rubbing against her leg and meowing. *It's probably hungry*, she thought. There was no cat food in the house. Reluctantly, she filled a saucer of milk and placed it next to the cat. The unwelcome guest would have to stay a bit longer until she could figure out where it belonged.

The ID tag was visible, and Lynne could again see the mobile phone number. As she leaned closer to Misty, she noticed that the tag was a bit worn; the number 3 was probably an 8, but half of the number had been worn away. A sense of relief calmed her. All she had to do was call the owner to come and take the cat away.

When she dialled the number, it reached a voicemail message: *'Hi, Michael Taylor is not available to speak to you, but if you leave a message, he will call you back during normal working hours, 9:30 am to 5:30 pm'*

She looked again at the business card that Michael had given her. As strange as it seemed, his mobile number was the same as the number on Misty's tag.

Chapter Fifty-Six

The telephone rang, as Lynne was staring at Misty, who had gone back to sleep in the corner of the kitchen. Lynne jumped when she heard the phone, as if jolted from a dream by the noise.

She walked over to the telephone and answered it, in a daze.

'Hello, Lynne?' It was Michael.

'Oh... Michael, I was just trying to get hold of you.'

'Yes, I know. I had a missed call on my mobile. Thanks for getting back in touch. I have been meaning to call you, but things keep coming up. You know how it is.'

Meaning to call me? Lynne wondered whether he was telling the truth. Her mind went back to what Mark had told her, at the cemetery; how Michael is supposed to be interested in her... But then she felt annoyed. *Mark is dead*, she reminded herself. And she was certain now, having been over and over it in her mind throughout a long sleepless night; that there was no way she'd seen Mark. It had all been some sort of optical illusion, brought on by stress, no doubt; or by this time travel. Her mind was so mixed up, she didn't seem to know the difference between reality and fantasy these days.

'Lynne, are you still there?' Michael's voice shook her from her deep thoughts.

'Yes. I was just wondering about... Oh, never mind. How are you?' She wondered whether it was even true that Mark had died, or if she had imagined the whole thing at the cemetery.

'I'm okay, in the circumstances,' replied Michael. 'I'm not sure if you've heard the news. I was going to tell you, but then I remembered that you were not really engaged to Alex, so you didn't really have any real interest in the heart donation. Um... Well, it's sad news.' She heard his voice break. 'Mark took a turn for the worse, shortly after the incident with Rachel, and then he was taken back to hospital. His body had started to reject the heart. It was unexpected. He'd been expected to live, because all the signs....' His voice drifted off. 'Oh, well, you don't really need to hear all of that.'

'I'm really sorry, Michael. I know Mark meant a lot to you.' The questions in her mind were slowly being answered. She had really seen Mark Cribbs's grave. She hadn't imagined that.

'We were like brothers. We were the same age, you see. My mum and his mum are sisters. They brought us up together. Most of my childhood memories involve Mark. We always stayed close even as adults.'

'I'm so sorry. You must be devastated.'

'It's hard, but life goes on, and all that.'

She could hear the melancholy in his voice.

Lynne noticed that Misty had woken up and was now drinking from the saucer of milk again. 'Um... Michael, have you lost your cat recently?'

'My cat? Not my cat... Mark's cat. How did you know?'

'That's why I called you this morning. I found the cat and called the number on the ID tag. But... it's your number... Why your number, if it's Mark's cat?' As she said the words *Mark's cat*, a shiver rippled through her at the realisation that the cat had been at the cemetery... At Mark's graveside.

'Mark didn't want people calling him, so we used my work mobile number, so that it wasn't a personal number on the tag.'

'Oh.'

'So, Misty's safe? Where did you find her?'

'Um... I was at the cemetery visiting Alex's grave yesterday. Misty followed me home.'

'Mark's grave is right next to Alex's. Wow. So, Misty went to Mark's grave? We thought she'd been run over or something. She went missing the day Mark was taken into hospital.'

'Well, when can you collect her?'

'Er... why don't I take you out to dinner tonight... er... as a thank you for finding Misty and keeping her safe. Then I can collect her tonight.'

Was he asking her out on a date? She found herself wishing he was. His voice sounded so soothing after all she had been through. He was like a real friend.

'That would be lovely,' she said, finding that she was smiling. She blushed.

'I'll pop over at about eight then.'

Chapter Fifty-Seven

When Michael asked Lynne to marry him, she was struck more by the date than by the question; the 28th of July. That was the last day she had been in real time before the time slip—if indeed that time had been *real*.

They had been dating for a few months, and she spent most of her time at Michael's house. She felt truly happy. Most mornings she had to pinch herself to find out if she was dreaming; he was *that* perfect. Her dream man.

Sitting opposite him in this expensive restaurant, seeing his eyes twinkling with the love he felt for her, she was worried that it was in fact a dream. Would she wake up tomorrow morning—either back in her previous hell existence, or in some other time—and find she would have to relive everything, like that *Groundhog Day* movie? *Please let this be real,* she thought, holding tightly to Michael's hand across the table, almost squeezing the blood out of it.

'Of course I will marry you,' she said.

He produced a ring. She was relieved to see that it wasn't the same engagement ring Adam had given her... or the one that Alex had offered her.

Her mind quickly flashed back to a memory of Adam and Paul's wedding. She had attended in the end. With Michael. If she was being honest, it was because she wanted to show him off. She also wanted to show Adam that she had moved on.

Back in the present time, she smiled at Michael as he placed the beautiful diamond ring on her finger.

She recalled how Sandra had shown her the ring Dave had given her last month, and how she had been slightly envious, wishing that Michael would ask her to marry him. Now, here she was. He kissed her hand. 'I love you,' he said.

'I love you, too.'

A waiter brought them a bottle of champagne, having overheard their conversation. 'On the house,' he said, beaming.

Things really seem too good to be true, thought Lynne.

'I think a June wedding would be good,' said Michael.

'Yes, lovely. That'll give me lots of time to prepare.' She thought of all the preparations she had made for her wedding to Adam. *Perhaps I'm a bigamist on some universal plane.*

At least it would be easy to arrange the wedding this time; she just had to contact the places she had used the last time. She would be avoiding the extra time spent on wild goose chases for perfect catering, flowers etc., because she already knew who she'd be using! *Going back in time is stressful, but has certain advantages.*

The next twelve hours or so would be crucial. Would she wake up on the "real" 29th of July, as it would have been; when she had found out that Adam was cheating on her, and she was stranded without a job or a permanent home, uncertain of her future? Or, would she wake up in the arms of this knight in shining armour who had come out of a fairy tale somewhere and rescued her? She sighed to herself.

'Lynne? Is there something wrong?'

'No,' she looked into his greeny-blue eyes, and said: 'I just wish I could gift wrap this moment and send it to myself whenever I'm feeling down.'

He laughed that contagious laugh of his. 'Oh, don't worry about that. I'll make sure you're never feeling down.'

'Is that a promise.'

'You bet.'

And she believed him.

Chapter Fifty-Eight

Lynne woke up the next day, to find Michael getting ready for work. She was so happy, she jumped out of bed, knocking poor Misty off from where she'd been snuggled up on the duvet. Lynne grabbed hold of Michael, not wanting to let go. 'I've made it!' she said, hugging him tightly.

'Made what?' Michael's face was full of confusion.

'You wouldn't understand if I told you.' Lynne looked up at him. 'Well, you might think I'm barmy if I told you. So I won't tell you.'

'I think you're barmy now, so you might as well tell me.' He giggled.

Lynne thought for a moment. 'Let's just say, I was going along the wrong road. I was lost. Then someone...' She thought of Mark and the dreams. 'Someone found me and led me to where I'm supposed to be. Like a guardian angel.'

'So, I take it you're happy we're getting married.' He smiled, and went over to the mirror to fix his tie.

'You have no idea,' she said, almost under her breath. *I might tell him one day...*

Epilogue

Years later, Lynne joyfully told her grandchildren about how their great-uncle Mark had come to her in a dream and led her to their grandfather. She had never told anyone up until then. Well, she had told Michael, once, when they were younger. He hadn't believed her. He told her she had a vivid imagination and should write a novel. 'It'll be a best-seller,' he'd said.

As she was well into her eighties when she related her tale to her grandchildren, and Michael had recently died, they all thought she was just grieving and finding a way to carry on. They humoured her, looking at her with sympathy. Lynne had suspected they would think she was becoming delusional in her old age. In a way, she preferred that, because she had come to think of her adventure as a dream. It was something sacred; her own secret. Looking more deeply into it and analysing what had happened, or *how* it had happened, would only make it something tangible. Then it would be ordinary. She preferred to think of it as something magical and unexplainable. It was a dream that had taken her on the journey of a lifetime. She had lived a long and happy life and would not change a thing. And she was thankful for the memories. Whenever she visited Michael's grave, she always made a special detour to visit Mark's grave, and also Alex's. She placed new flowers there and removed the weeds. She would never forget them.

www.ingramcontent.com/pod-product-compliance
Lightning Source LLC
Chambersburg PA
CBHW050923120626
46552CB00001B/17